DARING DRAFTSMAN

A COCKY HERO CLUB NOVEL

BY ALEXA PADGETT

Daring Draftsman is Book 3 in The Wright Family series inspired by Vi Keeland and Penelope Ward's *British Bedmate*. It is published as part of the Cocky Hero Club world, a series of original works, written by various authors, and inspired by Keeland and Ward's *New York Times* bestselling series.

To find out more about all the Cocky Hero Club World books and authors, visit: http://www.cockyheroclub.com

ISBN: 978-1-945090-39-4

Editor: Sarah Allan
Proofreading by: Charity Chimni
Photo Credit: Yafimik
Cover by: Chris Philpot

A sexy, new forbidden romance from USA Today bestselling author Alexa Padgett.

He was never supposed to be mine…

Nico Wright hates me because of my sister's actions. I hate him because of how he makes me feel. I'm all twisted up with attraction, longing, and a large dose of shame.

When I find out he's the architect I need to help me get the old theater turned into a proper dance studio, I have no choice but to use his designs to bring my vision to reality. As I spend with Nico, I realize he's the only one who understands how much I ache over losing my prima ballerina position at the Boston Ballet. He, too, had his dreams shattered by people who claimed to love him. Just like me.

I'm learning the real Nico. He cares too much. Unfortunately, I can't let him fall for me, the younger sister of his ex-fiancée who already cost him his job and his reputation.

Chapter One
Cassia

I rose on my tiptoes, searching for the familiar face in the crowd while doing my best to ignore the pain shooting up from my ankle to wrap around my knee. Someone in the crush of hot torsos bumped me, and I lost my balance. I clenched my jaw and exhaled a frustrated hiss between my teeth as I stumbled. I lowered down to my flat feet, still craning my neck, searching for my sister.

If my sister Amanda no-showed on me tonight I was never, and I mean *never*, giving her another chance.

"Hey, are you hurt again or something?" Amanda asked, appearing at my elbow. Her blond hair glinted in the light, framing her delicate features. Her makeup was simple and elegant, her dress cut low enough to show off some cleavage without being too revealing. And, as usual, Amanda had on a pair of stunning, sleek stilettos. My sister was always poised and put together—a skill I could only marvel at and aspire to.

"I'm fine."

She held out one of the lemon drop martinis she was carrying. I took it with a murmured thanks.

"You're grimacing. It makes you look constipated. You need to give that foot time to heal."

I gripped the glass more tightly. "It won't."

"Won't what?"

"Heal." I drank deep. "Not properly, anyway."

"Slow down. These drinks are strong. Come on. I have a table reserved."

Of course she did. I scowled, annoyed that the restaurant she'd asked to meet at was actually a nightclub. At least the location was neutral ground—she'd acquiesced to my insistence on that. I'd worried if she'd come to Grammy's house, I'd never get her to leave.

I trailed behind her, my aching foot forcing me to move without my typical ease. No doubt I looked like a tromping elephant. I felt like one, too, thanks to Amanda's cute pixie-ness and… life. After my shattered bones, my shattered career and shattered dreams, I hadn't spent more than eight hours pirouetting and leaping across the boards, and I was ten pounds heavier than I'd ever been.

Amanda seemed to have a sixth sense for when I was at my weakest; I never would have agreed to meet her if I hadn't been so lonely and overwhelmed by my life's rapid changes.

We settled into a booth tucked back in a corner, and I put my half-filled drink on the table in front of me.

Amanda placed her hand on the table, the other on top of the first, and studied me. "How are you doing, Cassia?"

She asked the question like she cared. "Well, I finished my rehab. As I mentioned, my foot didn't heal. Nothing like turning twenty-eight and retiring at the pinnacle of my career."

I dropped my attention back to my glass, unwilling to watch pity fill Amanda's eyes. I detested pity. Envy, jealousy, even hate

I could handle—*had* handled as the principal ballerina for two major companies over the course of my thirteen-year career.

But not pity.

And I'd seen way, *way* too much of it during the past few months.

"The doctor can't put pins in it or something?"

I drew a line with my fingertip across the wood tabletop. "No pins. That would further reduce my agility."

"There aren't any weird experimental procedures? Like…kelp or 3D printed bones?"

My jaw hardened as I raised my head to meet my older sister's stare. "No, Amanda. My career as a ballerina is over."

She settled back against the booth. "Well, that sucks."

I snorted.

"So, what are you going to do?" she asked.

"I officially moved into the house Grammy left me." I didn't add that I had to because *Amanda* had taken over the home—and bed—I'd shared with my ex-boyfriend. By the tightening of her lips, she surmised the reason all on her own.

"Grammy should have left half the house to me," Amanda muttered, petulance on full display.

I ignored that comment and continued, "I start meeting with architects this week to review their bids for the studio."

Her eyes widened. "Architects?"

"Yes. I can't use the space as it is now. Plus, if I'm going to incorporate the dance camps I want to offer, I need to have wheelchair access."

Amanda pursed her lips and something flashed in her eyes.

"Why didn't you ask me?"

I raised an eyebrow. "You were...busy." *Busy getting sued. Busy stealing my boyfriend.*

Amanda huffed out a laugh. Even though it was sardonic, it tinkled and a couple of men looked over, checking her out. "He dumped me, you know."

I licked my lips, unsure how to proceed. I downed another gulp of my drink, both enjoying and disliking how the alcohol burned its way down my throat. "I'm sorry the relationship didn't work out."

No, I hadn't been serious about Lowell, but the fact that he'd chosen my sister over me simply proved I was defective. Amanda had a freaking civil lawsuit against her—one she lost—for lying about sexual harassment, and Lowell *still* chose to date her.

So, clearly, I had serious issues.

"He insisted on keeping the dog we'd picked out together, too." She blinked back tears and grabbed a napkin to dab her eyes. It came away black, but her mascara didn't run. "Guess I deserved that."

"I don't think anyone deserves to be hurt, Manda."

She scrunched her brows together. Amanda looked a lot like Eva Mendez with natural gold highlights. My hair was a few shades darker, but I'd inherited our father's light gray eyes.

Her brown eyes always seemed so warm and welcoming, making Amanda easy to approach, to talk to, whereas I'd been told my gaze felt cold, watchful. My entire life I *had* been wary of others, and that started with my sister, who'd tried—and failed to derail my dance career. Not because she wanted to be a dancer;

she simply hadn't liked that I was dedicated to it—that I had a passion and a purpose.

I studied Amanda, noting yet again that she had the perfect build for dance. At five-foot-three and maybe one hundred and five pounds, Amanda was compact and athletic. Part of the reason my foot was smashed to hell was because my leap held more power thanks to my much longer legs, and I'd landed on my male partner's toe with enough force to shatter three delicate bones in my foot.

Those bones had healed over the past few months, but not well enough for me to dance with the elites of Boston or New York again. I'd tried after the mandated rehabilitation post-surgery but the intensity of the pain eliminated any grace from my movements.

Another drink might drown out the pain of losing my career. I might regret the alcohol tomorrow when I was in meetings, but now it seemed to be the only way to get through a conversation with my sister.

This time, it was Amanda who picked up her glass. She drained it and set it down with a determined click.

"I'm sorry, Cass. You have no idea how sorry I am. I'm so humiliated that I was stupid enough to think he'd take care of me. I…I was just in a bad place after losing my job in Manhattan and that stupid civil case."

Even her apology was about *her*. Some things wouldn't change, no matter how much I wished they would. I pushed my drink away, not wanting to add more to my list of woes—delicious as that list would be sliding down my throat.

"I wish I could believe you," I said. "And it would have been a better apology if you hadn't brought me to a club. You know I'm not comfortable here."

On top of that tasty tidbit of not-my-scene, my sister didn't deserve another chance with me. Lowell wasn't the first boyfriend she'd stolen, and I doubted he'd be the last. Amanda couldn't help herself if someone else had a shiny new thing. She had to have it, but she lost interest as soon as she did.

"I'm considering staying in the area. You know, to be closer to you and Mom," she murmured.

I sighed, dreading where this conversation was headed. Amanda wasn't nearly as clever as she assumed she was. As my mother used to say, "Amanda exists in her own world."

But even my mother quit speaking to my older sister when she started dating Lowell. My grammy insisted on it though I didn't much see the point. Amanda wasn't going to change. Thanks to years of coddling from both my parents, my sister truly did believe the world revolved around her—and that she could do no wrong.

But the civil suit she lost earlier in the year proved otherwise. Still, if that hadn't shown her the fault in her ways, nothing would. And Amanda had followed up being sued with stealing my boyfriend, so…yeah, she wasn't changing.

Ignoring Amanda's spiel for wanting to be closer to Mom, I looked around the swanky nightclub. The place teemed with well-dressed young people. It was crowded, but the music was low-key and the beat strong. I listened for another moment. Yes, this was totally danceable. Or sit-back-and-chillable. Not easy to pull off. The decor slid from pewter to silver with a few splashes of crimson to add warmth and interest. Overall, I'd say the club hit the mark of reflecting what its hip, urban customers wanted.

"So, you'll let me live in Grammy's house?"

There it was. My stomach rolled. She'd gotten me mellow with liquor before she popped her question—no doubt with Amanda, there'd also be guilt and tears. Pretty ones that made men want to protect her from me.

"No, I won't. There was a reason she left it to *me*," I said. My tone was even. Like I hadn't lived through the worst of betrayals—finding my sister clutched in my boyfriend's embrace the day I'd come home early because I broke my foot.

That day was the worst one in my life. I'd lost my career with one of the most prestigious dance companies in the world, and I'd lost my boyfriend and my sister mere hours later. Grammy had already offered me a place to recuperate from my surgery when I called her while I was in the emergency room. So instead of staying to hash out the details of my sister's lips—and other parts—locked with my boyfriend's, I jumped in a cab and headed to the nearest Amtrack station, where I bought a ticket on the next train heading to Providence. My grandmother met me at the station and offered me a hug and her prescription pain killers to help me get through the next couple of days until I could have the surgery back in Boston. Through tears of rage and pain I stepped into the first and popped the second.

"I know she did, and that was so selfish of her, of you." Amanda bit her lip, trying to contain a further outburst. I waited, impatient to be done with this conversation.

She raised her gaze, her eyes glassy with tears. "I…I don't have anywhere else to go." She seemed bewildered—as if she had no idea how to solve this issue on her own. "You know I was living with Lowell, and the new firm in Boston didn't hire me because of that stupid civil suit," Amanda said, exasperation weighing on her tone.

"You mean because the guy could prove you lied about sexual harassment?" I asked.

"Don't make the situation between us any weirder, Cass," Amanda chided.

"The situation between us will always be weird." I leaned my elbows on the table. "I can't trust you."

She sat back, her pink lips painted in a pout. "That's not exactly fair."

"It's not fair that I can't dance professionally anymore. It's not fair that I found you naked with *my* boyfriend. It's not fair that my favorite person in the world died, and it's *definitely* not fair that now, on top of all that, you expect me to share the house she left to me—and me *alone*—with you. But this has never been about fairness because if it was, we'd have to talk about our parents and how they treated us differently. But the answer is still no, you cannot live with me."

Before Amanda could respond, I picked up my glass and fled the table.

Chapter Two
Nico

"I'm heading out," Aidy said.

I pulled her in for a hug. "You did an amazing job with this space," I said. My pride in her accomplishments warmed my chest, and I gave her an extra squeeze.

The nightclub's mellow lighting and monochromatic color scheme added to the high-end vibe. The place was full but didn't feel excessively crowded, thanks to the well-spaced tables and the large dance floor behind the bar area. While the music thumped some bass-heavy-beat, the thick glass blocks Aidy had chosen muffled much of the sound, allowing the nondancers to continue to converse with ease.

She patted my back. When she backed away, she smiled widely and laughed. "I did, didn't I?"

"You hit this one out of the park, slugger," Knox, our brother, said as he, too, leaned in to hug Aidy.

Their happiness soothed some of the other emotions I struggled to avoid. Still, my good mood hollowed out a bit as I took in my younger siblings, their spouses, and their obvious contentment.

I clapped Ryder, Aidy's husband, on the back as he slipped his arm around her waist. Aidy seemed to exude more confidence from Ryder's nearness. Whatever it was, the two of them *worked* together. I hadn't been sure about their relationship in the beginning, but Ryder had proven to be exactly the man Aidy and my sweet niece Lilia needed. More, he was the husband and father they *deserved*.

As an added bonus, Thanksgiving was way more fun—almost like the old ones we'd had at our parents' house years ago—with Ryder and his aunt and uncle joining our meal.

From the gleam in Ryder's eye, I wouldn't be surprised if they announced another pregnancy soon. That thought brought a strange pang to my chest—like I'd missed out on something or lost a deeply personal thing.

Not that I was looking for a relationship or a child. I wasn't. I was a confirmed bachelor. The one who didn't do attachments or the whole life commitment thing that Ryder was currently rocking so well. I had my niece to spoil, but…hell. I was lonely.

Maybe I should get a pet. Something I could snuggle and pat and talk to about my day, who'd care about my comings and goings.

My brother-in-law cuddled my baby sister closer, his mouth whispering something into her ear as he led her from the club. Knox settled his forearms on the gleaming scored metal expanse that Aidy had custom-made for the space.

"She's really settled into her roles," Knox mused.

"She has. They suit her well. I'm glad she's happy."

I lifted my beer and drank deep. We were both in a mellow mood thanks to Pearlescent's smooth grand opening. When restauranteur Lear Scott approached us with her ideas for the place, she'd clicked immediately with Aidy. I would typically run point on our projects, but after seeing the women together, I'd passed this project off to Aidy, and she'd come through, big time. I was sure the reviews of the converted warehouse were going to be fantastic, and Aidy had added a big feather to her portfolio.

I couldn't have been prouder of her.

Being so many years older than Aidy, I'd expected to marry first. But Aidy, my baby sister, walked down the aisle. Then, even after my stupidity nearly ruined their relationship, Knox married the love of his life, Emmaline, just a couple of months ago. After a long sit-down between the three Wright siblings, Emmaline agreed to become our newest business partner. Granted, if I hadn't approved the option, Knox would have left the firm for the second time. And I wasn't sure Aidy would have stayed with me if I hadn't asked Emmaline to come aboard.

My siblings were paired off, happy, and that left me in the same position I'd been in for nearly ten years: alone.

At first because I needed to be. I'd needed to focus on Aidy—which I hadn't done well—and our company, which I'd brought back from the brink of bankruptcy twice. The second time was part of what led to the fissures in my relationship with Knox, but, hopefully over time, we'd work through his anger with me.

Knox seemed to realize that he was next to me and he shot Emmaline a glance. She was relaxed, but Knox no longer was. He'd yet to forgive me for not trusting her to have our firm's best interests at heart. My need to make her prove her loyalty hurt her feelings and blew Emmaline's trust in Knox. He'd had to work hard to rebuild it.

"We're going to head out," he said, his tone stiffening along with his features.

"You don't have to—" I began.

"We do," he cut me off. "We'll see you Monday." He turned away. "Are you ready, darling?" he murmured into Emmaline's ear. She shot me an apologetic shrug and said yes. As if I hadn't been chastised enough for not trusting her, for assuming Emmaline was like the other women who had moved through Knox and my lives, she had to go and be decent, honest, and empathetic. I didn't deserve her concern, and I knew it.

I smiled and dipped my head as they told me goodbye, not willing to add any more tension to our powder keg of a situation. I tracked them, happy for their happiness…and disinterested in returning to my lonely house where I'd spend another night rehashing the many bad decisions I'd made since I first met my ex-fiancée, Amanda.

I stared into my beer. Damn. I wished I'd made different choices then, and I wish I'd been smarter after she hurt and betrayed me. But I hadn't. And I was alone because of those choices; without my family to soothe the edges of the ache I'd never tell them I experienced. They didn't need to know how little I slept, worrying over each interaction when I'd made the wrong choice, taken the less noble path, let my anger, fear, or frustration override my common decency. My father would be disappointed in the jaded ass I'd become.

I pushed my beer aside. A thin, tanned arm settled onto the bar next to me, followed by a deep, heartfelt sigh.

I settled back into my seat, turning to find out who could have made a noise that so perfectly suited my own feelings.

Chapter Three
Cassia

A man shifted next to me, turning to face me. His expression morphed from pensive to alert.

His eyes were a shade of brown that lacked all the warmth of chocolate but were filled with swirls of pain and shadows that slowly turned into hot licks of interest. I shivered with awareness, enjoying that reaction.

"You look familiar," he said. "Do I know you?"

"I don't think so, and I don't know you," I replied with a smile that was mostly teeth. Dealing with Amanda left me frustrated, and I didn't want anything further to do with people tonight.

He sized me up again, lingering on my breasts. My jaw tightened. "Get a good look, 'cause that's *all* you're getting, buddy."

His lazy upward sweep accompanied an easy, unrepentant grin. "I need to be closer for the kind of look you deserve, especially if that's *all* I'm getting."

First, Amanda brought up our stupid shared ex, and now *this* guy flirted with me.

"Are you telling me you're interested in…" I lowered my voice as I let my long, coated lashes drop to half-mast over my eyes. "More than just one night?"

His brown eyes flared with shock, maybe even panic, the lighter centers now a starburst of lust and intense interest.

"I'm interested in you," he said.

Well, *swoon*. Someone bumped me from behind and I grunted from the pain in my foot as I slid forward. The guy I'd been talking to glanced over my shoulder, frowned, and rose to block the next shove. His arm pressed lightly against my back, letting me know that the push was fairly intense. That gesture was kind but he'd still eyed me moments before like I was a candy bar ready to be devoured—and tossed aside, no doubt.

"What did you mean? About more than one night?" he asked, close enough for me to feel the warmth of his chest against my side. Something in his tone...it dipped, almost as if he were disappointed in my racy comment. I wasn't in the mood to deal with anyone's opinion of me.

"Mmm... Marriage." I glanced up to take in his shock. I bit my lip to keep from giggling. "That's right. I want a man who wants to commit to *more* than a hookup."

He studied me, clearly trying to figure out what game I was playing. I wasn't sure yet, but my frustration with the night fizzled out. Talking to this guy was...*fun*.

"It's good to know what you want." He looked at me for a long moment, making it clear what he wanted. A shiver danced down my arms, ending with tingles of awareness in my fingertips. What would that beard feel like? His lips? They were firm, but soft. And his eyes...they were warmer now, like a cup of hot cocoa.

"It is," I said, feigning breathlessness. "It's soooo good."

He smirked, clearly amused by my ridiculousness. That made me smile back—a real one. I relaxed, enjoying this game I'd created. His breath caught as I grinned, and his pupils flared.

I was playing with fire with this one—and while I definitely wasn't interested in a fling, I wanted to continue our banter.

"So, can I count on you?" I fluttered my eyelashes. Teasing this guy was, at the moment, much more fun than dealing with Amanda. I refused to think of her, to let her ruin this moment.

"To…what, exactly?" he asked. "Save you from the people trying to shove you into the bar? Absolutely." His grin was lopsided, almost like he'd forgotten how. My chest warmed at the thought that I'd brought it out of him.

His voice was deep, rich, and silky. His dress shirt and tie screamed well-to-do. Not the bored, uber-rich trust fund fashion of my ex, but definitely a successful professional.

"To continue to enjoy your company? Again, yes."

I tilted my head, fully enjoying the conversation. "That's much appreciated." I leaned in closer, keeping it just between us. "I'll enjoy you keeping people from shoving me and your company right back while I take a breather from my sister."

"Sister?"

He turned with me toward the table I'd left, and Amanda tilted her head, watching the two of us. His eyes widened when she glanced at my companion, and Amanda's shoulders stiffened before she turned away.

Oh, that was interesting. *Now*, I was intrigued.

"You know Amanda?" His voice was tight; all pleasantness leached from his face. He moved with a woodenness I wouldn't have believed when, just moments before, it was supple and warm.

"Yes," I said slowly, trying to understand the switch that flipped with this guy. "We're related, hence my use of the word 'sister.' And if you're looking for a good time, she'd be the one—"

"Never," he snapped. "I'd *never* be interested in anything she had to offer."

My mouth gaped open. "Do you know—"

"You're like a shadowy version of her," he said, cutting me off. His head tilted, studying me. "Broodier, less vivacious."

I scowled because I hated being reminded of my beautiful sister. "I think you mean I'm the less attractive, *meaner* version." I showed him my teeth. We were right back where we'd started.

This time his smirk was surface-level, not the warm lopsided one that I already yearned to see again. That smile had meant something. Now…whatever this guy's history with Amanda, it wasn't pretty. But then, most people who spent time with her ended up with a negative opinion.

"If you think you'll meet your future husband in a bar, then you're not mean." He shook his head with…was that pity? "You're naive."

I glared. "I'm not naive!"

He raised an eyebrow as if to say, *really?* "A free piece of advice: I suggest you find a different path from your sister's. Because she definitely owns that one. Worse, it only leads to truly ugly places."

He turned away from me just in time for me to get shoved once more, right in the middle of my back. I stumbled—almost into the man I'd considered sexy and fun just moments before.

The burn of tears pressed against my eyelids. This man's insults hit their mark. I wasn't my beautiful, confident older sister, and I *was* naive.

If Lowell taught me anything, it should have been never to trust a man, especially around Amanda. I righted myself, wobbling a little in my pumps as pain shot up my foot and strode around the gorgeous, cruel asshole who'd ruined my night—and the few shreds of confidence I'd managed to rebuild since the Lowell disaster.

Maneuvering toward the table through the ever-growing seam of hot, sweaty bodies took time. Time I didn't have. How many people had they let in here in the last twenty minutes? Too many.

I was on the verge of crying because of that man's words. How he'd managed to find his mark with such deadly accuracy, I would never know, but he'd hit it. And I bled once more, always the one hurt by Amanda's actions.

I snatched my purse from the table—why'd I leave it there in the first place? He was right—I was naive *and* stupid.

But that man put me in my place. He'd shown me how ridiculous it was to flirt in a bar. I swiped angrily at my eyes as I struggled through the crowd, desperate to get away from Amanda and her sweet smile and cruel jabs.

"You can't just leave me here," Amanda said as I slid my purse on my shoulder.

"Yes, I can. Go home, Amanda. Stop ruining my life."

"It's not my fault you hit on a guy who has it out for me," she huffed. "He's such a dick."

In that, we could agree. I whirled from the table, unable to ignore the pain flaring from my foot and hobbled toward the exit.

Amanda and Bar Guy deserved each other.

"Cassia!"

I heard Amanda but I ignored her. I was in a bar in a city neither of us had ever lived in, and Amanda was already ruining this place, too.

"Cassia, come on… What about letting me stay with you?" Amanda yelled again.

"I already told you no," I shouted over my shoulder, but I didn't look back. I didn't want to talk to anyone, *especially* my sister. Or Bar Guy.

I just wanted my bed, my body pillow, and to be left *alone*.

Chapter Four
Nico

I scrubbed my palms over my cheeks, hoping it would help with the exhaustion I'd suffered all weekend. Then I pushed my way out of the car and strode from my normal spot toward our office building.

I'd watched Amanda's sister reel from my comments. Worse, once I stopped protecting her, someone shoved into her hard—hard enough for me to worry about her being hurt. But before I could come to her defense once more, she'd turned and walked away, shoulders back, gait proud…with *tears* in her pretty gray eyes.

Because of what I'd said? I hoped not, but I kept returning to my words. Because I hadn't thought through what I was saying—*who* I was talking to—and guilt ate at me all that night and the next.

"I was such a dick," I muttered.

Amanda's sister was an innocent bystander, the person I took out my anger on with little thought to how it affected her. I wish I knew how to get in touch with her, to apologize. To tell her that my bitterness and rage should have been directed at Amanda.

The more time I pondered our brief interaction, the more I realized there was no way I ever would have looked twice at

Amanda if I'd met her sister first. I wanted to—had to—get to know her.

"Dammit, Nico, let it go. She has to hate you. She *should*."

Maybe it was better to wish I'd never met either of them. That would make my life simpler. But no matter how many times I told myself that, I couldn't get the beautiful brown-haired woman out of my mind.

My steps stuttered when I heard a soft, pitiful mew. I glanced around, heart pounding. There it was again. I swallowed and tentatively headed toward the side of our building, where I'd heard the faint cry.

I crouched next to a damp piece of cardboard that seemed to have fallen out of the Dumpster.

"Hey, there," I murmured to the speck of fur. A tiny pink mouth opened and the pitiful mewl slid out.

"Where's your mommy, little baby?" I whispered, hesitant to reach out toward the kitten. I looked around, not seeing another cat. I hesitated before I headed back toward my car, hoping the distance would cause the mama cat to return. Good thing I'd arrived so early this morning—I had a couple of hours before my first meeting. I set my briefcase in the passenger seat and settled into mine. I sipped my coffee and waited.

The tiny cries were faint but still discernible now that I'd opened the car window. I finished my coffee, but there still wasn't a sign of the mother. I glanced at my watch. Nearly an hour had passed. I exited my car, briefcase in hand, and headed back toward the kitten, not my office.

It whined again, and before I realized what I was doing, I had the calico snuggled around my suit coat rubbing its downy head with my chin. "Hush, little one. I have you. Nothing bad will happen now. I have you."

"Who are you talking to?" Knox asked.

I turned, my briefcase bumping my thigh. He and Emmaline stared back at me, eyes widening as they saw the kitten clutched to my chest. Emmaline's features softened but Knox was worse. He loved animals.

"Aw. It's tiny," Knox whispered, clearly already under the kitten's spell. He glanced around, worry tugging at his brows. "Where's its mom?"

"I don't know. I waited for a while but she hasn't returned. He's been crying, under the cardboard. I think he's hurt. At least hungry."

"Well, don't just stand there," Knox exclaimed. "Take it to the vet."

"But I have a conference call in an hour—"

"Not anymore. Your baby takes precedence," Knox said. His tone threatened terrible retribution if I disavowed the kitten. I didn't want to say that, though. I rubbed my cheek against the kitten's little head again, beaming when the faintest of purrs revved through its body.

"Yeah, okay, if you're sure."

"We'll handle the meeting, no problem," Knox said, his features softening. Hopefully, that kindlier expression was due to relief about my caring for the kitten, not the fact that he didn't want me in the office.

Thankfully, a local vet squeezed us in. I closed my eyes as I waited for the vet to enter the small exam room I'd been ushered into. The sister's heart-shaped face called to me, her chin, small and pointed flowed from her sharp, blade-like nose. Between the two sat lush pink lips and, to the side, those high, wide cheek-bones. But it was her eyes, the light soft gray, like the moment before a fresh spring dawn, that caught my interest.

I wanted to forget that Amanda was connected to the first woman I'd been deeply attracted to in ages.

The door clicked shut as the vet entered, and the kitten's head popped up at the sound. He blinked, bleary-eyed. "Hi, I'm Dr. Shapiro. What do we have here?"

I'd gotten the vet's name from Aidy, who'd texted back heart-eyed emojis after she demanded a picture of the ball of fur who seemed to have settled in to sleep in my lap in the car.

"A kitten I found. He—I'm pretty sure he's male—was under some cardboard boxes."

"Let's have a look," Dr. Shapiro said.

I scooped up the kitten and placed it on the large metal exam table. Unable to stop myself, I ran my thumb over the small head, enjoying the silky feel of the furry ears. I'd missed this—a connection with another living being.

"I hope you're not too sick," I whispered.

The vet listened to the cat's chest and then palpated his belly. He opened the kitten's mouth and then used a penlight to check his eyes.

"You're right about him being male. I'd say he's seven weeks. A *little* young to be without his mama, but not the youngest I've seen. He's dehydrated and malnourished, which suggests his mother's been gone a while. My suggestion would be to let us give the little guy some fluids, his vaccines and, while he's here, we can neuter him tomorrow. I'll be sure to fit him in. That way, you can pick him up late tomorrow afternoon, barring any further issues, once I'm sure he's healthy and the procedure's over."

"Already?" I asked, surprised. My hand closed around the little body, my protective instincts in high gear. "Shouldn't we wait?"

The vet shook his head. "The sooner the better, really. They heal quickly and, ah, you know, can't miss what they can't remember."

I grimaced. "I'd remember."

The vet chuckled. "You're not the first man to say that."

My shoulders slumped. "We're the worst, aren't we?"

He smiled. "If you mean 'we' being the men, then, yes, we are."

I sighed. "It's for the best?"

The vet nodded. "He'll be more docile, more likely to stay home." He frowned. "You are keeping him aren't you?"

"Yeah. Fred found me. I want to keep him."

Dr. Shapiro raised an eyebrow. "Fred, huh? Well, why don't you talk to my receptionist about when to pick up Fred. She can also get you started with appropriate kitten food."

I ended up walking out of the vet's office juggling food, bowls, and even a scratching post the receptionist said felines enjoyed. I was pretty sure she'd up-sold me on most of it, but I wanted Fred to have the best of everything—including a fancy new name tag and blue leather collar I'd picked out. The receptionist let me put that on his neck before I gave him one more scratch behind the ears, my heart aching at his tiny purr, before I had to leave him.

I drove back to the office, trying without success to brush the cat fur from my suit. Sitting in traffic, my mind drifted once more to Amanda's sister.

I wish I'd asked her name. I wished I'd spent more time with her. Sure, lust licked through my gut whenever I thought of her, but I enjoyed her banter, her smile, the softness of her skin and the hint of laughter around her pretty eyes. I liked all of her.

I grumbled as I strode into the office, straight to the conference room where I was supposed to meet with a new client. I'd have to talk to Knox about how the first call of the day went, but for now I pulled out my file on the dance studio project and went over my notes, all while still hyper-focused on my run-in on Saturday night.

At thirty-four, my ability to manage myself seemed less likely. I ran a successful architectural firm. I managed to schmooze with wealthy patrons and help out at the local cycle club where I was a member, mentoring younger athletes. I offered my time at Rhode Island School of Design with a capstone course.

And I was *still* an asshole who didn't know how to keep his mouth shut. I wondered if I could find Amanda's sister. Apologize…

The door opened, and I spun toward it, shock slamming its fist straight into my chest.

Our potential client, whose name was Cassia Bevins, was none other than Amanda's sister. I never would have put the two together and not just because they had different last names. Cassia. Such a pretty name.

Her long, lean, bare legs were cut off by the knee-length black skirt. The seductive flare of her trim hips led into a deep curve at her waist and the silky green blouse covered her lithe shape.

"Shit."

Damn my stupid mouth yet *again*.

Cassia tipped her head to the side, her eyes flaring with anger and hurt. Her lips pressed tight before the right corner lifted the smallest amount.

"Seriously? That's what you have to say to me? Oh, you *are* a shit. And, clearly, this meeting isn't going to work out." She turned on her slim black shoes my sister called ballet flats and began a seductive hip-roll out of the room.

"Wait! Please don't go."

"I'm absolutely leaving," she called over her shoulder. Her lips were painted a pale pink. They were such a soft, innocent color but her body was that of a siren. No, a *goddess*.

My heart hammered. The glass wall reflected her image back, and she blinked multiple times, her chin quivering. Her breath caught as if she was about to cry. Again. All because she'd run into me a second time. I couldn't blame it on the lights or alcohol or her crazy beliefs that there was a man on the planet who walked into a bar expecting to find his soul mate.

"Just…just give me a minute. Please," I said, extending my stride to catch up with her. I managed to loudly smack my hand onto the doorknob just as she reached for it.

She sucked in a breath, a couple of tears leaking from the outer corner of her eyes. I wasn't sure if it was from the loud noise or if she now feared me. Just fucking great. Either way, this wasn't how I wanted the reunion between us to go. I took a step back, holding my hands out in supplication.

"I'm so sorry. I didn't mean to startle you. I just wanted a moment to talk…"

She dashed her hand at the errant tear and glared. "Stay out of my way. In fact, stay far, far away from me."

"Look—I'm really sorry."

"I don't want your apology," she said between gritted teeth. "All I want is to leave and *never* see you again."

"Cass—"

"No, don't you dare use my name. You can call me Ms. Bevins. Better yet, don't ever call me *anything*."

My heart pounded so hard at her words I wondered if she could hear it. "I'm sorry, Ms. Bevins," I said. I used my body to block the exit.

I tried to see her eyes but she'd dropped her chin to her chest and studied the distressed, reclaimed Brazilian hardwoods at our feet.

Fuck. I jammed my fingers in my hair. I couldn't have bungled this situation any worse.

"My sister found the flooring," I said. "You know Aidy, right? Isn't that how you ended up calling us?"

Cassia shifted her shoulders back and raised her face. The look she shot me was pure hate. At least now she didn't want to cry.

"Aidy is the best person I know here in Providence. Lilia is a treasure."

I smiled, thinking of my niece, ignoring the dig she'd just made at me. "Couldn't have said it better myself."

"Well, we agree on something. Now, please explain to your sister why I will not need your services."

My heart sank right back into my guts. "Please, Ms. Bevins, just give me a moment of your time. I was thinking about our conversation on Saturday, and I wanted a chance to apologize for my behavior then. Maybe we could sit at the table... opposite ends of the table...and...I *never* should have said that to you. I wasn't upset with you anyway, not that that excuses my behavior."

She stared back, stone-faced. "You just hate Amanda, and I'm colored with the same brush. Believe me, that isn't the first time this situation has arisen."

The tension in my shoulders eased. "Well, um, yeah...I...I don't like your sister." But at the look in her eye, I realized that wasn't the right thing to say.

"I mean, I'm sure she has nice qualities..." I was positive Amanda didn't.

Cassia's features softened a bit. "Look, I get you don't want to disappoint Aidy, but there is no way a meeting between us could be productive. You hate my sister, and I dislike you. And I don't want to work with your firm because of how you chose to talk to me Saturday."

"But...you could work with Aidy or Knox. Maybe his wife..." A new thought hit me. "Why didn't you ask Amanda to do your designs?"

Instead of answering me, she yanked her phone out of her purse. She must have called up a name, though I couldn't read it thanks to the glare on the screen, because she put the phone to her ear. She stepped away from me, all the way to the far end of the room. Her back settled against the warm, rich gray wall that

went amazingly well with the deep umber stain on the
wood floors.

"Hi, Aidy. This is Cassia Bevins. I wanted to let you know
that I'm not going to be using your firm to work on plans to
renovate and expand my studio."

She listened for a moment, watching me the whole time.

"Oh, no. I adored the designs. You couldn't have expressed my
wants and needs any better." Warmth spread through me at her
words. I'd created those plans, and I took great pride in the fact
she liked them. Cassia took a deep breath and her eyes narrowed.
"The problem is your brother. Oh, he's here with me now. And he
won't let me leave the room."

I heard a shriek from across the office. I managed to get my
hand off the knob before Aidy slammed into the room. Instead
of looking at her friend, her wrath was leveled on me. I stepped
back until I hit the wall behind me.

"What did Nico do?" Aidy said through clenched teeth.

In ten sentences, Cassia explained our meeting on Saturday,
our flirting, my cruel comments once I realized she was related to
Amanda, and our exchange here in the conference room just now.

"I'll deal with this," Aidy said to Cassia in a brittle voice. "I
deeply apologize for the situation, Cassia. I never, *never* expected
my brother to be such a jerk."

"Thanks," Cassia said, her voice tremulous. She touched Aidy's
shoulder before she walked out. Much as I wanted to go after her
I stood frozen, too shocked by Cassia's dislike of me to move my
feet. I mean, I deserved it, but *still*...I hadn't realized how much
of an impact my words, my actions, had on those around me.

Why hadn't I realized that?

Aidy waited for a beat, then shut the door and whirled to face me. I braced myself, unsure what type of eruption would occur. Aidy wasn't a yeller. She tended to internalize issues and then react in negative, often self-injurious ways—like binge-drinking in high school or staying with a selfish asshole of a boyfriend throughout college. Instead, I yelped when she gripped the front of my dress shirt. Her fingers squeezed, then twisted my nipple as hard as she could.

"You are going to fix this, Nico Warren Wright. Cassia's trying to help the community here, and we're landing this project because it'll be great PR. But, more importantly, she just got out of a terrible break-up that included her sister *banging her boyfriend*."

My mouth dried up. "Amanda screwed her boyfriend?"

Of course she did. I thought I had reason to hate the woman, but Cassia…Cassia couldn't help being related to her.

"She not only seduced him, but she also moved in with him— forcing Cassia to move out."

"That's horrible," I said.

Aidy stabbed a finger in my direction. "And now you've proven to be just as big of an asshat as he was."

I never cheated or kicked a woman out. I simply didn't have relationships with them. The fact that Aidy would compare me to a dickwad who obviously had terrible taste in women pissed me off. "Does your husband know you talk like that?" I asked.

Wrong response. Fast as an adder, she pinched and twisted my other nipple. This time I nearly doubled over from the pain, but I couldn't because of Aidy's iron grip.

"I call it like I see it. Don't condescend to me on top of the fact that you upset a really nice woman. I am so, so angry with you...until you fix this, you can't see Lilia."

She dropped her hands, turned on her heel and opened the door.

"You'd keep my niece from me?" I asked, rubbing my abused chest.

"No," she shot back, eye blazing, cheeks bright, and I realized Aidy had been keeping it together up until this moment. I'd never seen her this angry. I backed into the wall, hands out, to protect myself from Aidy's wrath.

"*You're* keeping you from your niece. She doesn't need to have such a shit for a role model. First with me, then Knox. Now clients. I don't know what's gotten into you, but you better figure it out if you want to have any decent relationships left," she hissed.

Chapter Five
Cassia

I swiped at the tears leaking from my eyes. Dammit. That was twice Nico Wright made me cry. *Twice*. And I wasn't a crier. Once I was old enough to understand that my parents focused all their attention on Amanda because they simply didn't care about me, I quit crying.

I hadn't cried when I caught Amanda snuggled on Lowell's dick. I hadn't even cried when I shattered the bones in my foot, or later, when the Boston Ballet revoked my principal dancer position. But the damn tears streamed down my burning cheeks as I stormed down the building's steps and headed toward my car, which was parked a couple blocks to the east. I'd gotten confused even with the GPS and decided it was easier to walk to the location than try to find the correct address while fighting traffic.

I took a deep shuddering breath, trying to control the anger ricocheting through me. Was I angry with Nico? With myself? Some, but most of my fury focused on Amanda. I gritted my teeth. She was a piece of work, one I wished many times I wasn't related to. But we didn't get what we wanted—at least some of us didn't.

A few months ago when my mother dragged Amanda with her to visit me after my surgery, Amanda had admitted she'd taken Lowell's call, pleased that he told her *she* was the sister he wanted to date. I'd stared at her, dry-eyed, when Amanda promised that they'd gotten carried away, but she'd gotten tired of waiting for Lowell to find the right time to break up with me.

I hadn't realized then, but my mother knew my sister lusted after my boyfriend and told *her* mother. I was the most pathetic person in the family, and that was why Grammy left me the large building I planned to turn into a studio, her Victorian, and a big chunk of change. I was also so grateful to Grammy for loving me when the rest of my family didn't.

My sister, according to Grammy's last letter to me, could suck it. *It* being any part of Lowell she wanted because I was done...*d-o-n-e* with men, with people. *Especially* with Amanda and the big jerk who'd made me cry, Nico.

I shrieked and nearly twisted the ankle of my bad foot when I jerked away from the hand that clamped down on my wrist. In my attempt to right myself, I stumbled back into the long, lean male body that now had his other arm wrapped around my waist.

"Whoa. Easy. I'm not going to hurt you," Nico said, his tone placating. "I'm trying to keep you alive."

I noted the multitude of cars whizzing past mere inches from my body. "I..." No words squeezed past my throat, but I couldn't look away. I hadn't realized...how could I have not noticed those cars, the noise?

"You scared me," Nico said.

I stumbled back and pain flared through my foot, up my leg, straight to my jaw. Before I could clamp it shut, a whimper drifted past my lips.

"What's wrong?" Nico's voice rose, worry seeping into it. "Hey? Are you okay?"

"No," I snapped. I panted, hoping the change in my breathing pattern would push back the black dots crowding out my vision.

This man brought out the worst in me. Sure, when I first saw him at the bar, I'd walked *toward* him, drawn by an ephemeral connection. His acorn-colored hair framed chiseled features and his broody lips settled in a short beard that was just the right side of scruffy. He was Lowell's opposite—golden skin and burnished hair to Lowell's dark locks and hazy blue eyes. That was, until Nico opened his mouth.

I tried to put weight on my foot but winced. At least I didn't cry out again.

Before I could speak, Nico lifted me into his arms. I raised my arms to his chest, planning to push him away but he stepped off the curb and I yelped, wrapping my arms around his neck.

"Where are you taking me—put me down!"

"I'm taking you to the clinic around the corner. My friend works there. He'll check out your leg."

"I don't want to go to another doctor," I gritted out. If I saw another doctor in my lifetime, it was one too many.

"You're hurt. I want to fix it."

"Maybe you don't grab women on the street."

"You didn't hear me when I called your name, and we've established you were about to walk into traffic. I didn't know what else to do."

Fair enough. I'd been too emotional to think straight, but the pain cut through my haze.

"Put me down," I pleaded, hating that people stared at me. I hadn't even let anyone carry me out of the ballet studio when the bones in my foot shattered. Heat gathered on my neck and shot up over my cheeks. "I'm too heavy for you to carry."

"You're not heavy," Nico said. "In fact, I'd say you're just right."

"Will you stop with the flirting and the nice-guy act?" I huffed. "We both know that isn't really you."

Nico frowned. "I can see why you'd think that. And I'll apologize again. And again."

"I don't want your apology because I don't want to be anywhere near you!"

He pushed through a doorway and strode up to the reception desk. "She hurt her foot. Is Dr. Hogue available? I'd like him to look it over."

I opened my mouth to tell him it wasn't necessary but his expression softened. "Please, Ms. Bevins. It would make me feel *much* better. And I'm covering the cost."

I relented because my foot throbbed. Maybe I could get some painkillers out of the deal.

The receptionist set down her phone. "I spoke with Dr. Hogue, and you're in luck. He's available before his next appointment, so let's get her into a room."

Wow. This place wasn't busy? Oh, right, it was after the first crush, just before lunch. I bet if we'd shown up an hour or two later, I'd have at least that long of a wait. I remained stiff in Nico's arms as he strolled through the waiting room and into the exam room. He set me on the padded exam table and stepped back.

A dull red appeared above his beard and he fidgeted, his face contorted into a contrite expression more suited to a small boy who'd been reprimanded for eating too many sweets.

"I really am sorry about your foot. And for scaring you. And for what I said Saturday, which I didn't mean—"

"I forgive you," I said, cutting him off. I didn't. I'd continue to mull over his comments on Saturday night for months, hurt each time. "You're a brooder, Cassia Bevins," my grammy used to tell me. "You need to learn to let things be."

Nico shook his head. "No, you don't. But I'll keep telling you until you do."

I threw up my hands. "What are you going to do? Follow me around like a puppy?"

"If I need to." His expression was so earnest, I believed he would, which wasn't at all what I needed. Why couldn't he just accept what I told him? I wanted to cross my arms over my chest, but I didn't—I couldn't let him see how much he'd hurt me by comparing me to Amanda.

I never let anyone see, mainly because few seemed to care.

Like Nico had already noted, I *was* the shadowy version of my sister, the one most people simply brushed off, ignored, or pushed around to get to Amanda's bright light. I always had been. What people failed to understand was that she was like an angler-fish, her beacon of bubbly good nature just another trick to draw in prey. She'd use the other person and spit them out, not because she had to but because she could.

Before I could reply, the door opened and a blond, built man in his early thirties walked in. What was it about Providence and sexy men? Clearly I'd been living in the wrong city.

He smiled at me, and I nearly smiled back—he was *that* potent. But he didn't give me the same zing of awareness as Nico.

I grimaced, hating that I was more attracted to Bar Guy the jerk than the kindly doctor.

"Good morning. I'm Dr. Simon Hogue. I see you have problems with your foot."

Nico moved toward the door, but I snagged his arm. My heart pounded and anxiety flooded through me. I hated visiting a doctor, especially since I'd had meningitis as a ten-year-old. There'd been so many needles, so much pain…Then, I broke my foot and I'd postponed visits, letting the pain get worse and worse because I was so scared about the surgery. I'd caused myself much more agony than necessary, yet I couldn't seem to cope with a doctor's visit alone. The mere idea of being in here, alone, at a doctor's mercy, made me light-headed.

"Don't leave," I said, forcing myself to meet his gaze.

Nico's brows shot upward. He searched my face for a long moment before he nodded. "If that's what you want."

I didn't *want* to be here; he'd brought me. "Thank you." My grip on his sleeve lessened, but I didn't let go.

"Want to tell me what's going on?" Dr. Hogue asked.

"I broke the talus and the left two tarsals a few months ago." The names of the small bones rolled off my tongue now—I'd learned their purpose in my foot to better discuss my issues with my former doctor who'd been affiliated with the Boston Ballet— not that it had done me much good. He'd breezed in and breezed out, not seeming to listen to my comments. That was the other reason I didn't like doctors. What was the point of going to see one if they wouldn't listen to my symptoms and complaints?

Dr. Hogue winced. "An accident?"

"Yes. I landed wrong after a leap. I'm—I was a ballerina."

"You were?" Nico said. He snapped his fingers then pointed. "*That's* where I saw you! I took Aidy to *Swan Lake* in Boston. I couldn't get over your leaps. I mean, you're tall," Nico said, eying my legs.

"I'm aware," I snapped. "I'm especially tall for a ballerina, and as the journalists and other dancers told me, it's probably why I shattered my foot." And my dreams.

Chapter Six
Nico

Dr. Simon Hogue glanced between us, his eyes filled with questions. He cleared his throat. "Well, let's look at the foot. Then, we can go from there."

"She stumbled over the edge of a curb, and then couldn't put any weight on it," I said, offering what information I knew.

Cassia frowned and opened her mouth, no doubt to explain that I'd actually been the reason for her latest injury. Instead she hissed through her teeth when Simon palpated her foot.

"That bad, huh? On a scale of one to ten, it would be…" He waited.

"Eight," she croaked, her face pale and sweat dotting her upper lip.

I bit my cheek. Her injury clearly hurt more than she admitted. Simon was a great doctor from everything I'd seen. My brother-in-law Ryder, a pediatrician at the same clinic, spoke highly of his skills and bedside manner, and I trusted him to see more than Cassia let on. Simon made a note with his tablet while she glared at me.

My shoulders slumped. I'd never get to see Lilia again. She'd grow up not knowing she had another uncle besides Knox. And it wasn't as if I were going to have my own kids. This was the longest I'd spent in a woman's company since…well, since Amanda, and Cassia hated me. After what had transpired between us, I couldn't blame her.

Simon settled back on his rolling seat. "Based on how tender your foot is, it's possible at least one of the bones hasn't fused together properly."

She straightened, her expression filled with fear. "As in, it's re-broken?"

Cassia's fingers flexed on my sleeve, gripping my dress shirt more tightly. Dammit, I didn't want her to be hurt, either physically or emotionally. She hadn't done anything wrong. I'd loved her flirting on Saturday, had been a very willing participant, until she brought up Amanda. As soon as I let my mouth run, I wished I could take back the words, take back the shame I'd seen on Cassia's beautiful face. She wasn't the person I was angry with— honestly, I wasn't even livid with Amanda anymore, *finally*. No, now my anger was self-directed, as it should be, especially after I'd treated Cassia so poorly.

"Let's get the X-ray first," Simon said, rising. He glanced between us. "I'll have the lab tech collect you in a moment."

As soon as Simon shut the door, I said, "I'm so sorry—"

"I don't want to hear it," she said, exhaustion lacing her tone. She massaged her ankle, her expression filled with consternation. "Moving here was supposed to be a fresh start."

"From what?"

She dropped her head forward. "My broken foot, which shattered my dreams of remaining in the Boston Ballet. Hell, getting to perform again at any level. Then, there's my sister stealing my boyfriend and *that* ending with her looking like the victim. Which, in all honesty, she was. Lowell is a pathetic excuse for a person. But now that she's not living with him, she wants to move in with me, and I…" She blew out a breath. "Never mind. I shouldn't dump all this on you." She offered a tight smile but her eyes remained cold, closed.

"That's…an extensive list."

She rubbed the center of her forehead, as if trying to shove away a memory or an ache there. "I could live with the rest of it, but not being able to dance…" Her chin quivered and her damp eyes met mine. Then she seemed to remember I was the reason for her current plight and straightened, turning her head away.

But I'd seen it—the brokenness of her dreams, the vulnerability of a hole in her soul. And oh, did I understand.

"I always wanted to build things," I said. "But when my parents disappeared, I took over my father's firm." I'd never admitted that before. Sure, I was a trained architect, but I'd already fallen out of love with the planning of the buildings before my parents took the last sail. By the time Amanda stole my designs, I'd known I wanted to be the one actually constructing the forms we made. That hadn't been possible, not once I became the sole breadwinner with a brother in college and sister still in high school. They'd both expected a place to work because Dad talked about us joining his firm.

A good place, one that would offer them the best chance to reach their potential. And keep them nearby, where I could watch over them, make sure they stayed healthy…alive. Something I hadn't done for my folks, and I regretted my decision to focus on a big career, be part of a power couple, as opposed to listening to my dad's excellent advice about finding what I loved, both the woman and the work.

I reached out, fumbling a little until I clasped her hand. She let me because she needed someone in that moment—just as I had all those years ago. Only I learned Amanda, the woman I'd planned to marry, was a scheming double-crossing backstabber.

Cassia wasn't any of those things, just a hurt and hurting woman. She accepted my touch as her shoulders heaved once, twice, until she was once again back under control.

"Thanks," she murmured. This time her smile held some warmth.

How could I have ever compared her to Amanda? This beautiful woman proved herself much different from the get-go. From all I'd seen since, Cassia had more mettle than most people.

I wanted to fix her circumstances. Not because Aidy told me to, but because Cassia *deserved* better than her current situation.

Chapter Seven
Cassia

Shock reverberated through me.

"Tarsal tunnel syndrome," I said, wrapping my mind and tongue around each syllable.

"You'll have to see a podiatrist to confirm, but I'm pretty confident," Dr. Hogue said. "What I don't understand is why the doctor at the ballet didn't suspect based on your symptoms."

I looked away, abashed. "Probably because I didn't go to a follow-up appointment." At first I refused, but then, grammy fell ill and I'd been much more concerned about her wellbeing than my own.

Simon nodded. "That would explain the situation."

I nibbled at my lower lip. "So, the sharp pains, the pins and needles sensations…"

"Are being caused by the damage to the tibia nerve. More than likely it was inflamed when you broke your foot." His steady brown eyes met mine. "It's a good thing you came in when you did because if you start treatment now, we can prevent permanent damage."

I licked my lips, my chest quivering. "And…the prognosis?" I whispered.

Dr. Hogue tilted his head. "I can't say for sure—you'll need to schedule with the specialist, but most treatments allow for significant—if not full—recovery. That doesn't mean you'll get to dance professionally—at the Boston Ballet—again," he hastened to add.

I nodded absently. Sure, I missed the rigor of my days, the fluidity of the movements, but I didn't miss the competitiveness, the politicking, the critical comments, reviews, and everything else that removed the joy from ballet.

"But I *could* dance?"

Dr. Hogue patted my hand. "I don't see why not. Eventually. Once the injury heals."

I smiled so wide my cheeks hurt. I threw my arms around Dr. Hogue and hugged him tight. "Oh my…thank you!"

"He's married," Nico said.

I let go of Dr. Hogue, my cheeks flaming but a small smile tugging on my lips—one Dr. Hogue returned. He, too, had heard the jealousy in Nico's tone. "Sorry."

Dr. Hogue chuckled. "Nothing to apologize for. My wife's in medicine as well. She understands the excitement of better-than-expected news. But, for the record, I'm very happily married. *Very*."

I nodded. "Gotcha. And I wasn't…I wouldn't…"

Dr. Hogue laughed again. "I wouldn't either." He softened the comment with a smile. "Now, let me get you the name of the podiatrist I think will be best able to work with you. Be right back."

When he left, I flopped back onto the exam table and stared up at the ceiling, heaving a deep sigh. I gave myself that one long, deep breath. I'd ignored the pain, fearing the tarsal hadn't healed properly but this…this was better than I'd expected.

"I'll be able to dance," I said with a smile. Energy poured

through me, and I wanted to leap up and slide into a fouetté or a grand jette.

"You miss it," Nico said.

I started again. Damn. I kept forgetting he was there. I glanced back, seeing his hooded eyes, taking in his relaxed posture as he leaned against the wall.

"Don't you have better things to do than stare at me?" I sniped. Sure, he'd been nice—since he scooped me up on the sidewalk. But that didn't mean I forgot how he'd treated me before.

"No. Nothing's more important than watching you reclaim your dream."

I rolled my eyes. He pushed off the wall, stepping closer. He touched my cheek with the tip of a finger—a featherlight touch that I did *not* feel straight into my chest.

"There's a fire in you, a lightness… You thought dancing was gone forever."

"You know what it's like to lose your passion," I whispered.

The corner of his mouth tilted up. "I do."

"It's…a relief, but also the biggest rush."

My breath puffed out, and it had nothing to do with him dropping his hand. My skin did not tingle where he'd touched it.

He tilted his head. "I wouldn't know that part." But he smiled, and it held deep sadness. "I'm so glad you don't have to lose your dream, Cassia. *So* glad."

I bit my lip. No, I shouldn't be warming up to Nico Wright. He'd been an ass to me. No matter his reasons, one person shouldn't disparage another, shouldn't make them feel bad about themselves. Though I didn't know the whole story, I sensed that whatever went down with Amanda was why he lost his dream.

And that sucked. No wonder he didn't like her—and me, by extension of our shared parentage. Yet, he hadn't been rude or difficult today. I had. Because I didn't want a repeat of Saturday night.

So, really, I was as much to blame for the situation as he was.

"I'll donate my time," he said, stepping back. He slid his hands into his dress pants' pockets.

I frowned. "What are you talking about?"

"For your dance studio. I'll donate my time. We'll make you the best version you imagine. One you're excited to dance in."

I blinked up at him, uncertainty swirling through me, leaving me lightheaded. "Why?"

"Because some dreams are absolutely worth fighting for. And yours is one of them."

Chapter Eight
Nico

I had no idea what led to my rash announcement that I'd work on Cassia's studio pro bono, but it had nothing to do with concerns about spending time with my niece—or Aidy attempting once again to rip off my nipples—though both were valid concerns.

"Cassia?" I asked.

"Mmm?"

I'd meant to walk her to her car, but she'd turned bleary-eyed and I worried about her driving. So, Cassia was settled in my passenger seat, her head leaning back against the headrest. Her dark hair lay against her cheek and over her neck. She wasn't yet asleep, but she wasn't totally awake either.

Never had such rightness come over me as the decision to help Cassia crossed my mind. My declaration came in response to the flow of euphoria that bubbled from Cassia at Simon's pronouncement that she might well dance again. I wanted her to keep that glow, and the best way to do that was to create a space where she could dance—where she'd shine and give others her light. How could I have assumed Cassia was the shadow version of the sisters? She held so much light, so much burning, beautiful passion for ballet.

She'd striven for her dream. She'd reached it, held it, nurtured it. That was way more than I could say for myself.

I shook my head, still shocked I was driving Amanda's sister home. First, I adopted an alley cat—kitten—and now this. Today couldn't get any weirder.

Well, it would if I had to see Amanda. My knuckles whitened against the steering wheel. I'd situated Cassia in the passenger seat of my high-end sedan while she was still shocked by the good news Simon shared. Otherwise, I was pretty sure she would have fought with me about driving her home.

My phone beeped. No doubt Knox or Aidy replying to my text about getting Cassia home. My nipples ached in response to the thought of Aidy, but her reaction to my helping Cassia thus far had been positive.

"Your sister's staying with you?" I asked.

Cassia snorted. "No way. She wanted to, because it would be easier than trying to fix the problems she created in Manhattan." She raised a hand to her mouth and covered her wide yawn.

I rearranged my hands on the steering wheel. "I see."

"You already know she's an architect."

I should probably tell Cassia that I'd lived with Amanda—that she'd kept *my* apartment after I was fired from our firm and had to move back to Providence after my parents' disappearance. I should, but I didn't want to rehash those ugly memories, not when I was finally putting them to rest.

"Yes. That's why I wondered why you hadn't asked her to help with your studio."

Cassia sighed and looked out the window. "Owing Amanda anything, even a favor, is exhausting. Plus, her work is…rigid. There's a corporate-ness to it, which won't work for kids. Aidy's, however, was playful, boisterous…it made me want to move. Like I could be free in the space—like I could be me and that's what I want for the kids I plan to teach."

I bit my cheek as I nodded. I'd been the lead on this project from the get-go, not Aidy, mainly because my sister's long-overdue honeymoon took precedence over work. But Cassia had contacted Aidy originally, which was why Aidy sent over the initial designs. I'd planned to handle it so that Aidy could focus on the next boutique hotel with Emmaline—something the two women had been coordinating for months.

"Amanda's here because Lowell kicked her out. Well, no that's not why. Our mother's angry with her and Mom's husband won't let Amanda stay with them. He said she needs to take responsibility for her actions."

"She does."

"Agreed. But Amanda thinks because Mom and I have rolled over in the past, we'll do so again," Cassia said on a sigh. "But *I* won't."

I nodded.

"And for the record, we were never close."

"You weren't?" I asked. That may explain why Amanda never mentioned she had a sister.

Cassia shook her head. "She's five years older. The age gap was large when we were young, and Amanda never had much interest in bridging it." A deep V formed between her brows. "Why am I telling you this?"

I shifted in my seat, wondering the same thing. "Because I'm a great listener."

She giggled until she snorted. She clapped her hand over her mouth but didn't stop laughing. "I think that codeine Dr. Hogue gave me went to my head," she mumbled.

Yeah, it definitely had.

"Why do you have different last names?" I asked.

"I legally changed mine when I began to perform. I liked the distance from Amanda and from my parents." She yawned. "They never cared about me, so why should I keep their name?" She slumped against the window and passed out. Soft breaths puffed between her parted lips.

I knew she wouldn't have told me half of that—*most* of that—if she hadn't been on painkillers. Cassia kept her emotions close, and I began to understand why.

The slight rattle—not quite a snore—coming from her nose made me smile despite the ache in my chest at her words. This woman was cute. No, she was much more than that. Cassia was lithe, beautiful, naive, independent, bright, prickly, and advocated for herself.

She enthralled me, and if I hadn't given both Aidy and Cassia my word, I'd run from her. Because in that moment when I pulled up in front of her sprawling Victorian and met her sleepy-soft expression, I knew *nothing* good could come from my intensifying infatuation with Cassia Bevins.

Chapter Nine
Cassia

I slapped at the hand lightly tapping my cheek, then growled at the resulting pain in my fingers.

"Cassia...come on, Cassia...Cass...you have to wake up." The voice was deep, warm, like a thick, downy comforter.

"No," I mumbled closing my eyes tighter. "Sleepy. It's so hard to sleep."

A deep, heartfelt sigh was followed by a soft puff of air against my cheek. "I don't know how to get in your house."

I kept my eyes closed, enjoying this silly game. "With keys."

"Smart ass."

"I have a nice ass. I worked hard for it, but it isn't smart." I yawned. Why was this pillow so hard? "If it was, I wouldn't have let Lowell touch it."

"That codeine wiped you out."

I didn't bother to answer because the darkness pulled me back under. I was vaguely aware of strong, delicious arms lifting me to a warm, solid chest. I sighed, contented, as my cheek touched my cool pillowcase. I'd splurged earlier this month on linen sheets—white ones that softened with each washing. I snuggled into the cloud-soft perfection.

Fingertips brushed the hair back from my temple, and that deep voice spoke in low tones nearby. I liked the voice—it was masculine and soothing… For the first time in months, my foot wasn't throbbing or tingling. Oh, glorious, pain-free sleep! I slid fully into the welcome darkness with a smile tugging at my lips.

I sat up, blinking, my foot pulsing with pain. I bent forward, intent on clasping it, but I didn't manage because my foot was wrapped with an ACE bandage under an ice pack, and all that was wrapped in a towel.

"What…"

I was in my room in Grammy's house—the first-floor bedroom off the stairs. I'd chosen that room to minimize the stairs, which helped me manage the pain. I was clothed, my lashes stuck together like I was still wearing makeup. The room—and the world outside—was dark.

Really dark. I shivered as I pulled up my sheet and down-filled comforter. My teeth chattered as I realized I had no idea what had happened; I didn't know what time it was or who put me to bed.

I gritted my teeth and swung my legs to the floor, crying out when my left foot touched the hardwood.

Footsteps clipped down the hall toward my door. The door creaked open as I slunk back. A man. Large. Backlit. My breath puffed and serrated.

"You're awake."

The switch flipped and the overhead light flared. Nico Wright stood near the door. He had rolled up his dress shirt's sleeves, showing off his tanned and toned forearms. His typically neat hair was a mess—from fingers or sleep, I couldn't tell.

"What…what happened? Why are you…how did I…" I

frowned, unable to collect and hold a full thought.

"I took you to see Simon—Dr. Hogue—at the clinic. He gave you codeine-laced Tylenol, and you fell asleep." Nico shifted. "I didn't want to leave you…I was worried about your reaction, especially after you refused to wake up for lunch…" He trailed off, his cheeks turning a dull red.

The same heat seemed to travel from his cheeks into me, and it warmed my chest and the back of my neck. Nico Wright, the man I'd built up to be a heartless cretin, had been *worried* about *me*. We stared at each other, the moment pulsing, growing with more realizations: Nico *wasn't* unfeeling; he cared deeply. Maybe *too* deeply. He lashed out in an effort to protect his fragile, squishy heart whereas I pulled inward to do the same.

And if that were true, then Nico might actually *like* me… No, that was stupid—absolute garbage logic people told little girls to allow them to continue to let boys, and later, men, treat them poorly. I *knew* this because I'd seen it play out time and again in ballet, where the lead male dancer strutted around like a rooster in the center of his flock of hens.

"Um. Well, thanks. I mean, for making sure I didn't have a reaction to the pain meds."

Nico cleared his throat. "Simon said you'd be thirsty when you woke. I…uh…I left you some water."

"Right. Thanks." I looked away from him and noted the can of sparkling water on my nightstand, one of my reusable towels folded neatly underneath it.

I bit my lip, trying to hold back the emotions rioting through me.

"So, if you're okay, then I'll just go…"

"Have you eaten?" I blurted.

He stepped back. "No. I didn't feel right raiding your kitchen."

"Then, let me make you dinner. As a thank you for babysitting me all day."

"I couldn't just leave…"

But he *could*. Lowell had. My sister and mother had. No one stayed with me, *for* me, except Grammy. But now she was dead.

I added Nico Wright to the list of people who'd cared enough about me to watch over me. The same man I'd castigated all weekend and this morning—to his face—cared for me. Burning shame rolled across my nerve endings. I, of all people, should know that the cover had nothing to do with the book underneath. People assumed my silence meant I was shy, or worse, stuck-up, and disinterested in their conversations. People saw Amanda's bright, bubbly personality and reasoned she was as caring as she seemed open.

Both were wrong—my reserve was a direct response to Amanda's seemingly outgoing cheeriness that held such dark, painful undertones. I held myself back to cope, but people, including Lowell, were attracted to Amanda's beauty and poise because they didn't understand she was a Venus flytrap ready to pounce on the unsuspecting victim.

"You don't have to go out of your way," Nico said, tone brusque. Clearly, gruff was his default setting. I wondered why he chose to act grumpy and disengaged when he was clearly so thoughtful.

"I'm not. I haven't eaten today, and I'm hungry."

Not quite the truth. I *hadn't* eaten today, but my body had long since grown used to being pushed to the limit of endurance with minimal nutrition. Just another aspect of professional ballet I wouldn't miss.

For some reason, I wanted to spend more time with this man—a man who, just hours before, I would have happily shoved out my door. More than happily. But that was before he showed such concern, then tenderness for my injury. But what really got to me was his absolute desire to ensure I was happy. All this from a person I barely knew.

He seemed to be thinking the same thing because he studied me so long, I worried he simply wouldn't answer. Embarrassment welled, and my face heated as I waited for his rejection.

"I'd like that," he said, his voice quiet. "But only if you let me get you dinner. I'm sure your foot needs the rest, and I never bought you a drink on Saturday, though I wanted to."

And just like that, Nico Wright turned from a man I could possibly like to one I could fall for—hard.

Chapter Ten
Nico

I shouldn't have agreed to stay for dinner. Oh, I wanted to spend more time with Cassia. I craved the opportunity to get to know her better, to watch her dance, to see her eyes blaze with passion. But I shouldn't. She was Amanda's sister, and I could not forget that relationship. Just because Cassia said the two of them didn't get along didn't mean they weren't alike in some way…and thinking like that exhausted me.

I was tired of always believing the worst in someone. For tonight, at least, I wanted to enjoy a beautiful woman's company, bask in her smile, and enjoy a meal with someone special.

Mainly, I didn't want to be alone.

I'd realized how often I was lonely when the vet had called to say that Fred would need to stay at the clinic for a few more days due to how slowly he was responding to the fluids. I'd been looking forward to taking the little guy home with me, to letting him snuggle on my bed.

All these thoughts ran through my mind at breakneck speed while I placed an order at a local restaurant. As I stood looking out the living room windows, waiting for the food to be delivered, I told myself to gather my suit coat and leave before Amanda Krantz's sister managed to dig her claws into me. But I didn't move.

Something about Cassia called to me, and I was compelled to know she was on her way to healed. I'd determined to build out her dance studio, not just for Cassia, but for my dream, too. I could prove my capabilities as a contractor: I would showcase a beautiful studio space that I built, not just designed.

While I'd never be able to fulfill that dream full-time, I could at least dabble in my own interests. There was no harm in trying to reach a goal, right? Especially since I was doing what Aidy asked me to do—make things right with Cassia.

I grappled with my duty versus my desires even as I deposited the bag of food on the glossy white engineered-stone counter. I approved of the softly beveled edge, liking how it gave the space a more refined crispness. The hunter green cabinets were a bold choice, as were the built-in hutch and pantry units, but the kitchen, at least double the size of a standard one for these houses, appeared homier for the touches.

I glanced up, noting the slight indention of previous nails that showed the edge of what would have been a tiny kitchen and the much grander dining room. Taking out that wall created a more modern aesthetic, showcasing much of the first floor in the open concept popular with current entertaining trends. I noted the small-paned windows were new but kept the vintage charm of the house.

The warm smell of garlic and herbs perfumed the air, and I inhaled, groaning softly. I was *starving*. I'd missed lunch and, at eight-thirty, it was well past my typical dinner time, too.

"Do you know when the house was built?" I asked Cassia once she'd cautiously made her way into the kitchen. While she was clearly strong enough to manage the crutches, she wobbled a little, as if unused to them. Much as I wanted to go to her, to steady her, I determined by the set of her mouth that she'd refuse my offer.

She shook her head. "No clue, but it's been in the family for generations."

"Oh?"

"Yeah. The Bevins House is part of the historical registry, which is why Grammy was so careful about her remodel."

"Your contractor did a fabulous job of staying within the house's original scope—and its historical building codes."

She blushed, dropping her eyelashes. "Right. Of course you'd know all about that, huh?"

"It's my job to know," I said. "And I'm impressed with the work. Do you know who did it?"

She busied herself pulling down plates and glassware. "No idea," she said, her tone defensive. "I wasn't living here at the time."

"I didn't mean to upset you." I rocked back on my heels and heaved a sigh. "Though, it appears I'm good at it. Well, that and causing you pain."

She handed me a plate and motioned to the three entrees I'd ordered, along with the large salad and the mouth-watering pile of garlic bread.

"You didn't. Not really. You saved me from stepping into traffic—for which I'd be much worse off than my aching foot. And now I know what's wrong with it." She smiled, but it dimmed and she shook her head. "I wish I'd been here, then, is all."

"Why's that?" I asked.

"Grammy did a lot for me, and I…" Her lips thinned. "Get some food while it's hot. You have to be starving. Thanks for buying. You've more than made up for any issues between us."

She was clearly rattled. Because of my question? I frowned at her obvious unease.

"I don't think I have," I said. I wanted to insist she go first but I'd already made the situation between us awkward. Instead, I swallowed the request, inwardly cringing at my mother's horror of me cutting before a lady and served myself.

"You need a bigger plate?" she asked, a smile gracing her lips and her eyes dancing.

"Missed lunch." I popped a slice of garlic bread in my mouth and topped my dinner with two more pieces. I might not have Knox's skating and weight-lifting regimen, but I managed to cycle about three, sometimes four hundred miles each week and row in the bay on the weekends. I was in decent shape and didn't need to worry about the calories I consumed. I liked it that way—just as I liked buttery bread and baked goods. *Especially* baked goods.

My mom had made the best cookies, soft and warm with just the right amount of sugar and a hint of cinnamon.

I pushed the thought aside and settled into a ladder-back dining chair. The oak wasn't my first choice—I didn't like the heaviness of the grain—but it went well with the Shaker-style cabinets and the vintage schoolhouse light fixtures. I was a fan of the red oak floors, which shone with a recent polish.

While nothing here had the same clean lines of my preferred

Scandinavian aesthetic, I felt surprisingly comfortable in the homeyness of Cassia's space.

Cassia filled her own dish but then looked doubtfully across the expanse of floor. I watched her suck in a breath, but I rose and slipped the plate from her hand before she could start the trek to the table with it. She shot me a shy smile even as she hobbled toward her seat. She latched onto the back of the chair and eased down with obvious relief.

"Good thing you've got an appointment with the orthopedist soon."

She blinked up at me, her large eyes wide. "Right."

She stared down at the table and fiddled with her fork.

"You don't remember?"

A blush stained her cheeks, blooming a lovely shade of pink. "I don't," she whispered. Like it was some evil secret. No, she didn't know she'd told me about changing her name—about her sister and parents leaving her.

What had her childhood been like? Not the happy, loving one I'd known. Yet, while Cassia remained guarded, she wasn't bitter like I'd become.

"That's not surprising," I said. "The medication Simon gave you hit you pretty hard."

She bit her plump lip, still refusing to lift her head. I didn't like this sad, slightly cowed version of Cassia.

"Simon said the same thing when I talked to him earlier, but he also said that you need to alleviate the pain enough to sleep."

"I'll be fine," she said, her voice hardening with resolve.

"I'm sure you would be, but I hate that I'm the reason for

your most recent bout of pain, which is why I'm taking you to the appointment. That way, you can take your medication if you want to. Or not."

Her eyes searched mine, wary. I deserved that. All of it. I'd spent so long locked in my misery and bitterness that I'd forgotten people could be kind, caring. But my siblings' relationships were testimony to finding the kind of love I'd dreamed about as a kid—the kind my parents had shared once.

The ache at the thought of them expanded, as did the paralysis associated with learning I was in charge of my teen sister and my father's architecture company. I'd barely been out of school myself, still learning about design, function, and basic client meetings when I was thrust into the roles of full-time caregiver and business owner. To say I hadn't been ready was an understatement. To say I fucked it up…well, everyone knew that. I was still dealing with the fallout with Aidy, and Knox remained distant, thanks to my treatment of Knox's wife.

I deserved his enmity, but I hated that I'd caused so much more pain and turmoil when all I'd truly wanted was to have my siblings look up to me like they used to. Like the big brother they could trust with their woes, one who would help them fix their problems. Instead, I'd caused more problems for them.

I leaned forward, catching her fingertips in my hand and rubbed my thumb gently over the tender skin there. Sure, I was doing this more for me than for her, but it was a good deed. And I needed to do more of those in general. Maybe then I could let go of my guilt and frustration. It went back a long way—first to Cassia's sister.

"Please. Let me do this. Let me help you. Just until you have the pain under control."

Her tongue darted out to touch the corner of her mouth. "Um…"

"You need the medication to sleep because sleep will help you to heal. You hate the doctor—that was clear earlier—and you need someone there to ask questions. I spent part of the afternoon reading up on your injury."

"My injury?" she squeaked, eyes widening further. "Why would you do that? Why do you even care?"

Everything I did seemed to freak her out. I nodded slowly, trying to act reassuring. "I don't think your doctor in Boston provided you with the best treatment based on what you told Simon. I think it was maybe because you didn't know what questions *to* ask."

She swallowed, inching her hand out of mine. I mourned the loss but understood. Self-preservation ran deep. And to her, I was still the asshole from the bar. I hated that. I'd do anything to make her see me as the person I was.

"Were you on medication then?" I asked.

Before I could delve into my reasoning, she said, "I was. And you're right. I didn't have anyone with me, and I didn't know what to ask the doctor. Nico, you're running your business. I couldn't possibly ask you—"

◄ ▬▬▬▬ ▮▮

"I offered. And I'd really like to help you." My hands clenched. "I messed up. With you, I mean. Not once, but *twice*. And I hate that you think I'm the kind of man who'd intentionally hurt someone, but especially you. I've felt terrible all weekend; the guilt was suffocating, because I knew—I knew you didn't deserve what I said." I firmed my jaw, lifting it a little. "So, please, let me do this for you. It's for me, too."

"Your food's getting cold," she said, her voice soft. "I know you're hungry."

I was, but I also wanted her to answer me. She shifted in her chair and picked up her fork, running it through the sauce on her plate.

I bothered her, maybe even intimidated her. I sighed and picked up my own fork, trying to ease some of the tension from her elegant shoulders.

We—well, I—ate in silence but the tension still brewed.

"How long have you known Aidy?" I asked.

Cassia smiled. "We met in…I guess it was eighth grade. I spent the summer with Grammy that year and the next one, too."

I nodded. That made sense. "Her dance phase. Mom took her to lessons for about a year or so."

"Right. That's where we met—at a summer camp. She's very graceful. I think she could have gone far."

I shook my head. "She was still searching for her thing. She wasn't passionate about dance. Not like she is about interior architecture."

While Aidy'd been proficient and even graceful during her ballet phase, she never showed the level of passion for the discipline that Cassia did. I'd watched a couple of Cassia's performances on YouTube, mesmerized by the deft grace of her movements, the sheer bliss on her face as she executed complicated maneuvers. She made each leap, each twirl, seem effortless, but I knew it wasn't. I'd been at home that summer and seen how hard Aidy had worked to perfect the form.

Aidy hadn't loved dance like that—she reserved that devotion for Ryder and Lilia. She brought that mindset to our work, specifically her focus on interiors that were as comfortable and inviting as they were environmentally friendly. I respected my sister more with each passing day for the *very* reason I'd been so hard on her years before: she'd searched out her passions, not willing to settle for anything less than what brought her true joy.

I hadn't done that. I'd gotten a degree in architecture because I hadn't known what else to do with my life. I liked it, sometimes I even loved it, but I didn't have the same affinity for textures that Aidy did. And Knox, who showed such skill, gave up his driving passion for hockey to help out when I needed him.

I couldn't change the truth that my siblings had more diverse talents, more drive, than I did. I was an architect because I'd felt like Dad expected me to take over the firm. I was the boss because I was the oldest. But I'd learned over the last year that my being older and technically in charge didn't make me the best for those roles.

The same restlessness I'd been fighting for years ate at me once more. I detested the unsettling feelings that reminded me of the days when I'd worked twenty hours, desperate to hold together my dad's firm, his legacy, all while missing my baby sister's slow descent into her own grief.

"Since we're trading information, you knew Amanda when she lived in New York?"

I nodded, mainly because I was busy swallowing the bile that rose in my throat. Why did she have to bring up Amanda? I'd been having a nice…no, a *great* time. Now, my appetite disappeared and my mood tanked.

"And you were one of the people who testified against her in the civil suit?"

I sighed even as I met her stare. "Yes. And I know that could be problematic because I'm not sorry that my testimony might have cost Amanda that case. She deserved to."

Cassia chewed her bite thoughtfully. After she took a sip of her drink and patted her lips with a napkin, she said, "She did."

Huh. I'd expected her to argue with me. Once again, I wished I'd met Cassia first. If I had, there's no way I would have asked Amanda out.

My life would have been so different. Better. Richer. Maybe Cassia would still be dancing. Maybe…maybe she'd have been okay with moving back to Rhode Island with me and we'd have rescued Aidy from her grief.

If only…

"Are you okay?" Cassia asked.

I looked up at her, cataloging her shiny dark-brown hair and cautious gray eyes, her delicate features, the grace, and economy with which she moved.

"I am." I refocused on my plate and worked my way through the meal with a pleasant methodicalness that we interspersed with small talk about the house and her studio.

"Why do you want to set up a studio?" I asked.

"Because dance is my passion." Cassia took a sip of her drink, and I appreciated the long line of her throat. Everything about this woman was elegant. She licked her lip to catch a bead of water that settled between the pillowy softness. My breath caught at the sight, blood pooling in my groin.

She glanced up at me, and, watched me as if she knew what I was thinking. My heart hammered against my chest as heat swelled under my skin.

I wanted Cassia. Badly. I hadn't desired a woman in months, maybe a year or longer.

She smiled a little, ducking her head, her cheeks suffusing with color. I sliced off another bite of chicken, eager to get some much-needed calories into my system.

"You need to eat all the food you bought, Nico. It's only fair, considering I'm still groggy from pain meds and not used to such rich meals."

I swallowed my bite, already taking another bite of the pasta on my rapidly-clearing plate.

"Did you have a specific diet while you danced?"

She nodded as she poked her fork into her salad. "I wasn't perfect. I'd cheat sometimes, not follow the nutritionists' meals." She let out a long sigh.

"I like chocolate," I offered.

"Who doesn't?" she shot back, a smile curving her lips.

"Weirdos," I said. "Can't trust people who don't like chocolate."

She laughed, and the happy trill settled over me, warming my chest. Contentment welled up, and on its heels was anxiety I wasn't sure how to manage. I didn't date women because I refused to trust their motives. I wouldn't. Never again. I'd been blind-sided by Cassia's *sister,* who'd turned on me without a second's thought, costing me my job and my reputation in New York. Worse, Amanda made me second-guess all my relationships, not just the one I'd thought I was building with her. And unless something changed, there was really no way I could trust *Cassia*.

Chapter Eleven
Cassia

Nico's face slid into neutral yet somehow harsh lines as he once again lowered his lids, hiding from me, I was sure of it. Disappointment hit hard. I couldn't figure Nico out. He could be mean—cutting—but he was also the man who'd carried me to the doctor, cared for me, worried over me, bought me dinner… I wanted *this* version of Nico to stick around.

"I should head out soon." His motions were precise as he cut off a piece of his chicken and popped it into his mouth. He chewed slowly, his attention roving the room, but remained silent, each moment closing him off further.

Once again, I wondered what Amanda did to this guy. I was sure it was *something*—definitely bad—but he refused to talk about her. Not that I could blame him. I had my own stories about Amanda I was too ashamed to share with others.

I sighed and pushed my food around my plate. My appetite waned as I considered my current problems—my leg wasn't healing properly, and if it didn't, there was no point in pursuing my studio. Yes, I could hire other dancers to teach, but that wasn't what this new dream was about. I wanted to make a difference—*me*. I needed to show girls they were worth more than what culture said about their bodies. Technically, I was too tall, too heavy to be a ballerina, yet I'd made principal in a renowned corp. It had taken years of additional hours in the studio, years of focus and drive and belief in myself when only Grammy cheered me on.

Now, however, I was too old and too injured to make a triumphant return to the stage, but that didn't mean I was willing to give up on all my dreams—or any of the girls I'd met over the years.

I'd made promises I wanted to keep. Pledges to children who'd never plie or arabesque because their bodies required additional support or simply wouldn't support them. That didn't mean they didn't want to dance, didn't feel the music all the way to their souls.

I clenched my hands into fists, remembering Amanda laughing at me all those years ago.

"But you're too big," she'd said, her tone patient, bordering on condescending, when I'd piped up about my desire to perform as Odette in *Swan Lake* on the ride home for the Boston Ballet. "Only petite girls, like me, do ballet. I mean, how is the guy supposed to hold you up? You'll probably weigh nearly as much, if not more, than he does."

Shame from those words burned up the back of my throat and up my neck and cheeks as I remembered my mother's response. She'd turned around from the front seat to look at me, concern, maybe even pity in her eyes.

"Manda has a point, sweetie. Maybe there's something else you'd like to do?"

I'd jutted my jaw, and Mom groaned. "You're just setting yourself up to be hurt."

Oh, I'd been hurt, but that was physical. I flexed my toes and winced, hating the stabbing pains that lanced up from my foot into my calf. But those were nothing compared to the slices of my heart both my mother and sister carved out of me from the time I was in seventh grade.

Sure, I'd wanted a big sister I could look up to—one who helped me with my hair and chatted with me about boyfriends, gave me fashion advice and bought me tampons. Instead I'd gotten Amanda. Narcissistic, self-absorbed Amanda.

I'd been shocked when she'd announced she planned to go to architecture school. I'd been less surprised when she called me last year, in tears, because a former lover decided to sue her in civil court when she stole his ideas—after accusing him of sexual harassment.

"But...but...he looked at me," Manda had wailed. "I *know* he wanted to touch me."

"Did he touch you?" I'd asked. "Grope you?"

She sniffled prettily. Even Amanda's tears were pretty, mostly because she didn't care enough to really let herself go, to really feel the pain of whatever was supposed to be bothering her enough to have a true ugly cry.

"That doesn't matter. He wanted to, and that makes it sexual."

"You tried to ruin a man's *life*, Manda. Of course he was going to be pissed about that." And rightfully so.

I'd hung up the phone that night as disappointed in my big sister then as I was when she stole Lowell a few months later. Or when she tried to weasel her way into Grammy's will.

"Do you mind giving me a key to your storefront?" Nico asked. "I'd like to get the final measurements so that I can put in an order for the mirrors and flooring.

My fork hit my plate with a clang before it clattered to the table then to the floor. I'd been so lost in my thoughts, I'd completely forgotten Nico was there.

"Um, sure."

Heat once again swamped my cheeks. I started to bend over, but Nico was faster. He snagged the utensil from the floor and stacked it atop his plate.

"Want me to get you a new one?" he asked.

I shook my head. "I'm not that hungry."

Nico frowned. "You barely ate. Is the medication making you feel weird?"

"I'm fine."

I refused to look at him, not wanting to see his censure—or worse, pity. He rose from the table, clearing it despite my protestations, and slid the dishes in the dishwasher. I let him because he seemed intent on doing so and because my foot ached deep inside. My jaw tensed. Nico closed up the containers and wiped down the counters.

"You take it," I said as he moved to place the food in my fridge. "I still have most of mine left to eat, and you paid for the food. Let me get you that key."

He hesitated before saying, "Thanks."

"Thank you for the meal. And getting me in to see Dr. Hogue today."

Nico opened his mouth, as if he wanted to say something but snapped it closed. He nodded with stiff formality and collected his bag of food. I rose, awkward and ungraceful on the gangly crutches, but I managed to get to the key rack and plucked off one of the keys under the printed address. My grammy had been organized, bless her, and she'd loved the label maker I'd bought her a few years back. The key, too, had a shorter label on it with just the street number.

I turned, but Nico was behind me. I wobbled a little, shocked by his closeness, and dropped the key into his outstretched hand.

"That's my only copy," I said.

He frowned. "It's not smart to give me your only key. I'll get another one made and swing by to give you the original back."

"I know that." I inhaled, my head still a bit foggy. "I had another one, but it's gone."

He pursed his lips, no doubt once again thinking I was a fool. I didn't mention that it might have fallen out of my purse at the bar. A plus was I was pretty sure that key didn't still have the address on it.

I shivered. Well, Nico would be there first in case someone managed to figure out where the lost key went to. Served him right. He did deserve some irritation for the hurt he'd caused me.

"I'll be in touch soon, Cassia."

I shook my head. He wouldn't. I'd call tomorrow and ask Aidy to take over my project—which I really should have thought of earlier. Except...I had the feeling that Nico had been more involved with the original renderings than I'd anticipated.

In fact, I'd gotten the sense he'd created them. If so, then working with Nico might well be the smarter option, especially since he'd offered his services for free. I'd be a fool not to take him up on that deal.

By the time I managed to make my way to the front of the house, he'd already closed the door behind him. Part of me wanted to steer clear of Nico. He'd apologized and I'd accepted. We didn't have to work together; I didn't need to see him again. But, for some reason, my stomach felt hollow at the idea of never seeing his sexy smirk again.

Chapter Twelve
Nico

Before dawn had fully broken on Tuesday morning, I drove over to the building that housed Cassia's soon-to-be-dance studio. I wanted to see what I could handle myself and what I'd need to farm out to some of the subcontractors we used directly for smaller jobs. The space felt larger than I'd expected from the original plans—definitely big enough for the four classrooms, which were already in place but dated, and an eighty-seat auditorium that needed an overhaul. Many of the seats were tattered, faded red vinyl popular in the sixties and seventies. I pulled up the specs on my tablet and realized that only two of the studios needed ADA updating along with the bathrooms. The theater was the big overhaul.

I flipped over to my renderings for the space and reconsidered my original vision through the eyes of a ballet aficionado—which I wasn't. Not even close. I'd taken Aidy to that show because she liked the ballet, but I'd made a point to watch a few more shows on my TV last night and had a better sense of stage sight lines. Yes, they'd all been Cassia's performances. No, I didn't feel too weird about that at all. Cassia was the reason I now enjoyed ballet. Well, I liked her dancing. She had these amazing, long lines that seemed more capable of poetry than the typical compact dancer, and her legs...those mile-long legs were sublime in tights. She was strong but graceful, and I wanted to watch her dance again, which meant I had to give her the best possible theater.

I called my ADA subcontractor. "Hey, Abel. I have a dance studio that needs some updating. Do you have any time you can spare to take that on soon?"

"Let me check the schedule. You said dance studio?"

"Yeah. For a former Boston Ballet ballerina." Pride pinged through my chest, much as it had done when Aidy walked across the stage to accept her master's degree.

"Huh. Interesting. My four-year-old Lainey's got low muscle tone in her legs. We've been looking for something to strengthen them. Ballet's good for that."

"I read that yesterday in an article Cassia—that's the dancer— was mentioned in. She set up camps for kids with ambulatory issues. I guess movement helps with range of motion and the kids' confidence."

Abel said, excitement lacing his tone. "That's what the physical therapist said. Man, this is *perfect*! If I can get in there, how soon do you think this ballet dancer will be opening up her studio?"

I frowned. "Well, the biggest hurdle to opening is the dance space and bathrooms, but the auditorium or theater or whatever ballerinas call it is the real disaster."

I kicked at one of the hinges on the nearest chair, wrinkling my nose as rust fell from the joint.

"It's got to be fifty years old. The stage is ragged, which can't be good. This space will need a full reno."

"If I could get some of my guys to help out after other shifts, you think we could knock it out faster? I mean, I have to ask them, but they know about Lainey's issues. I bet because it's odd hours, I can talk the guys into taking their normal rate, maybe less. They know how worried we are about Lainey."

"Wow, that'd be fabulous, Abel. Let me know what you can set up. I'm sending you a message with the specs now. I'll talk to Cassia about the first draw later this week, which would set us up for a start date maybe even by the end of the month."

"I'll be on the lookout. Thanks, Nico. Lainey's going to be so excited. She loves tutus and frilly shit. I can't wait to buy her ten more dance outfits."

We discussed my original budget and how we could maximize its use. I hung up, grinning.

"Got you a discount and a customer, Cassia," I murmured as I typed in some notes.

Finished, I headed back out toward the front door. I locked the space behind me and slid the key ring back into my pocket, hustling toward my car for a cross-town client meeting.

———————————

I spent the rest of the day in meetings but managed to put in another call about proper dance flooring. I'd pulled specs on a basket-weave semi-sprung wood floor for the main stage, which I still felt was the best choice. But my flooring contact suggested the vinyl semi-spring Marley floor, which would be easier and less expensive to install.

"Is it good for ballet?" I asked.

"Yep," Dave said. "All kinds of dance, really. People are putting in unfinished sprung floors beneath the Marly, which saves some big bucks and these vinyl options are heads and shoulders above the old floors, and the sports sprung floor will mitigate injuries."

I perked up. "How does it do with nerve damage?"

"No clue, but I'll send you the information I have, as well as the contact at the factory."

"Yeah, do that."

I spent a long evening coming up with the best options for the four classrooms. "Right on," I muttered as I set down my pencil and stretched my arms up, trying to alleviate the tightness in my shoulders. I glanced around the office, shocked to find the space quiet and dark. My eyes widened when I realized it was after ten. No way I could call Cassia with the good news tonight but I'd definitely chat with her tomorrow.

That was my plan...until I received a call from the foreman of one of my projects before seven the next morning letting me know that the contractor hadn't shown up in the past couple of days to hand out assignments.

"I'm stuck with a less-than-productive crew, and we're really falling behind. I don't know what to do, Nico. Marcus isn't answering my calls."

I sighed, scrubbing my cheeks, wincing at the bristles there. "I'll come out there this morning. Give me half an hour." I rose and stretched. "Make it an hour. I need coffee."

As I pulled up in front of another client's large residence, I frowned at the lack of noise coming from the building. I strode up the front walkway, noting the ripped-out chunks of concrete but the lack of removal. That created a clear safety hazard and needed to be addressed immediately. I found a group of subcontractors lolling around in what used to be a kitchen. They glanced over at me, seeming unperturbed, and went back to eating, drinking, and chatting. At nine-fifteen in the morning.

Before I managed to open my mouth, Clark Vance, the foreman, strode into the room. His scowl was deep and dark enough to make the men around him straighten.

"I told you I wanted that concrete cleaned up," Clark said.

I came to stand beside him, and he glanced over, his eyes burning with anger until he recognized me.

"Nico," he said, running his hand through his sweaty hair. "Damn. How long have you been here?"

"About thirty seconds."

"Well, as you can see, this job's gone sideways. Marcus is currently in charge now that Jeb's out, and he seems to be skipping this job site. I think he's still angry about your sister's treatment toward him on The Mac job. Or her comments to him here earlier this week."

I shrugged, though a wave of uncertainty flowed down my spine. Aidy had been on location this week? I really didn't like that I was just hearing about *that*. "I don't care what nasty he's got up his ass. Aidy had every right to kick him off The Mac job, and I'll be sure to discuss this issue with Jeb."

Clark swallowed. "About Jeb…"

"What?" I asked. Fingers of iciness licked up my neck, gripping at my skull. "You mentioned he's out—on vacation?"

"He had a heart attack."

The grip tightened. "I hadn't heard."

"That's because Marcus was supposed to tell you. You

know, play nice with you since you're the biggest architecture firm in town."

I gestured over my shoulder to the men hanging out. "Instead, he let these guys sit on their asses, wasting time and money for my client."

They started to grumble. I turned back to face them. "You didn't do *any* work this week. I know, because I was here Sunday evening. That means you're not getting paid."

The low grumbles turned into outraged bellows. I held my ground, thankful that Clark stood next to me, but unwilling to bend. I couldn't stand laziness, and I wasn't about to start.

"I've got my steel-toed boots in the trunk of my car. Let me get those on and we can take the tour of the place. I'll be sure to make a list of what should have already been completed and what I expect by week's end."

I held each man's gaze, waiting until the five of them dropped theirs. They shuffled off after Clark gave them assignments—the first of which was to clear the busted concrete from the front walkway.

Clark rubbed his hand over his brow. "Such a way with people, Nico," he muttered.

"Well, they weren't doing the work they were contracted to do. What did you expect from me?"

His shoulders slumped. "I'm expecting them to grumble more then decide en masse to quit. Construction is booming right now, and there's no way they're going to accept less pay."

"The person they should be angry with is Marcus. *He* cost them their paycheck."

Clark shook his head. "They won't see it that way."

"Then, it's best they go—along with Marcus."

"That's the kicker. Marcus wants to buy the company from Jeb. This is Jeb's second heart attack, and it's requiring bypass surgery. No way he can handle the stress."

"But Marcus is a shoddy selfish prick who does subpar work." And I was sure he pocketed the difference between the material costs of what he was supposed to buy and what he did purchase.

"He's also Jeb's nephew. So, it makes the most sense for him to buy out Jeb."

"Buy him out, huh?" I moved toward the front door where I heard the crash of concrete into the large metal Dumpster. Another load hit, but then the voices rose.

"Yeah, we don't have to take this shit," one of the guys said. "Marcus never makes us work this hard."

I stepped around the doorframe and stared at the speaker. "Glad to know you've quit. I don't want your subpar work on my project."

"I didn't say—"

"You did. You also mentioned Marcus doesn't require you to put in a full day's labor, which is what the clients are paying you for. So, again, it's good that you quit."

The beefy guy's hands fisted and he snarled, but before he could come at me, his buddy caught his arm. "Let's go. Marcus has three other job sites. We'll go to one of those."

The crew of five guys headed toward their trucks and drove off, tires squealing.

Clark cursed under his breath, his expression panicked. Two

more workers, who appeared to be electricians based on their tool belts, sauntered out to stand next to us on the porch.

"Good riddance," the smaller of the two—a young woman in her early twenties—said. "They've barely lifted a finger."

"But they have managed to get in our way," the older woman said on a sigh.

"Good to see you, Lauren," I said. I glanced expectantly at the younger woman.

"Hazel Sato," she said. Her hair was a couple of shades darker than Cassia's, almost jet black, and her nose and cheeks were dusted with freckles. She exuded fiery independence I respected.

"Nice to meet you, Hazel. I'm sorry these guys haven't allowed for a decent working environment. Clark and I plan to discuss our options."

As glad as I was for the crew to be gone, their departure would set us back a solid week—a week we didn't have. The clients insisted on the final date and offered a large bonus if we hit it. A bonus I was now considering using to buy Jeb's construction company, which meant I needed this project to be on time.

"Would you be willing to hire more women?" Hazel asked.

"Of course," I said. "As long as they can do the work and do it well."

Hazel's eyes lit up. "I have two sisters who do finish work, and they're looking for a crew here in Rhode Island. We all live on the east side, near our parents and aunts and uncles. But they mostly work out of Boston or New York, which makes for long-ass commutes."

"If you can get them here and I can review some of their work and a reference or two, I think they have a great shot of being on the team," I said.

"Jeb's wondered why more females weren't applying with his firm," Clark muttered.

Clearly, because of Marcus's behavior. The snake. He couldn't get control of the construction company—not if I wanted to have a reliable option in Providence. Up until Aidy had problems with Marcus last year, Jeb's company had been dependable. It was also the largest outfit in town with few other options. If we couldn't work with Jeb, we'd be competing with crews who most likely lived and worked in larger surrounding states.

I'd worried over this for years—taking on bigger, more high-profile jobs meant needing bigger, more robust construction crews. Jeb's was pretty much the only option. But, from what Clark told me, it may no longer be one.

Hazel shook her head. "They don't want to work for Jeb again."

"Why's that?"

Hazel hesitated. "There's harassment."

A chill swept over me. "More than cat-calling? Were your sisters ever touched?"

Please, Jesus, say no…

She shook her head. "But there were plenty of lewd and specific comments."

Clark muttered a few choice curse words while I swallowed. "Was this on one of Wright and Associates projects?"

Hazel considered that question, eyes narrowed, before she shook her head. "Nah. That happened about five or more years ago, while I was still in high school. They didn't want me working for Jeb's crew, but I'm taking night classes at the local university, and I couldn't make the courses if I was in Boston."

I blew out a relieved breath.

"Would you be willing to call them?" I asked. "Maybe they'd be willing to work for me."

"You?" Hazel asked, eyes wide.

"Well, if you can't work with Marcus, and Marcus doesn't make his guys actually work, then the issue becomes mine. So, yeah, working for me." I closed my eyes. "Once I have the proper paperwork in place."

"I can ask," Hazel said.

Lauren grinned. "I'd be interested in working with Wright Construction. I don't mind you being a hard-ass because I know you're fair. And that's all I've wanted—a fair working environment."

"I'll see what I can do," I said.

I tipped my head to Clark, and he fell in line beside me as I headed toward my car. I shrugged out of my suit coat on the way, already re-arranging my afternoon so I could get the concrete menace off the front lawn—and eliminate the chance of a lawsuit.

"How good of a chance is there Jeb'll sell to Marcus?"

"Good," Clark said.

"Why not to you?" I asked.

Clark shook his head. "I'm fifty-three. We just got our youngest out of the house. Sure, I need to pay her tuition, but I want to retire in the next few years, not take on the burden of a new business."

I nodded.

"But Marcus is bad for the workers like Hazel. She didn't say it, but I've heard the inappropriate remarks, seen them pat her ass…it's hostile, which is why she's excited to get her sisters and cousins here. They're good workers—they did the Loughlin Bank reno in Jamaica Plain."

I nodded, familiar with the art deco style that had been so carefully restored. "That's a great piece for their portfolios. Do you think Jeb would consider another offer?"

Clark shrugged. "Who's got that kind of cash lying around to be able to make a better-than-market offer?"

I finished the mental tally of my assets, of the projects I was currently in charge of, and how taking this on would give Wright and Associates a much better reputation, thanks to the quality of the craftsman who completed our visions.

"Me. Possibly. If you think Jeb would be willing to look at it."

"It'd have to be a damn good offer," Clark said.

My heart thrummed hard in my chest. "I know."

Clark gave me a hesitant nod, doing nothing to alleviate my worries. "Can't hurt to try."

Chapter Thirteen
Nico

I stared, grim-faced at my computer screen, bombarded by shock. In his curt email, Jeb had refused my offer. I'd given him an extra twenty percent over the current market value. *Twenty* percent. That was really more than I could afford, but I'd planned to figure something out.

Clearly, my actions today screwed me—but, worse, my family. I'd managed to piss off Marcus, his subcontractors, and had no way to finish the renovation on time to get the signing bonus Wright and Associates needed. I didn't want to tell Knox or Aidy, worried they'd be angry with me for causing problems—especially when the situation with Cassia wasn't resolved.

But it was meeting time, and they both sauntered into my office, along with Emmaline, before I had time to organize my thoughts.

"Um, I thought we were meeting in the conference room for our working lunch."

"Change in plans," Knox said. He pressed a kiss to Emmaline's temple before tipping his head toward one of the chairs. He took up position behind it, a sentinel there to protect his queen. Not that I would disparage Emmaline. I never had. Em was talented. She was also still leery of me because I hadn't trusted her in the beginning. But, then again, I didn't trust anyone with the company—not even myself.

"Okay. Why's that?"

"Because you're acting weird and haven't been working twenty hours a day," Aidy said. "Lunch will be here soon, by the way. I ordered from Vincent's."

"Mmm," Emmaline said, patting her stomach. "I'm starving."

"I never worked twenty hours a day," I scoffed.

"Eighteen," Knox countered. "You're a workaholic who seems to think nothing can go right if you're not the one touching it or overseeing it. And we're tired of that mentality."

I swallowed down my immediate retort and tried to consider Knox's point. I inhaled slowly, let the breath out even more cautiously, aware of Aidy's concerned expression. Em touched Knox's wrist and gave him a small shake of her head, no doubt telling him to cut down on the posturing.

"I appreciate your comments, but you have to understand that until a couple of years ago, I *did* have to touch everything because we were locked in a court battle for our designs."

This time, Knox scowled even as he flinched, hard.

"That's been resolved, and once it was, we made it back to profitability, but those years were hard. Very hard." I laid my hands on the desk. "I took out a second mortgage on my house and this building to pay legal fees."

"What?" Knox exploded. "Why didn't you tell me that before?"

"Because you were wallowing in your guilt, and it didn't seem productive."

Knox's scowl darkened. "I had a right to know what you were doing with our assets."

"All of which were available for your perusal in our accounting software," I shot back. I closed my eyes and leaned my head against the chair.

"This is why Nico didn't tell you," Aidy said to Knox, coming to my defense. "After the mess Dad left the firm in and then your mistake in trusting Melinda, it's no wonder Nico's felt the need to hold everything together. He *literally* has."

I opened my eyes and shot her a thankful look. She returned it with narrowed eyes. "That doesn't mean Nico's always done it right."

Exhaustion weighed on me. "No, I haven't. And I'm sorry for that."

"Well, what about these mortgages?"

"The bonus for The Mac project paid down most of what we owed on this building," Aidy said.

"You've been in the accounting software," I said.

She nodded. "Ryder and I talked. We want to make sure you're not bearing the financial burdens alone, Nico. I'm going to put my share of the next bonus back into the company so that we can either finish paying off this building or apply it toward your house."

I waved that off. "I'll deal with my house."

"You won't," Knox snapped.

"What my husband is trying to say with such obvious tact," Emmaline stepped in, "is that he and I will also help pay down the debts incurred because of *his* actions."

Knox nodded, his mouth set in a grim line.

"You don't have—"

"You're right; we don't," Knox interrupted, his tone sharp. Then he sighed as he looked down into Emmaline's upturned face and his expression softened. He turned back to face me.

"Look, I'm pissed at you. And you deserve that. But I also finally realize how much you've sacrificed, how much stress you've carried to make sure we had a place to work. A good place, with a strong reputation." Knox's tone was filled with respect. "You've managed the near impossible, Nico, building this firm up twice over. Sure, you fucked up with Aidy, and with Em and me, but now I can at least better understand why. So, you're going to accept some help from us because we're *all* tied to this firm, and you should never have taken on the financial risk for my mistake."

I wanted to ask if that meant he'd forgive me, but I didn't. Now wasn't the time for that conversation.

"I did mess up, with all of you, and I'm very, very sorry." My voice was thick, my heart heavy.

Emmaline shifted in her chair. "And I forgive you. I want us to get along, Nico. To be a family." Her smile was tentative. "I miss that opportunity."

"Me, too," I said, choking up.

"All right," Aidy said, clapping her hands. "This is too much emotion for me." She waved a hand in front of her eyes. "Damn hormones. Everything makes me cry."

"But you're not pregnant anymore," Knox said.

"I know, butthole, but that doesn't mean my hormones magically returned to pre-pregnancy levels. Ryder said it usually takes about six months for hormones to rebalance. Clearly, I'm taking longer than the average."

Knox held out his hands in supplication. "I'm sorry. Really. I didn't mean to upset you."

"Then don't tell me how my body's reacting to shit wrong," Aidy snapped.

I struggled to maintain a neutral expression, made worse by Emmaline's twinkling eye and bit lip. Thankfully, our reception-ist Nannette stuck her head into the office to let us know our lunch had arrived. We filed out to the kitchen and each grabbed a plate, though I walked over to our central area and made sure the rest of our staff also had the opportunity to eat. Then, the four Wrights took our plates into the conference room. I hesitated for a moment but settled into a chair next to Aidy, eschewing the head-of-table seat.

I cleared my throat. "Well, as fascinating as it is to learn about the mysteries of the human body, I…er, *we* have a prob-lem," I announced. I clenched my fork, wishing my stomach wasn't in such knots.

The three sets of eyes locked onto my face as I explained the situation at the Victorian reno. My neck prickled and my face went both numb and stiff somehow. When I finished, Knox smirked.

"You have the floor, Aidy-pie," he said, satisfaction oozing from his tone.

I blinked at him, surprised that he seemed…he couldn't be *happy* with this turn of events. He twirled his fettuccini onto his fork and winked at Em, who blushed prettily. Clearly, I was missing something.

"I spoke with the Van Michaels on Tuesday morning. Where were you, by the way?"

"Looking into Cassia's dance studio building. I…ah…lost track of time."

Aidy hid a smile behind her bite.

"And how's *that* going?" Emmaline asked.

Em raised an eyebrow. "I saw him pull her back from the oncoming cars."

"Look at you," Knox said, eyes widening. "A real hero."

I shot him a withering look. He smirked but it didn't hold any heat. Maybe…maybe we were finally putting my mistakes behind us. I could hope.

"We need to discuss the Van Michaels," I said, trying to get us back on track—and away from further talk about Cassia. I had no idea how she was doing and that bothered me. I wanted to make sure she was taking her medication, that she was eating. The need to talk to her ate at me, but I did my best to ignore it because I half-expected her to call Aidy again and demand I remove myself from her project.

I didn't want to do so—I appreciated what she was doing, more so now that I understood how deep her passion ran. Helping her achieve her dream seemed to settle something in me.

Plus, I enjoyed looking at her. I adored her smiles and laugh. She intrigued me to the point I almost didn't care she was related to Amanda.

Almost.

"I went to their property."

I glanced up at Aidy, a frown building between my eyebrows. "When? I didn't know that. Was Marcus there? Did he hassle you? Are you okay?"

"Calm down. Knox went with me," Aidy said.

"Just as the muscle," Knox said. "Aidy handled the client, Marcus's douchery, and the rest of it."

"I couldn't have done it without those muscles," Aidy said with a laugh. That made Emmaline sigh and grab Knox's hand, kissing his palm.

This whole family-run business thing was getting on my nerves. Too many moments of affection and cuteness for me to tolerate. I shoved a large bite of food into my mouth and chewed slowly. The others did the same.

"What happened with Marcus? And the Van Michaels?" I asked after I'd sipped from my water.

Aidy tapped the table with her fingernail. "I plan to interface with them moving forward, which I did yesterday. I would have told you—"

"But I was on site, cleaning up the last of the mess out front so that it didn't become a liability."

"Thanks for that," she said, face serious. "And so you know, the Van Michaels fired Jeb's company this morning." She sucked in a breath. "I spent most of Tuesday on the phone. I talked with the Carlisles, the Modern Art wing, the Sorensons, and the Roth-schilds, and they've all expressed confidence in us but displeasure in both the rate of work and the finish. When I told them about my conversation with Marcus, they each expressed interest in finding a different contractor, which I've forwarded to Jeb."

"That's half their business," I exclaimed. No wonder Jeb was in the hospital with bypass surgery.

"That explains why he refused my offer to buy him out," I said. "He must have thought I was working in concert with you."

"Buy him out?" Knox leaned forward, his elbows on either side of his cleared plate. "What are you talking about?"

"He's worried about the projects," Emmaline murmured. "Getting them finished in time."

I nodded. "That's exactly what I'm worried about—our reputation—"

"Is based on the quality of the finished product, *not* the deadline," Aidy said. She held up her hand when I opened my mouth. "I'm not saying getting it done on time isn't important. Rather, I am saying that I'd prefer to build a relationship with a contractor who can actually work well with us and meet deadlines than with a double-dipper who skimps on materials."

"And doesn't stare at your boobs," Emmaline added.

"Preach, sister," Aidy said, offering Emmaline a fist bump.

"But that leaves us with a huge hole in completion—and out a lot of money if we don't figure this out," I said. I shifted in my seat, overtaken by the same antsy feeling I'd had when I found out how deep in the hole Dad was.

No one had a solution to the issue, but all three of them had calls out to construction crews in the area and into New England, looking for a couple of companies that would work to our aesthetic—and work ethic. At this point, we had to hope someone was willing to step up.

My stomach was in knots. Dammit. This was playing out just as I'd feared.

"I, uh, talked to Hazel Sato and Clark Loomis on Wednesday," I told them.

"Oh?"

"Yeah. Clark called me out there first thing. Clearly, I didn't know you'd already talked to Marcus."

Aidy bit her lip. "Sorry about that. I should have kept you in the loop."

I waved off her concern. A year ago, I would have been pissed. Now, with all the projects we were juggling and my erratic hours, I couldn't be upset.

"Maybe we can send an end-of-day message to each other to make sure we're all caught up on what's going on," Emmaline said. "That's what Knox and I do, over dinner."

Aidy smiled at her. "'Good idea. Yeah, I can do that."

"Me, too," I said. Mainly because I wanted to know what else I'd been missing. Clearly, the three of them were spending more time together than I was with them. Em and Knox made sense, but I felt a little crushed that Aidy, too, was closer with Knox and Em than she was with me. When she was little, I'd been the brother Aidy sought out. I'd loved taking her to the beach or on long hikes. Aidy had always been up for an adventure, the first to try something new.

I missed doing those exciting things with her. Hell, I missed having people I could call on a whim to do something with. But since I'd been back in Providence, it seemed like all I did was put out fires. If I wasn't on one of my bike rides, I was in the office.

Or in my home office.

My social life, just like my family life, had suffered.

"Clark's not interested in working for Marcus, nor is he interested in taking over Jeb's business. That's why I made the offer."

Knox nodded. "Smart. We could have let Clark remain the foreman and fed him projects."

"That was my hope, but he declined. He's not in a bad position with Marcus, so he'll stay there. Which leads me to my conversation with Hazel Sato. She's an electrician." I explained what Hazel said about her sisters and the harassment they'd borne. Aidy and Emmaline both grunted, sour expressions on their faces.

"So, if I can get a new business permit and everything switched over to, say...Wright Construction, we can move forward. I think."

Knox nodded his head, thoughtful. "That lets us better control the pipeline from initial client request straight through to completion. And make sure it's done to our specs."

"I can reach out to some more construction workers to see about putting together a local crew," Aidy said. Then she sighed. "But I'm already juggling this new hotel project, my clients, and Lilia."

"Which is more than enough," I said. I hesitated. "Your family comes first."

She raised an eyebrow, and I knew she wanted to clap back but she held her tongue. I stared down at my plate, reminded of my meal Monday night with Cassia. I nearly told Aidy she was Amanda's sister, that I was torn by my interest in her with my need to protect myself, and my family, from Amanda.

Instead, I said, "I know you think I put the business first, but it's all we had left of Mom and Dad, their legacy to us. I couldn't fail them."

"I've been thinking about that," Knox said. He stretched out his legs and leaned back in his chair. "And you didn't fail the business because Dad nearly did." He shot a glance toward Emmaline, and I knew then that they'd discussed something, something potentially big. "It should never have fallen to your shoulders to stabilize a failing venture, Nico. Hell, from the contracts Dad talked about, the business shouldn't have been failing at all."

"True, but it was." I didn't want to delve into my concerns as to why that was. "What do you think about me taking on a construction business?" I asked.

I met each of their three sets of eyes. "I'd be out there in the field, not here, bothering you guys. I mean, if you feel like you can handle the clients, which I'm sure you can…" I trailed off, hating how I was rambling. My heart thumped and I squeezed my hands into fists.

Aidy pressed her lips together and laid her hand on my shoulder. "Is this something you *want* to do, Nico, or something you feel like you *have* to do for the business? For us?"

"I…"

"Because you built this architecture firm into what it is," she continued, shooting Knox a shut-up look. He pressed his lips together and nodded.

I breathed in through my nose, enjoying the terrifying flutters bubbling in my belly as I considered starting a new company—

my company. One that wasn't tainted by my father's lies, my own failings with my siblings.

"I…I think I want to take on construction." I didn't want to admit how tired I was of being the boss-man of my siblings. Each time we disagreed felt like another rip in our familial relationship. Plus, excitement bloomed at the idea of being outside, out of a suit, actually working with my hands. That thrill pulsed under my skin.

Aidy, Emmaline, and Knox shared a long, silent communication. "You're still the principal here," Knox said, meeting my gaze. "And you always will be, if you want to, that is. But I think this is a good opportunity to broaden our income and our reach, so I'm in, willing to do what needs to be done."

"I'll need you to take over my projects," I said. "Except Cassia's. I promised to work on that one myself." Well, I'd promised to do the work pro bono, and I wanted to. I enjoyed manual labor, feeling my muscles warm. I'd loved watching the space—Cassia's dream—slowly unfurl into reality. Based on the number of projects I'd pick up just from Wright and Associates, I'd be able to afford to give Cassia my time. Excitement flickered over my skin at the thought of spending more time with the beautiful ballerina.

Knox rose and stuck out his hand. "All right, brother. We're with you. A team."

I pushed out of my chair and clasped his hand, surprised when he pulled me in for a back-slapping hug. "A team."

I exhaled a shaky breath, shocked by the relief coursing through me. I'd needed to be part of a team, needed to share some of the burdens I'd carried. And now I was.

Chapter Fourteen
Cassia

For the few days after Nico took me to see Dr. Hogue, I took my pain meds and got out of my comfy bed only long enough to eat, drink, and go to the bathroom. Maybe it was the emotional exhaustion of the last year or maybe my body simply needed the time to heal. Whatever the reason, I never got around to calling Aidy, nor did I respond to Amanda's increasingly frequent voicemails—in fact, those I ignored altogether. I considered answering when my mother called, but I didn't. I hadn't seen her since Grammy's funeral, and I refused to allow my sister to live with me. Mom's potential guilt trip about "poor Manda" wouldn't change that. My sister had hurt me and taken advantage of me for the last time.

On Friday, when I woke, my foot throbbed but at a manageable level, so I took a long, hot shower. I dressed in a flirty, linen wrap dress Grammy had bought me last year for my birthday. It hit a couple of inches above my knees and the sky-blue fabric complemented my skin tone and eyes. I slid my feet into a pair of bronze ballet flats—no sandals for me. I was a ballerina who specialized in en pointe, and my feet had borne most of my weight on my toes for nearly two decades. A simple pedicure couldn't ever fix that kind of brutal use.

I eschewed any makeup and styled my mass of dark waves atop my head, a normal style for when it wasn't pulled back in a tight bun. I loved long hair, enjoying the weight and the repetitive action of brushing it, but I hated how the strands caught in my lashes or lips.

I'd hobbled to the kitchen and set the electric kettle to boil when a sharp rap via the old-fashioned knocker sounded at the door. I sighed, uninterested in talking to anyone. I needed to head into the former library, with its dark wainscoting and bookshelves, and come up with some feasible plan for my ballet school.

I opened the door, frowning at the empty porch. I grumbled to myself and turned back inside. The glint of metal caught my eye. My mouth dropped open at the set of crutches leaning against the cedar shingles.

"What…"

"You're going to need them to get around." I whirled back to face the porch and Nico, who stood there. "These are easier on your hands and wrists than the ones Simon gave you earlier this week."

His hair was still a little damp but it was brushed back from his face, showcasing the sharp line of his jaw and the bold planes of his face. His eyes were clearer today, free of the shadows that seemed to haunt him earlier in the week.

"Why are you here?" I asked.

"To take you to the orthopedist."

"But…"

He shook his head, even as a faint smile teased the corners of his mouth. "I was pretty sure you didn't remember this conversation."

"I remembered I had an appointment. I just don't know the

time. I planned to call in a few minutes to get that all sorted out. You don't need to take me."

"Oh? So you have someone else who can get you to East Providence in an hour?"

My shoulders slumped. "I'll drive myself."

"With no car? Unless you managed to get it back already, though I didn't see it in your driveway."

My cheeks heated as I realized I hadn't thought about my car in days. Just as I'd never managed to call Wright and Associates and ask Aidy to take over my project. *Not smart, Cassia.* "Um…"

"You told me when I was here earlier this week that your car was in the Whole Grocers lot."

I clamped my jaw. It seemed like each time I was near Nico, he proved once again how I was failing at life.

"I'll take an Uber to pick up my car. I need groceries anyway."

Nico surprised me by holding out his hands. "I really want to help you."

I folded my arms over my chest. "How do I know you're not doing this because Aidy made you?"

He grimaced. "You don't. And she threatened to never let me see my niece again if I didn't make nice with you, so yes, that's a factor. But after I went home the other night, I couldn't stop worrying about you—how you managed to get yourself to bed, if you'd taken your pill, if you were sleeping, had you locked the doors. So, I'm here, and I want to help."

I stared at him, trying to gauge his motive. The kettle whistled. I sighed. "Are you trying to send some weird karmic voodoo to get even with Amanda?"

His smile caught us both off guard. "Hadn't even crossed my mind."

The kettle continued to shrill.

"You going to get that?" he asked.

"Yes, I need some coffee if I'm going to deal with you."

"You could just let me have my way." He flashed a charming smile that warmed my insides and my belly fluttered with…possibilities.

My response to this man was ridiculous.

"I don't think I can."

He nodded. "I respect that." I started to turn but he touched his fingers to my arm.

"Please use the crutches. Just until you're sure about what you're dealing with. If there's even a chance they'll help, then…" He put his hands in his pockets. "I've seen you dance. Once in person and a few times this week while I was researching and working on those ADA specifications you requested. Your body…it's poetry. The world needs that kind of beauty. Don't let your anger or pride keep us all from that pleasure."

Well, hell. He had to go and compliment my dancing. That had been the one place I felt secure—beautiful, confident, capable, strong. And Nico had connected with my emotions. I was *poetry*. My stomach shivered at his words because they mattered. Why, how, I wasn't sure, but they did.

I grabbed the stupid crutches and shoved them under my armpits. Ugh. I was going to chafe the skin there once again.

Somehow, Nico weaseled his way back into the house—fine, I let him—and went so far as to fill my French press with coffee and the hot water from the kettle. He poured us each a travel mug—mine with a splash of cream and agave nectar, his black and bitter—before carrying them out to the car. I frowned, trying to be annoyed by his taking over the task but secretly pleased he'd thought of me. He'd said I'd kept him up the other night.

Yeah, I was a glutton for punishment. An attractive man showed me some attention, and I turned into goo, no longer standing up for myself. I grabbed my purse and slung it across my body, wondering how I was going to correct this hideous flaw in my character.

Nico stood next to the passenger side of his sleek black car, the door open as he waited for me. I liked his attention. A lot. Even though he was only here because of his personal agenda, I still enjoyed it.

I slid into the car and he grabbed my crutches, placing them in the back seat.

"How'd I get an appointment so soon? I mean, it's in the same week as my referral."

Nick shot me a glance. "I asked Simon to get you in quick but only with a highly reputable doctor. It just so happened Dr. Elliot had a last-minute cancelation." He shrugged. Part of me wondered if he was telling me the whole truth. Then, I pushed it from my mind. My bigger concern was what this Dr. Elliot would say during the appointment.

But, as I sipped my coffee, I wondered which man was the real Nico—the one I'd met at the bar or this solicitous version.

Panic rode me hard, making my stomach flutter and my palms sweat when the nurse called me back.

"Come with me," I said, turning toward Nico.

My heart thumped hard against my ribs as he studied me. Dammit, was he going to make me beg? I squeezed my eyes shut and licked my lips.

"If that's what you want," he said.

I opened my eyes and sawed out some of the horrible tension that had built up inside me. "I don't like doctors."

"I figured that out," Nico said, rising. He helped me up and handed me the crutches.

"I had meningitis as a kid and had to spend a while in the hospital. My mom was busy with my sister…"

Why was I telling him this?

His face remained neutral but I caught the flash of anger in his eyes before he turned away. "So she left you, a little girl, there alone?"

I'd been the one to start this conversation. "Yeah. I know my fear's irrational…" I crutched toward the nurse.

"I'd say it's totally rational. You were scared and alone and didn't understand what was happening. Any time you go to the doctor reminds you of that experience." Nico waited for me to pass by the nurse.

"Are you sure you want me to come with you?" he asked, giving me an out.

The panic drilled into my mind, seeped from my pores. "Yes," I whispered.

He settled his hand on my lower back. "Okay."

His easy acquiescence allowed me to ponder the multiple facets of his personality instead of the upcoming prodding and possible needles. Nico kept up a steady stream of small talk, mostly about my studio, which kept me from giving in to the panic that nipped at the edges of my consciousness.

The orthopedic surgeon, Dr. Elliot, knocked a few moments later.

"Hello, Cassia," he said.

He was a studious-looking man in his mid-fifties with salt-and-pepper hair, skin beginning to weather with interesting character, and sharp gray eyes. I liked him immediately, in part because Nico seemed so relaxed around him. But that was stupid. I shouldn't put my trust in Nico.

"Hello," I managed to push past my stiff lips. Nico inched closer to where I sat on the exam table and took my hand in his. I uncurled my fist and laid my palm against his, slowly relaxing enough to answer Dr. Elliott's questions. After a brief physical exam and another moment where he showed us the X-ray, Dr. Elliott confirmed what Dr. Hogue had already told Nico and me: my foot and ankle never healed properly. Part of that was my fault for not going to follow-up visits.

I tried to assimilate all the information he offered but my mind continued to whirl with the realization the ballet's doctor hadn't noticed that—or hadn't cared enough to ensure my body would mend.

"So, there's a chance that I could get past the nerve issues?"

"Better than a chance," Dr. Elliot said. "My guess is that with rest and appropriate physical therapy, you'll get nearly your full range of motion back."

"Excellent," Nico said, smiling broadly at me. Damn, happy Nico was *beautiful.*

I smiled back. Feeling more confident, I said, "So, what's the regimen you think best?"

"I'll have my nurse bring you those orders," Dr. Elliott said. "I just need to finish with your chart. It shouldn't take more than a few minutes."

"Okay."

I hugged my elbows as a faint ringing built in my ears. The door opened and closed, and I glanced up, blinking in surprise to find myself alone with Nico.

I licked my lips. "I thought I was okay with losing that part of my life?" I bit my lip and shook my head. "And it's not *just* the dancing. It's my ability to teach…I have kids counting on me…when I announced my retirement, the kids were devastated, much more so than my colleagues. But when I said I'd open a studio, they were so excited…"

"Look at me, Cassia," Nico whispered.

I didn't want to, but my gaze clashed with his, softened at the compassion there. Slowly, he slid his hand around the back of my neck and cupped the base of my skull. His thumb smoothed over my hair, the caress soothing. "We're going to make sure you get to teach. We're going to make sure your studio is open and a success."

"How…"

He leaned in and pressed his lips to my forehead. My breath stuttered. This was yet another side to Nico. One I never antici-pated. So much tenderness poured out of him.

"Let the reality sink in. Let yourself believe in the future."
He stepped back. "Will you be okay if I go get the car? I know
your foot aches and I don't want you to have to walk further
than necessary."

I nodded, not sure how else to respond. He turned on his heel,
his long, confident stride eating up the length of the hallway.

"Damn, girl. How'd you get so lucky?"

I turned, eyes wide, to find the nurse leaning against the door
frame, fanning herself with a sheaf of papers.

"What?"

She handed me the documents.

"Your PT regimen, plus Dr. Elliott's pain plan. Based on what
you told him about the codeine, he wants to keep you on a mix-
ture of Tylenol and Advil."

"That's not what you were talking about a minute ago," I said,
frowning.

She grinned. "I was talking about your man. He's so focused
on your recovery, on your goals."

"He's not…" My cheeks flamed. Had my longing shown on
my face? I cleared my throat. "He's not mine."

She raised an eyebrow and her eyes sparkled. "From what I
just saw, he sure thinks he is."

Chapter Fifteen
Nico

The more time I spent with Cassia, the more our commonalities and interests presented themselves. I saw the vulnerability she buried down deep, a vulnerability I understood only too well because I felt it, too. Not that I'd been able to even own up to my limitations. Up until this year, my siblings had needed me to be strong and confident and not fuck up *more* than I already had when Aidy needed me as a teen and Knox needed me to be a compassionate leader. Now, though, both Knox and Aidy were happy, so I felt the vise grip on my own issues slipping. Not that I wanted to fall apart; I didn't. I just…wanted to not always have the answers, make the decisions—have so many people look to me for answers I didn't have.

It was part of why I hadn't minded taking on the chore of visiting job sites, which I'd done prior to collecting Cassia and would do more of later today. Those field trips allowed me to get away from the icy politeness in the office.

"Nico."

I whipped around at the sound of my name, my steps faltering when I saw Bridget, Simon Hogue's wife, hurrying across the orthopedist's waiting room toward me.

"What's wrong?" I asked, panic licking its way up my gut and seizing in my lungs.

She shook her head. "Brendan broke his arm."

"What? How? Is he okay? Should I call Simon? What can I do—"

"We're okay." She rested her soft palms on my forearms encased in my suit jacket. "The break is weeks old now. We're just getting the cast off."

I deflated. "Oh. Okay. Well, good. Simon didn't mention that yesterday when I saw him." I frowned. I liked Simon and thought we got along well. Still, I hadn't really considered the lack of closeness to him—to anyone—until Cassia slid into my life.

"He mentioned you stopped by." The gleam in Bridget's eyes told me Simon mentioned I'd stopped in with a woman. "And I really appreciate your willingness to help." She blinked her big blue eyes up at me, and a bit more of the tension seeped from my body.

"So…what are you doing here?" she asked. "Did a driver clip your bike?" She studied me, seeming to seek out injuries, and gratitude warmed my middle. Bridget was special.

"I brought in a…" How did I describe Cassia? She wasn't my client. She wasn't even my friend—mainly because I couldn't let her be. "One of Aidy's friends," I finished.

Bridget raised her eyebrows. "Who?"

"The woman I'm sure Simon mentioned I was with at his clinic earlier this week. Her name is Cassia Bevins."

Bridget frowned. "Her name sounds familiar."

"She was one of the principal dancers in the Boston Ballet." My chest puffed up, as if Cassia's successes were something I could take pride in.

What was *happening* to me? My mind must be cracking. The

stress from cobbling together a solution to get some of our projects up and running had clearly messed me up.

Bridget pursed her lips. "That's not it."

"She plans to open a studio here and wants to do come classes
with kids with special needs," I offered.

"Yes," Bridget said, her face brightening. She became more
animated. "That's it. Aidy and Emmaline told me about her
at brunch. I saw a news story about her—this must have been
when she was still with the Boston Ballet. She taught all those
little girls a beautiful dance. Is she going to be able to host her
camp this summer?"

"Um…"

Bridget's son was called back by a nurse. Bridget sighed and
turned away. "I want to hear more about her program. It sounds
fabulous. I'm hoping to get our girls into it once they're a bit older."

I ran my fingers through my hair. I'd really boxed myself into
a corner, telling people about Cassia's studio, and I had no one to
blame but myself. I hoped she wasn't annoyed with me. I didn't
like how I felt when Cassia was upset with me.

I headed out to get my car, still pondering how best to ne-
gotiate my relationship with Cassia. Much as I wanted to get to
know her better, my past with her sister was an issue—one I'd
need to address.

But did I want to?

When Cassia came out of the building, I opened her door,
and settled her into the seat before stowing the crutches in the
back again. I rounded the rear of my car and steeled myself
against sitting in the small, enclosed space with Cassia once

more. Her light fragrance tickled my senses, and longing wended through me. I wanted to drive away, to leave Cassia there so I didn't have to face these feelings any longer.

"No one asked you to help me," Cassia pointed out. "Me, included in that. So you don't get to glare death rays out the windshield."

I laughed, caught off guard by her bluntness. This woman was so different from her sister—elegant and forthright, unwilling to bullshit me just because it was easier that way. And, despite how harsh her sentiments could be, I wanted nothing more than to hear what Cassia would say next.

"I…have a lot on my mind," I said. It was a bit of an olive branch, the best I was able to offer in that moment.

She smoothed her skirt. "You're not the only one."

I glanced over as I slid to a stop at the light. "Because of your foot? Or because of the studio situation?"

She snorted. "You don't really want to help me," she mumbled, looking out the side window.

"I already told you that I did—"

"But you don't like me. Because I'm related to Amanda. You didn't want to accompany me to the doctor today. You only did that because Aidy threatened you with not seeing Lilia."

She sighed. "I'm not sure I'm capable of taking on this big of a project, not right now with months of physical therapy in front of me. And that's no guarantee I'll ever be able to teach well, let alone dance again."

I didn't like the idea of Cassia giving up. She needed to fight for her goals. "I *do* want to help you."

"Why Nico? You barely know me and our interactions haven't been stellar." Her shoulders folded inward. "The only other person who *could* help me with this project is my sister. But, in asking her, I'd be giving in, letting her think her behavior's okay. Or worse, acting like her—manipulating the situation to get my way." She sighed, her expression bleak. "And I'd rather lose this dream than behave like my sister."

Chapter Sixteen
Cassia

"Wh—what do you mean by that?" Nico's voice caught, and I studied him from my periphery. His agitation was more apparent with each passing breath.

I was surer than ever that Amanda was responsible for at least some of his high-walled grumpiness. I fiddled with the hem of my skirt.

"It's the reason I didn't ask for her help initially—well, one of the reasons. She's a manipulator, and it's all caught up with her. She was sued in a civil case because she claimed a guy…well, that's not important—"

"I beg to differ. Her claim was *extremely* important," Nico said.

I raised an eyebrow. "Um…okay. Well, Amanda said that guy sexually harassed her at work, but she'd been dating him. So, yeah, there were touches that other witnesses saw, which made the guy look bad. But Amanda only said all that to get access to his work, which she then passed off as her own." I shook my head. "Knowing Amanda, that wasn't the first time."

"What if I told you it wasn't?" Nico asked. "That I was *sure* she'd done it before?"

I studied him. What was he admitting? I waited but he remained tense and quiet. "Because I'm her sister, you've wondered if I'm the same. If I take and take, hurting other people, never concerned about their feelings. I would, too," I added when he glanced over to me. "But I can assure you that I'd *never* stoop to lying or cheating. I grew up with Amanda—I know *exactly* what she's capable of and how detrimental her actions are."

No one had ever bothered to ask me what it was like to live in Amanda's wake, where the people she discarded happily turned on me because they couldn't get back at her.

As he slid to a stop at the next light, he studied me. "Not even to get your ballet studio?"

I stared at my hands. "There's no way I'd find joy in the space. It would be tainted by the lies and other people's hurts."

Nico was an enigma; he remained difficult to read but thoughtful and caring when he didn't shut down and hide behind the thick barricade he'd erected around his true self. I knew from Aidy that Nico used to be easy-going, fun, but all that changed after their parents disappeared while sailing in the bay.

That type of tragedy, and the subsequent fallout, would change anyone. Clearly, those losses reshaped Nico. I wished I'd known him before—the kindhearted, fun-loving man who'd always been there for his sister.

But maybe it was for the best I hadn't met him then—*that* version of Nico was one I'd fall for.

I didn't have any time or interest in love. And I'd keep telling myself that.

"Do you mind if we make a quick stop?" he asked.

I shook my head; part of me still seemed dazed by the good news from the doctor. Sure, I'd missed a follow-up appointment, but my team of doctors specialized in ballet. No one had mentioned the possibility to me. Had that been intentional? I bit my lip, hating even the thought that someone in the ballet wanted me gone badly enough to let an injury fester.

When Nico pulled up in front of a veterinarian's office, I gaped. "Why are we here?"

Nico ducked his head and mumbled something.

"What's that now?" I asked.

He glanced at me over his shoulder, his feet already on the pavement. "I want to check on Fred."

My brows drew together in confusion. "Does Fred work here?"

"No. He's my cat. Kitten. I dropped him off earlier this week."

My eyes widened. "Oh, no. Is he sick?"

"He was. I mean, he was malnourished and needed surgery." Nico's lips mashed flat. "I wanted to get him yesterday, but Dr. Shapiro wanted me to wait until this morning."

"You have a kitten? This I've got to see."

Nico sighed, muttering something about how he should have taken me home first. "Hold on. I'll get your crutches."

He gathered them from the back seat and handed them to me, waiting for me to move away from the door before shutting it. He strode ahead to snag the door handle before I could but let me go into the waiting room first.

The receptionist smiled. "Ah, Fred's going to be so glad to see you."

Nico's expression pinched. "Is he okay? What happened? Did he have a reaction to the surgery? Why didn't you call me?"

"He's fine, but he's been crying off and on this morning."

Nico fidgeted with the edge of his suit coat, his gaze darting toward the backroom. He kept silent as the receptionist stepped away from her desk but he began to pace the waiting room, back and forth, watching the door that led to the back. Finally, the vet popped out with Fred in his hands.

Nico rushed forward, careful not to bump my legs or crutches from where I'd sunk into a chair near the door. He plucked Fred from Dr. Shapiro's grasp and the soft, pitiful whining stopped. I couldn't see much, thanks to the tiny cone encircling the cat's head, but I imagined Fred must be looking up at Nico. I wished I could see the color of the cat's eyes.

"I'm here, little guy. Don't worry. I won't leave you again."

"Well, I think Fred's glad to hear that, too," the vet said, his tone wry. "Good news is I've done all I can for the kitten now. He needs some daddy time, apparently."

"What do you mean?" Nico asked as he snuggled the tiny furry body up to his neck and rubbed his cheek against his fur. My jaw dropped. Goodness. Was there anything sexier than a man and his pet?

If so, I hadn't seen it.

"He hasn't been this calm since you left him."

Nico's brows drew low and his hand stilled for a moment before he continued petting the little body. "He's been upset the whole time? Why didn't you call me? I would have come. Any time—"

"He's slept well, and I needed to be sure about parasites, which I am now," the vet interrupted. "No, no, I meant since he started feeling better from consistent food and water. It's been obvious that he was searching for you since we came into the office this morning."

"Did you miss me, Fred?" Nico murmured, nuzzling into the cat's furry neck. "I missed you. I've thought about you all week."

Nico happened to catch a glimpse of me as he cuddled the kitten, rocking his body just like Aidy'd shown me with Lilia. Dull red crept up his cheeks, but he didn't stop snuggling the kitten.

The vet smiled at me. "You've got yourself a softie right here. Is he always this bad when someone he loves is out of his sight?"

I cleared my throat, at a loss of how to respond. "I've never seen him react to any animal or person like this before."

The vet nodded. "Sometimes it's like that—an unbreakable bond that hits hard and fast. I always appreciate those because they're so special."

"I'll say," I whispered. I leveled Nico with a look heavy with speculation.

Once Nico paid the bill, he tucked Fred into the crook of his arm and led the way back to his car. "Damn. I don't have the cat carrier. I must have left it at home."

"I'll hold him," I offered.

"Thanks." Nico carefully transferred the kitten to my lap once I gave him my crutches.

"Why did you name him Fred?" I asked once Nico was situated in the driver's seat.

Nico tugged at his jacket's sleeves. "Um…my dad always wanted a cat when he was a kid. But his mom and brother were allergic, so Dad never had a cat. He told me he pretended his slipper was a cat, and he named it Fred. He took it everywhere with him for a year, maybe longer."

My heart ached for the man who clearly missed his father so much he wanted to name a kitten after a shared memory. I hadn't had any of those with my father; he'd made it clear for as long as I could remember that I was my mother's problem—not a child he'd wanted. "This is your chance to make it right."

"Something like that."

I tickled Fred's tiny chin and the little cat purred for me before twitching his ears. I laughed.

"I think he likes you," Nico said.

"Guess so."

The rest of the ride was quiet. "Let me take you to dinner," he said as we turned into my street.

My eyebrows shot up. "What?"

His lips quirked a little, but I caught the underlying uncertainty. I swear he wanted to fidget.

"Dinner. The meal in the evening, after work, where two people—"

"Why?" I asked. Confusion poured through me, along with alarm bells. I'd just been thinking Nico was a man I could care for, fall for, and now, he was asking me out? "You don't like me."

He inhaled through his nose. "Actually, I really like you. *That's* been the problem."

"That doesn't make any sense," I said.

He pulled into my driveway. "I have a history..."

When he didn't say anything more, I leaned in, desperate to know about this past, the reason he was so jaded, so closed off.

"A history?"

He opened his car door and stepped out. I struggled but managed to resettle the kitten in the seat and get myself out of the car.

"Maybe my suggestion wasn't a good idea," he said even as he handed me the crutches.

I shifted backward. "You don't get to decide if it's a good idea. I do."

And there was that damn attractive lip quirk that made my stomach all melty.

"Oh? And why's that?"

"Because you asked me to dinner, on a date, so I get to decide if it's a smart idea of me to accept."

"I see." His expression was solemn, but the mirth in his eyes gave him away.

"Smart ass," I snarked.

"Weenie," he shot back.

I gasped. "I've never been a wimp. Not once!" I raised my chin. "Fine. I'll go to dinner with you. On a *nice* date."

Nico swallowed, shuffling his feet. "Cassia—"

I crutched into my house and turned to face him. "We can talk about my dance studio. It'll be a write-off for you, and I get to eat out at an elegant restaurant. Win-win and no one gets hurt."

I wished I could believe that, but I'd just have to do my best to make it so.

"Goodbye, Nico. I'll expect you here, Saturday night, at seven. For our client meeting."

I shut the door before he could say anything further—or before I could second-guess my choice. Because I was pretty sure I'd just made a ridiculously bad one.

Chapter Seventeen
Nico

Filled with a renewed sense of purpose and unwilling to allow our projects to languish, I'd managed to get the proper insurance and business license to operate a construction firm throughout the week.

Between calls and trips to city hall and other governmental offices, I set up Fred with a cozy bed in my office. The scratching post from the vet had pride of place next to it. I'd even gotten Fred one of those cat condo structures—after researching the fuck out of them to make sure he'd use it and like it—so he could lounge in luxury while we watched the Tour de France or soccer. Not that Fred seemed overly interested in the thing. He'd sniffed it a few times and climbed on it once.

Thankfully, through the rest of the workweek, Hazel Sato had been an invaluable help. Since our project was shut down until we had the proper license and insurance, she stood patiently in some of the courthouse lines, waiting to get paperwork filed or signed when I had client meetings.

Finally, Friday evening, after I'd taken Cassia to the doctor, we received the proper documentation. I let Hazel know I planned to reopen the Michaelson property to labor and anyone who wanted to start working on Saturday was welcome.

That morning, I pulled on a pair of jeans I hadn't worn in

years because I spent most days in the Wright and Associates offices and wanted to look the part of the successful partner. I smiled at the softness of the denim, but the tightness in the seat and waistband had me frowning. "Well, I guess all those bike rides haven't added up to quite the same weight as in college," I said. "Good thing this new career is going to keep me active."

I poured my coffee and made sure I was on site before the rest of the crew showed up, hoping to hide some of the exhaustion lingering on my face.

No reason to let anyone else know I wasn't sleeping well. I was thirty-damn-three, a man in my prime, well past this awkward teenage obsession over Cassia's smile, her silky hair, and soft skin. Hell, even the rich tone of her voice left me vibrating with desire. But the worst was when I closed my eyes and her dancing filled my mind. The fluidity of movement, the sureness of her steps and gestures seduced me—and I readily embraced it.

I could barely stand to wait until tonight to see Cassia again. I'd dated before Amanda, though not much since, and while I'd been attracted to girls in high school and college, nothing compared to this persistent, clawing need to be in Cassia's presence, to see her smile, hear her voice. I ran my thumb along my hammer's top as I frowned at the space. I didn't like this level of neediness I felt, but I couldn't change it either.

"Only way there is through," I muttered. I threw myself into the demolition. I'd spent the last hour knocking down the interior studs that separated two rooms we wanted to turn into a larger great room. The problem was that one of those studs was a support beam—and of course it was in a position in the room that blocked the sightlines we'd planned on to the kitchen and back deck. I left that beam and returned to shoveling the pieces of drywall and two-by-fours into a wheelbarrow.

There was something about physical labor that put everything in perspective. At times, when I was sitting at a drafting table, I forgot the actual creativity that went into solving problems on the site. But most of the people I worked with were smart, thoughtful, and dedicated to their craft. At least, the group who showed up at the Victorian reno site were. Hazel hadn't been kidding about the group of women interested in working on the project—without Marcus's toxic comments and poor work ethic.

I counted heads twice. "Seventeen," I said, my head spinning. "You brought me *fifteen* additional workers. On a Saturday."

Hazel nodded as she shoved her hands into the back pockets of her coveralls. A satisfied smile played across her lips. "I told you there were women who wanted to work."

"Where's Lauren?" I asked, expecting to see the older woman.

Hazel pursed her lips. "She said she was done with construction. Her husband's wanted her to retire for a while, so she decided to."

"Can't say I blame her after what you told me."

Hazel shrugged. "Lauren's pushed hard for change. We wouldn't be here without her. But she's been hassled or paid less for her expertise her entire career."

My mouth felt as though I'd just inhaled a bunch of sawdust. "How much *less*?"

She raised a thin eyebrow. "You'd be surprised by how many contractors knock off a few bucks per hour for women."

"That's not happening on this project," I said, my tone as adamant as my resolve. "In fact, if we can get the project back on track, I'll do my damnedest to find some bonuses in the budget. They may not be huge…"

She gave me a firm nod. "Good. That'll go a long way to show you're serious."

Before I could ask her what I was serious about, she turned to the women who had fanned out around us in the dusty, jumbled, soon-to-be great room.

"Who's ready to get to work?" Hazel called. "For full pay?"

A loud cheer split the quiet morning. "I guess I have a crew," I murmured. I'd thought I'd said that quietly enough not to be overheard, but Hazel turned toward me. "I hope you have plans for this group of ladies after this job. Some of them didn't go to their other jobs or side gigs for a chance to be considered first for any full-time slots."

I swallowed hard. "I will, depending on the quality—"

"Be prepared to be wowed."

Before I could even blink, Hazel stepped forward, clapped her hands, and began to divvy out assignments. This small woman had leader written all over her. I stood back, taking in her leadership style, assertiveness, and no-nonsense vibe. She was tough but thoughtful.

Yeah, Hazel was definitely a woman I wanted around—one I was sure Aidy and Emmaline would enjoy working with. And I was pretty sure Hazel would have the same respect for my sister and sister-in-law that they'd have for her.

Excitement swelled alongside hope. If this project actually met its initial deadline, then I'd have more money and more opportunities for Hazel and the team she'd assembled.

I glanced around at the busy hum of work, a smile building along with excitement and hope. Yes. We were *doing* this. Wright Construction was in business, and I was finally—finally—doing what I loved most.

Chapter Eighteen
Cassia

I smoothed down the flowing, asymmetrical skirt, wishing I could wear heels.

"You're being ridiculous," I whispered into the mirror. I leaned in closer, noting that my eyeliner over my right eye was smudged. I grabbed a Q-tip from the glass jar on my vanity and touched it up.

"You should not be going to all this trouble for Nico," I said. "You really shouldn't."

And yet, I'd straightened my hair, shaved, and even used one of those facial masks that promised glowing skin. I wasn't sure if my skin glowed, but my cheeks were pink and my eyes were bright. I'd put on a knit skirt that cut off a couple inches above the knee in the front but trailed down to my ankles in the back. My top was a turquoise silk shell with embroidery at the V-neck. I slid into an elbow-length bolero with the same embroidery. My ballet flats were the same soft dove gray as my skirt. I could say that I'd worn this because I loved it—true—but I'd put it on because it was one of my nicer outfits that showed off my legs—my best asset—and hugged my curves.

I'd just turned away from the mirror when I heard the thud-thud-thud of the knocker. I frowned at the clock. It was half-past six, and while I appreciated a man who showed up early, I wasn't interested in one who would railroad me into hurrying just to meet his agenda.

I swung open the door, ready to offer Nico a piece of my mind, but snapped my mouth shut when I saw Amanda there. She'd called many times over the past week, but I'd ignored each one. Still it galled me that she'd come to my home. I clearly didn't want to talk to her.

"What do you want?" I asked.

"Is that any way to talk to your sister?" she asked.

I raised an eyebrow and leaned into the doorframe, keeping hold of the door's handle.

"If my sister had ever shown me an ounce of support or love, I'd say no."

She tipped her head, taking in my outfit. "You have a date."

"I have a business dinner," I said, tone firm. Maybe, if I said it with enough conviction, I could convince myself this meal was just about business.

"On Saturday night?" Amanda scoffed.

She was right. It was a date. More, I *wanted* it to be a date. I lifted my chin.

"My life isn't your concern. Why are you still in Providence?"

"I had my interview on Thursday. I didn't get the job."

"I'm sorry to hear that."

"Are you?"

I sighed. "What do you want Amanda?"

Her shoulders curved inward. "Mom isn't speaking to me."

I shrugged.

"And it's because of Lowell. If you talked to her, told her you're not mad—"

"I am angry with you. You betrayed me. Lied to me. Were the worst possible sister to me you could have been."

Her eyes filled with tears. "I don't have anywhere to go."

I forced the concern and pity from my heart. "That's too bad. But you burned this bridge with me, too, Manda. I'm not forgiving you for cheating with my boyfriend. Again. And if you want Mom's forgiveness, then you better work it out with her."

Amanda's lip quivered. "You'd kick me out?"

"You don't live here, so I can't kick you out. But, for the record, that's exactly what you did with Lowell. I *lived* with him, and you had no problem boxing up my clothes and things."

She scowled. "I never knew you held such a grudge."

"I didn't either. But I've reached my limit with you, and I don't intend to change my mind."

She narrowed her eyes. "You're a bitch, Cassia."

I met her eyes, though my heart thundered. "Maybe. But I learned from the best."

Amanda spun on her heel and flounced down the steps toward her car. It was a cute little Mercedes convertible, and it appeared to be the same one Lowell had bought for my birthday. The man was too lazy to trade it in, so no doubt he'd given to my sister when I mailed him back the keys.

She rolled down the window and flipped me off before speeding down the street.

I shut my door and leaned against it, closing my eyes. I inhaled, then exhaled, trying to recover from the quakes working their way up my extremities. I crutched my way back down the hall to my bedroom. After a long moment's debate, I picked up my phone and dialed my mother.

After three rings, I was just about to hang up when I heard her voice. "Cassia! This is a surprise. Everything okay?"

"I'm not sure," I ventured.

She made a noncommittal sound. "Does this have something to do with your sister?"

"Yes. She came to the house tonight, practically begging for me to let her stay here." I went on to impart the rest of the conversation, still unsure what I expected from my mother. Mom sighed.

"That sounds like Manda. She told you that I've cut her off, right?"

"She mentioned you didn't offer to let her stay there."

"No, it's more than that. Martin refuses to have anything to do with her. After he and Grammy sat me down, made me really look at what she's done to you, to herself, to those poor men in Manhattan… I'm mortified I had a part in her behavior."

"Men? There was more than one man?" I asked.

"Oh, dear. Right, you wouldn't know. I guess you were touring—in London or Europe or wherever. That was the beginning of this whole mess. Martin was so angry then."

Martin was my mother's second husband, a nice man who enjoyed rowing and mountain climbing nearly as much as he liked growing his stock portfolio. He'd never approved of Amanda's actions or dramatics. This came to a head after the civil suit, when he flat-out told Amanda she wouldn't get any of his money or support once she admitted to "rearranging" the facts of the case to make herself look more like the victim.

"That's part of why Martin's put his foot down. Manda said

that young man asked her to marry him, let her move into his apartment and then…well, you know what she does."

The disapproval dripping from my mother's tone startled me.

"I'm…surprised you're sticking to your mandate."

Mom sighed. "That's because I always did indulge her. I know I did—and as Martin pointed out, often at your expense."

My throat felt tight, thick, and my eyes achy. Calling her now hadn't been smart. I sniffled and dabbed a tissue at my nose. "I don't know what to say."

"You know what I realized after your grandmother pointed it out to me? Manda's never apologized for her behavior. I mean, she'll say she's sorry, but that's to get what she wants. She's never once been contrite about ruining those men's reputations, about stealing your boyfriends, about talking to the Boston Ballet about you dancing."

All the air was shoved from my lungs. "She did *what*?"

"You didn't know? Oh my goodness! Seriously?"

"Mom, what are you talking about?" I asked, urgency flooding my every cell.

Mom made a choked sound. "She was at dinner with Lowell. This is after…well, she…you know."

"She had sex with him in *my* bed."

"Er, yes. After that. Lowell took her to a dinner, which happened to be hosted by one of the ballet's biggest contributors. She let it slip that you'd been thinking about moving to London—"

"No, I wasn't!"

Mom sighed. "I know. I *know*, Cassia. But you know how Amanda is…"

Yeah. A lying, cheating horrible excuse for a person.

"No wonder they were so keen to cut me from my principal-ship. It also explains why the doctor didn't bother to follow up with me. They just wanted me gone."

Because of my sister.

I clenched my jaw. Damn her. She never cared about how her offhand comments and half-truths—sometimes flat-out lies—impacted others.

"You didn't get proper care?" Mom gasped. "Oh, honey. Come back to Boston. I'm sure there's something Martin can do, some strings he can pull—"

"I'm okay. Now. I actually have a proper diagnosis and am getting healthy."

"Are you sure?"

I considered this for a moment. Sure. I wanted my mother to help me. But I was fine. I liked being able to dance what I wanted, when I wanted...and I enjoyed eating food—bread, chocolate. I liked the business I was going to build here. I wouldn't think about Nico because he didn't deserve to be on my list of reasons why I was content with the shift in my life. And I was content. Happy even. Perhaps Nico could be the icing on my new-life cake. Eventually.

I realized my mother was still talking, so I refocused on her.

"The type of behavior is why Martin says he's had enough. And...I have, too. Amanda needs to grow up."

My mood soured. I'd heard my mother spout all this before. While she talked a good game, she'd never followed through before. So, I doubted she would this time.

"I have to go," I said. My shoulders slumped. The last thing I wanted, now, was to deal with a crowded restaurant. If I hadn't insisted he take me, I'd cancel our business dinner that wasn't a date.

My head ached and my stomach remained knotted, but I'd seen Nico's headlights flash through my bedroom window and any moment he'd knock on the door.

As much as I might not want to go, I'd forced this issue yesterday and needed to woman up to the consequences.

My mother told me goodbye, and I tried not to fixate on the fact she hadn't told me she loved me or that she was sorry for how she'd treated me. That wasn't something she'd ever done with me, so I shouldn't miss it. I couldn't.

I slid my phone into my purse and collected my crutches, walking down the hallway just as Nico knocked. I opened the front door, unprepared for Nico's appearance. Sure, I'd seen him in a suit and tie, but I hadn't seen him prepared for a date.

He wore a dark gray wool suit that had to be from a high-end designer. His shoes and belt were black, glossy, clearly freshly polished. His white dress shirt was crisp, probably linen, and unbuttoned at the collar, flashing tantalizing hints of the hollow of his throat and his collarbones.

His acorn-colored hair was styled back off his forehead, throwing his cheekbones into starker relief. I bit my inner lower lip as I looked him over.

"You clean up well," I said.

His smile turned warmer but remained enigmatic. "So do you. I love the skirt."

I curbed the urge to twirl or to flirt.

"Thanks."

His brow furrowed, and he reached up, tucking a few wayward strands of my hair behind my ear. "What's wrong, beautiful?"

I sighed, loving the compliment but unwilling to melt further for this man.

"I'm not up for another round of anger and resentment tonight," I said, barely suppressing the urge to nuzzle into his hand. I wanted to burrow into his warmth, but we'd drawn lines—ones we weren't good about not crossing. I was Nico's client. He was adversarial with my sister.

"I have a question," he said slowly.

"All right."

"How do you feel about takeout? We can head back to my place…" At my wide-eyed look, he rushed on, "Or to your studio, somewhere that's quieter. We can still get some work done but it'll be low-key."

"Why are you willing to put up with me?" I asked, exhaustion creeping over me. "I know you're still angry with Amanda."

He considered that for a long moment. "I've been angry with her for a long time, yeah, but…well, that's history. *Ancient* history. It helps to know that she got her comeuppance and that you know how she behaves—that you don't condone it. But, really, the kicker has been me examining all that baggage and realizing that she was never who I thought she was, who I wanted her to be. And I was selfish and short-sighted, blinded by my own family issues, unwilling to believe I could have fallen into the same trap."

Troubled by his tone, I locked my door and started down the

steps. He stayed close but didn't touch me—a silent presence that would support me, catch me, if needed.

"What trap?" I asked, unable to bear the pain in his expression.

He opened my car door and waited until I settled in before he took my crutches and stowed them in the back seat. From there, he rounded the car's hood.

"My father had an affair. I found out about it a few months before my parents disappeared."

"I'm sorry to hear that," I said.

"Yeah, well, the worst part was how in love he pretended to be with my mother. Except now, I think he might have truly been in love with my mom."

He started the car and reversed out of the driveway. I watched him manipulate the gear shift as he settled the gearshift in drive. I liked his hands. His fingernails were neatly buffed, his fingers long and elegant, the palms large. Capable hands, not unlike those of my former partner at the ballet. Hands like that could hold me, keep me secure from falling.

"If he loved her, why did he cheat?" I asked.

Nico sighed. "I've wondered that myself for years. And I still don't know the answer. But I think he did love Mom, and I think he regretted being unfaithful. But that's not the point of my story."

"Oh?"

He shook his head. "I went looking for a woman dedicated to her career."

I shifted, a weight pressing against my stomach. "And you met Amanda."

"I'd already met her—we worked together. It was comfortable,

easy to take her out for drinks, which progressed to dinners…
I figured my parents had love but my dad screwed it up, so I
wouldn't bother looking for that. Why should I? It hadn't worked
for my parents."

His eyes fell into a shadow as he pulled up to a stoplight. "I
can't believe I'm telling you this. I've never even told my siblings
about my father's infidelity."

"Why not?"

He shrugged. "What's the point? My parents are gone. Telling
my brother and sister our father wasn't the stand-up guy we
thought him to be…they already know about the company's
issues. I didn't want to further tarnish their view of him."

I remembered Nico's story about his cat—he named his kitten
Fred for a father who had cheated on his mother, hurting Nico
in the process. Some of Nico's conflicted emotions made more
sense. He'd loved and respected his father, clearly very much, but
the man broke that trust with his son as much as he did his wife.
My own father was an unfeeling jerk, at least when it came to
me, but as far as I knew, he and my mother simply grew apart.
Her attempt to save their marriage—me—backfired spectacularly,
making everyone miserable enough for my father to simply quit
us. I couldn't blame him for looking for comfortable, could I? I'd
done the same with Lowell—wanted a man who supported the
arts, who looked good on my arm. I hadn't bothered to search for
deeper because I didn't believe in it. Like Nico.

The realization rocked me. I was messed up—*more* messed up
from my childhood than I'd thought.

"But it would lessen your burden if you told them. I can tell that it bothers you."

"Yeah, well, it was the first of many of my choices that bother me. I have to live with all of them because I can't change them."

"Would you? If you could?"

He tapped his fingers on the steering wheel. Once we were stopped at the next light, he turned to face me.

"I think that I can't change the past," he said, as if just coming to the realization. He studied me for a long moment, long enough for heat to pool in my belly and lick up into my chest.

"But I can and do want a much different future. A happier one."

Chapter Nineteen
Nico

Talking with Cassia proved easy. She never interrupted, even when I rambled. I felt seen, heard, in ways I hadn't…maybe ever. And telling someone else about my father's affair? It was like a deep well of poison had been lanced from my chest. Up until the moment I finished saying the words, I hadn't realized how much of a weight they held over me.

I'd loved my father, even worshipped him. He'd been the epitome of what I'd thought a loving husband should strive to be. He took my mother for spontaneous weekends away. He brought her favorite flowers, and coffee in bed.

He also screwed a twenty-five-year-old receptionist who I fired the moment I took over the company. That's when I discovered my father had been paying her large sums of money every month to keep her from telling my mother about their affair. The young woman, Stacey, had tried to seduce me, but I'd refused to re-hire her. Or have sex with her.

The receptionist had been pretty, but my mother was *beautiful*. She focused her world on my father and us and built a home. The fact that my father threatened all that for—I hated to think about him with another woman, but that's what happened. And she extorted most of the profits from the business thereafter.

I touched the tip of my tongue to my upper lip. "'Maybe that's why I'm so jaded," I said.

"I definitely think that's why you're jaded. Well, that, and because my sister obviously screwed you over."

I sighed, surprised by how much lighter, freer I felt. "Tell you what—let's not discuss your sister anymore. Like I said, she's in the past, and I'd really prefer to keep her there. Now, do you still prefer to get dinner to go? Or would you like to be wined and dined?"

I pulled into the parking lot and slid into a space. I put the car in park and turned to face her.

"What do you prefer?"

I shook my head. "This is about you, Cassia. I want you to be comfortable. Happy." As I said the words, I realized just how true they were. Maybe the reason I'd been adversarial toward her wasn't so much about Amanda in the beginning as the feelings she'd ignited during that initial exchange. I loved talking to her. I loved watching expressions play across her features. I thrilled at her laugh and ached at her sadness. I'd never felt emotions so deeply before, not for someone else, and I wasn't sure what to do with them—how to manage them.

By not facing them, just as I hadn't confronted my father's infidelity, I wasn't learning how to deal with these cataclysms in my life. Clearly, I needed to spend more time dealing with my problems and feelings head-on. While uncomfortable, that was the only way to actually grow.

And I wanted to grow. I aspired to find happiness and purpose again. I was on the cusp of it—maybe because of Cassia, maybe not. But if nothing else, she was my friend. As I took in the delicate shell of her ear, the sharp line of her jaw, the softness of her plush lips, I realized I wanted to continue confiding in her. I'd missed intimacy—yes, the sexual kind but perhaps as much, the emotional one.

She hesitated, hand on her seat belt. "Let's go in."

I smiled with approval. "Good call. The tables are spread out and the noise is minimal. I asked for a table in the corner and an extra chair."

At her confused look, I said, "For your crutches and in case you wanted to put your foot up."

Her features softened. "Oh. That was thoughtful."

"You deserve it," I said, my tone gruff. I wanted to touch her cheek again; I wanted to run my thumb down her soft skin and press it to her plump lips. I yearned to lean forward and kiss her.

But that would be crossing a line—the line I'd set between us. Cassia deserved grand romance and a man without a huge pile of baggage with her family.

I opened the car door and stepped out into the night. I looked up into the sky, enjoying the twinkle of the stars and the soft kiss of moonlight.

Had I made the right choice by not telling Cassia the depth of my relationship with Amanda? I didn't know, but I was sure I didn't want to rehash those dark emotions. I retrieved her crutches and opened her door. When she smiled up at me, I determined to focus on her tonight, giving her the evening she deserved.

Then, I'd have to let go of the dream—the future of light and laughter that Cassia created.

Chapter Twenty
Cassia

Nico turned distant and introspective as we entered the restaurant.

Maybe he wasn't up to staying? "If you don't want to eat here—"

"No, sorry, I do," he said. "I've been looking forward to this all day. It's what got me through a gnarly bathroom demolition."

"Wait." I slipped into the chair he held for me. "You *worked* all day?"

He nodded.

"Hard manual labor—and now you're out with me? Aren't you exhausted? We can just grab takeout, let you put your feet up—"

"I'm good, Cassia. Really." His eyes brimmed with excitement. "I love that type of work. It was invigorating. I had more fun than I've had in..." He swallowed down some emotion and his expression turned wistful. "I had fun," he murmured.

"*Destroying* things was fun?" I raised my eyebrows, trying to infuse a bit of levity.

He smiled, taking the road out of his memories. "For me, it was."

Fair enough. "So, what else do you do for fun?"

Our conversation was interrupted by a waiter, who set down chilled glasses of water and handed each of us a handwritten menu. "The special this evening is scallops cooked in brown butter over a bed of saffron Israeli couscous with haricot verts sautéed with garlic and macadamia nuts."

My mouth watered and I nodded. "Sounds great. Could you give us a minute to decide?"

He nodded and stepped away. Nico's dark head was bent over the menu, but he lifted it a moment later.

"That special sounds awesome," I murmured.

He leaned in closer, and I enjoyed the opportunity to meet his brown eyes. "I agree. Want to share a bottle of wine? Maybe a French Sauvignon Blanc?"

I shrugged. "I don't know wine or alcohol well. It wasn't really part of my nutrition plan."

"Do you miss that strict eating schedule?"

I smiled as I reached for my water. "You first. I asked you what else you do for fun."

"Oh. Right. I like to ride my bike." He shrugged. "I used to play rugby in college—that was a blast. And I like chilling with Fred."

"How is the little guy?"

Nico's smile brightened his whole face, causing my breath to catch. "Great. He slept most of the day. He likes his new bed." He glanced away and cleared his throat. "Well, he liked it after I put one of my T-shirts in it."

"Just like a human baby," I said. I set my water back in its spot. "No, I don't miss the rigidity of my former diet, but I'm also not used to eating what I want, when I want. It's weird." I wrinkled my nose.

He studied me for a long time, no doubt taking in the slight hollow below my cheekbones and the soft roundness of my chin. My overfull lips.

"I like looking at you just as you are today. And I like that, with me, you can try new options, expand your taste horizons."

I shook my head, a rueful smile tugging at my lips. "I like to be active. I like to feel fit, firm, and strong. Not being able to dance…" I bit my lip as confusion and desolation bubbled within me.

Nico reached forward, touched the back of my hand with his fingers. "I want to be the reason you forget your sorrows, if only for a little while. I want to sweep my thumb across your lower lip, to nuzzle into your neck…"

My breathing hitched, my focus locked on Nico. My heart pumped a rickety rhythm, his words, that flash of desire in his eyes making me lightheaded.

No, this couldn't be happening. Not with him. What had we been talking about?

"It's hard to lose the familiar, the comfort of a routine," I said. My voice came out a little ragged, like my body didn't want to let go of the notion of him.

His lips quirked a little, just a hint of white teeth. "True. But you're not losing the ability to dance, Cassia. It's just postponed."

The waiter came back and we both ordered the scallops. Nico asked the waiter for some wine choices and we settled on an unoaked California Chardonnay that he claimed went beautifully with the seafood. He brought the bottle, which he opened with a flourish. Nico gestured toward my glass. "Make sure she likes it."

My wide-eyed stare turned to a glare, but Nico just smiled at me. "I want you to get the most out of the meal, and that means enjoying your glass of wine. "

I sipped from the small amount the waiter poured after a sniff. I tilted my head back and made a faint moaning noise. Why hadn't I known wine could taste like this? What else had I been missing in my life? "It's *good.*"

Nico's attention fixated on my mouth, eyes burning brighter when my tongue darted out to catch the last drops from my upper lip.

"You are gorgeous, so bright, and authentic. That's what I love most about you, Cassia: you don't hide your reactions, your delight."

He blinked a few times, as if he'd realized what he'd said. The waiter poured wine into both of our glasses, breaking the spell woven by Nico's words. Part of me wanted to keep the young man from stepping away.

"We should talk about the studio," I said.

Nico shut his eyes, his lashes brushing his cheekbones. "I'd become so jaded, so used to burying my feelings or lashing out to keep people at arm's length that I'd forgotten the possibility of simply enjoying my life." He opened his eyes and met mine. "You're reminding me. And I fucking love it."

"I'm not...I'm not ready..."

I wasn't ready to admit how much I cared for this man. I didn't want to know what Amanda had been to him.

Nico settled back, his expression pinched. He picked up his wine glass. "I understand."

I smiled but it wavered. Today had been emotional. I picked

up the wine glass and sipped again, needing the relaxation it might offer.

"I was thinking we might repurpose the seats from an old movie theater in a nearby town. The building's slated to be knocked down, so we could get them dirt cheap."

My shoulders relaxed. "That's an interesting idea. But, it's sad to think of it being torn down," I said, frowning. "There's no way to save it?"

Nico shook his head. "It's been neglected for a long time. I was surprised the interior's in as good of shape as it is. The seats will be a big step up from the vinyl ones you currently have. They'll need to be reupholstered, but Aidy has contacts there, and after the bid she gave me yesterday, I'm confident we can cut the initial expenditure from the estimate by twenty, maybe twenty-five percent."

I grinned. "That would be amazing, Nico."

He rubbed his chin. "Well, I kinda want to impress you." His lip curled up a little. "Is it working?"

I leaned forward. "Yes."

Our food arrived and we ate while the conversation flowed easily. Once we'd finished, Nico pulled out my chair and offered me my crutches.

Once at his car, he held open my door, his expression intense. "I don't want to be the villain in your story," he said, tone fervent.

I leaned my armpits into my crutches and touched his cheek. "You're not."

He nodded. "Good. That matters to me."

He drove me home and we were both quiet. But the silence

wasn't stilted or uncomfortable. I'd enjoyed the evening more than I'd expected. More than I should.

He opened my door and handed me my crutches once more. "I'll walk you up."

I smiled, enjoying his display of gentlemanly behavior. Once I opened the door, I paused, nerves building in my belly. He leaned in and pressed a soft, gentle kiss to my cheek.

"Goodnight, sweet Cassia."

I tipped my head back, the pulse in my neck pounding as my lips parted. His gaze dropped to my lips and he looked pained as he stepped back.

"Damn, I want to kiss you."

Instead, he turned on his heel and headed toward his car. Once behind the wheel, he stared at me. After a long moment where my confusion turned to acceptance, I stepped inside.

Only then did Nico start his car and pull out of my driveway, leaving me alone in my big Victorian, alone and lonely, and close to tears.

Chapter Twenty-One
Cassia

My mother called me the next morning after the date with Nico. "I wanted to check in on you," she said.

I bit back my initial response of *why?* That wasn't nice and she seemed to be trying. I appreciated the effort, but, at the same time, it was nearly thirty years too late. I'd needed her when I was a child, so confused about my parents' relationship, my place in the family.

But brushing her off felt wrong—like the way she'd treated me. My family confused me. "Thank you. I'm fine."

"Did you have a nice time last night?"

I frowned as I stared down into my coffee mug. I had. Talking to Nico proved easy. He was much funnier, much kinder, when he let down his guard. I'd seen the man beneath the mask, and while it might be wishful thinking, I didn't think many people did. But then, instead of kissing me as I'd hoped, he'd left. And I was…bereft. That was the word for it.

I was completely let down.

"Yes. My business dinner went well. I think we're going to come in under budget on the project."

My mom chuckled. "I'll believe that when you can show me the final bills. Our kitchen reno was double."

I set down my coffee, thankful I hadn't taken a sip. "I don't have double," I said. My chest felt tight.

"You're probably right," Mom hastened to say. "If your contractor says he can do it for less…"

"You don't believe that, though."

She sighed. "I'm not helping you this morning. Look, Cassia, if you need money, you can always ask us."

I shook my head. "I don't want to. I should do this on my own."

"And that's *why* we'd give you the money," Mom said. "You've never come to us with your hand out." *Unlike Amanda.* Neither of us needed to say that, but the words still hung there. "You've always been independent, capable of making your dreams a reality, but Martin and I would love to be a part of your dream."

"Hopefully, it won't come to that," I said. I ran my fingertip down the outside of my mug. "I start physical therapy tomorrow."

"Oh? That's good, isn't it?"

"Yes, it should be. And I forwarded my current medical information to the Boston Ballet's doctor. I clipped on a note letting them know I'd heard about Amanda's comments. I don't expect anything to come of it, but it felt like the right thing to do. I wouldn't want that situation to happen to another dancer—hearsay has no place in decisions like this."

"You're right. And I'm glad to see you taking charge, standing up for yourself."

I picked up my mug and took a fortifying sip. "What gives, Mom? Really? You're never this supportive. I don't think we've talked twice in a week since I turned fourteen."

"I still can't believe you were a freshman in high school, carrying those courses along with ten-plus dance classes per week."

I shrugged. "It's what I knew. What I loved. And it's a good thing I kept it up because I just managed to get my BA in dance before my prima ballerina designation was stripped from me."

Mom sighed. "I'm so glad you took Martin's advice to get a degree."

I hadn't taken Martin's advice. I'd always wanted a college degree, and, thankfully, being at a large company first in New York and then in Boston allowed me to take advantage of my university's connections with the ballet corps. It also helped that more universities were making programs easier to fit around dancers' hectic schedules.

"I think that's part of why Lowell cheated," I blurted.

"He cheated because he's a lowlife pile of scum," Mom said, anger vibrating through her tone.

"True. But I was rarely available. Between rehearsals and my college classes, I didn't have much time to spend with him. And when I was home, I was exhausted."

"That's on him, Cassia, *not* you. A mature adult would have discussed concerns with you, not started an affair behind your back." Venom dripped from Mom's staccato words.

I'd never asked about her and my father's relationship, but based on her anger and her response to Amanda, I was beginning to have a much better sense of why my parents divorced. I'd never understood the dynamic in our house, where Amanda was the perfect, golden child, spoiled, petted while I'd been an afterthought—if I was lucky.

"I was just thinking—"

"No," Mom said. "Lowell and your sister don't get a pass for

cheating. Ever. That's a coward's way out of a situation, especially if you hope you'll get caught." She took a moment and
responded again with more of her typical serenity. "You didn't
do anything wrong. I'm not saying you did everything right,
but you didn't make them betray your trust. That's on them,
and they need to own that."

Well…okay, then.

She sighed. "Look, I know I haven't been there for you, not as
you deserved. I know this is probably too little, too late and you
have every right to question me and my motives. So, I'll just have
to show you I care by calling more, being involved more."

I sucked in a long breath. "I…don't know what to say."

"Let's leave this here for now. Not that you asked, but I'll tell
you anyway: Martin's taking me to brunch at the marina. Something about a tour on the bay with some of his colleagues. So, I
should get off the phone."

I wasn't sure what to think or do about this woman. She
wasn't my typical Mom.

"Sounds fun," I said.

She laughed. "Sounds dull. I'm not interested in stock futures,
but the scenery is pretty, and I do like a mimosa."

"Have fun."

"What are you doing today?"

I rolled my eyes. This is what my mother did—said she needed to go then introduced a whole new topic.

"Nothing much. Collecting my car from the grocery store.
Actually getting groceries. Laundry. Maybe if I'm feeling motivated, once I run my errands, I'll head over to the studio to get a

better feel for the changes Nico wants to make."

"Who's Nico?" Mom asked.

"The contractor building out the studio."

"Oh. Well, good. For a moment, I thought… Never mind."

"What?" I asked.

"Nothing. Not a worry at all. Have fun and we'll chat soon."

I told my mother goodbye, unsettled by her sudden concern and then dismissal of worries at Nico's name.

— ▬▬▬

My PT the next morning started at eight, but I was more than happy to start the healing process. I dressed in stretchy leggings and a flowing yoga-style top with a large cutout in the back where the straps crisscrossed. My sports bra was heavy-duty—the only type I had and probably unnecessary for the easy movements we'd do today.

Still, I didn't want to be unprepared, which was why I also packed a forty-ounce bottle of water and a banana.

My session started with my therapist, Nell, and me alone in the expansive gym. She worked my ankle and foot, checking the range of motion. Thankfully, the days I'd been off the foot seemed to have alleviated the worst of the inflammation, and I executed each of Nell's requests with ease.

Toward the end of the session, Nell needed to grab a higher level of resistance band and left me alone on the pads. I bit my lip, wishing I could jete and plié to the soft strains of Brahms. Instead I lay on my stomach and used my arm muscles to push myself up into a half pushup, my elbows close to my body. Then, I whipped my right arm around and settled on my palms, chest high, heels off the floor. My stomach muscles tensed and quaked as I pulled them into my chest. From there, I extended my left leg into the splits and kept my right knee tucked to my chest. I switched legs, keeping the motion slow as I worked out tightness and kinks in my hip flexors. I pressed hard into my left palm and swung my right arm over my head while my uninjured foot propped up my body, holding a side plank.

Once my arm shook from the position, I slowly eased onto my shoulders and spun, like the kids who do break dancing. I wasn't a great modern dancer, but I'd been in enough dance classes to have picked up a few moves.

"That was so cool!"

I dropped down, my chest heaving, sweat trickling down my cheeks. I glanced over at a sandy-haired preteen, a tall, gangly kid that showed promise of his height to come.

"What else can you do? Can you teach me that move?"

"Brendan, what did I tell you about interrupting her?"

The boy's mom offered her apologies, even as she juggled twin girls who seemed desperate to dart away from her—and each other. "I'm Bridget."

"Cassia. No worries. I was just messing around."

"But you can breakdance," the boy, Brendan, said in awe.

I chuckled. "Hardly. I know a few moves."

"Can you teach me?" he asked again, hopeful.

"Your arm is still healing," his mother said, exasperation and affection crowding her features.

"You like to dance?" I asked Brendan.

He shrugged. "Not weird stuff or girly stuff, but yeah, I like to do things like your dance—that seemed like it required lots of muscles."

"It does. I wasn't sure I'd be able to do them. Not now."

"Why's that?" Brendan asked.

"I've been hurt for a while."

Brendan grimaced. "I know how that feels. I'm dealing with this stupid broken arm, but Mom and Pops said that with the physical therapy, I'd heal faster and better."

"Too right, young man," I said with a laugh.

"And get back on the diamond in no time," his mother added.

I gathered my crutches and a towel, wiping my face. One of the twins beelined toward the door, so I dropped my unneeded crutch and grabbed her, tickling her tummy when she would have otherwise cried. I kept the other crutch under my arm to steady my weight as I brought the toddler to my hip. I spun us, using the ball of my foot all while making silly noises. Instead of bursting into tears, the little girl started giggling like mad.

"Here you go," I said, offering the child to her mother. Bridget took her back but then sighed when the baby fussed. I moved toward them and settled on the bench. Bridget shook her head as the toddler crawled back into my lap.

"Clearly, she's happiest with you."

"She's a doll," I said, smiling down into the tiny, shiny face grinning back at me. She kicked her legs, so I grabbed her arms and made various movements. The little girl squealed with delight as we created an interpretive dance there on the side of the room while her big brother worked on his wrist and arm strength. The other little girl drowsed in Bridget's arms.

"I know who you are," Bridget said.

I raised my eyebrows in question.

"Nico brought you into Dr. Elliott's office, right?"

I nodded.

"I thought so." She smiled seeming satisfied.

"Nico was friends with the doctor who initially saw me—Dr. Hogue."

Bridget laughed. "That's my husband."

I shook my head. "Providence is so small compared to New York or Boston. I can't believe you're married to my doctor."

"Get used to the closer ties. I'm also friends with Aidy and Emmaline. We all get together for brunch at least once a month. After our yoga class. Though, I can't imagine you needing yoga to stay fit."

"I do yoga," I said. "I like the yin practices because they help alleviate sore muscles."

"Have you ever tried Bikram? Hot yoga?" Bridget asked.

I shook my head.

"Well, if you want to give it a whirl, Aidy, Em, and I are attending a class tonight. It's at seven and then we may grab a drink afterward—the drink probably being iced tea or some infused water because we sweat. A lot." Bridget grimaced. "Not my favorite part, but I feel so amazing afterward. Like I'm lighter. And I have all this energy."

I looked down at my leg. "I'm not sure how much I can do."

Bridget turned thoughtful. "Well, you could always try it out. And if it doesn't work for you, then you can pause. But most of it is on our hands and knees or on our backs, so I think you'd be okay."

I nodded, enthusiasm building in my belly. "I'd like that. I've missed the exertion—and the highs from it."

"Great!" She began to gather her diaper bag and strap the toddler she'd been holding into the stroller. I handed her the second child, while she rattled off the address, which I entered into my phone.

She waved as she pushed her stroller toward the exit, and I finished my session with Nell. As I gathered up my belongings, my muscles tugged a bit, and I grinned. I felt good—healthier than I had in a while. Plus, I'd made a friend.

I eased out of my car at the yoga studio that evening, thankful my foot and ankle hadn't been put to the test while driving. My nerves pulled tight already and dealing with additional pain atop my anxiety of making new friends—hopefully—while unsure of my body's capabilities… It was like I was five again, and three inches taller than all the girls in my ballet class.

"Cassia!" I lifted my head out of the back seat of my car, arranging my crutches, and looked toward the soft patter of feet. Bridget stepped up next to me and beamed.

"I'm so glad you decided to join us."

I nodded. "I'm nervous," I admitted.

"I can't imagine why. You're a professional dancer, so more flexible and in better shape than any of the rest of us."

"I *was* a professional."

Bridget tipped her head to the side. "If I quit my position at the ER, I'd still be a nurse. And if Aidy quit working at Wright and Associates, she'd still be an architect. So, you're still a ballerina. That role will always be part of your identity."

Something must have shown on my face, something vulnerable that cracked at her words, because Bridget smiled, her eyes filled with understanding.

"Don't give anyone else power over your self-worth and capability," she said.

I repositioned my bag on my shoulder. "Those are wise words."

She laughed. "I'm the oldest of the group, so of course I'm the wisest."

I smiled, happy to have this lovely woman fall in step next to me as we entered the studio. I greeted Emmaline and Aidy, who were chatting near the doors to the yoga studio. A wave of sultry air bathed my skin, and a fine sheen of perspiration bloomed.

Oh, this was going to be interesting.

"Nico said he smoothed things over with you," Aidy said as she settled onto the mat next to mine.

"You mean he went too far and plans to do the project pro bono."

Aidy shook her head, frowning. "I don't get him sometimes. He can be so thoughtful, like he was with you. But now with the new company he's started and the vandalism on one of our sites, I just don't know which version of Nico will show up." She frowned.

"Vandalism?" I asked.

She sighed. "Mostly petty stuff. Stolen lumber, broken windows." Her brows tugged in tight. "We've never dealt with that before. It sucks."

"I bet."

Her frown persisted. "It's probably just petty thieves or bored high school students." She smiled but the worry cast a shadow over her features.

"Let me guess, he's taking it as a personal affront and wants to single-handedly bring the bad guys to justice."

Aidy chuckled. "That does sound like Nico."

I shrugged but my ears burned. I didn't, not really, but I understood and admired his sense of justice. He would have to detest the damaging behavior that set back his plans. If it impacted Wright and Associates, he'd be like a bloodhound with the scent, doing whatever he could to ferret out the perpetrators and eradicate the threat to his family.

I wondered if Aidy saw Nico's dedication to her. I cleared my throat. "Must be something else, having two big brothers always concerned about your well-being, your livelihood, doing all they can to preserve that."

Aidy's eyes widened. "I used to hate it, but now... We talked, you know. Nico and me. We still talk at least once a week. If I were to bring this up to him and thank him for looking out for me, he'd grumble and deflect." She eyed me again, this time with more interest. "You really know my brother."

I shrugged. "I had a self-absorbed sister prone to dramatics, which made me pay attention to the people around me. How they behaved impacted Amanda and, therefore, me." I bit my lip. "I can only wish for the kind of connection you have with your siblings." Not that it mattered—Nico didn't want to spend time with me and my fascination with him was a waste of time and energy. Still I couldn't get his concerned expression as he'd held me to his chest out of my mind.

"Hmm. I get the sense your 'paying attention' is more than envy," Aidy murmured.

Class started so I didn't have to say anything, but I couldn't stop thinking about how their father's betrayal of their mother impacted Nico. If the fiancée hurt him or left around the same time, it was no wonder Nico was so closed off, so rigid and difficult to reach.

That didn't make his initial behavior toward me acceptable— but I understood better. Enough at least to accept that the man I had dinner with on Saturday was the true Nico. And I enjoyed the fact I was one of the few who spent time with that version of him. He was smart, talented, hardworking, and attractive.

I breathed through the transition to what the instructor called one-legged pigeon, the beginning of the cool-down period after holding goddess pose with arms in a V. My thighs had held me well and my ankle didn't ache at the continued pressure on my leg, but my foot tingled with the beginnings of pain, so I was thankful to get off of it.

I strove to force Nico out of my mind. I rested my cheek on my stacked palms, thankful for the heated space. No one would know I was blushing because of my sensual thoughts about Nico's mouth. I'd wanted him to kiss me on Saturday. I still did, if I were honest.

Something told me that our connection would be explosive, and I was caught between desperation to find out and fear of just how easy it would be to fall further and harder for Nico.

Chapter Twenty-Two
Nico

About a week after her appointment with Dr. Elliott, my schedule brought me within a couple of blocks of Cassia's house. I'd *just* managed to wrangle my need for her back under control. That's what I told myself, but I also couldn't stop myself from driving by. She was outside, on the sidewalk at her mailbox. So much for me sneaking past.

I slowed my new acquisition. It was a late model heavy-duty, four-wheel-drive pickup truck without some of the flash of my sedan but lots more cargo space for the tools, bolts, and drywall I seemed to need at every turn.

I wouldn't have bought it so soon because I really wanted to pay down what I owed on my house, but I needed a pickup, and Knox and Emmaline had handed me a check earlier this week that did a lot to lighten my financial burden. Once I'd cashed it, buying a new truck—using my nice sedan as a trade-in—had fit in my budget. I grinned, happier than I'd been in years.

I loved this truck—loved what it represented. I loved that it was electric and could generate enough power to run a TV and a blender. Not that I'd tested that possibility with Knox and Ryder…more than once.

Okay, we'd been playing with how many appliances were could plug into the truck all week, and so far, we hadn't managed to drain its battery.

"Hey," I said as I rolled to a stop.

She smiled as she leaned further into her crutches. "How's it going?"

"Great, actually. I was in the neighborhood…"

She broke out in giggles and the back of my neck heated even as my lips quirked.

"Totally *not* a line. I really was in your neighborhood. We're doing a massive renovation on a Victorian around the corner."

I gave her the address, and she sobered. "I love that house."

"Me, too. And now the interior won't be from the later 1800s. We're adding some more light and knocking out a few walls. Kind of like your place."

She nodded. "Good. I like the flow of the rooms here."

"Me, too. I did some digging, and I found out my father designed the plans."

Her eyebrows went up. "Did he? Well, no wonder you and your siblings are so talented."

My smile tightened, just as it always did when I thought of my father. Up until those last few months of his life, I'd wanted to be him, but after he and Mom disappeared, not only did he leave me, but he also destroyed my belief in him. In love.

"You got an hour?" I asked.

Shit. I clamped my jaw shut but the words were out there.

"Why?"

I cleared my throat. I was a successful man in my thirties. I could handle driving Cassia around, spending an hour with her. I hoped.

"I was thinking we could swing by your studio and I could show you the new flooring. It should go in tomorrow."

"Okay. Just let me grab my purse."

She crutched toward the door and I took a moment to enjoy the long, smooth lines of her legs, thanks to the shorts she wore. They were a dark linen, loose, but ended mid-thigh, giving me a wonderful view of most of her legs.

"How's your foot?" I called as she locked her door.

As she moved down the porch steps, she smiled, bright and animated. "Good. Physical therapy is definitely helping. I have extra stretches and exercises that I do at home. And Bikram yoga has been fabulous! The heat really helps the tendons stretch, releasing tension."

"Bikram, huh? I think Aidy mentioned something like that."

Cassia nodded. "I met Dr. Hogue's wife at the physical therapist's office. She's the one who suggested I attend the class."

I filed that tidbit away, wishing Aidy had told me she'd been seeing Cassia. And…what? Pumping my sister for information about my crush was juvenile. But I'd missed Cassia.

The past week should have cooled my interest. Instead, I'd thought about Cassia each day. Multiple times. Even when I fell into bed, more exhausted and fulfilled than I'd ever been after twelve hours on the job site, I still spent minutes, sometimes hours, reliving our conversations, the softness of her skin under my lips, the scent of her hair.

Just like in those memories, I sank further into Cassia's commentary about yoga versus therapy or ballet. I listened, rapt, as she spoke. Her gestures, tone, facial expressions, her giggle all called to me. I fisted my hand to keep from stroking back her dark hair where it caught the glint of light.

This was more than infatuation. I was falling for this woman, hard. And I loved and feared every single second of it.

* * *

I drove her to the studio, forcing my attention to the road. When we pulled up, I opened my truck's door with a soft sigh of relief. The faint scent of her shampoo as well as her arm on the center console, mere inches from mine, warmed me. I maintained control over my reaction, but this was the first time since early high school that I worried I'd embarrass myself.

Never before had a woman left me so out of control and wishing for more. I took in a deep breath of the sun-warmed air. Once I was sure my legs would hold me, I stepped from the truck and met Cassia at her door, her crutches in hand.

"Thanks." She smiled up at me, and my breath caught. She was lovely. Her skin smooth, eyes gleaming, teeth white and straight, a perfect face for Roman statuary.

"Sure thing," I said.

I waited for her to brush by me before I shut her door. I bit back a groan as I followed behind her, enjoying the shift of her long hair between her shoulder blades and the sway of her hips.

Desire pooled, warm and deep. I stepped up beside her and inhaled her scent. I wanted this woman. I would *always* want this woman.

"So, what made you choose this place?" I asked.

Cassia cast me a glance. "I didn't. My grandmother did. Grammy was the only family member who truly supported my dream to be a prima ballerina."

"What about your parents?" I asked.

Cassia shook her head. "I haven't seen my father since I was... maybe a teenager, I guess? That's when Amanda left for college."

"Why wouldn't you see him after that?" I asked.

"Because he loved Amanda, was a present and doting father for her. I was—You know, it doesn't matter."

I stopped in front of the closed glass-fronted door. "I care. And I'd like to know. If you're willing to tell me."

She looked over my shoulder, her lips pressed tight and her eyes unhappy, lost in a memory. "There's no easy way to describe this. Amanda was my parents' favorite. I was the kid that they had to try to salvage their marriage. That didn't work and we were all miserable for it."

"Did they...did they tell you that?" Anger burned under my sternum.

"They didn't need to. Some things are obvious."

She pulled out a key on a chain with the Boston Ballet logo. Below that was a tiny ballerina—Cassia—with her left knee at ninety degrees to the floor, her hands in a perfect shape above her bun. She unlocked the door and stepped inside, clicking on a light. I followed, surprised when I bumped into Cassia's hip.

"Where did you get that?" I asked.

"I found it in my grandmother's desk. I gave you my spare, remember?"

"I do. And I made you a copy." I settled my hand at her waist, steadying her. Not that she needed it. I wanted another excuse to touch her, even if it was through her T-shirt.

"That's this one." She held up the key.

"Oh, so the ring was in your grandmother's desk." I smiled. "You look cute as a figurine."

She stiffened. Had I offended her with my comment?

"I'm—"

She held up her hand, head tilted to the right, eyes narrowed. After a long pause. "Never mind. I thought I heard something," she said. "Like a closing door."

I peered around her, focused on the space, not Cassia. "I'll walk around, make sure everything's clear," I said.

Cassia laid her hand on my arm, her warm fingers branding my skin. That constant desire revved into overdrive, and my breath shortened while my heart pattered.

"It's okay. I'm sure I'm being silly."

"No, I don't want you unsafe. Wait here." No way I was making her step further into the building. "Better yet, here are my keys. You can sit in the truck until I'm sure it's safe."

She shook her head. "It's okay, Nico. There's no need. I'm probably just imagining things."

I opened my mouth to argue, to let her know I wanted to support her, to let her know I heard her concerns, but was that something I should do? I was the contractor, not her lover. I didn't have rights to her emotional well-being. In this, she was the boss. So if she said she was fine, I shouldn't push her.

"All right. Where do you want to start?"

"The theater," she said.

"Well, that's the room that needs the most work," I said even as I noted the excitement in her features. "To the theater."

The auditorium took up the entire side of the building, minus the bathrooms. Cassia peeked inside the first bathroom, then crutched more fully into the space, so I stepped in behind her.

"I don't know why there's water there," I said, pointing toward the floor beneath one of the sinks. The tile was wet, a puddle formed at the base of the wall.

"We had it shut off when Bonnie was here earlier. She's one of our plumbers. She was measuring for fixtures and found a minor leak under one of the sink bowls. I know she turned off the water because I was the one in here looking for the splice in the line. I couldn't find one, which is why we left the water off. So, there shouldn't be more water there. That's at a different sink." I frowned, uncertain as to what would have caused this new leak.

"I'm sorry, Cassia. I don't want you to think badly of my crew or me. I'll talk to Bonnie and get the issue straightened out."

Cassia nodded, seeming far away. "I'm excited to see the new faucets and countertops. It'll be much more modern."

Pretty much anything was better than the pink tile and turquoise sinks, but I kept my mouth shut, still concerned about the water issue. I shot Bonnie a text as Cassia slipped past me and toward the theater. This time, I was sure I heard the faint snick of a door sliding shut. I turned to the right, intending to head down the hall toward the studios. Someone must be here, in the building. My heart pounded as I strode toward the first door.

No one was there, and the room was as we'd left it. The old floor had been removed, the new subflooring and vinyl wood pallets settled in the corner. I moved to the next room and poked my head in, cautious of what I'd find. Nothing. It looked like the first studio.

In the third room, I caught my breath. There was an article of clothing on the floor. I stepped closer, my gut clenching. A bright red silky bra lay on the pallets.

"Nico?" Cassia's voice slid closer.

Heart pounding, I tucked the bra under the edge, away from the door. My heart hammered at what it meant—someone on my team had been here, in this building, doing something that removed their underwear.

Holy shit. My ears rang. This was *not* good.

Chapter Twenty-Three
Cassia

Nico strode out of the far studio, a deep scowl tugging at his thick brows.

"Is there a problem?" I asked.

He seemed to ponder that. "I'm not sure. But I plan to figure it out."

"Okay." I smiled at him. "The new seats are amazing! I wasn't sure when you told me, but I love them."

I wanted to bounce up and down but managed to restrain myself when pain darted up my heel and into my thigh. Nerve damage hurt more than the actual break. Worse, it proved more challenging to heal because my foot felt capable of use...until I overdid it.

"Can you tell me more about the flooring? What's the schedule for that? When will the bars go in? And then can you show me why there's so much wood on the stage?"

Dear me, this man was worth every penny I was paying him. More. Not that he'd take it from me, but I'd been smart and set my budget thirty percent lower than what I had to spend. Sure, I hoped to keep some of the money, but I'd learned from Amanda's comments over the years and hadn't wanted to totally max myself out from the start.

That's why I was sure I'd be able to pay Nico's contractor share as well as his employees' salaries.

Nico swallowed down whatever was bothering him and smiled. "Ah. You saw that." He tapped his finger to the tip of my nose. "That was supposed to be a surprise."

"It was. It is. Now, what's it for?"

He chuckled. "We'll discuss the flooring and scheduling, like you asked, and then I'll tell—"

"Nico!"

He threw his head back and laughed.

Dear me. The man was stunning. His eyes sparkled, his face lit up. Happiness radiated off him, much like the glow of a fire on a cool autumn night. I wanted to snuggle in closer, to be surrounded by the cozy feeling only he evoked within me.

He led me back toward the theater, seemingly unaware of the emotions battering my chest. I wanted him. Badly.

───────

"I need help with the step up," I told Nico while he stowed my crutches in the truck. His eyes widened a little but he held out his hand as he neared me. I waited until he was close—close enough for me to witness his pupils dilate and his nostrils flare—before I slid my fingertips along his palm. I clasped his hand and bumped out my hip, making sure it grazed his thigh, before I settled myself on the seat.

"Thanks." I smiled at him, all bright sunshine. His lips remained compressed for a moment before they quirked up in a reluctant grin, his gaze searching mine.

By the time Nico rounded his truck's hood and settled into his seat, I shivered.

"I want to seduce you," I blurted.

My cheeks burned, and I kept my face forward so I didn't have to look at him.

"I want you to want me but I'm worried that if I tell you that, you'll push me away again, and that's going to hurt. But it's true. I want you to ask me out. I want you to invite me to your home, to let me play with Fred, to tell me more of your secrets so that I'm comfortable sharing mine…"

Chapter Twenty-Four
Nico

Cassia's obvious misery touched me. But at the stoplight, it was her bright, sad eyes that made me lean over the console and place my hand on the back of her neck. I tugged her toward me, so close.

"I want the same thing," I murmured before I closed the distance. I slid my lips across hers, beginning to open my mouth, needing, desperate for my tongue to touch hers, to know her taste.

A horn honked, followed by another. I pulled back, cursed, and pushed my foot on the gas, easing us into the intersection. I cleared my throat and glanced over. Cassia had her fingers up to her mouth, her eyes glazed, her face slightly lax.

"Cassia?"

"Hmm."

I waited until she turned to face me. "I've wanted to kiss you for a long time."

"Have dinner with me," she blurted. Once again, her cheeks flared cherry. "I'd like to share another meal—"

"Like a date."

She dropped her hand finally. Her lip gloss was rubbed off. Probably on mine now. I grinned at the thought.

"Yes, like a date. I want to date you." She shifted, facing me more fully, her eyes wide, expressive.

I only managed a quick glance before I returned to watch the road. How had I ever compared the two women? Sure, Cassia was related to Amanda, but they were vastly different.

"I'd like that, too," I said. I grinned, a lightness settling over me. "I've wanted that since the bar." I grimaced. "Sorry for being a dick."

She shrugged. "I could have handled that better, too."

"No, that's on me—"

"Stop," she said, raising her hands. Then, she laughed. "It's over. Done. We're here now, and I like your company. I simply enjoy you, Nico."

"Ah, Cassia, same goes. And thanks for being brave enough to say it."

"Well…I wasn't brave so much as feeling guilty."

"I'll take that, too."

"Nico?"

"Yeah?"

"Promise me something."

"Of course,"

"Promise that we'll always be honest with each other? It's important to me, and I want to be able to trust you, and…" She gave a tiny shrug. "Honesty is important to me."

She blinked her big, soft eyes at me. And I melted. "I get that, honey. I promise." I raised her hand and kissed her knuckles. "Let me take you home, make you dinner."

"But I asked you—"

"And you can play with Fred while I make dinner," I said, cutting off her objection.

She squeezed my fingers as joy built in her eyes. Damn, I liked *that* look. "Sold."

"Good."

Chapter Twenty-Five
Nico

Fred loved the attention Cassia heaped on him. I enjoyed Cassia's company. She sat at the bar, Fred snuggled in her lap.

"Does he ever go in the condo?" she asked, glancing back at the structure in pride-of-place next to the couch.

"Nope," I said with a grin as I washed some spinach leaves. "That asshole jets up and down the stairs like a gymnast but he won't climb anything he's supposed to."

She tickled his chin. "Sounds like every cat I've ever met."

I added more broth to my risotto and continued to stir. "Did you have pets growing up?"

She shook her head. "No. Well, Grammy had an old beagle. His breath was atrocious but I still liked to pet him."

I frowned as I noted her stroking Fred's ears. His eyes were closed in bliss and he purred loudly. "You like Haddock?" I asked.

"Sure. I like most seafood."

Twenty minutes later, dinner was on the table. Cassia washed her hands and settled into the seat at the head of the table I'd left for her.

"This is your seat," she said.

"Yes, but I don't have crutches."

"You could have let me help with something," she said. "Like setting the table.

"You helped by keeping Fred occupied." I leaned in and clasped her hand with mine. Her skin was warm, soft, and I gave in to the need and kissed her knuckles. "You're healing. Keep doing that, okay? I really can't wait to see you dance again."

She swiveled her hand from my grasp and cupped my cheek. "You say the sweetest things."

I turned and kissed her palm. "It's easy with you because I mean them."

While we ate, I regaled Cassia with stories from my childhood. I enjoyed remembering the happy times in my family. Fred jumped up on the table and attempted to sniff my plate. I picked him up, him meowing loudly in protest, and set him in the laundry room.

"Sorry. He's never done that before."

Cassia smiled, patting her stomach. "He knew he was missing out on something delicious. I'd be sad if I was him, too."

"I don't have anything for dessert."

"I don't need anything else. This was delicious, Nico. Thank you."

"You're welcome. I like having you here." I should tell her more about my relationship with Amanda. Instead, I refilled my wine glass. Worry sat large and heavy, a boulder between my shoulder blades.

I wasn't just attracted to this woman; I cared for her, deeply, which meant I needed to tell her—soon. She deserved the chance to make a choice about whether or not to see me again.

Those thoughts roiled through my mind as I drove her home. I planned once more to kiss her cheek, but Cassia had different plans. She turned her face and her sweet, plump lips slid over mine. I groaned, my hands cupping her hips, as I shuffled in closer. I was desperate for more of her—just as I knew I would be.

Her tongue touched the seam of my lips and I groaned, completely under Cassia's spell. I tilted my head, deepening the kiss. She tasted like the wine we'd shared but also of something spicier and sweet—something distinctly Cassia.

I pulled back a little, opening my eyes to find her head tipped back, eyes closed, a blissful expression on her face. I tugged her closer, unsurprised when her crutches clanged to the porch. I peppered tiny kisses to the corner of her mouth before I rubbed my cheek against hers.

"You're not going to get to seduce me, Cassia. I want you too much for this to be anything less than mutual. But there are things we need to discuss."

A frown formed between her brows and she pressed her fingers to my lips. "Not now. Please. Tonight was perfect," she pleaded, her eyes beseeching.

I brushed my lips over hers again, unable to deny her. Her sweetness remained on my lips long after I drove home. I ached with worry about how she'd react to my news.

My exhaustion concerned Hazel enough for her to seek me out. "I…have a lot on my mind," I said, my thumb smoothing over my hammer. That was becoming a soothing gesture, and I didn't like needing it.

Hazel stood next to me, clasping a clipboard, "You know what I think? You got trust issues, boss."

I nodded. "I really think I do." I signed off on the order she'd shoved against my chest. "So, you don't know anything about that bra at the studio site?"

"No, and I'd tell you 'cause that's weird. I'll talk to the women." She met my gaze, hers dark. "This is a good gig for us. We're not going to screw it up."

I scratched my cheek. "Then how did the bra get there?"

She shrugged. "Could have been one of the workers who brought in the flooring or other materials."

I sighed, some of the strain easing from my shoulders. "I hadn't thought of that."

Hazel shot me a stink eye. "Could have been kids who broke in. Installing those fancy cameras will tell you if it's your problem."

"All the work sites are my problem."

"That's a lot of responsibility to heap on your shoulders. Goes with the lack of trust. So, here's a question: you going to do something about that?" she asked.

We were on site of the Michaelsons' remodel—cataloging the smashed first-floor windows and the loss of our finish wood. Instead of completing the final details, the crew spent half a day getting a handle on what needed to be redone—a lot—and what we could salvage—not much. But we were back on track, and I'd ordered some expensive surveillance equipment for this site and our three other largest ones. So far, we hadn't dealt with more issues, but that didn't mean I would let my guard down. That statement was part of what caused Hazel's response.

She'd tucked her hair back into a nubby ponytail and one of those exercise headbands and wore a pair of baggy overalls cinched in by her tool belt. Her steel-toed boots thumped across the gleaming hardwoods as she checked each electrical socket one last time. Thankfully, I'd built in a couple of extra days before the client showed up for the final walk-through, and we'd definitely be able to meet that deadline—as long as there wasn't another issue with the property.

One of the benefits of being the architect and the contractors was I could handle the punch-list process, freeing up Knox, Aidy, and Emmaline to conduct client meetings for other projects—or to complete designs. So far, our new arrangement had improved Wright and Associates' productivity, and the company had been able to take on two more big projects. Our revenues were healthy, and mid-term projections were good. As promised, my siblings had both given me a portion of their paychecks to improve my finances. I'd managed to swallow my protests and say thank you.

"But you have to admit I have reason to worry," I said.

"Meh. There's always something. That won't change. The question is whether you want to worry forever or focus on issues you might be able to address."

I pondered Hazel's words. A breeze fluttered through the new, open windows. These had a more traditional style than the broken ones, and I liked the look better. In fact, the entire project made me proud.

"You did good bringing in your ladies," I said.

Hazel rolled with the change in subject. "Yeah. All they needed was a fair shot." She raised her eyebrows. "Parity creates opportunities."

"Yeah. You all worked hard. I can't believe we're going to actually get those bonuses."

Hazel rose from her squat next to an outlet. "We had incentives. And not just the money. I've had multiple women tell me this is the best working environment they've ever been part of. You did that."

I shook my head. "Not alone."

"You created the opportunity." She tilted her head to the side. "You're a good man, Nico."

Those words, along with Hazel's comments about trust stuck with me as I drove down the street. I had the last check from the homeowners in my pocket and one less set of keys on my keyring. The accomplishment settled warm and pleasant over me.

Maybe that's why I took the turn to Cassia's.

Except I knew it wasn't. I wanted to see her face. To kiss her lips. To inhale her scent. Just to be near her.

So I parked in her driveway and headed to her door. Her smile matched mine when we saw each other through the beveled glass.

"Hey," she said once the door was open.

"Hey yourself."

"I just wanted to see you."

Her smile widened. "I like being seen by you."

"Want to grab dinner?"

Her eyes sparkled with delight, and I wanted to ensure she always looked at me like that. "I'd really like that," she said, her voice soft.

I stepped in closer, aware that I'd spent the day on the work site. I cleared my throat as I tugged at the hem of my T-shirt.

"Cassia, I…" I swallowed. "This, what's between us, means something. To…to me."

See? I was trusting her.

Her face softened as she leaned forward on her crutches so that our chests brushed—almost as if she needed the connection between us as much as I did. "I get it, Nico. And, I feel it, too."

I released my breath. "Okay. Good. Yeah."

⸻

I called Cassia the next evening and asked her to dinner again; my stomach knotted as I awaited her response. I'd had to leave a message, and I didn't much like the anticipation each time my phone rang.

She replied a couple of hours later. "I just got out of PT," she said.

"How's that going?"

"Great! And, yes, I'd love to come to dinner. But you have to let me do something this time."

"Want to bring the wine?" I asked.

She sighed. "I'll bring it and a salad."

"Perfect. Seven?"

"Sure, I'll see you then."

I smiled the rest of the afternoon, something Hazel picked up on but didn't mention. She was turning out to be my favorite employee, ever.

Cassia arrived at seven on the dot. I'd showered and changed into some khakis and a button-down shirt. Cassia wore a denim skirt with a frayed hem, black ballet flats, and a top with a large bow looped near her left shoulder. She looked casual and elegant.

I held open the door, inhaling sharply when she brushed a quick, soft kiss across my lips as she crutched into the living room. A canvas bag swung from her wrist. She settled it on the counter and her purse in one of the bar chairs. I liked having her things in my house. I loved her greeting.

I wanted more of all of this—with her.

"How was your day?" she asked. I opened the tote she'd brought and pulled out the wine. "My day was good. Want a glass?"

"Sure."

"How did your day go?"

"Well, actually." She smiled. "I made it up to the attic and went through some of Grammy's boxes."

"Anything good?"

She shrugged. "Just stuff. But it was fun to look through." She headed toward the basket where I kept Fred's toys. He yowled as he pounced, and I smirked at his antics.

"He likes that string," I said with a laugh.

"No kidding," Cassia said. She smiled as she picked up her glass of wine and sipped. "He's fun."

Fondness spread through me. "He is. I love having him here to greet me when I get home." I strolled closer and slid a small tomato—her favorite, she'd told me before—against her lips. Her pupils dilated and her breath hitched as she parted her lips. I rubbed it across her lower lip one more time before resting it there. She opened her mouth wider, her eyes never leaving mine.

Feeding her was sensual. Passion rippled over my nerve endings, soaking me in desire.

And yet...we ate, we talked. For hours. She insisted on cleaning up so I settled in my chair, Fred in my lap. I admired Cassia's motions, the fluidity of her body, as I sipped the red wine we'd had with the salmon. Even cleaning was sexy—when Cassia did it.

"Will you come to the bay with me tomorrow?" I asked.

She glanced over her shoulder. "You're not sick of me yet?" she joked.

I set my wine glass on the table. "I don't think I'll ever tire of talking to you, Cassia."

She ducked her head, but she wore a pleased grin. "Okay."

I smiled. "Thanks for cleaning up—"

"You fed me," she cut in. "This is the third time now. This was the least I could do."

"I like having you here, in my home."

She glanced around. "It's a great space."

Not as great as hers. Her house had character, vivacity. This place was cool with its Swedish design and monochromatic color scheme. Aidy called it clinical.

After Cassia went home that evening, I noted the lack of homey touches at my place. Up until recently, I hadn't realized how frozen I'd been.

Cassia brought me back to life. Now, it was time to close the last chapter of my past and focus on her—my future.

Chapter Twenty-Six
Cassia

Nico took me to a quiet inlet the next morning. Because of my foot, he'd ensured there was a decent boardwalk before helping me from his truck. He handed me my crutches, which I resented even though I knew it was helping my foot to heal. This thing I hated to use would once again give me back my greatest love. I tucked some windswept tendrils behind my ear as I looked out at the small, rolling waves as they foamed against the brown sand that slid into the dune-studded shoreline. Homes dotted the beach, many snuggled into the grass-tufted hillocks a few hundred feet from the water. Sunlight sprinkled through the large, white clouds, glistening on the placid water.

"It's beautiful."

"This was my family's favorite spot," Nico said, voice quiet. "Our house was just down there." He pointed toward a blue-shingled two-story Cape Cod with a broad deck.

"What a great house."

He nodded, his eyes sad. "Selling it was hard."

"I bet."

He inhaled slowly, relaxing. "I haven't been back in a long time."

"Why's that?" I ambled forward, assuming it would be easier for him to talk if we were moving, him showing me around. This conversation seemed like a shift into something deeper with him, and I wanted to facilitate that.

"I was angry."

"Understandable."

"There were a lot of changes in my life. I know I was younger and wasn't really prepared for the roles I needed to fill. I didn't know how to bring Dad's company back from the brink."

I leaned against the railing and turned to face him. The sun warmed my cheek and neck. We were both in casual clothes, though bundled in long sleeves and, for me, a fleece jacket, thanks to the cool spring breeze. "But you did."

He leaned his elbows on the wooden ledge and looked out. The sun glinted off the golden tips of his eyelashes. "Yeah. But it was too high a cost," he murmured. "I nearly destroyed my relationship with Aidy in the process."

I reached over and squeezed his hand. He turned it and clasped my palm to his. I liked Nico like this—open, contemplative, a bit soft, vulnerable.

"I came here to tell them goodbye—to let the past go."

I leaned against him and he shifted, absorbing more of my weight. I enjoyed watching the gulls dive and dart through the endless blue sky. After a few minutes, Nico sighed. "Thanks for being here with me today."

"Glad to."

He turned toward me. "There's something else I need to do—to tell you about how I know your sister." His Adam's apple bobbed.

A weight settled in my stomach, low, hard, barbed. I really didn't want to hear this.

"So, are you ever going to tell me all the juicy details between you and Amanda? I mean, I think you mentioned you were dating," I said lightly. "You didn't sleep with her, did you?"

My heart pounded as I waited. *Please don't say it.* I gritted my teeth because if he had…the hurt was there, already growing with just the thought of him being with Amanda.

He cupped my cheeks and stared into my eyes. "Amanda was a mistake I'm thankful to have moved on from."

My heart continued to patter in my chest. "I get that it was a while ago, but I don't understand—"

He kissed me. Settling his lips over mine, he brushed them back and forth, desperate. But he pulled back, unwilling to drop this again. He seemed to memorize my face.

"You're in front of me; you held my thoughts, my heart. I'd worried weeks ago, when I first met you, that you might be able to break through my barriers. You did. And I wanted you to. I wanted you to see *me*."

He paused, swallowed hard, then once more. "Your sister and I lived together for about a month."

My stomach turned, my head spun. I clenched my fists as a breath hissed from between my teeth. "She moved in with me after I proposed."

Chapter Twenty-Seven
Nico

She stepped back, out of my arms, shivering even as the sun shone down. Sweat broke out on my scalp, my lower back, my armpits.

No, this couldn't be the end. She had to understand...

"I didn't love her," I blurted. "I mean, maybe I thought I did. She was so charming. But she's not you, Cassia. You have to know—"

"That I'm her shadow? Isn't that what you told me at the bar?" she tossed back. Another long deep inhale.

Everything seemed to stop—my heart, my breathing, *everything*. Like when I found out my father cheated on my mother and then bankrupted his company to pay off his mistress, to keep his secret from her. He was willing to destroy everything to keep from getting caught.

I never wanted to be like him, but in that moment, I understood his response. Shame flared hard and hot within me. I didn't want to be like that—like my father.

"I'd like to go now, please," she choked out.

We walked back to the car in silence. I tried to help her in, but she shook her head hard. "Don't."

My throat ached but I didn't touch her. At least she was letting me drive her home. Maybe she'd let me come inside and we could talk.

I glanced over at Cassia as I drove back to her place. I opened my mouth to say something, but I closed it again. What *could* I say? Cassia, for her part, stared out the front windshield, huddled into the far corner of her seat.

I wished, more than anything, that I could take back my words, but then a lie would fester between us. I'd done the right thing for us. If there *was* an us, which wasn't looking great at the moment.

She threw open the truck's door before I managed to come to a complete stop. She hopped down and grabbed her crutches. One look at her tight, set features, and I knew she wouldn't invite me inside.

"For what it's worth, I'm sorry," I said.

She met my eyes for a brief moment before she looked away. Her jaw tightened. "Me, too."

She slammed the door closed and hobbled up the path and steps. I waited, willing her to turn around, to give me something. No such luck.

She let herself in and shut the door without a backward glance.

My mood at work the following Monday was blacker than ever. Even Hazel avoided me, and I got it. I was acting like a douche. I slammed the sledgehammer into the wall. Drywall exploded in a thick cloud of dust and chunks of gypsum. I hauled back and brought the hammer through the wall again, this time connecting with a stud. It cracked and groaned under the force of my blow. I gritted my teeth and sent the hammer forward again. And again.

All the while hating that I'd caused the lost, sad look in

Cassia's eyes.

"Guess now's not the time to tell you there was another round of vandalism, huh?"

I dropped the hammer and turned to face Aidy.

"Now's the perfect time. I'm already angry."

She nodded her sleek, styled bun toward the wall before fanning her face as dust particles caught on the breeze and drifted toward her.

"How bad is it?" I asked.

She pursed her lips. "Not good."

"Did anything come up on the cameras?"

She nodded. "Yeah. The police are looking for the guy who did it."

I leaned the sledgehammer against the wall and took Aidy by the elbow. Not that I didn't think she was capable of walking through the demolition zone by herself—she more than was—but because it made me feel better to touch her. To know someone wasn't completely repulsed by me, and my former choices.

"What's the likelihood he's caught?" I asked.

She shrugged. "Not great."

"And the odds we can prove the guy's got some kind of relationship with Marcus?"

Aidy scowled. "It's got to be worse than finding the guy."

We reached the open landing that led down to the first floor or up to the third. I tipped my head back and stared at the coved ceiling. When that did nothing to release the tension in my body, I massaged the back of my neck.

"All right."

"We'll get this figured out, Nico."

"Sure."

"And we'll stop Marcus."

"Uh-huh."

"And...I saw Cassia last night."

I looked away from the ceiling and back at Aidy. "Yoga?"

She nodded. "She was miserable. Distracted."

"Because I told her I'd had a sexual relationship with her sister."

Aidy's lip curled. "She told us. And, yeah, that would do it."

I paced the landing. "I'd change dating Amanda, proposing to her, if I could. *God*, I would. But I can't, and Cassia's hurting and I can't fix it and I'm just so...*gah*!" I slammed my palms against the wall, letting my chin drop forward onto my chest.

"Want to come to dinner tonight?" Aidy asked.

I dropped my chin toward my chest, so damn tired. "You said I couldn't see Lilia until I fixed things with Cassia. And things are not fixed."

"But you did fix the professional issue. The fact that you fell in love with Cassia—no one was expecting *that*, Nico." She clasped my wrist with her warm palm. "And you did right by telling her the truth. I know it was hard, and you're both hurting... but you were right. So, I figured you'd need some baby snuggles. Maybe some puppy kisses. I mean, Rosie's tongue is nicer than Fred's, right?"

I nodded, my throat tight. "Yeah," I pushed out. "I really need that."

Chapter Twenty-Eight
Cassia

After my yoga class on Sunday and enduring Bridget, Aidy and Emmaline's concerned looks, I scrambled out of the room and drove home. Without changing from my yoga clothes, I crawled into bed and pulled the sheets up over my head. I was being ridiculous, and I knew it. But it didn't stop me from ignoring the world.

And my phone when it chimed.

Someone knocked on my door, then rang the bell, and I ignored that, too.

I spent three days—three full days—wrapping my head around the fact that Nico knew my sister better than I ever would.

And I *hated* them both for it.

I detested myself for caring so much. By the end of day three, I was disgusted with myself. I created lofty ambitions; I strove for my goals and executed them. I was used to working through challenges. Except, now, it wasn't just my foot that hurt, but my heart. I hadn't cared this much when Amanda slept with Lowell, so why did the idea of Nico having a relationship with my sister years ago bother me so much?

It just did.

I didn't even feel like myself anymore, so I climbed in my car and started driving. My stop really shouldn't have been a surprise, though I sat in the car, trying to calm my heart for a good fifteen minutes before I managed to knock on the door.

My mother opened it, mouth open with shock. I never visited—why would I?—but I wanted answers.

"Cassia, this is a surprise."

"I'd apologize for just showing up, but ending up here kind of surprised me, too."

My mother pursed her lips while she looked me over. "Have you washed your hair this week?"

That's what concerned her? "Maybe."

She sighed. "You can shower while I make some tea."

I remained on the porch, shifting from one foot to the other, trying to hold back the words until I couldn't anymore. "What made me so much less lovable than Amanda?"

My mom shut her eyes tight enough to crease her Botoxed forehead. "We'll talk after you've cleaned up."

I'd made it out of bed, and I'd managed to drive myself to my mother's large home. Being clean enough not to offend someone's nose seemed like a reasonable next step. So, I walked into my mother's husband's Back Bay mansion and up the stairs to one of the four guest rooms. I spent so long in the shower, the hot water ran out and my skin pruned.

When I opened the shower door, I noted the change of clothes my mother set out for me—red leggings and an oversized black tunic that fell to mid-thigh. She'd even found me a camisole with a built-in bra in my size, and clean underwear. While we were similar in body shape, I had a more generous chest—her euphemism for calling me big-breasted. Still, I appreciated the clean clothes as well as the toiletries and hairbrush.

Once my hair no longer dripped, I combed out the tangles and swiped on some deodorant. After a long look in the mirror at my shadowed eyes and thin face, I took a deep breath. I stepped from the bathroom on a mission to finally get the answers I deserved.

I stopped short, surprised to find my mother sitting on the chaise lounge under the window in the bedroom attached to the bathroom. She had a photo album open on her lap. She patted the seat next to her.

I moved toward her, my knees weak, which was a real problem on crutches. "This is your sister's baby book," she said.

My throat constricted and I slammed my eyes shut, unwilling to let more tears fall. I shouldn't cry over Amanda, but there was a lump in my throat and I swayed. I had to be dehydrated and, somewhere, deep in my body, hungry.

My mother cupped my hand as she placed a mug in it. "Drink this."

I started to shake my head, but she lifted my arm so that the mug pressed to my lips. I gulped the warm, soothing mint tea. My lids fluttered and my eyes opened to find her looking at me with concern.

"Better?"

"Yeah," I rasped.

"I'm showing you this for a reason. I think I see why this would be hard for you…but bear with me, okay?"

I set the mug back onto the coaster on the spindly table next to the chaise and lowered myself to the edge of the seat. I placed my hands between my thighs, palms touching, and forced myself to look at the book my mother had created for Amanda. She'd never made one for me.

In those first pictures, my parents were happy, their eyes and smiles beaming as they held up my infant sister. I swallowed down the hurt as my mother continued to flip the pages of the book.

"We were very much in love," she said, her thumb swiping over their happy, fresh faces in a photo that showed my mother holding Amanda and my father with his arms around them both. He had his lips pressed to Mom's forehead and she smiled so big and bright at the camera.

I remained silent, throat aching too much to speak.

"I had a miscarriage before her, then two after. That last one was when things fell apart." She sighed, flipping to the back of the book. Amanda's wild toddler curls flew in every direction, but my mother's eyes were sad, distracted. My father wasn't looking at either of them—he was staring at the person behind the camera.

"Who's taking the picture?" I asked.

A hint of a smile played across her lips as she picked up a still-full mug and handed it to me. I sipped.

"Noticed that, did you? Most people look at Amanda; she was a precious child." Mom's voice changed. "That was my best friend Jill."

"Was?" Jill? I'd never heard of the woman.

"Mmm. Your father had an affair with her—one I found out about *after* I was pregnant with you. He'd planned to leave me for her, and I honestly think he told me in the hopes I'd miscarry. So he could leave me without guilt."

I choked on the last of my tea. "That's horrible."

Mom rubbed me between my shoulder blades. "Yes. Jill was also pregnant, see."

Horror coursed through me. "I have a sibling?"

Mom shook her head. "*Jill* miscarried that time, not me. It was…" She pursed her lips, old pain shadowing her eyes. "That was a bad time."

"And I was the result."

"You were a child *I* made in love. I just didn't know how to get past your father's cheating." She closed the book with a solid *thunk*. "I never made you a book, and I regret that."

"I thought you resented me," I murmured. "I always felt like I was the reason you and Dad split. That if I hadn't come along, you would have been happy because you both doted on Amanda."

She turned to face me so that our knees bumped and clasped my hands in hers. "My mother set me straight on that when Amanda took her own desires too far. First there was that business in Manhattan with the man she was living with—"

I swallowed the lump of barbed emotion. "Nico."

Mom sighed as she nodded. "He talked to you?"

"Yes."

Mom pondered that. "Good. Yes, good. I'm glad he told you."

"Are you?"

She canted her head. "It means he's honest. You can't build a relationship on lies, Cassia. At least, not one that will last." She sat for a moment. "But I was telling you about my mother and Manda. So, your sister derailed Nico's career, then, finally, the next or the next or the *next* man filed a lawsuit, and, as you know, there was that horribly embarrassing public breakup with Lowell."

Her mouth twisted. "My mother pointed out Amanda behaved *just* like we'd raised her—to take what she wanted, when and how she wanted it. And why wouldn't she? She was used to getting her way because it was easier to shower her with love and be angry at your father for being a cheater." She pressed her lips together. "Unfortunately, I never stopped to consider how much my actions toward your sister and your father hurt you, and I…I don't have a good reason. Not a good enough reason. I'm not sure there is a good enough reason for how you felt during your childhood. *You* were never the problem. It wasn't until I met Martin that I realized just how much I'd let your father's betrayals take from me. And by then, you were doing *so* well."

I stared down at our hands. "I thought you…" My lower lip trembled but I forced the words past my lips. "That I was—that I *am* unlovable."

Mom pressed her fingertips to her lips as concern flooded her eyes. "I did such a number on you."

I shrugged. There wasn't anything to say to that.

"Oh, Cassia, I am so, so sorry."

I shrugged again.

"You have to know, my anger was toward your father, toward Jill. That my *best friend* had intimate knowledge of him and betrayed me…" Her mouth twisted and her eyes hardened. "That's not something I could ever forgive. I haven't spoken to Jill in nearly thirty years, and I never will again."

I looked down at the floor, staring at the space between my bare feet. "I fell in love," I whispered.

"Oh, honey." She smiled. "That's great!"

"With Nico." At her gasp I shook my head. "I know his relationship with Amanda was years ago. But I can't get that out of my head—that he—that she…" I closed my eyes and the tears pressed too hard against my lids and spilled down my cheeks.

"I just wanted someone who was *mine*, who loved *me*." My tone turned fierce as anger, hot and vicious, surged. Damn Amanda for taking everything from me.

"But he had to ruin what we had together."

"Did he?" Mom asked.

I scowled. "It's like what you said about your friend. Nico and Amanda have intimate knowledge of each other, and I'll always have to compete with that."

I didn't want to say the next words, but they were true. "Every single time I've competed with Amanda, I've lost. "

Mom raised her brows. "You coming here makes more sense," she murmured, her eyes sad. "I can't tell you what to do." She rose. "Well, I guess I could, but it wouldn't necessarily be the right thing for you—or for him."

"You said it yourself," I said, my tone as stubborn as my jaw-line that refused to loosen. "You won't speak to Jill again."

"Because she *chose* to cheat. She betrayed my love for her for her own selfish reasons. She was jealous. Is that how the situation occurred between you, Amanda, and this man?"

As much as I hated to do so, I shook my head. I didn't want my mother to be right. I wanted…I didn't know what I wanted. Well, I did. I wanted Nico to take back the words, the hurt they caused. But he couldn't. As Mom said, Nico was honest. And his integrity was one of the things I loved about him.

"Then, I don't see how it's the same."

"He's seen her naked," I cried. My anguish spilled over and I gnashed my teeth. "She's seen *him* naked. If they ever sit across the table from each other, they'll be able to remember. And I…I'm not perfect like Amanda."

Mom snorted. "Your sister is *far* from perfect—either in personality or in body. You're the one who worked so hard, dancing for hours each day—"

"Not anymore."

"Don't be petulant, Cassia," Mom chided.

I looked at the floor and took a moment to let those nasty feelings go.

"Look, Amanda's not in your kind of physical shape. And she really doesn't have anything she's exceptional at—like you do with ballet. She doesn't have your drive, your willpower. And she's the one who's been sued *and* dumped on national TV. Honestly, you can't be further from perfect than that."

Mom pursed her lips as she studied me. "You're welcome to stay here tonight, but you will have to talk to resolve your relationship with Nico. Talking to your sister…well, that's your choice. And I vote strongly that you don't."

"What?"

Mom pressed her lips tight. "Amanda needs to grow up. She needs to change before…" Mom huffed. "Your sister is making terrible life choices. That's partially my fault, but she needs to learn there are real and painful consequences for her actions." She blinked up at me. "Martin thinks you'll do much better in life—

you already have. Just…consider what you want and what you need from your relationship with Nico."

I wrapped my arms around my waist, wishing it would make the sharp pains there dissipate. I hated everything—every single thing—about the current situation. They were naked together. They kissed, and touched, reveled in their building passion, made each other reach peaks of pleasure.

I hadn't done that with him. Once again, Amanda had something that mattered to me. She'd had it first and ruined it.

I locked my knees unwilling to collapse back on the chaise, unwilling to fold inward yet again. That's what I'd wanted for days, but now…now I just wanted to move past everything that had happened.

I wanted the heartache to dissipate.

When I turned back to the door, it was shut. My mother had left me once more. But this time, she'd been right to. I lay back on the bed and stared up at the ceiling, considering what my mom had shared.

And what it changed.

Chapter Twenty-Nine
Nico

The puppy kisses from Aidy's Australian shepherd, Rosie, were sweet, but it was the cuddles with my niece Lilia that I appreciated the most. I happily changed her diaper and fed her a bottle, all so I could spend more time with her after dinner. I loved watching her eyes slide closed as sleep overcame her sweet, tiny body.

"You're good with her," Aidy said, her voice quiet. She leaned her hip and shoulder against the doorframe to the room.

I pressed a kiss to Lilia's little forehead. "She's easy to love," I said. I rose reluctantly and set her in the crib, tugging the blanket up over her rounded tummy.

"She's gotten so big," I said, staring down into her cherubic face.

Aidy sat next to me, deep contentment and love etched into her face. "Already over a year old," she murmured. She smiled up at me, the same smile I used to see on Mom's face. "It goes by so fast, Nico."

The words, too, were ones I was used to my mother saying. I put my arm around Aidy's shoulder and squeezed her into my side, then pressed a kiss to the crown of her head. "Love you, Aidy-pie."

She wrapped an arm around my waist, tightening our embrace. "Love you back, big brother." She glanced up at me. "You want this, don't you?"

I looked around the nursery, at the toys spilled from the toy chest. The tiny clothes peeking out of the closet. I could hear Ryder humming as he washed the dishes down in the kitchen. "Yeah."

"With Cassia?"

I pressed my lips together. "She's the *only* person I want this with. She's my light, Aidy."

Aidy rested her head on my shoulder. "Then, it'll work out."

Clearly, Aidy put out the SOS because when I stepped out of our latest project—the vandalism hadn't been as extensive this time—I found Knox nearby, his yellow hard hat gleaming in the sun.

"Are you babysitting me?" I asked.

"I'm checking in on our project. Just wanted to update the client." He hesitated. "But, yeah, Aidy told me about your issues with Cassia. Sucks, man. Especially since you did right by telling her the truth."

"I fumbled that," I said with a sigh. I shoved my hands in my pockets, too glum to find pleasure in the steady hum of the saws or the hammering coming from inside. I squinted up at the large house.

"Maybe. Or maybe this has less to do with you and more to do with her."

I frowned. "What do you mean?"

"Em was terrified of losing someone else in her life. Understandably so."

Knox turned on his heel and headed back toward the trailer. I followed. It had taken most of the abuse by the vandals but was still functional—especially after a coat of paint covered the obscenities that had been spray-painted on it. Once inside, he tossed off the hard hat, which landed on my desk, scattering papers. I pressed my lips together so I didn't yell at him for messing up my piles.

"She lost her parents and her fiancé. Getting her to open up to me was hard. When she found out about how we were testing her, it gave her the push she needed to run. But the desire had already been there."

I rubbed my knuckle along my scruffy chin. "Because Emmaline's fear overwhelmed her, and I fed it," I admitted. "So you're saying that Cassia isn't going to trust me because her last boyfriend was a fucking moron and cheated with her sister."

"I don't know how deep Cassia's insecurities run, but having a sibling betray you is pretty difficult to overcome." Knox's expression, full of frustration, also held understanding. "I played a part in what happened with Em. I went along with your decisions because I was dealing with my own shit."

I shoved my hands into my pockets. "I'm still sorry for—"

Knox raised his hand. "I know. I knew it when you told me where to find her. I was just... I was angry because I was scared."

The same emotion roared through me, but I battled it back, sighing deeply. "Yeah. I've been scared for a long time. And it's easier to be angry than to admit I'm afraid."

Knox grinned. "Look at us. We're making serious progress." He settled into one of the semi-comfortable chairs and swung his ankle over his opposite knee. "What's had you scared? It wasn't just taking on Aidy. She was a good kid—at the time."

I slid into the chair across from him and tapped my fingers

on the desk between us. When I left, it would once again be cleared of paperwork, all filed appropriately. As much as I liked the organization, it was Hazel's obsession. She was the best thing that had happened to our fledgling construction company. I tried to tell her often, and I planned to pay her accordingly after this job concluded.

"No, Aidy wasn't what worried me. Not initially."

Knox tilted his head, waiting.

I sighed, still wrestling with whether to share the news. "You know the business was a mess financially. Well, that's because Dad was having an affair, and he nearly bankrupted the company to pay off the woman. And—and—what if he made the sailboat capsize? What if he decided that was a better way to deal with his shit choices than to actually tell Mom?"

The words poured out of me in a thick rush, much like sludge from a formerly broken pipe. I blinked at Knox, shocked by how much better I felt to have shared that awful secret, my deepest concerns.

Knox leaned back in his chair, let it swivel back and forth as he stared up at the ceiling. "I wondered."

"About what?"

"Dad. He took me to all my practices, right?"

"Yeah."

"But, after he dropped me at school, or whatever, where did he go? Mom made a few comments over the years about Dad being impossible to catch in the mornings."

"You think he was screwing another woman *all that time*? And using your…" I broke off, lip curling. "That's worse than what I thought."

"And we don't know if it's true. But I wondered. Still, Mom didn't know."

I dropped my head into my hands. "What if she did?" I asked. My voice was muffled by my palms, so I forced my head up. "What if she's the reason the boat capsized? She was the better sailor…"

Knox leaned in and placed his hand on my forearm. "We'll never know, which sucks. *Hard*. I'm pissed that I don't know. But I do know that we can't marinate in those possibilities. You have got to let that go. They're gone. Whatever—however—it happened, they're *gone*."

I swallowed hard. "I'm *so* angry with him."

"Me, too." Knox sat back and placed his palms behind his head. "And I'm mad at you for not telling me how bad things were with the firm. I would have—"

"I didn't want you to have to give up your hockey career. I was already taking over for Dad because I needed out of Manhattan. I was going to have to do the work to stabilize the company, so why should you get sucked back into something you didn't love?"

Knox narrowed his eyes. "I've wondered about that, too. Are you finally admitting you don't love architecture?"

I let out a breath as I nodded. Another huge weight lifted off my shoulders.

"But you took on the firm, the debt, *all* of it."

"Because it was Dad's legacy. Because you loved to create. Because Aidy was making noise about being part of the firm. Because it was all we had left of Mom and Dad."

Knox jutted his jaw, then shifted it left, then right. "I didn't go into the draft."

My chest ached. He'd been such a talented forward. He would have gone in the second round, if not earlier. He'd have fame and money—money we'd never make as professional architects. "I'm sorry you gave up your dream."

Knox shook his head slowly. "I'm not. I mean, at the time, it *sucked*. I wanted to play in the NHL more than anything. and that didn't feel possible." Knox considered me. "Probably how you felt about taking over Dad's firm to begin with."

Knox turned contemplative, then a slow smile broke across his face. "But…now? No way can I imagine not having Em in my life. *No way*, man. And we've done well," Knox continued, satisfaction radiating off him. "Lots of accolades. That last one was basically the Stanley Cup of architecture."

I smirked. "That one did feel good." I sobered, sitting forward. "You sacrificed a lot."

"So did you. I just didn't realize, and that makes me feel like a dick."

"I wish you hadn't had to know." I sighed. "What was the point of me doing all that if it still cost you your dreams?"

"I wish I'd known you didn't want to be an architect."

"That evolved. Probably in part from Dad's mess, but also because I was never happy in Manhattan. I never would have wished what happened to Mom and Dad to happen, but I think…I think having to move back to take care of Aidy saved me from some bad years. I can't believe I ever considered Amanda as someone I'd want to spend my life with." I shuddered, my skin crawling at the prospect. "We wouldn't have been happy."

I rose and grabbed some waters. I handed him one.

"And now Cassia."

Unease still weighed me down. "About that… I really screwed up."

Knox leaned in. "Want to tell me?"

I frowned. "Don't you have a meeting?"

Knox waved me off. "Em and Aidy will handle the clients. Look, I'll text them that I'm helping you work through your relationship issues."

I grunted, concern and embarrassment congealing into a hard knot in my gut as I watched him type into his phone.

"Stop with the assholery," Knox said, slipping his phone back into his pocket. "And start talking."

Chapter Thirty
Cassia

Sometime in the night I woke in the deep, quiet dark, knowing what I wanted. I lay on the expensive, thousand-thread-count sheets and stared up at the fancy coved ceiling of my mother's guest room.

Getting the result I determined I needed might prove tricky. But I *knew*. I rolled over, mashing my face into the pillow, and screamed.

I rolled over and fell back to sleep, this time, without dreams.

The next morning, I strolled into the large, airy dining room, and dropped a kiss on Phil's balding head. He set down his coffee mug and the *Financial Times* to focus those sharp eyes on me. He wore a well-fitted charcoal three-piece suit, the vest covering the beginnings of a paunch that his hour each day at the gym no longer managed to offset. His shirt was a blinding white, and cufflinks winked when he brought his ceramic mug to his lips.

"Hey, honey. I heard you get up, so I made you a coffee."

"Morning. Oooh, thanks!"

"You look like you have some sparkle today," he said. He grinned so I smiled back. Martin was easy to love—thoughtful and generous. But it was his kindness toward me that had disarmed me and made me fall in love with him over the years. I'd been more excited than my mother when Martin proposed.

"I do?"

I snagged a bowl of fruit my mother had set out for me, along with a latte. Martin had one of those expensive coffee machines that cost more than most people's monthly mortgage. I took a long sip and savored the rich, milky brew. Yeah, it was worth the cost.

"You have the best coffee," I said on a deep-felt sigh.

Martin chuckled. "Visit more often. That way, it's old hat."

I smirked as I took another sip of my delicious drink. "What are you up to today?" I asked.

"I plan to enjoy breakfast with you, catch up on your doings, then I need to head into the office."

Martin ran a large accounting firm. While my eyes crossed at the spreadsheets, Martin thrived on the numbers. And he'd provided my mother with a wonderful life for the past ten years.

"Mom's off?" I asked.

"She ran to the farmer's market to get you some of those pastries you like."

I picked up my mug. "I definitely need to visit more often."

I hummed most of the drive from Boston back to Providence, too nervous to sing along to music on the radio. My thumbs tapped on the steering wheel as I chewed my lip. I should probably call Nico, tell him I wanted to talk. Instead, I drove toward the studio hoping to find him. He needed to know that I wanted him.

Him for *him*.

Still. Badly. No—desperately. That was why I would set his former relationships with Amanda in the past, right where Nico said it belonged. I had to because the alternative was to give him up, and I just couldn't do that.

But maybe just showing up would undercut him in front of his employees. I parked in the Whole Grocers parking lot, my hands shaking as I pulled out my phone. Most of a week gone since we'd last spoken because of my insecurities. The insecurities I *still* couldn't quite let go of. I rolled my eyes even as I yanked open my door.

"Chocolate," I muttered, giving in to my love for the confection—one I hadn't indulged in since I was a teenager. "I'll get him a damn bouquet of the stuff."

So I did. I winced at the final cost…and the side-eye from the checker and the older woman behind me as a pimply-faced teen shoved yet another chocolate bar—salted caramel and almonds in that one, yum!—into the bulging paper sack.

I accepted the bag and my receipt but before I could slide off, the older woman tapped my shoulder. "Might want to reconsider too many of those at once. I mean, your figure…"

No one had a right to tell a person to watch their weight, their figure, no matter what they looked like. I gritted my teeth then let it go. *Whatever.*

Still, her words burned. Because they weren't just *her* words, but the words of countless dance instructors, other dancers…my sister.

"Oh, it's okay. I work out about eight hours a day on a slow day," I smiled, all teeth, as I patted my stomach. "But thanks for worrying about my ass."

I giggled about the look on the woman's face all the way to my car where I settled the bag of chocolate and pulled out the caramel and nut one. I ripped it open and took a big bite.

"Damn, that's good," I moaned.

The older woman pushed her cart up to the Mercedes SUV next to my sedan, her face a mask of disapproval just as I was about to take a second bite. So I bit into it, a generous amount that had her sniffing.

I laughed again, feeling lighter than I had in a long time. What I'd said could have gotten me fired, ended my career, and it was so freeing to finally put the judge-y women in their place.

Next up, visit Nico. I dropped the rest of the candy bar in my lap and headed toward my studio, hoping my nerves would calm down if I saw him.

"Nico's not here," Hazel said when I pulled up to the site. I'd met her the last time I showed up with Nico, about a week ago— just before he told me about his former relationship with my sister. I'd liked her then, and now wasn't any different. "He had to go check on another one of our sites that was hit."

My heart pounded. "Hit...as in...?"

"They broke the windows and ripped out wiring. It's going to be a bitch to fix, both in time and materials. We'll have to cut out drywall we'd already taped and bedded." Hazel slammed her screwdriver back into her belt, her scowl growing. So I did the only thing I could think to do—I passed out the chocolate bars to the crew. Well, half of them.

"The rest are for Nico," I said.

"Hope the sugar improves his disposition," Hazel muttered.

I chewed on my inner cheek. "Has he been...difficult?"

"He's trying not to be, but...a grumpy bull would be more

pleasant than him right now."

My chest tightened. "Because of the break-ins?"

Hazel shrugged. "Those suck and are costing us serious money and time, setting back schedules." Her dark eyes searched my face. "But no, I think this has everything to do with you. Oh, and that bra and pair of silk shorts he found in the second room."

I frowned. "What are you talking about?"

Hazel covered her mouth, her large eyes now saucer-size. "Oh, he's going to kill me."

"You found a bra *here*?"

"Yeah, that first day he had us come in. He reamed the team and me out for behaving unprofessionally, but it wasn't ours." She rolled her eyes. "None of us can afford La Perla."

There was only one person I knew who could, and I didn't like where my mind—and insecurities—took me.

Chapter Thirty-One
Cassia

Once in the driver's seat, I took out my phone and dialed his number.

"Cassia."

His tone was soft but clipped, and the chocolate felt like lead in my stomach. I inhaled sharply, then choked.

"Cassia? Are you okay?" His voice grew in volume with concern. "God. Talk to me. Please. Are you hurt? I'll call Knox. He'll get to you faster than I can—"

My cheeks burned and my eyes watered. "I'm…okay." My voice sounded like a seventy-five-year-old after a whole bottle of moonshine and seven packs of cigarettes. "Something in my throat."

"You scared me."

"Why would Knox be able to get to me first?" I asked.

"I'm across town."

"Why are you over there?" I asked. My voice was closer to normal but my throat still burned.

"I missed you and keeping busy has helped. You really want to talk about me being at a job site?"

I fiddled with the candy wrapper. "Um…yeah?"

"Dammit, Cassia. Giving you space was the hardest thing I've ever done."

"I miss you, too," I whispered. "Nico?"

"Yeah?"

"I want to see you."

"Really?"

The hope in his voice made my stomach settle and my heart race. "Yeah."

"Want to meet me at my place?"

My entire body relaxed and warmed. "Sure."

I beat him by twenty minutes. Enough time for my nerves to return.

But the moment he exited his truck, he was all I could see. Then his hands cupped my cheeks, his callused palms warm and steady, and he kissed me. The soft brush of his lips, dry and comforting, over mine had me closing my eyes and leaning into him.

"I need you, Cassia," he said against my lips. "I need you."

I opened my eyes. "Wait." I pressed my hands to his chest. My stomach rolled. "I need to ask you something."

He nodded, eyes wary.

"The bra at my studio…you're not…you haven't been…Nico, I *need* you to be honest with me."

He cupped my cheeks, staring deeply into my eyes. "I will always tell you the truth. I promise."

I nodded. "All right." I swallowed, trying to wet my dry throat. "You didn't see Amanda, did you?"

First confusion clouded his eyes, then his face took on a pained expression. "I haven't seen your sister. I don't want to see your sister. Why did you ask about her?"

I released a lot of tension with my next breath. "Because she wears La Perla."

"What's that?"

"The bra Hazel said you found."

"Oh. Oh…" His eyes widened. "*Fuck*—it hurts that you'd think I'd ever be with her."

"Okay."

He raised an eyebrow. "Okay? Really?"

My lips still tingled from the touch of his. I licked them, enjoying his faint taste. "You have a history with her. So do I." My stomach cramped.

I didn't want to have a deep conversation in his driveway. "Take me inside, please."

"Yeah. Of course."

He led me through his garage and into his kitchen where Fred wound around his legs, meowing demandingly. Nico bent down and picked up the kitten, hugging him close.

"Want a drink?" he asked me. He bent to peer into the fridge, and Fred leaped to the ground, walking away, his tail pointed straight upward.

"There's sparkling water and beer."

"Sparkling water," I said as I eyed his delicious ass. Nico in a suit exuded professionalism and urbanity. But Nico in jeans that cupped his butt and showed off those thighs was something else. Heat curled in my lower belly, as rich as the chocolate I'd eaten earlier.

That reminded me. "Oh, I have something for you."

"Later," he said, handing me the drink. "Talk to me, please.

What can I do?"

I set the drink on the counter and met his gaze. "Nothing. At least nothing *else*. You did the right thing by telling me and I needed to process. But I'm not willing to give you up. You—you matter to me, Nico."

"Ah, Cassia, you matter to me, too."

I stepped in close, my heart hammering. "I'm sorry it took me time to work through my issues," I whispered.

He nuzzled my neck. "I understand. I think I would have felt the same way, if our roles were reversed." He scowled. "Actually, I might have to break Knox's face just because I thought about the possibility of you two together."

I laughed, easing more of the tension that had built the entire ride back to Providence. "He's married. Happily."

Nico shook his head. "Yeah, but…" He blew out a breath. "You amaze me. Your willingness to forgive humbles me. Thank you for being here. For being with me."

I hugged him tighter. "Nico?"

His lips smoothed down my neck, sending shivers of pleasure in their warm wake.

"Do you think I can seduce you now?"

He reared back. "Cass—"

"I know. It may be too soon. But I want you and I want you to be mine. Totally." I nipped his ear.

"I don't want to rush with you," he said. "This, what's between us, matters too much…" His hands slid down to my waist, then up over my ribs to the underside of my breasts. "Let's watch a movie."

"Can we make out while we do that?" I asked.

He picked me up and my crutches fell to the ground. "Absolutely."

―――――

Nico had been right. That wasn't the moment for us to be together. That didn't change how frustrated I was, though. The only solace I had was I knew Nico felt the same way.

I considered taking matters into my own hands, but I also enjoyed the lusciousness of deferred gratification. For now, especially when he kissed me so softly, so sweetly. I lay in his embrace, safe and hot—too hot—and…happy.

Nico made me happy. And horny.

―――――

Sometime later, I woke in Nico's arms, my neck stiff, when Fred sniffed at my cheek. We'd fallen asleep on the couch. I squinted at the blue screen on the TV, even as I raised my arm to pet Fred's soft head.

"What…" Nico lifted his bleary head from the couch cushion and winced. "Fuck. My neck."

He pulled me in closer so my hips were tight against his pelvis and my ass was back on the cushion. "It's worth it, though, to hold you." His voice was gruff from sleep…and maybe the growing erection pressing into my hip.

I smiled as I rested my cheek on his pec, still stroking the cat. This was what I'd always wanted.

"Come to bed?"

I lifted my head, studying his sleep-softened features. I raised my other hand and caressed his lips. "Yes."

He smiled even as he pressed a kiss to my fingertips. We untangled ourselves from the couch with Fred hopping lightly to the ground, tail swishing as he led the way down the hall. By the time I'd brushed my teeth and donned Nico's T-shirt, Fred had settled in the center of the bed. Nico came out of his closet in just his underwear, and my breath caught, my hand still holding up the sheet where I'd slid into the bed.

He was rangy, not bulky, with long, defined muscles that flexed and shifted with each step. He yawned, running his hands over his face as he strode toward the bathroom. Once the door was closed, I flung my head back against the pillow and gasped at the tug of desire in my belly.

Moments later, he exited the bathroom and crawled into bed next to me. He moved Fred, who yowled in protest and then snuggled up against my side. He slid an arm across my waist, his thumb drawing lazy patterns up and down my ribs.

"Night, Cassia," he murmured.

I turned my head, counting his eyelashes before studying his strong nose, soft lips. I settled into the realization that while I lusted after Nico's body, this closeness was what I craved even more.

"I'm glad I'm here."

He hugged me a little tighter. "So am I. Thank you for coming back, for staying."

I closed my eyes, warm and content. "There isn't anywhere I'd rather be."

───────

Over the next couple of weeks, the work on my studio neared

completion. I'd been giddy to hand Nico the final check yesterday, which he'd told me was too much.

I smiled. "That includes your fee."

"But I was doing this for free—"

"I took your architectural services for free." I winked. "And you've more than paid off our initial meeting. So, we're good. You have total access to Lilia again, too. I made sure to clear it with Aidy."

He pulled me in close, holding me as though I was a Ming Dynasty vase. This man's love for me was so clear. How could I have missed it?

"I don't want your money, Cassia. The construction business is booming. I'm making more than I did as a partner at Wright and Associates."

I folded my hands around his. "This is fair, Nico. It's right. And it's yours." I kissed him. "Now, get out of my way and let me enjoy my classrooms before they fill with students."

He laughed. "We still have the rest of the fixtures to put in and—"

I waved him off. "Gonna dance now that my foot will hold me. I have kids showing up next week." I bounced on my feet— and didn't feel a shooting pain up my leg. "I have forty kids already. Forty! And both my ADA classes are full."

That made me happiest.

"Lainey's excited," Nico said. "That's what her dad told me when he was checking on the floors yesterday."

"Good. I am, too. And that family is the reason my classes are full, so I've offered to comp them the first year of tuition."

"Wow. That was generous," Nico said, blinking. He smiled broadly. "You, Cassia, are amazing."

The next day, a reporter called to ask for an interview. When I explained about our biennial shows, she asked "May I have a ticket? I've always been interested in dance."

"Of course," I said, but nerves skittered up my spine. Sure, the show was still months away—we needed to open and hold classes before the kids could perform.

Still, this was my first time on the administrative side of the shows, and not being able to control the performance caused sweat to bloom along my back.

Hours later, I settled back on my yoga mat, sweat once again dripping from my skin. This time, because of my efforts in the steamy room. The only downside was the single stiletto I'd found in the first classroom Nico had finished. It was in the closet where I planned to keep basic props, under the pile of brand-new scarves.

The shoe was a size seven. Amanda's size. And I couldn't help but think she had a pair of those particular heels. Perhaps to go with that La Perla underwear?

For the most part, the hour-long class relaxed my muscles and eased some of the tension from my mind. Aidy and Bridget noted my expression after class at the restaurant as we settled onto our typical stools, large glasses of water in front of us.

"What's got you so tense?" Bridget asked.

I sighed as I ran my fingertip down the side of the glass. Before I could decide what to say, Aidy piped up.

"Nico."

I glanced at her, eyebrow raised. Defensiveness swelled, but

I wasn't sure if I wanted to protect Nico or if my frustration stemmed from my need to shield myself. "Why would you say that?"

"Because you're quiet. And because he just finally told me about my dad's affair. Why am I always the last to know about stuff in my family?" Aidy grouched as she slumped back in her seat.

"I didn't know my husband was having an affair," Bridget said.

"Dr. Hogue?" Shock and fury wound through me in equal parts and I was ready to kick him in the balls.

Bridget shook her head, her eyes gleaming with love. "No, not Simon. He's wonderful. But I'm so glad you girls have my back." Bridget chuckled. "I was married before. Brendan is my son with my first husband."

"Oh." Clearly, I still had lots to learn about these women.

"My point was, it's not always easy to know. I had no idea what to look for—he was good at keeping secrets. And you, Aidy, were a teen, probably preoccupied with your own life."

Aidy nodded with a sigh. "Oh, I was definitely self-absorbed. But that doesn't explain why Cassia knew."

"Nico told me a couple of weeks ago when he was trying to explain why he was so angry for so long."

Aidy stabbed her straw around her glass. "When you take that hot mess in conjunction with the fact that his fiancée not only kicked him out but got him fired from his firm, I guess I can understand a lot more of his bitterness."

It was my turn to totter off to the water dispensers. Except I set my glass in the dirties bin and headed toward the locker room. I was collecting my bag when Aidy strode in. "You didn't know about his fiancée?" she asked.

A weight slammed into my gut. "I knew. He told me. I just…I *hate* thinking about Nico with my sister."

She pursed her lips. "Ryder and I met, became close, while he was dating another woman." She sat next to me on the bench and stared down at her hands. "I hate the idea of them together, but then, I was pregnant with Lilia, had just ended a relationship… How could I hold Ryder's experiences in life against him when I had my own past to wrestle with?"

Bridget entered the room and settled on my other side.

"I totally get what you're saying," I said. "Just as I know how I feel about him. It's just…Amanda's difficult."

"Makes me glad I don't have a sister," Aidy mumbled.

"Me, too." Bridget smiled. "Except I consider you both like sisters. And Calliope and Emmaline. We made our own band, and I promise never, never to see your significant others naked."

Aidy giggled. "I like this pact. Mainly because I never want to see my brothers nude."

"Yeah, you get the best part of that deal," Bridget said with a wink.

I rummaged around in my bag and pulled out some of the chocolate bars I'd purchased and stashed in my bag. "Want one?"

"Oh! Give me one." I let Aidy take the dark chocolate mint one she wanted and then held out the others to Bridget, who plucked a chocolate, almond, sea salt from the options.

"I adore chocolate," Aidy whimpered.

"So, back to your original question of why I'm stressed…" I told them about the bra, the shoe, and my missing key from the night at the bar.

"So you think Amanda's staying in your studio?" Aidy asked. "Like, living there?"

I shrugged. "My mom won't help her. I won't help her. She lost her job and apartment in New York."

"Do you think…" Aidy paused. She shoved a large bite into her mouth and picked up her items. "Gotta go," she called back in a garbled voice over her shoulder.

I raised my eyebrows at Bridget, who shrugged. "I don't know what she's thinking or doing."

"All right," I said.

"Thanks for the chocolate."

I smiled. "Any time."

"No. Don't you dare make this a thing. No more chocolate bars."

"You just said you like them," I said.

"That's the problem."

"I have another issue," I blurted. Then, I nibbled my lip. "Never mind. I'm pretty sure I need to figure this out on my own."

She bumped her shoulder to mine. "You're not alone, Cassia. You haven't been for a long time."

Chapter Thirty-Two
Cassia

The issue with wanting sex but not being brave enough to ask for sex was…

"I'm living in hell," I whispered to the mirror after my shower the next evening. Mirror-me nodded, astute in the ways of the world I myself wasn't. Clearly. Because if I was, I wouldn't have spent the last few weeks tortured in a sensuous daze as Nico wined, dined, and romanced me…without ever giving me what I really needed.

His cock.

My cheeks burned with the heat of my blush, but I met mirror-me's eyes. "I want sex. Badly."

I leaned in closer to my image. My makeup was subtle and light. My hair fell in thick waves over my shoulders and down my back, caught behind my right ear with one of my grammy's silver combs. My dress skimmed my body, not tight but definitely hinting at my curves, stopping two, maybe three inches below my butt to best show off my long, toned legs.

Because my foot no longer ached, I wore low-heeled close-toed sandals. Dr. Elliott expected me to stop using my single crutch within the week. I shifted more weight to my previously-injured foot, beaming because I didn't feel a tingle or twinge. I looked as good as I could—hopefully, good enough for seducing my man.

"I hope he wants me as much as I want him." I bit my lip. "No more excuses for postponing our sexy times. I need orgasms. I deserve them." With one last nod at myself, I turned from the mirror and grabbed the hated crutch as I headed toward my bathroom door.

Nico planned to make me dinner at this place tonight. I enjoyed his cooking and playing with Fred, who'd grown so much these last few weeks. But I didn't intend to do any eating—not until after I orgasmed into blissfulness anyway.

The drive to Nico's was as nerve-wracking this time as it was when I told him I wanted to keep seeing him. I shoved thoughts of my sister out of my mind. I hadn't seen any further sign of Amanda, nor had she called me again. At Nico's insistence, we'd changed the locks of the doors to the studio and my house.

I'd also used the past few weeks to advertise my grand opening and hire another dance teacher and an office manager. Both started in a couple of weeks—once the floors were laid. The theater would be completed last because the reupholstered seats, a big splurge in my budget, were taking longer than we'd hoped. But there'd also been a delay in the lighting needed to complete the auditorium.

I couldn't believe my studio would open so soon.

I also couldn't believe I was still celibate and craving Nico's body with an ever-increasing obsession. "Tonight's the night."

After I parked in what had become my spot, I grabbed the bottle of red Nico liked and headed toward the porch. I knocked. Nothing.

With a frown, I knocked again, harder.

Nothing.

I stepped back, nibbling my lip. That's when I saw the yellow post-it. I bent down and read: Cassia,

Come on in. I arrived later than expected and jumped in the shower.

I shivered in anticipation at the thought of Nico's wet body. "Tonight is definitely the night."

I let myself in, careful to lock the door behind me. I gave Fred a quick scratch and after I dropped my tote on the kitchen counter and my purse in its usual spot at the bar. I crutched down the hall. I entered Nico's bedroom just as he opened the bathroom door, a roll of steam encasing him for a moment before it dissipated. My breath caught. He was more toned now than he had been a few weeks before. His biceps bulged and his abdomen was taut beneath the dark blue terrycloth of his towel.

"Nico," I said.

"Hey, Cassia." He grinned, his pleasure at my appearance warming me. Not that I needed any warming.

My blood pumped hot and thick. I settled my crutch against the wall near the bedroom door. I shut the door, my attention never wavering from him as he strode toward me, the bulge between his legs growing.

Just before he reached me, I blurted, "We're doing this. Now."

He stopped, his brows tugged tight over his nose. "Doing what?"

I stepped forward, pressing my palms to his pecs. I let my fingertips slide down his chest, over those abs I planned to lick soon, and tugged at his towel. I rose onto my tiptoes.

"Well, I plan to do you," I whispered in his ear.

His breath caught, his towel fell, and I wrapped my fingers around his erection.

"Cass—"

"Yes?"

He made a garbled noise as I rubbed my thumb over his tip. His hips jerked. "Don't stop."

"Didn't plan to."

"I…hell…I want you, Cassia." He finished the sentence with his teeth grinding together, his head falling backward. "*Fuck*. I'm desperate for…you."

"Excellent. Because I need you, too."

He widened his stance as he pulled me tight against his body, and I needed to shift my hand to continue to touch him. I kept my movements slow and firm, not unlike his drifting hands as they cupped my bottom. His eyes darkened, his pupils blown wide. "This, you, matter. Mean everything."

He took my hand, trembling, as he led me to his bed where I tumbled backward, the coolness of the duvet a welcome glide against my overheated skin. I stared up into his eyes as they burned—for me.

"Cassia," he said. His throat worked as he struggled to control his desire, but behind the tensed jaw and flared nostrils, tenderness shone from his eyes. "You're sure?"

I gripped his wrists and swiveled my pelvis, hating the barriers of cloth between us. "I want you, Nico. Yes, I want you inside me, but I want *you*. The man you hide from the world. I love your kindness, your concern for your family, your dedication. I might even love the brusqueness that I first found so off-putting now that I understand why you pushed me away."

He bent in closer, his nose running down the length of my cheek. "I was wrong to do that. So damn wrong. I've never felt anything more beautiful, more *right*, than being with you."

He lowered his face until our lips touched, a tantalizing brush of flesh. I shivered, needing, desperate for more. He slid his hand to the back of my neck, his palm cradling me as his thumb stroked along my cheek from chin to ear.

I arched my neck as he skimmed my skin once more with his thumb. His lips continued to drift over mine in soft caresses. My pulse pounded and heat gathered, warm and rich in my pelvis. I softened further, relaxing into his embrace even as I pressed my tongue to the seam of his lips. I licked along the bottom edge of his lower lip, my tongue tantalized by the softness and the rasp of the tiny hairs on his chin.

He opened for me, and I delved deeper into his mouth. He groaned and I tilted my hips to better cuddle his straining erection. My hands slid from his sides up his neck to the silky hairs at his nape. I speared my fingers there, loving how the strands wrapped around my digits. My tongue slid along the side of Nico's, and his flavor suffused my mouth.

His scent, his taste, bloomed over my senses even as cravings burned through my middle, blasting outward, making my arms quiver. He tipped his head, slanted his mouth, and loved me.

This kiss was tender and burning with passion. My pulse ratcheted higher, higher, even as the soft, gentle glide of his lips and tongue soothed a deep ache in my chest. My breath caught and Nico pulled back.

"You are so beautiful. The most beautiful person. I want you, Cassia. I need to be closer to you."

I slid my leg up the back of his, over his calf, thigh, buttocks. "Yes. I need that, too."

My core warmed further, nearly burning with intensity as my body burst into a light sheen of perspiration. He continued to kiss me in long, slow glides. I melted into the sensation, feeling drunk off the endorphins he brought forth. The world shrank so that just the two of us mattered.

Nico rose over me, his hands drifting down from my collarbones to my breasts, over my ribs, stroking my waist, and I whimpered. Catching the edge of my dress, he pushed it upward, bunching it at my chin. I moved to sit up, but Nico settled a hand on my stomach. "Let me do this."

"I have to look ridiculous."

"You are stunning." He pressed a kiss to the swell of my left breast, then my right. "Absolutely divine."

Nico drew down the cup of my bra so that my tender flesh puckered further, then he suckled and nipped, licked, and kissed my chest down to the waistband of my panties.

"You with me? You still okay with this?"

"Yes. Yes, *please*."

Nico chuckled. "You're not much of a talker."

"I react best with movement."

Brow quirked, Nico smiled—slow and deviant and devastating as he slid my underwear over my hips and down my thighs.

I shivered, my skin shocked by the heat of his palms and the coolness of the air.

"I can tell. Look at you." The tone of his voice held the same awe as his eyes. "You're all muscle—long, lean, so toned." He ran his finger along the indention of my thigh, up the taut curve of my hip.

"You should have seen me when I was dancing eight hours a day," I said.

Nico's eyes flashed to mine, expression solemn. "Don't. Please. Don't diminish the work and care you've taken with yourself. You're *stunning*. I'm so fucking impressed and a little intimidated." Even as his fingers continued up, over my abdomen, back to my breasts, he shook his head.

"And so turned on. You're beautiful, Cassia. Not just your body." He kissed along the column of my throat. "You. You are so amazing."

I shifted, restless, lips parting as I exhaled. Nico kept his touch light, a mere whisper over my skin, and each caress inflamed my desire. I bit my lower lip, unsure.

"Let me hear you, Cassia. I crave your sounds, your whimpers, your sighs. Give them to me."

I shook my head and clenched my eyes shut. Too much. He overwhelmed me in the best possible way. I bucked, struggling with the sensations that intermingled with the emotions. I unfisted my hands from the sheets and cupped his cheeks, tugging him closer.

I kicked off my panties and hooked my right ankle around his knee, turning us over. He shifted to his back with a grunt, his hands never ceasing their massage of the back of my thighs, my butt. I pressed my breasts to his chest, my core to his erection, restless energy making me grind, seeking friction, seeking a release from everything fizzing inside me.

I reared back, my hands gripped his sides. He ran his palms over my hair, my cheek. I halted to nuzzle into his hand.

"Let me love you," he whispered.

I bit my lip again, searching his eyes.

"Please let me love you."

I shook my head. His words. I'd never felt like this, needed like this. Was the driving force behind my need for him passion or love? Lust licked through me, tightening my muscles, but he softened it.

I sat up and removed my dress and bra before I slid my palms up his muscled legs, enjoying the thick, solid weight of his quads, the stability of his patella, the indent at his hips—the sturdy girth of his erection.

I licked my lips, transfixed by the mushroom tip. I leaned down and he groaned when my hair skimmed his thighs, his belly. He jackknifed when I slid my lips around his erection, taking him deep into my mouth.

"Holy. Cassia. Sweet...Ung..."

I suckled the tip, swirling my tongue. Before I could slide back down, he had me on my back, and I stared up into his glazed eyes, loving the gentleness in his fingertips and his features as he caressed my face, my neck, my breasts, down over my belly to my folds.

Again and again he touched me, learned me, cherished me. I shattered, my skin warming, blooming under his ministrations.

He rested on his elbow next to me, kissing my lips as I soared up and over the next peak of pleasure.

I quaked, broke, and cried out his name.

"My beautiful Cassia," he said. He rolled on a condom and slid into my welcoming body. He held still, not breathing, steady but for the shiver in his shoulders. I wrapped my languid legs around his back, hooking my ankles there.

"You feel so good. This…this is what I…"

He kissed me again, more aggressive, his tongue and teeth marking me. I shifted, undulating my hips. He held firm, rooted deep.

Breaking the kiss, his chest heaving, he slipped his hands in both of mine, our palms as close as our bodies, his strong fingers a promise, his expression filled with forever as he rocked us both to a powerful orgasm that left me breathless, my defenses shattered, my heart his.

Chapter Thirty-Three
Nico

I cradled Cassia in my arms. My chin rested atop her head, my arms snug around her back, her breasts pressed to my chest. I'd asked if I was hurting her, holding her too tightly, but she'd simply cuddled even closer. She was so perfect for me.

I shifted so I could stare up at the ceiling. Falling in love remained scintillating, and I had every intention of being the lovesick fool. Cassia deserved the romance, and I *deserved* the beautiful opportunity to give it to her. But, even as excitement and joy mingled, a deep ache formed in my chest. Cassia would never meet my mother.

If my father hadn't been a cheating scumbag who'd nearly destroyed our family, maybe my mother would still be here. But even as the familiar anger built, Knox's voice sounded, reminding me of his words about Emmaline. He wouldn't change his path because it might not have led him to her.

I needed to let my bitterness go. Life was messier and much less in my control than I liked. I inhaled the soft, floral scent wafting from her hair even as I vowed I would let her know every day, with words and my actions, how much I cared for her. How much better and stronger she made me.

That meant overcoming not just my bitter resentment toward my father and toward Amanda but Cassia's feelings of inadequacy when she compared herself to her sister as well. I couldn't imagine how she couldn't see herself as I did. Cassia shifted closer, throwing one of her trim thighs over my abdomen. I groaned as her soft breast pushed into my biceps. My body roused, more than ready for another round.

"What's wrong?" she murmured, her voice heavy with sleep.

"I…"

She pulled back, face fearful as she searched mine. "Do you… regret tonight?"

My arms tightened. "No. *Never.*"

"Then what is it?"

"This has been the best night of my life," I whispered. "You're the best thing that's happened to me." I grabbed her hand and placed it over my heart. "I could never feel this for anyone but you." I turned so I hovered over her. I needed to look into her beautiful eyes when I said, "I love you. You're the only woman I've ever said that to."

I paused, letting my words sink in and not wanting to bring up her sister at this moment by name. But Cassia needed to understand what I was telling her.

"That I will ever say that to," I finished.

Her face softened and she touched trembling fingertips to my cheek. "Oh, Nico…"

My heart stuttered and panged that she didn't say it back, but I was patient—rather, I had to be. I kissed her, showing her with my body that I meant those words and intended to worship her.

And I did until she cried out my name, quivering with pleasure.

Then, I started over and did it again.

Chapter Thirty-Four
Cassia

I stretched, deliciously sore, smiling as I felt Nico's lips brushing over mine. I opened my eyes to find him hovering over me, already dressed.

"Oh." I pushed upward, out from under him. "Do you need to go to work?"

He grimaced. "Soon. But Hazel's covering the daily assignments. Not that the ladies need our input. They know what they're doing."

He handed me a mug filled with coffee and a touch of cream. I sipped, noting the bitterness had been removed with a touch of sweetness—a bit sweeter than I normally drank, but Nico did his best and remembered I added agave nectar to my coffee.

"Is it okay? I didn't have that nectar stuff you used, so I added some honey."

I took another deep drink and sighed, smiling. "It's perfect."

He grinned back. "Good." He settled against the bed frame, his long legs encased in faded denim, his feet bare. He had nice toes and long, elegant feet. I was glad mine were under the sheet.

"Will you eat breakfast with me?" he asked. "Then, you're welcome to stay here if you don't want to head home. Whatever you prefer."

I turned my head to study him. "You don't mind me being in

your space?"

He shook his head, a small frown forming. "Why would I?"

"Because…I never have before. I mean, after we slept. This is new." I motioned between us.

He set his mug on the nightstand before gently removing mine from my hands. He took my warmed fingers in his bigger hands and focused on me. "I love you, Cassia."

A warm jolt hit my chest at his words.

"And I want you in my life, in my home. All of that. So, no, I don't mind you being here. I want you here."

"I…"

A hint of sadness crept into his eyes before he handed me back my coffee and kissed my temple. "Why don't you finish that and come to the kitchen when you're ready? I was thinking of making eggs and toast. You okay with that?"

"Yes. Sounds great."

My voice was strained and Nico picked up on it—at least if his drooped shoulders were any indication.

I slid from the bed once he left the room and headed to the bathroom. Dammit.

"Why can't you just admit how you feel?" I grumbled, glaring at my tousled, sexed-up image in the mirror. "Stop being a weenie, Cassia. He bared his soul to you."

With a nod at mirror-me, I drank another swig of my coffee and took a short shower.

Once clean, I realized I didn't have my overnight bag, so I headed out into Nico's room. He'd made the bed and left a robe on the edge of it. My heart stumbled and then beat faster. It was these little gestures that mattered so much.

I slipped my arms into the robe, holding it close to my nose to catch Nico's faint scent. I grimaced down at my bare feet, but decided not to cover them. Nico deserved to see all of me.

"Now, Cassia. Tell him." I folded the towel, hung it on the rack, and grabbed my empty coffee mug. I headed down the hall to the kitchen and walked right up to Nico where he watched the toaster.

"I love you, too," I said. My voice wobbled. "And that scares me…"

He pulled me into a hug so my cheek rested against his T-shirt-clad chest. I sighed, closing my eyes, enjoying the softness of the cotton and the warmth of his body.

"I don't ever want you to be afraid of me or with me." He kissed the crown of my head and just held me, long after the toast popped.

Finally, I disentangled myself from his arms. "There are parts of me that aren't pretty…" I pointedly looked down at my feet.

"Your feet were your tool," he said. "I've already smashed my thumb with a hammer too many times to count and ripped the skin off the back of my hand on a broken piece of wood. Are you going to tell me I'm too ugly for you?"

I shook my head, my throat clogged with emotion. He cupped my cheeks.

"None of us is perfect, Cassia. We just have to be stronger than the fear and our mistakes."

I clutched at his shoulders as I lifted my lips to his. The kiss was soft, soothing. Exactly what I needed.

"Thank you for that. Now, how about you feed me breakfast so I don't get you in trouble with the boss man."

Nico chuckled. "This is one of the cases where it's nice to be the boss man."

"Well, then, I'll have to see how much trouble I can get you in." I winked, stepping back.

"Can you join me at the studio today?" Nico asked, his expression filled with excitement. "I have something to show you."

"Of course."

I followed his truck with my car. Hazel waved at us from the doorway, all smiles, as Nico led me to the back studio.

They'd laid the floor.

I covered my mouth, tears flooding my eyes.

I knelt and touched the floor, my fingers reverent. "This is incredible. It's better than I hoped."

His smile turned bashful. "I wanted you to have something great."

I took a deep breath as I stared at my face in the long mirror. I was in sneakers, yoga pants, and a T-shirt—not the best dance attire. But I steadied myself. After a long moment where I let my eyes slide closed, I thought of my favorite music—and began to spin. Nothing too hard, because while my foot felt better, it was still tender. After my fourth spin, I moved into a jete and then slid into an arabesque. My heart raced from exertion and exhilaration. I released back down to the floor and opened my eyes. Nico stared at me, admiration and desire burning from his brown eyes. Behind him, Hazel gawked.

"You're amazing," she gushed.

"She really is," Nico said.

My cheeks heated. "Not really—"

Nico strode toward me, his palms cupping my cheeks, his fingers threading into my hair, his lips on mine.

"You're amazing," he murmured, his features softening.

I skimmed my fingertips down his cheeks. "And you're too good to be true."

"Only with you."

"That's true," Hazel piped up. "He's hell on wheels to work for." But she shot Nico a wink as she sauntered off.

He grumbled but I could hear the affection in his voice. Those two enjoyed each other's company and respected each other's abilities. Nico deserved a partner like Hazel—just as she did him.

"Thank you for this, Nico," I said.

"In another week we'll be all finished."

◄ ▬▬▬▬▬▬▬ ▮▮

That night, I joined him again at his place where I made him dinner and told him about the classes I planned to offer at the studio.

"Bridget suggested that I post flyers at the nearby schools, maybe offer to do some demonstrations for the classes to drum up possible clients," I said. "She thinks that'll fill the rest of my empty spots."

Nico smiled before he went back to his linguini with clams.

I tilted my head. "What's that look?"

"I'm glad you've made friends with women who care about you," he said. "And you're already successful. You haven't even opened yet, and you already have full rosters."

"You're right," I said. "I'm so very lucky." I smiled at the thought of Bridget, Aidy, Emmaline, and my new dance instructor, Lynn, who I'd met at the yoga studio. "I was friendly with the dancers in Boston but we weren't close. It's nice to have friends who truly want what's best for me."

He reached over and picked up my hand, squeezing my fingers lightly. "You deserve those friends. You deserve to be happy."

I slept wrapped up in his arms once more, and the next morning, he made me breakfast. The day after, he made me dinner and I made him breakfast. That morning, I enjoyed packing him a sack lunch and telling him to "Have a good day, dear!"

His laughing eyes and deep, sultry kiss made me want to turn the brown bag into a ritual.

The following week, when my studio opened, Nico stood beside me.

I vibrated with nerves—mainly excitement.

"Look at what you accomplished," he whispered in my ear. "Look at all these kids who want to learn from you."

Tears of joy filled my eyes. I smiled up at him. "Thank you for making this possible."

He shook his head. "You did that, Cassia. I just cleared a bit of the path."

He pressed a soft kiss to my temple and strode off. I sighed, wishing I could go after him—that I told him how much I loved him.

"He's rather special, isn't he?" Mom asked.

I gasped and then threw my arms around her. Her own arms held me loosely, almost as if she were afraid I'd jerk back. "You came!"

"Nico invited us." She patted me once more, pride rolling off her in waves. "I just wish you'd done so."

I sighed. "I'm trying. I need to do better with you. I will..."

Martin pulled me into a side-arm hug. "Don't worry. We're both thrilled to bits and so very, very proud of you, darling girl."

My mother was making an effort with me and I should reciprocate—not so much because she wanted me to or even because it was expected—no, I wanted a relationship with my mother, and working through these awkward moments was the only way to get there. "If you don't mind waiting a couple of hours, I'd love to take you out to dinner to celebrate this."

Mom's eyes lit up. "Mind if I sit in on your class? It's been years since I've seen you dance."

I squeezed her fingers. "I'd really like that."

The next morning, not long after I arrived at my studio, Aidy called me.

"Where are you?" she asked.

"At my studio."

Ten minutes later, Aidy flung open my office door. She stood there in a well-tailored blue pantsuit, her strawberry blond hair pulled back in a low tail. She narrowed her eyes at me. "Do you have anything incognito?"

I blinked at her. "Like your suit?"

"No, not like this. I have a meeting with a client that I may be late for, but this can't wait."

"These are my only clothes here. I'm planning to teach in a couple of hours, so I have on my workout gear. Why? What can't wait?"

"The stakeout. You need something drab, which is why I brought you this." She tossed me a boring oversized college hoodie. Probably Nico's. "Put this on."

I slid my arms into the sleeves as we rushed out the door. I barely had time to lock up before she shoved me into her car. "Aidy, I don't understand."

"I'll explain on the way. You're going to watch Marcus's offices. Bridget's already there. I roped her into this because she was closer and had the day off." She winced. "But I think he'll notice a lady with two active babies hanging around soon."

"Why am I staking out the office of your former construction company?"

Aidy started the car and we headed out. "That bra at your studio...La Perla. That's expensive."

"I know."

She nodded.

"That's why I swung by there. I took these." She pulled out her phone at a red light and scrolled through some photos of Amanda heading into this building. "You were right about Amanda staying in Providence."

That didn't surprise me. My last conversation with my sister hadn't gone as she wanted. She wouldn't have let that go. She'd also said she didn't have a place to stay. So, she must have swiped my key—my missing key—from my purse that night at the bar.

I ran my tongue over my teeth, jitters working down my arms. Amanda lying and manipulating wasn't new, so why did this hurt me?

"Wow."

"It gets worse." Aidy shoved her hair out of the way.

"Amanda's working for Marcus?" I scrunched my nose. "They are two peas in a pod."

"Maybe." Aidy drew out the sound. "I think your sister's the one who's been defacing our work sites."

Chapter Thirty-Five
Nico

"I need you," Cassia said the moment I picked up my phone.

"Hey, honey." I pressed the phone harder to my ear as one of the contractors began loudly nailing the drywall into place. "I'm kind of in the middle of something. Can I call you back?"

"No. This is important."

I scowled even as I hustled from the building. "Okay, that's better. What is it?"

"Can you come by Wright and Associates?"

My stomach hardened. I hadn't been in the offices in weeks—and planned to keep it that way. I much preferred my new arrangement and always would. Wright and Associates was the legacy I'd felt obligated to protect, but that had turned into a prison of bitterness. Clearly, I'd been doing a lot of soul-searching over the past few months, and I was happier than I'd been in years, maybe ever. The fatter bank account helped, but, mainly, this work suited me. Hazel was the best foreman I'd ever worked with, and my siblings, Emmaline, and the Wright and Associates clients were all effusive in their praise toward my crew.

Everyone was happy, especially me. Yes, Cassia was an integral part of that *joie de vivre*, but so was taking charge of my future, my passions.

Still, if Cassia needed me at Wright and Associates in the

middle of a workday, it must be serious.

"Is something wrong with one of my siblings?"

"They're fine. And, Nico?" Her voice broke. She sniffled. "I'm so sorry."

I hopped into my truck, my heart pounding. "What could you possibly be sorry for? Unless you're breaking up with me," I half-joked but trepidation slithered down my spine.

Everything had been going so well, but I knew Cassia still worried about me sticking around, about her sister's actions and past behavior—and what Amanda would do to us.

"No, I don't want to lose you." She swallowed thickly. "Ever."

Thankfully, our work site wasn't too far from the building that housed Wright and Associates. Much as I wanted to ask her more questions on the phone, Cassia was clearly upset. I needed to hold her, reassure myself we were okay.

She met me in the doorway, wearing my college sweatshirt she must have stolen from my drawer and leggings, her one arm wrapped around her waist. She sprinted into my arms and clutched me tightly, her lips seeking mine, even as she said over and over again that she was sorry.

"What's going on?" I said, pulling back, studying her. "You're worrying me."

Her eyes were red-rimmed, her nose pink at the tip. "It's Amanda." My heart sank at the name. She'd forever be my deepest regret—and mistake. Cassia's typical graceful movements were jerky, almost uncoordinated. I hated that her sister could affect her like this.

Cassia grimaced. "She's been living in my studio."

"*Still?* Even after we changed the locks?" I placed my arm around Cassia's shoulders and led her into the building, out of the wind. She continued to shiver, so I ran my palm up and down her arm.

"I don't know if she is now. Have you found more stuff?" Cassia asked, tipping her head back to meet my gaze.

"Not that I know of. I already put in an alarm system, so you don't have to worry about her doing any harm."

"That's not what has me so upset." Cassia continued to walk toward the conference room—the one where we'd had our second ill-fated meeting. My feet became heavier with each step.

"Why *are* you upset?" I asked, a chill sliding across the back of my neck.

"Because we're pretty sure Amanda's working with Marcus," Aidy said as we stepped through the door.

I grunted. "That sucks but it's not really surprising." I didn't say that was because both Amanda and Marcus were terrible people, and like belonged with like. I wanted to but I didn't. Saying that might hurt Cassia's feelings, and she was already upset.

Cassia tipped her head back, her lip quivering. "That's not what I meant. Aidy and I are convinced Amanda's the one vandalizing the job sites."

My breath whooshed out and a buzzing hit my ears. "She... *what?* How can you be sure?"

"We aren't completely. Yet," Aidy said.

"Not following." I settled myself into one of the chairs at the table. Instead of moving to the chair nearby, Cassia dropped into my lap. I scooped her even closer, nuzzling into her hair, my chest warmed that she's let me comfort her.

"I guess I should start," Aidy said. "Cassia told me about the missing key and the lingerie you found there, so I've been driving by her studio, making a point to go each time I'm out." Aidy clicked on her computer, which brought up grainy images of Amanda using her key to get into the building.

I growled. "She stole that from you."

"She did," Cassia said. "But that's not the worst part. We don't know what she did inside because I don't have cameras in there, but we do know this…"

Aidy pressed a button and another still shot showed Amanda with Marcus. The next image showed them in a clinch, the final one of them kissing.

"That's at your studio?" I asked.

Cassia nodded. "And Bridget and I staked out Marcus's offices today. Amanda was there."

I grunted. "While that sucks, it's not conclusive that Amanda is in any way involved in the vandalism."

Cassia took a deep breath. "I heard them talking today."

Fear sliced through my chest. "Do I want to know how you were able to get close enough to do that?"

Cassia shook her head. "But I will say that holding a plie underneath Marcus's window for that long was killer on my thighs." She waved a hand. "But that's not the important part. They were discussing how to get back at you—make you hurt, Nico. And me, too. Amanda's upset that my mom and Martin were at my grand opening. So, I think they're going to mess up my studio."

I clutched Cassia, not wanting her to go through the frustration and loss associated with vandalism. Our job sites were just that—jobs—except for Cassia's. Because her studio mattered to her, it mattered, deeply, to me.

Cassia licked her lower lip. "Marcus wants to hurt you financially and Amanda wants to wound me both financially and emotionally."

"Why did you start looking into Amanda?" I asked. Even I, knowing how devious the woman could be, never considered this level of petty nastiness.

Aidy tugged at her lower lip before she shrugged. "Marcus's eyes that time at The Mac—they promised retribution." She shivered. "And, once Amanda showed up, I just felt like she was involved. The bra's what clinched that for me, but it still took me weeks to get those pictures of the two of them together. So, it's not like I'm very good at sleuthing."

"I'd say you did a damn fine job." My eyes narrowed and my lips compressed. "But I don't want either of you doing anything unsafe. Marcus has already bullied you and expressed interest in assaulting you, Aidy. He's dangerous."

She shivered, her hands coming up to rub her biceps. "Agreed. And I think Amanda's egging him on."

"She doesn't like doing the actual dirty work. She'd rather he be to blame. At least, that's always been her MO up until now," Cassia said.

I bit my tongue to add that Amanda didn't like doing much except taking credit. While that might be true, the thought wasn't productive. We needed to focus on actionable steps, not get caught up in bitterness.

"What do we do?" I asked.

Aidy tugged at her lip again. "I think we head over to the studio tonight and catch them in the act."

I shook my head. "I don't want you near Marcus."

"And I don't want to be near him. But we need evidence. The police can't do anything without it, and they don't seem interested in investigating the leads we've tried to give them."

I scowled. "Because all we've had is a hunch."

"Not anymore. Now we have a connection and the conversation Cassia overheard."

I wanted to tell Cassia and Aidy *no*. I wanted them safe. But they'd found the piece of information that could stop the damages to our job sites, reputations, and our finances—they were already part of this and were looping me in as soon as they had solid evidence. I closed my eyes, needing a minute to absorb the emotions swirling through me. My fear would have to take a back seat in this case.

"What do you propose?" I asked as I refocused on my lover and my sister.

Aidy's eyes sparkled. "Oh, I'm so glad you asked. How do you feel about spending some quality time with your significant other tonight?"

I nodded. "I'm always down to spend time with Cassia."

Aidy pulled up a new screen—a slide that detailed times and interactions.

"Ryder and I will sit out at the hotel project. You and Cassia can take Marcus's offices, and Knox and Em will watch the studio."

"What about the rest of our projects?" I asked.

"Well, if we feel the need, we can expand our scope, but I thought these were the most important places to start."

My sister's organization impressed me but her investment, not just in finding the vandals, but in my relationship with Cassia, humbled me.

"You think Knox and Emmaline will help out?" I asked.

"They're already on board."

I shot her a thankful look and she smiled.

I hugged Cassia to my chest, my heart thumping wildly. "If you're sure…"

"It's the only way to catch her, Nico. It has to be red-handed."

Chapter Thirty-Six
Nico

"Nico? Knox. Em's on the line with the police. Marcus and Amanda just broke into the studio."

I gripped the back of my neck with my free hand as I swore.

Aidy and Cassia had been correct. Amanda's pettiness extended to intentionally hurting her sister. I closed my eyes, hoping that the damage done to the space wasn't too great. That was the part of the plan I'd hated—Cassia's insistence that Amanda be caught in the act.

While I understood the rationale, and the need for evidence against her, I hated that we'd have to fix whatever Amanda broke. And of course Amanda would go for the theater, something Cassia had that was hers.

Fuck. *Fuck.* Cassia was going to be devastated.

"We're on our way," I said, pushing words past my stiff lips. I looked down at Cassia, who was curled into my side. "You heard that?"

"Yes."

"Cassia, the damage..." I closed my eyes, pressed my thumbs against them.

"Could be extensive," she said. She squeezed my fingers. "It's okay, Nico. I really do have a plan for this."

My heart twisted. "But you insisted on paying me for the renovations, so it's not like you have extra cash lying around to re-do the space again—"

"You're right. But, please, trust me." She touched my cheek. I let my forehead fall against hers.

I started the ignition, trying to ignore my sweaty palms and the noxious anxiety coiled through my guts. The next hour would test Cassia and me in ways I wasn't sure we were ready to be tested. We rode toward the studio in silence.

The officer at the studio's door dipped his head at us as I led Cassia toward it. We'd run into each other at the last two construction sites.

"How bad is it?" I asked.

Cassia slipped her hand into mine, squeezing gently. I was too nervous to return the gesture, but I was sure she noted how my hand shook.

The officer grimaced. "Not good. But on the plus side, thanks to the call, we caught a couple of people inside. One bolted out the back and we haven't caught him yet, but the woman—she claims she had the right to be there—that she left the door open and the guy attacked her. She also claims she's the one who called us."

I scoffed.

"Nico!"

I turned at the sound of my name, blocking Cassia from Amanda's view. Amanda struggled to get out of the officer's hold. Her hair was a mess and she was wearing sweatpants and a thin sweatshirt covered in tiny flecks of spray paint. I'd never seen her in such an outfit before.

My stomach pitched. The interior was going to be bad. I

inhaled sharply to keep from hyperventilating.

"Nico!" She lunged toward me, her hands positioned behind her back in what I assumed were handcuffs. Her brown eyes rolled wildly, like a spooked horse's. "You *have* to help me. Tell them Cassia's my sister. Tell them I have every right to be in that building."

"What are you doing here?" I snapped. I had to play my part. "Cassia never gave you a key."

Amanda's eyes widened as she seemed to realize I wasn't going to rescue her as she'd hoped. "I…"

"Cassia *never* gave you a key, but one went missing. Months ago, straight from Cassia's purse the night she saw you."

Amanda sputtered.

"Did you steal the key from Cassia's purse?"

"*I didn't have anywhere else to go*," Amanda screamed. She ducked her head, shoulders shaking. "I'm broke, thanks to that civil suit. My mother isn't speaking to me, Lowell booted me, and my own grandmother cut me out of her will. My sister refused to let me live with her—"

"Maybe because you screwed her over when you screwed her boyfriend?" I asked, sarcasm lashing through each word.

Amanda turned to face me, mascara smeared down her cheeks. "Get off your high horse. It's not like you even care about Cassia— you're just using her to get back at me for dumping you."

My entire body tightened. *Don't let Cassia believe that. Please. Don't let her.*

I shook my head and opened my mouth to say more when I heard Cassia ask in a tremulous voice, "Am I interrupting?"

"We lived together," Amanda said, stepping closer to her

sister. "He asked me to *marry* him, did you know that? I bet he
never told you—"

Cassia kept her eyes locked on mine, letting me see the hurt
building, building, building…crashing across her features. She
swallowed and locked everything down. "Actually, he did." Her
voice was raw. "He was honest with me about that."

"Thank you," I said, as I lifted my hand to trail my fingertips
along Cassia's cheek. "I wish I could change that part of my past.
I hate how it hurts you, but you have to know that Amanda never
mattered to me like *you* do."

"Oh, sure, beat on the woman who's already down on her
luck," Amanda griped.

"Shut up," I growled, finally turning away from Cassia. "Can
you *not* think about yourself for five seconds?"

Cassia turned to the first officer we'd met, who still stood
beside her. "As you heard, my sister stole the key to this building and has been living here without my permission. What's the
charge for that?"

Clearly uncomfortable with the situation, the cop stuttered
out something about breaking and entering, criminal trespassing,
and possibly larceny.

Amanda's eyes widened further and her jaw dropped.
"You cannot be serious!" she shrieked. "I never would have
stayed here if you'd been a good sister and let me live in Grammy's house!"

Cassia tipped her head to the side. Her jaw trembled, and I
ran my hand down her back, desperate to soothe her.

"And my studio wouldn't be spray painted, and I don't even

know what else if you hadn't taken what wasn't yours. *Again*." Cassia turned to the officer. "Emmaline Wright called in about Amanda entering the premises. We should have a video to corroborate it."

Cassia waved Knox and Em over, both of whom stood, lips pressed tight, anger emanating from them as they clutched their phones. Knox gave a small shake of his head. I wasn't sure if that meant the cops had taken too long to get there or the damage was going to be difficult and expensive to fix. Didn't much matter which it was—they were basically one and the same. I groaned, running my fingers over my face.

"Will you please get her out of here?" Cassia asked, her voice hard. "I'll fill out whatever I need to against her later. Right now, I need to catalog the damage to my business."

"Please come with me, miss," the officer said to Amanda.

"Why should I?" she asked, petulance dripping from her tone. "You just want to put me in jail or whatever."

The officer raised an eyebrow, his expression stern. "Let's go. *Now*."

He led Amanda away, ignoring her griping and crying and arguing.

"Cassia…" I didn't know what to say, how to ease whatever came next. Part of me wanted to lash out, but releasing my anger on my siblings and Cassia wouldn't make any of us feel better. I reached forward to cup her cheek and she sighed, closing her eyes as she leaned into my touch. "This *sucks*." I held her tighter. Still completely unsure what to do, what to say, I dropped my cheek against her hair. "I love you."

"I needed to hear that." She let her fingers drift across my chest, over my heart. "I *really* needed to hear that. Okay. Let's go see the newest damage my sister wrought."

Chapter Thirty-Seven
Cassia

The destruction to the classrooms was minimal. The theater, though, was in shambles. I continued to stare blankly at the mess that used to be my beautiful stage. My chest felt like it had been sliced by a dull knife as my eyes filled with tears. "I poured so much effort and money into this dream and she ruined it."

Because my sister would never love me. I drew a deep breath. She would never love anyone but herself. She didn't want me to be happy.

"No, Cassia. No. It's postponed, but I'll do everything I can to make it right," Nico said. His hand was still in mine. I could feel him shaking. He kept glancing at me, concern stamped on his handsome features.

I let out one more long, painful breath. "I'm sorry we didn't officially connect Amanda to Marcus," I said.

"*That's* what you're worried about?" he asked, incredulous.

I nodded. "Yes, of course. I know the vandalism has been cutting deeply into your profits, Nico. I don't want you to hurt—"

He cupped my cheeks and kissed me. It was long, slow, an owning, a sharing, a thank you, all rolled up into one. When he pulled back, he settled his forehead against mine.

"Don't do that, please. Don't try to shoulder my problems. I can't stand for you to accept that burden."

"But—"

"*Please*, Cassia."

I sighed. "I'll do my best."

"That…nutter dumped ammonia on the floors," Knox said as he strode toward us. He shot me a look of apology, but I just shrugged. He wasn't wrong about my sister. In fact, his insult was much nicer than the words I was currently screaming in my head.

"Amanda knew it would do the most damage." Nico's eyes turned to the mess, desolation creeping into them. "Do you think it's salvageable?"

My heart was hollow. "It's probably not. Amanda wanted to ensure I'd need to sell Grammy's house in order to pay for the repairs here."

"What? Why?"

I raised my eyebrows. He was riled, clearly angry—at my expense.

"Because Amanda didn't get the house. Therefore, I shouldn't have it."

He drew back, confusion tugging at his brows. "That literally makes no sense."

"Welcome to being related to Amanda."

"Fuck. I almost married that disaster," he whispered. He shuddered. "I'm really, really glad I didn't. And I'm so sorry you had to grow up with her."

Warmth exploded in my chest and I flung my arms around him, and I grinned.

In this moment, I saw that, he, too, had placed me at the top of his priorities. He didn't just love me—he truly, deeply aspired to make me happy and fulfilled.

He grunted. "You realize your good mood doesn't make sense, right? I mean, I'm glad to see you smile, but I'm not letting you sell your house just so you can pay me to fix this mess—"

"Then you sell your house and move in with me."

"We definitely need to talk about that statement." He scrubbed his palms over his face before peering at his brother. "Let's see what we can hook up to spray it off."

They strode away, faces set with determination while Aidy, Emmaline and Bridget, who'd shown up moments before, led me toward the back of the space. I blinked, trying to focus on the now.

"Anyone have a trash bag?" I asked.

Emmaline snorted as we all stared at the stuffing exploding out of the ripped seats. So much for the beautiful new upholstery. "We need a Dumpster. But we can't touch anything until the police give us the all-clear."

That hollow feeling tried to expand. My shoulders slid down and forward and I struggled to swallow. I managed a wan smile. "Thank you for being here tonight. Aidy, Bridget. I know it was hard to get away from your family."

"You're family, sweetie." Bridget's expression shifted, became more determined. "Now, let's find out what we can do tonight and what has to wait for the police."

Aidy's husband, Ryder, strode over. "Not much tonight," he said on a sigh, obviously having heard Bridget's comment. "But we'll all be back tomorrow, first thing."

Nico and Knox joined our group, feet and shoes damp, expressions grim. "They let us hose off the ammonia because it's a fire hazard, but we can't touch anything else," Nico said. "We used a couple of the big brooms still in the back to push as much of the water off the wood as possible. I don't like that it's on the concrete back there, but it's better than on the wood. Here's to hoping that was enough."

"We have to give statements to the police," Knox said.

"We'll call in some help, Cassia," Aidy said. "Things might get crazy for a few days, but we'll get this right."

Chapter Thirty-Eight
Nico

Cassia's phone rang as we drove home from the police station. She glanced at the screen, her eyes widening.

"It's my mom."

"Well, answer it," I said.

"Yes, I know Amanda's been arrested," she said to her mother instead of a greeting. "I'm the one who pressed charges."

I wished I could hear what her mother said in response. Cassia must have realized this because she put the phone on speaker.

"...the type of behavior Martin warned me about," Cassia's mother said, her tone tremulous. "I'm so sorry she destroyed your studio, Cassia. That's unconscionable. Martin and I will be in Providence first thing tomorrow to help you sort this out."

"You don't have...you know what, *thank you*, Mom." Cassia sighed. "I could use the help."

"You're welcome, sweetie. I don't want you to worry. Amanda needs to face the consequences for her behavior."

Cassia's face slackened in shock but then she set her jaw and nodded. "I agree."

After a few more minutes of chatting, Cassia hung up. "This is *totally* surreal. All of it. I can't believe Amanda would intentionally hurt me like this. But I also can."

We were at her house, so I pulled into the driveway. I'd wanted to bring her to my place to snuggle with Fred, but I knew she needed to be around her familiar things. So, for tonight, Knox and Emmaline were ensuring Fred's care, and I was taking care of my girl.

I exited the truck, coming around. By the time I got there, she was already standing outside , so I shut the door and caged her against its side.

"Did you mean it? About moving in together?"

She nodded, her eyes never leaving my face. "I did."

I cupped the back of her neck and kissed her. Our tongues tangled in a warm, wet dance.

I rested my forehead to hers.

"That means everything to me, Cassia."

She leaned in and said, "Then, I'm glad I asked."

My lips curved against hers. "Not as glad as I am." I brushed my lips across hers. I could *feel* my eyes dancing, features blooming with joy. "I like being asked important things by you."

She raised an eyebrow. "Makes you feel special."

"Very." I held her so that I felt her heart thump against my chest.

She gripped my shirt. "Will you take me to bed?"

"I'll take you to *our* bed."

At her perplexed look, I swept her into my arms. "Any bed we're in is ours. We're a team. Got it?"

She nodded. "I think I do."

I pressed kiss after kiss to Cassia's lips, breasts, belly, murmuring over and over how much I loved her, how we'd work through this setback, how much I loved that she'd asked me to move in with her. She reached the first peak fast and the second, and when we came together it had a dreamlike quality. I held her close, needing to feel her reassuring warmth and the soft puff of her breath on my skin even as I slid into sleep.

I woke the next morning before sunrise to find Cassia missing from the bed. The sheets were cold on her side. I rose, padding naked down the hall, and found her in the kitchen. She sat in the dim light, a mug of half-drunk coffee next to her. The tip of her nose and her eyes were red-rimmed.

I scraped another chair closer to hers. Once settled in it, I wrapped my arm around her shoulder. With a deep sigh, she dropped her head to rest against my chest. "Today's going to suck."

"It might." I lifted her mug and took a sip, shuddering at the chilled beverage. "You've been up a while."

"I woke up, wondering if I was being petty toward Amanda. I don't want to be—I don't want to be anything like her, Nico. Maybe I shouldn't press charges. Maybe this is just me, being mad she had you first."

I smoothed her hair. "Do you know what I thought when I first realized you were related to Amanda?"

She shook her head but remained snuggled against me. Her limbs were loose and her breathing slow and steady. I took those as good signs.

"Well, the very first thought I had about you was that you were gorgeous. I liked how quick you were with a comeback. Once I got over the shock that you were related to Amanda, I realized that you shone with this inner light Amanda never had. The more I got to know you, the more I realized that Amanda had to be the way she was to make sure you gathered up all the goodness, all the kindness, all the light she strode past, unseeing, or tossed aside because she was too self-absorbed to understand the gifts she'd been offered."

Cassia tipped her head back. I was glad to see her eyes were clear, her expression open. "I'm not sure I believe in good being the flip side of bad. Look at you and your siblings. You had a rough patch, but for the most part, you're all thoughtful, caring, decent people."

I raised my eyebrow. "Just decent?"

"You took a while to get there."

I sighed, shaking my head. "You're right. I treated you terribly, and I hate that. But it's what I expected from someone related to Amanda. The fact that you're so much better than her boggles my mind. So, I get that you're worried about doing right by her now. That's why I know you will—because you care, Cassia. Even now, when she clearly doesn't deserve your kindness."

I kissed her. She wrapped her arms around my neck and straddled me, which led to some hot chair sex that I'd be thinking about all day.

* * *

We arrived at the studio before seven, and I wasn't surprised to find Hazel and my crew already at work clearing out the damage to the theater. I still couldn't believe how much they'd managed to destroy.

Hazel pushed a few strands of hair from her eyelashes as she jumped down from the stage area.

"I think it's salvageable, but it's going to take a deep sanding. It's a good thing you sprayed that crap off before leaving last night." Hazel's eyes blazed. "I mean, who messes up a place for kids? Especially those with special needs?"

I zipped my lips, deciding that was rhetorical.

Hazel grumbled and huffed, going on about how important these classes were. "I maybe could have been a ballerina if we'd had someone like Cassia teaching," she said.

I bumped Hazel's shoulder with my elbow. "You're the right height."

"Stop with the short jokes," she said, then laughed. "I'm too short to be a dancer. Good thing I like electricity."

"And managing the crew. Thanks for getting them all here," I said. My eyes turned misty.

Hazel scoffed. "Like the ladies didn't jump at the chance to help out your lady. You know they love Cassia. She's the chocolate bringer."

"I hope you like her for more than just the snacks," I said, frowning.

"She keeps your grumpy butt in check." Hazel raised an eyebrow.

"Good point. I like that, too. Let's take a look," I said. Hazel led me toward the steps, and we climbed the stage.

I glared at the strips of peeling finish, annoyed all over again with Amanda's actions. The floor had been gorgeous—smoother than satin and perfect. We'd taken such care to get it right the first time, and here we were fixing it, again.

"Makes you want to take a swing at her knee with a ball-peen, doesn't it?" Hazel said.

"Can we get a sander in here today?" I asked.

The floor would be the biggest fix, but it was doable. Aidy and Emmaline had calls out for theater seats, which would require another round of upholstering. All in all, we'd manage to get it put back together soon. Definitely before Cassia's first recital.

I clenched my fists, wishing the guy who'd fled the scene last night had been found. I knew, deep in my gut, it was Marcus. And he deserved to pay for the problems he'd wrought these past few months just as much as Amanda did.

"Aidy's making a list of equipment. She works wonders," Hazel replied.

"That she does."

My phone rang and I stepped out the back door, lifting my chin at Knox in greeting as he and Emmaline slid past me.

"Mr. Wright? This is Mark Ilston, the detective with Providence PD. I wanted to let you know that we've brought in Marcus Jones for questioning."

"You have?" *Finally.*

"Yes. Ms. Krantz implicated him as a co-conspirator during our questioning last night."

"Did she now?"

"Ms. Krantz has been very forthcoming with evidence. She stated Mr. Jones dumped the chemicals on the stage and ripped up the seats in the theater."

Satisfaction settled over me like a thick parka in the middle of a snowstorm. I doubted that fact—I was sure Amanda damaged the property, too, but I was pleased Marcus would be charged with some of the crimes. That ought to further hurt his business. Maybe the foreman Clark would buy out what was left of the contracts. Or I would. Yeah, I'd purchase those and expand my business, making sure Hazel and my crew had first dibs on the projects they wanted to complete.

"Good."

"We'll keep you posted, but I thought you'd want to know Mr. Jones is the prime suspect for the vandalism of your job sites."

"Yes, I did want to know. Thank you."

We said our goodbyes and I stood there, eyes closed for one more moment. It was over. Wright Construction was going to pull through and be better—stronger—for these past few months of strife. Just as Cassia and I would be.

Chapter Thirty-Nine
Cassia

"I'm so sorry this happened," Aidy said as she joined me where I stood toward the back of the theater. I wasn't much good with power tools, and I couldn't bear to look at the words my sister painted on the mirrors down the hall. I needed to find a project, but, at the moment, I couldn't seem to move into action.

It looked worse in the light of day. But the sheer number of people helping to erase it lifted my battered heart.

Her baby, Lilia, was strapped to her chest, the baby's gummy smile broken by four teeth and lots of drool. Her hair had thickened, turning a shade or two darker than Aidy's gorgeous strawberry blond. But the baby had the same dimples and big, innocent eyes. She cooed as she kicked her feet and waved her arms.

"Out! Up!"

"She wants you to hold her," Aidy said, apology lacing her tone.

"You know I love babies."

"Yeah, but this isn't really the time, is it?" Aidy looked around, consternation settling over her expression. "Sorry, I couldn't get a sitter today, so I'm not here for the actual tear out. I'm going to the specialty stores to see what I can buy as soon as Nico gives me a list."

She squeezed my hand, ignoring Lilia's soft but steadily increasing whines.

My lower lip quivered and tears spilled over my lashes.

"Thank you," I whispered. I scrubbed my hand over my cheek. "I can't believe you all showed up. I don't…" A sob bubbled up.

"Hey, this is what families do," Aidy said gently. "We take care of each other. It'll get worse looking but then, it'll get better—*be* better. One step at a time, okay?"

"Yeah. Sure." There was so much to do just to make the spaces functional for classes on Monday. I rubbed my palm over my forehead.

"It's overwhelming to take in," Bridget said, frowning. Simon stood behind her, concern tugging at his expression.

"Need a seat, love?" he asked.

A hysterical laugh bubbled out of me. "There aren't any. At least none you can sit in, which is terrible and ironic and…and… my *sister* destroyed my theater." I threw my arms around Bridget. She gripped me tightly, patting my back, and letting me get out this first storm of emotion.

Once I calmed, I accepted the tissue Simon handed me. Bridget swiped the hair that stuck to my cheeks back.

"Better?" she asked.

I shrugged. "I could use a drink."

Bridget nodded, eyes solemn. "No doubt. But maybe after we get a bit done around here, okay?"

The damaged space was now teeming with people, not just the Wrights or even Nico's all-female crew. There were my two dance instructors, who'd I'd emailed last night. Simon and Bridget and even their son Brendan were there, determined to help. The rest of the women from our yoga classes, who Hazel was leading off toward the classrooms to get the horrible graffiti off the mirrors. Everyone assured me that it might take some time and elbow grease, but was a rather easy fix.

And my mother and Martin, both standing out in their well-tailored tops and slacks. I hadn't seen Martin in tennis shoes, ever, and he didn't disappoint today—his wingtips were shiny and terribly out of place.

"We're not much for the manual part of the labor," he murmured, after giving me a long hug. "So, your mother and I decided to bankroll the costs."

"And provide meals for the crew," Mom piped up.

I leaned back in and hugged her again. "That's really generous of you."

She squeezed me even tighter. "You deserve the best, Cassia. We'll make sure you have it."

I nibbled my lip as my emotions waged. Finally, I said, "I'm going to press charges against Amanda."

Mom swallowed hard even as she nodded, her mouth pinched. "She deserves to pay for her behavior. You have my full support to press those charges."

I hadn't really expected Mom to stick to her comments when Amanda needed a place to stay, but Martin had. Now, though, hearing her tell me she supported my decision, caused some of the brittleness in my chest to ease. We might not ever have an easy relationship, but we were working toward a good, healthy one.

A moment later, Nico caught sight of me and jumped off the

stage. He made his way toward me. I met him in the middle and wrapped my arms around his waist.

"My mom said they want to pay the costs for fixing this," I mumbled against his chest.

He stiffened, so I leaned back and looked up at him. "I want to fix the studio for you," he said.

"You are. You called in your whole crew to work here today."

He dropped his forehead to mine. "You don't get it. How much I care, how much I want to give you the world."

I focused solely on him and touched his cheek. "You have. This…" I waved my hand. "This is a hiccup."

The strained lines faded from his expression and determination set in. "Damn straight. Your theater is going to be even better now."

"I know." I grinned. "I can literally feel all the love in the space. How could it not be perfect?"

Epilogue
Cassia

Tears blurred my vision as the thunderous applause reached me. I stepped out from stage left, my knees trembling as shouts erupted, then stomping feet. I glanced down, noting Aidy, Ryder, Knox, and Emmaline beaming up at me. Simon shoved his fingers between his lips and wolf-whistled. Bridget laughed as she clapped, but it was Nico's warm brown eyes that captured my attention. His pride washed over me in a warm cascade, like sinking into a hot tub in winter.

We'd created this—he and I. We'd managed to bring my vision to life. I raised my hand with a flourish, turning toward the dancers. Their small faces beamed with excitement and happiness as they bowed at the waist as I'd taught them. Sabine wheeled forward, accepting the giant bouquet that Nico handed her, then she pushed her wheelchair toward me. I covered my mouth with my hands, shaking my head.

"Without you, we wouldn't have a recital. You believed in us, Miss Cassia."

I bent down and pressed my cheek to hers, leaving both wet. I wasn't sure whose tears caused the dampness, and it didn't matter. Sure, this goal had taken longer to achieve than I wanted. Many times, I'd wanted to quit. But the joy on the kids' faces, the pride from their families as they continued to cheer, made it all worthwhile.

Every bit of the worry, the setbacks, the second-guessing. We'd created a beautiful ballet. Limited movement hadn't limited my students.

That's what I'd changed my studio's name to after we finished the repairs to the theater: Limitless.

Nico hung back, nearby but out of the way as I accepted more hugs, flowers, and congratulations from the parents and students. Finally, the theater emptied and I turned to face him.

"Thank you," I murmured, walking straight into his open arms, my own wrapping tight around his waist.

"This was all you, Cassia."

I leaned back and met his eyes. The turbulence that used to be so visible had eased behind the happy sheen of contentment. He cupped my cheek and I nuzzled into him.

"You continue to amaze me. You fought so hard for what you wanted."

"So did you," I whispered. "You're the most in-demand contractor in the state. Everyone knows you're the best—and honest."

"So, you're okay with being married to a construction worker?"

I blinked as Nico lowered to his knee. He took a deep breath, his hands trembling as he dug in his shirt pocket and pulled out a beautiful yellow-gold ring with a large solitaire. The diamond sparkled, and I appreciated each glint and refraction of light.

"Will you, Cassia? Will you marry me? Will you let me slide this ring on your finger so that everyone knows you're mine?"

I nodded and he pushed the ring on my finger. His fingers

caressed it, then my finger, as he rose.

"Aidy and Em went with me to pick it out," he said, his voice hesitant. "*I* picked it, not them, but I wanted to make sure you'd like it. If you don't, we can always go back and find something you'd rather wear."

I couldn't stand his babbling. Nico didn't babble. He was steady, solid, often immovable. That caused tension at times, but it also stabilized his family when they needed it—when I needed it.

I slid up onto my toes—not quite to *en pointe* because, while my foot was healed, I still didn't push myself to my former limits—and captured his lips with mine. He deepened the kiss, holding me with gentle hands, making sure I knew I was treasured, loved, desired.

I pulled back, breathless.

"I'm honored to marry you, Nico." I slipped my hand in his and headed toward the door of the theater. I turned off the multiple sets of lights and locked the door. I faced him again, my happiness bubbling through me.

"I have a confession," I said, once we were both in his pickup. I settled back against the plush comfort of the heated seats.

"What's that?" he asked, turning to look at me.

"I like you better in jeans than in suits."

His face flashed from shadow to light as he pulled through the empty lot. "You're sure? I mean, Martin's a bit put out I'm not back at Wright and Associates. He feels like that career path makes me a better catch."

"Martin's just jealous you can use a jigsaw. And, anyway, you're still an owner in that firm *and* always will be whether you exercise your rights or not. On top of that, I understand the importance of using your hands. You've seen my feet—they're the tools of my trade. How could I not respect each nick, bruise, busted nail, that comes about as you create something new or restore something to its former glory?"

His smile grew with each passing moment. "I needed to hear that," he said.

He'd reached our driveway—ours now, not mine.

"You want to live here, right?" I blurted.

He turned off the engine and faced me. His warm palms slid over my cheekbones, soothing me. I gripped his wrists. His gaze dropped to my engagement ring before returning to my eyes.

"I want to live where you're happiest. That's here. I'll sell my house. But…"

"But?"

"I do want to make some changes to the master bath."

I giggled. "Add a tub?"

"And a decent-sized closet. I hate cramming my suits—"

"Jeans. You wear jeans now."

He kissed the tip of my nose. "Not to client meetings."

"Okay. You're right. You need more space for your suits."

"Don't forget your dresses. I *love* your dresses."

My smile widened. "And my dresses."

"And lingerie. I'm building you an entire set of drawers for frilly, sexy-as-fuck undergarments."

Heat pooled low in my belly. "I like how you think," I whispered. My breath stuttered. "A whole set of drawers just for my unmentionables?"

"Oh, I'm mentioning them. I fucking love your ruffle-butt panties, Cassia. They're a wet dream come to life."

He shifted away from me, "Don't touch that handle. I'm going to pluck you out of this truck, carry you inside and lay you out on our bed. I'm going to feast on every inch of you before I come deep inside your body."

And he did just that as sweat bloomed across my sensitized skin as I screamed his name.

"Going to keep you doing that," he panted. "For years."

My toes curled as he pumped his hips, my core clenching with each thrust. By the time he orgasmed, I'd come twice. Yeah, I could definitely, *definitely* look forward to each of Nico's promises.

ACKNOWLEDGMENTS

Jen and Kate, you two are the best—the best!—beta readers EVAH. I'm so, so humbled by your enthusiasm for my work (and sexy heroes!)as well as the time and effort you put into making the story as special as you two are. Thank you for your help. I truly never, ever want to publish without you. You rock!!!

Sarah, I still can't believe the mess that happened with this manuscript. Thank you for your insights and your expertise. And I'm so, so sorry Microsoft and Apple quit talking during this project. That was not fun.

Chris, it doesn't matter what I throw at you, you simply say, "yes, I'll help you." I'm so lucky to have you in my life. Thank you for your support. It means more to me than I can express.

Charity, I can't imagine how much harder publishing would be without you and Mantha cheering me on. I so appreciate you both. I hope I don't ask too much of you. And, yes, the hockey book is coming. Soon.

ABOUT THE AUTHOR

USA Today bestseller Alexa Padgett's books have garnered accolades from prestigious organizations, including *Kirkus Reviews*, National Indie Excellence Awards, and *Publishers Weekly*.

Alexa spent a good part of her youth traveling. From Budapest to Belize, Calgary to Coober Pedy, she soaked in the myriad smells, sounds, and feels of these gorgeous places, wishing she could live in them all—at least for a while. And she does in her books.

She lives in New Mexico with her husband, children, and Great Pyrenees pup, Ash. When not writing, schlepping, or volunteering, she can be found in her tiny kitchen, channeling her inner Barefoot Contessa.

Magnetic Medic
Book One in The Wright Family Series

A sexy, new brother's best friend romance from USA Today bestselling author Alexa Padgett.

He's my brother's childhood friend. I'm pregnant with another man's baby. What a time to fall in love…

Coming home seemed like a good idea at the time. My ex-fiancé split, I was almost done with my master's degree, and I was already working at the family architecture firm. When I move in next door to pediatrician Ryder Mackay, I'm not expecting the connection—or the passion in his eyes that I feel deep in my soul. He's the best doctor for my baby, but he's *not* the guy I need.

Still, the way Ryder looks snuggling my puppy—and my infant daughter—to his rock-hard chest makes me wish this sexy, smart, compassionate man was *mine*.

Maybe, it's pregnancy hormones. Or…maybe *this* magnetic pull is ***forever***.

Arrogant Architect
Book Two in The Wright Family Series

A sexy, new forbidden romance from USA Today bestselling author Alexa Padgett.

For the first time in years, I want…

I want Knox Wright. My best friend's brother, my boss…the man who breaks my still-shattered heart.

Knox was a college hockey legend and, now, he's one of the most successful architects in decades. I was the new hire whose desperate need to move on from that night drove me to succeed.

I never should have accepted the position, not once I looked into Knox Wright's eyes and felt the heat deep in my belly… but I did. Because Knox makes me feel alive. And as I fall under Knox's spell, our relationship turns intense and deep…and secret. When our affair runs the risk of being exposed, I ***face a far more intimate betrayal than I ever expected***.

Deep in the Heart
Book One in the Austin After Dark Series

Remembering the music I love… lets me forget a past that haunts me.

I thought realizing my dream of country music stardom would chase away the ghosts of the past. But I didn't understand how the horrors of war would imprint their scars on my heart… leaving me a shadow of the man I used to be.

Haunted by regret, filled with a rage I can't control, I destroy my favorite guitar.

A J. Olsen original. The only instrument that allows my fingers to caress my music into creation.

Now, I need a new one, and in order to get it fast, I have to work with her—Jenna. She stirs something deep inside me. Something I haven't felt in years.

When I stare into her breathtaking eyes for the first time, I see struggles that echo my own. The kind of torment that colors a woman's soul. But I'm drawn to her—I just can't stay away.

As our emotions start to blossom, creating a magic that rivals the music, Jenna's dangerous ex reappears to play a reckless game. Between his lust for revenge and the unreasonable demands of my record label, we can't catch our big break.

And unless we can both heal the wounds that remain shuttered in darkness, we'll lose *everything*.

Broken Rose of Texas
Book Two in the Austin After Dark Series

She aches to make her own music...but I burn for the perfect revenge.

I never thought a late-night Scrabble game would blow my world apart. Moving letters. Keeping score. Swapping words and desire with a mystery woman who makes me fantasize of things I have no right thinking.

I can't get involved.

I won't.

Despite the pull of her lush curves and the electric crackle of chemistry between us, I resist. Regan has aroused something far more desirable than revenge, and I can't get sidetracked by my pesky feelings. Not now that my plot to pay back my best friend's heartbreaking betrayal finally snaps into place, and I vowed years ago to see it to the bitter end.

And that means no emotional entanglements. *Even* for her.

Until a vindictive smear campaign aimed at Regan is followed by a bombshell that blows my world apart...and our fragile relationship crumbles.

Unless we both go all in and trust each other, we won't be able to pick up the pieces.

Austin By Morning
Book Three in the Austin After Dark Series

From the moment I see Kate Grace, I can't wait to find out if what they say about redheads is true... Not only are her wild ringlets entrancing, she's sweet and sassy, with slower, sexier curves than a Texas back road.

Too bad she's also country music star Camden Grace's baby sister. Camden holds my chance at a comeback in his hands, and he doesn't want me—or my bad attitude—anywhere near Kate.

I don't have time for all these thoughts about Kate, anyway. I must focus on my son's future. I failed him once, but I'll do anything to prove how much I love him. *Anything.*

Even if that means giving up my dreams of a music career and another chance to kiss Kate's soft, luscious lips. Ike comes first. I promised, and my word is my vow. I'll *never*, ever break it.

Yes, even if I have to give up a chance to work with the biggest names in the music industry, and even if I have to walk away from the only woman I'll ever love...

Sweet Solace

Book One of the Seattle Sound Series

Betrayal Broke Them Once...

We can't afford to indulge in this attraction, but our connection burns too brightly to ignore.

Dahlia

My husband was the second man who betrayed my trust when he left me alone to raise my daughter. Asher was the first. I found solace from both in my novels, writing about the hero I'd lost. But in those bestselling books, Asher-I mean my hero-didn't shatter my heart the way he had in real life.

Asher

There were so many things I couldn't say to Dahlia when she was seventeen. But I've never forgotten the only girl I ever loved. My voice and song-writing talent made me a star. Fame extracted its price. Now I have another chance—the chance to restore her faith in love. The chance to find it for myself.

I'm not letting Dahlia go now that I have her in my arms again.

Between Breaths
Book Two of the Seattle Sound Series
2017 Readers' Favorite award winner and
The Romance Reviews Top Pick.

Hold You Close
Book Three of the Seattle Sound Series

Many Sounds Of Silence
Book Four of the Seattle Sound Series

From The First
Book Five of the Seattle Sound Series

Striker's Waltz
Book Six of the Seattle Sound Series

When We Fell Down
Book Seven of the Seattle Sound Series

A Moonlit Serenade
Book Eight of the Seattle Sound Series

Midnight Dance:
Book Nine of the Seattle Sound Series
A Seattle Sound Series Romantic Suspense Spin-off

Moonshine Eyes
A Seattle Sound Series novella, Book 10

Until The Moon Ends

BOOK ONE IN THE BLUSHING MOON TRILOGY

KITT LYNN

LUPO PUBLISHING

ISBN: 978-1-958309-06-3 (Paperback v2)

ISBN: 978-1-7377356-1-8 (eBook)

For more information visit www.kittlynn.com

V 2.0

Creature Guide

Ashmores - Tree-like creatures that live in the trees in the Faeland forests. They are vicious and deadly, often attacking anyone that dares to touch their trees.

Bethir - Large lizard-like animal with jagged teeth and a scaly body. Mostly found in the cursed lands they tend to eat the dead or dying.

Elves - Like wolf-shifter they see themselves as superior to other creatures. Targon elves have green skin and tend to be more violent than their brothers, the Azzuro elves.

Kunzite crystals - Found throughout Havre. Pinkish crystals that grow in clusters underground and make everything from the land to the air very cold. But they also give the area a calm and serene atmosphere that anyone walking through them will find relaxing.

Luminite crystals - Bright yellow crystals that emit a tremendous amount of heat. They are harvested and used frequently within villages.

Mountain Men - (aka, Rock men of Gygax). Men made of rocks that live within the mountains throughout Havre. Their origin is believed to be the result of witches and fairy folk that bewitched the mountains to aide during the Great War with the humans.

Rouges - Werewolves with no allegiance to a pack or village. Frequently they are banished from villages, and branded to prevent them from entering any other were-colonies. The actual brand varies based on the village, but traditionally a "R" on the neck or somewhere visible.

Siren - Magical humanoid creatures. They can shape-shift into other beings and tend to eat more challenging beings like alphas and elves. They are considered very dangerous.

Were-wrack - Mutated shorebirds that feast on the dead and dying in the dry lands. They have been known to be bold enough to even attack a pack of alphas.

The Enchanted Lands of Havre

To see a larger version of the map of Havre, visit www. kittlynn.com.

For Bo.

And Bryce. Always for Bryce.

The Omega Origins

IT HAS BEEN SAID that hundreds of years ago, werewolves roamed free, dominating the land and all other creatures. Men that easily slipped into their wolf form at will, they were savage and unforgiving. Destroying anything that crossed their paths.

Humans kept their distance from the unhinged animals until a young noblewoman found herself lost in the enchanted forests. A werewolf found her and they fell in love, and she birthed twins. The first beta and omega.

The omega, unable to transform into its wolf, was a gentle creature, fragile and obedient. The perfect mate for the more aggressive alpha werewolf.

The beta had more beastly characteristics but could only shift into its wolf when the Moon hung at her fullest. Calm and smart, the child held the perfect balance between human and wolf.

The birth was hard and bloody, and the noblewoman died, her body unable to handle the horrors of birthing beasts. But she left behind a new breed of weres, creating a fragile balance between wolf and man.

The villages grew, bursting with werewolves of all kinds:

Alphas, betas, and omegas. And soon, the humans realized the wolves finally had a weakness. Their mates, the omegas.

The humans attacked, slaughtering hundreds of the gentle creatures, pushing werewolves almost to the point of extinction until the fairylands came to their rescue. Fighting the humans and staving them off. Reclaiming Havre as a land of enhancement and magic.

To protect their kind from any further attacks, the alphas locked their omegas away in villages fortified with large border walls, shutting them in and keeping them safe.

Prologue

HAXA COULD SMELL the old wolf just outside her home. His guards' heavy footsteps thumped against the soft forest floor and echoed throughout the floorboards of her home. They were purposely loud, alerting the surrounding wildlife of his presence and forcing her attention from her book. *How could a predator be so damn noisy?*

"Witch!" a loud voice boomed.

Slowly, she closed her book and set it softly on the table, closing her eyes for a moment before getting up. She wrapped her shawl more tightly around her to help ward off the cold winter air as she made her way across the room.

"Witch!"

With great reluctance, Haxa peeked outside. Her home was set deep inside an old, cracked willow tree, making it well hidden and secluded. She wasn't fond of visitors.

An old wolf dressed as a man stood before her. He was much older than the last time she saw him. His black, thinning hair showed a shiny circle of dark skin along the crown, and his beard was filled with silver streaks of grey. It contrasted wildly with his deep, brown skin.

His attire for such a trip was needlessly extravagant. Dark blue, flowing robes, a thick leather overcoat, and a golden breastplate. He rested a massive hand on a heavy sword slung from his hip with polished rocks and gems encrusted in the handle.

It was all a little much.

"Ares," she nodded from the safety of her hovel, tucking her frizzy blonde hair behind her ear.

"I need to speak with you," the Alpha leered at her, his teeth flashing violently despite the smile on his face.

Haxa opened the door and glanced around at the dozen or so guards flanked at his sides. She wondered what could be so important that bringing such a show of force was necessary. She briefly thought of denying him entry, but it was pointless. He'd order his guards to break down her door, destroy her home, and so much worse.

"Only you," she said firmly. "No guards."

"That will not do, and you know it," Ares said, a low growl rolling off his chest to convey his displeasure.

"I think putting myself in the presence of one werewolf is more than enough. Besides, what can one weak woman do to an Alpha such as yourself?"

Ares' chest swelled, and he smirked. "Only us," he nodded.

She opened her door, allowing the wolf entry. His anxious guards shifted and glared at her, a few even baring their teeth. Smiling, she reveled in the faint scent of fear that drifted through the air around them. She might have posed no physical threat to the werewolves before her, but her powers were undeniable even to them.

"Witch," the old wolf said, dropping his heavy body into her chair. It creaked under his weight. "I have found myself in need of your services."

He grabbed her book off the table and thumbed his dirty

4

fingers through the pages, leaning his head slightly to the side as he squinted at the writing.

"What can I do for the King of Wolves?" she said, placing her hand on the book and gently pulling it from his hands.

"A prophecy —"

"I don't do prophecies," she interrupted. "That kind of magic isn't for me."

The wolf shifted, and his eyes narrowed. It was interesting the things that would drive such beasts over the edge. For creatures so obsessed with control and dominance, a simple interrupted thought had the effect of a sword through their gut. It always brought a smile to her face.

"I don't give a shit what magic is for you," he seethed. "I need a reading."

"I simply don't do that. Witches pull themselves to certain spells, and those never have —"

The old wolf launched himself across the room and grabbed her by the throat, pulling her feet off the floor. Desperate for air, she swiped at his face and dragged her nails over his hands, drawing blood. The skin across her face became hot and tight as she gasped over and over again. Her chest constricted and tears blurred her vision.

"I didn't ask what you could or couldn't do, Witch!" he roared in her face, spit flying out around his growing fangs. His eyes glowed a deep red, like the blood trickling down his arm. "I suggest you pull out one of those books you love so much and figure it the fuck out."

He released her, letting her smack hard into the floorboards. She reached protectively for the raw skin of her throat as she gagged and coughed, sucking in as much air as her lungs would allow.

Pushing herself into the wall, she used it to help her stand on shaking knees. Ares settled back into the chair, a look of pure satisfaction on his face. She wanted to claw his eyes out.

"What exactly is it you need?" she spat, her voice rough. She brushed a hand through her greying, blonde locks, moving it out of her face.

"The Magpie came across a prophecy, and his interpretation is...lacking."

He reached into his robes, pulling out a piece of rolled-up parchment and tossing it on the table toward her. She inched forward, watching the old wolf carefully. A smile tugged at the corner of his lips.

"So you just want to know if this is a warning?" she asked.

"Is it a warning? The Magpie seemed to think it was a foretelling."

"Nothing is ever really foretold. Everyone has a choice as to what —"

"Just fucking read it!" Ares growled, slamming his fist into the table.

Haxa repressed the urge to roll her eyes. The angry impulses of wolves truly made her wonder how they had survived this long.

She stared at the text on the weathered piece of paper, reading and re-reading it. The old wolf shifted, growing restless, and she could feel his sharp gaze on her.

"Get on with it!" he roared.

"It's a foretelling of how to preserve your empire," she said calmly, settling the parchment on the table.

Ares stood up, the Alpha practically shaking with anticipation

"How?" he asked.

"Kill the children marked by the blushing moon."

Revenge is a confession of pain.
—Latin Proverb

The Madra Village

Tzidal

I STOOD at the edge of the field, watching the old woman sob and wail, her arms coated in a thick layer of sticky blood. She rocked to and fro on her knees, her hair falling from its tight bun and into her tear-streaked face. My wolf whimpered as she ghosted her trembling hands over the shredded remains of her only son.

An alpha, one of the village guards, wrapped an arm around the poor woman's middle and pulled her away. Her painful screams sliced through the cool afternoon breeze, making my heart ache.

It was awful watching her grief unfold, but I couldn't pull my eyes away. The devastation pulsating off the poor woman was too consuming. It demanded my attention.

The hair along the back of my neck prickled as I sensed a familiar presence at my shoulder. I didn't bother to turn when my closest friend hooked an arm around my waist.

"It's just so horrible," Sade whispered. "I can't believe something like this could happen here."

Nodding, I watched the guards carry away the grieving mother, and tossed a few blankets over the mangled corpse.

Even though Madra was one of the larger werewolf colonies, our village was still very safe compared to many surrounding cities. Alphas settled fights and grudges outside the border. Things like this just didn't happen within our walls.

"Omegas!" the guard yelled, causing me to jump. "You don't need to see this. Go on."

"He's right, Tzidal," Sade whispered, pulling at my waist. "We don't need to see this."

I nodded silently in agreement and allowed my friend to lead me away, lacing our fingers together. My mind raced as she babbled and gossiped the entire way into the village square, but I couldn't focus on her words. I knew the dead wolf. Sander was a massive alpha. Tall and strong. He was known for showing off the scars on his chest and back that he obtained from one of his many fights beyond the border walls. He would not have gone down easy.

What disturbed me the most was the state of his remains. Whoever did this had no compassion in their bones. Sander's body held deep, ripping gashes all over his torso and legs. The kind of wounds that injured but didn't kill. His attacker clearly played with the alpha, inflicting a disturbing amount of pain before ending his life.

Why would anyone do something like that?

I tried blocking out my disturbing thoughts and focusing on Sade's excited chatter, but fear swirled within me, making my wolf whimper and skin itch.

When I woke this morning, I could feel a change in the air, thinking it must mean my mate would be returning home soon. Now I wondered if that feeling could have had an angrier meaning. Something dark had found its way into the village, and it scared me to think what might happen if it wasn't found.

I shook my head and tried focusing on better things. My mate, Korban, was due home any day now. He left only a month after our mating to patrol the northern border for the King, something our younger alphas did every year. The passing months without him had been agony. I was a mated omega living with my parents, who frequently forgot I was no longer a pup. I had lingered at the border gates almost every day since the trees started to bud, waiting for him to return.

Sade and I made our way into the village square and toward the stores. The merchant house was bustling. Lots of gruff wolves were stocking up on supplies and growling aggressively at one another when certain items appeared to be in short supply. The whole space was crowded, loud, and hot.

I waited patiently at the counter for Sade to pick up supplies for her father. I hoped she would be quick so we could get out to the gates. I wanted to ask the scouts if they had received any sign of our alphas returning.

"I heard the Winter Wolves are returning today," Sade cooed as if reading my mind. She leaned over the counter, kicking her feet playfully behind her.

"What? When did you hear that? How could you not tell me?"

"My brother heard it from the scouts last night when he was on duty. They should be home some time today or tomorrow."

My heart raced with anticipation at the thought of seeing Korban's beautiful face and feeling his large hands roam all over my body. I closed my eyes, lost in the memory of our last night together. I unconsciously pressed my thighs together, and my spine tingled. Forcing my eyes back open, I was suddenly all too aware of the throng of hostile wolves rushing around me.

"Good afternoon, Beta Dane," Sade said as she slid a list of supplies across the counter to the old wolf.

"Omega Sade, Omega Tzidal," he nodded. "How are you today?"

"Excellent, thank you," Sade chirped.

I nodded politely and glanced sideways at a large alpha a few feet from me. He dragged his gaze up and down my body, licking his lips slowly. I flipped my long, dark hair over my shoulder, showing off the prominent mating bite just beneath my ear. The alpha eyed it hard before turning on his heel and stomping away.

"The store seems filled with a lot of unknown wolves today," I said, watching the alpha disappear out the front door.

"I take it you didn't hear about Sander?" Dane asked.

"We saw him," Sade whispered, her brown eyes deep and sad.

The beta gasped. "They said it was just awful." His face was grim, but a slight trace of excitement flashed in his eyes at discussing such savage news. "Apparently, his sister found him completely ripped to pieces. The Pack Alpha is offering a hefty reward for the capture of whoever did it. He doesn't like the idea of wolves capable of such things taking up residence in his village."

"It's true," I said. "His attackers weren't kind at all."

"They think it might have been rogues." Dane gave me a pointed look. "So don't stray far from the village center," he warned.

We both nodded quickly. Omegas barely had the strength to fight off a cold, let alone savage alphas.

"Are you excited for Korban to return?" he asked.

"Oh yes," I smiled at the beta's sudden turn in topic. He

obviously wasn't too eager to return to his other, more aggressive clients.

"I heard they might be returning any minute."

"Really?!" I yelled, bouncing on the balls of my feet.

Not waiting for the beta to respond, I ducked through the crowd, right out the door, and straight to the front of the village, abandoning Sade behind me. I reached the large iron gate and looked around, biting my bottom lip in anticipation.

Alphas stomped through the streets, some hauling large kills. A few betas tended to their shops, haggling with customers and shouting out prices to attract onlookers. But the most excitement came from a group of omegas. They were bunched together in a tight group next to the gate, chatting and giggling. A few spoke excitedly with the aggravated guards. The energy they radiated was a bit overwhelming.

I sat along the side of the road, several paces down, deciding to keep my distance. I had nothing against the other omegas in my pack, but the attention they were receiving from some of the nearby wolves made me uneasy. There were too many strangers wandering around the market today.

The day wore on, and it felt like I had been waiting for hours. The crowd around me began to thin as dusk settled. Alphas ventured out of the gates to patrol the surrounding area, taking most of the noise with them. The majority of the shops closed for the day, and most of the omegas gave up on waiting for their mates and shuffled off to their homes.

I picked up a few small pebbles at my feet and tossed them, watching them bounce and skip across the dirt. Once there were no more within reach, I huffed loudly and rubbed the back of my neck.

"Patience, my sweet omega."

I spun around. "Korban!" I squealed, flinging myself into his open arms and wrapping my legs around his waist. "You're home," I whispered, burying my nose deep into his neck.

"I'm home," he laughed. The vibrations radiating off his chest caused my toes to curl.

He looked good. He looked tired but so very good. His sandy hair had gotten so much longer, and his complexion was very dark. The last several months of roaming without shelter had left his perfect skin an even deeper shade that called to my wolf. I wanted desperately to lick every inch of him to see if he tasted the same.

Korban tangled a hand in my dark, wavy tresses and gently pulled my head back. He looked over my face, and his eyes settled on my lips. He smiled briefly before plunging into my mouth.

He tasted so sweet.

To The Meadow

Tzidal

KORBAN'S HANDS groped my thighs and roamed to squeeze the curve of my backside. "Let's go home," he growled against my mouth.

"No!" I urged. "My parents..." I gave him a coy smile.

Since Korban had to leave so soon after our bonding, we had decided to wait to claim our own home until after he returned. Being a newly mated couple and forced to keep our hands to ourselves when my parents were home was more than challenging. So instead, we frequently ran off to the edge of the boundary line to talk and make love.

It was the perfect place. A small open meadow with a few willow trees that had grown together to create a curtain of privacy from any onlookers, not that there ever were any. No one liked to venture that far away from the village square, especially after dusk.

"Shall we go to our spot?" Korban asked, kissing along my neck and sucking softly over his mating bite.

"Yes," I gasped, arousal already pooling between my legs.

Korban chuckled, deep and rough in his chest. *My goodness, how I missed him.*

He sat me on my feet and grabbed my hand, pulling me through the village. I giggled and sprinted after him. My alpha was barely running while I was almost out of breath. His long, toned legs carried him quickly past the shops and cabins and into the tree line. He held my hand firmly in his, pulling me gently behind him.

We raced through the brush and past the wooden bridge over the stream and deep into the woods, stopping when we finally caught sight of the cluster of willows. It was just as it had been last fall. Only now, the buds on the low-hanging branches were green, signaling a new beginning. The last of the day's sunlight settled beyond the trees, leaving only the glow of the Moon to illuminate everything around us.

I leaned into my mate as he pulled me off my feet. He kissed my neck, carrying me behind the curtain of branches. In the center of the willows, a soft patch of grass grew, lush and thick. A sweet patch of land, perfect for secret passions.

"I missed you," Korban moaned against my lips, running his thumb along my jaw.

"Show me," I whispered.

He pressed me firmly to the ground, kissing me hard. His lips were soft and warm, urgent and strong. I kissed him back, moaning against his hungry mouth. Our tongues moved together, twisting and teasing as one.

Korban sucked on my bottom lip, letting it snap gently back into place. Then he groaned low in his throat, taking in my flushed appearance.

He quickly pulled off his shirt and pants before turning his attention back to me. He took hold of my waist and dragged his hands up my stomach, pushing my shirt up with them. He stopped just beneath my breasts and paused, giving me a wicked smile.

"Stop teasing me, you brute," I giggled.

He let out a quick chuckle before pulling my shirt off, exposing my breasts. He hummed as he looked over my naked flesh. My body tingled from the look in his eyes, and I pressed my thighs together.

Moving back over me, he sucked at the mating bite on my neck. His firm chest pressed into mine, his skin soft and warm. "Fuck, you smell so good," he moaned. "So fucking good."

His deep voice vibrated against my skin, making my core burn with desire. I reached out, clutching his shoulders, needing him closer. I ran my fingers over the broad expanse of his back, gasping when he pushed his hard length against my hip.

"Korban, please," I begged, my breath quickening by the second.

It had been so long. Too long. I needed to feel him. Smell him. Make love to him. *Now.*

My core pulsed with anticipation as he slowly pulled my pants down my legs. His hands grazed over my skin, goose-bumps dancing in the wake of his touch. He moved over me and pushed his face into my stomach, inhaling deeply. Sucking long and hard just beneath my belly button, he left a dark, beautiful mark.

"I need you," I moaned as he sucked each one of my nipples into his mouth. I gasped and threaded my fingers through his hair, then tugged at the roots, pulling a deep rumble from his throat. The vibrations washed over my skin, and my core tightened in anticipation.

Sensing my desperation, Korban grabbed my thighs and wrapped my ankles around his waist. He slid his cock between

17

my wet folds, moving the tip up and down and circling my clit before sinking deep into my hungry body.

"Ugh!" I gasped, loving the way he stretched me open. "Please, alpha. Please...move."

He quickly obliged, rolling his hips forward. I moaned, long and wild. I could feel every inch of him deep inside, throbbing hard with each snap of his hips. The coil in my stomach began to twist and burn, my eyes watering at the intense sensations he was pulling out of me.

"Oh, baby," he growled in my ear.

He palmed my breast and pulled at my nipple, rolling the sensitive bud between his fingers. I yelled out and arched my back as his thrusts picked up, becoming more forceful and frantic. My core tightened, dangerously close to shattering apart into a million pieces.

"Korban...ugh...please, faster," I gasped, fisting his hair.

He growled and began pounding into me harder and faster. My body tensed, and thighs shook as I unraveled around his thick girth. The ripples of my orgasm rushed through my body, prickling along my spine and curling my toes.

My mate growled loud and deep above me as his hips hammered against my spiraling body. His thrusts became sloppy and he suddenly stilled, his knot taking hold. A gush of fluid pushed out around his throbbing member as he filled me deep to bursting.

"Fuck," he mumbled, throwing his head back, his eyes closed. "Fuck, I missed you."

His chest fell gently on top of me, and he pushed his nose into my throat. My flesh pulsed in the aftermath of my orgasm as he sucked and nosed at my sweaty skin. I had longed for this, his smell, his taste, his passion.

Korban kissed me, moving our mouths together in perfect

unison, softly tasting and feeling me. When he pulled back, all I could see was love.

He gently bumped his nose into mine, then moved down to trace my lips with his tongue, inhaling my breath.

"Never leave me again." I wrapped my arms around his neck and kissed him softly.

I couldn't help the tears that clung to my eyelashes. It was so stupid wanting to cry, but my whole body thrummed with emotion. My mate was home, and I would get to feel his arms around me every night from this moment forward. Bliss was the only way I could describe how I felt right now.

My alpha held me gently as we waited for his knot to go down, whispering and kissing in the moonlight.

"I got you something," he mumbled against my skin.

"Yeah?"

He slowly pushed himself up, causing me to wince when he was finally able to pull out of me. I was already too empty, wanting to feel him fill my body again.

He grabbed his pants and pulled something small out of the pocket. "We traveled near the sea while we were up north, and we met a neighboring pack. Some of their omegas prepared gifts for us as a thank you for protecting the borders." He grabbed my wrist. "They call this a pearl."

He opened his hand and placed a small blue stone tied to a leather strap into my palm. I looked at it carefully. It didn't resemble any of the rocks we had here. It looked soft, and it shimmered. It was beautiful.

"I love it," I beamed.

He smiled wide and took the beautiful gift from my hand. He placed the leather strap around my wrist and tied it securely in place. I moved my wrist around, watching the moonlight reflect off the surface of the pearl.

"Tzidal," he sighed, pressing his hand to my cheek. "I love —" He stopped abruptly, his body going tense.

Crouching down, he swept his eyes back and forth over the tree line in the distance. My body tensed, and I reflexively curled into myself. I didn't know what he heard or smelled, alpha's senses were so much better than omega's, but whatever it was, it wasn't good.

"Put your clothes on," he said in a firm, hushed tone.

I pulled my shirt over my head and moved to reach for my pants but froze when Korban shifted into his wolf. His bones glided into place and dark fur rippled across his body. The towering grey werewolf that stood before me sniffed the air and growled.

His aggressive stance scared me. Whoever he sensed, it wasn't a member of our pack. It was a stranger, possibly someone dangerous. I moved back against one of the willows, my heart racing.

All I could think about was Sander and Beta Dane's words from this morning.

His sister found him completely ripped to pieces.

Within The Willows

~

Tzidal

A SHARP HOWL echoed across the dark sky, making me shiver. I wrapped my arms around myself, feeling exposed and vulnerable. My pants laid on the ground not far from me, but I didn't move for them. Too frightened of the things I couldn't see.

Korban's wolf slowly stalked past the willow's long branches and out into the meadow. Yellow eyes flashed, watching us just beyond the tree line. I whipped my head around frantically, trying to find anyone else watching us. A second pair of eyes flashed in the dark, and I whimpered.

The meadow, while small, was completely open outside of the cluster of willows. There was nowhere to go or hide. If I ran, they'd see me.

Two dark creatures stalked their way out of the forest, teeth bared and hackles raised. The thick smell of alpha over-whelmed my senses, overpowering Korban's soft scent and causing my wolf to panic. I laid on my stomach and peeked up over the grass, desperate to be as small as possible.

One of the wolves, black and massive, lunged at Korban, but he quickly dodged the attack and sprinted straight for a tan wolf. He jumped onto her back and bit down, causing her to yip and flail.

I covered my head with my arms and cried, fear coursing through my veins, making me tremble uncontrollably. The pounding in my ears thundered so loudly I could barely hear the growls and snarls of the wolves ripping into one another. My nose caught the faint scent of blood and my breath caught in my throat. An image of Korban lying injured or lame barreled through my mind, but I shook my head, trying to shove it away.

He'd be able to fight them off. Right?

A yip pierced the air, and a painful tremor ran down my spine. I whimpered, desperately wanting to crawl into myself and disappear.

"What do we have here?"

I spun, then kicked away from the large, naked alpha. He towered over me, his bulging muscles flexing with each step.

"Hello there, little omega." An evil grin spread across his pale face, his bloody teeth on full display. "Why don't you come with me?"

I jumped up and ran as fast as I could through the branches and out into the meadow. The evil wolf's laughter rang in my ears as I pumped my legs, willing myself to be faster. I could see the other two unknown wolves in the distance but not Korban. He was gone...just gone.

I stopped abruptly, not sure where to go. There was no way I could outmaneuver three alphas. *Where was Korban? Where was my mate?* Tears poured down my cheeks as I sunk to my knees. Fear completely overtaking me.

"Come on," the evil alpha said as he walked up behind me and grabbed me by the hair.

He dragged me toward the other two wolves. I swiped at the hand tangled in my hair as I repeatedly tried to stand, but he walked too fast, jerking my body with each step. My small frame skidded across the uneven ground, and my hip smacked into a sizable rock before he finally came to a stop in front of the other wolves.

I let out a quick sob. The fierce, tan wolf pinned Korban's wolf form to the ground beneath her. She snarled at me, then sunk her claws deeper in his back, making Korban's wolf yip. Blood poured freely from his shoulder, and he had deep claw marks down his side.

"Korban!" I yelled out. I tried to move toward him, but the evil alpha held my hair firm in his grip, jerking me back.

A black wolf moved toward me and shifted, rolling his shoulders as he straightened up. He stopped just in front of me and studied my face for a moment. He was tall and muscular, a typical alpha, with rich, dark skin and soft green eyes. His eyes didn't feel right for the torment he was inflicting. It was almost like he felt bad.

"Let her go," he said firmly to the alpha holding me hostage.

"Shift, or we'll kill her," the evil alpha spat at Korban, completely ignoring the order and holding me firmly in place.

A soft whine left Korban's throat before he melted back into his human. The tan wolf removed her claws, pulling a deep grunt of pain from my mate, then stepped away. Korban laid motionless for a moment, breathing slowly and deeply. He was covered in sweat and grunted hard when he finally pushed himself up onto his knees.

"What the fuck do you want?" Korban demanded.

"You're marked, aren't you?" the black wolf asked, running a hand through his short, thick black hair.

"Marked?" Korban squared his shoulders, head held back.

I couldn't help but think how strong he looked, even overpowered and forced to his knees. But it wouldn't take him long to regain the upper hand. I knew my mate. All he needed was one good opening, and he'd kill them all. He would protect me.

"Show us your fucking mark," the evil alpha roared, snapping my head as he spoke. A whine left my lips as tears rolled down my cheeks once more.

"Hida!" the black wolf yelled. "She's not our target. There's no need to hurt her."

"You're too fucking soft, Byriel," he sneered.

The evil alpha, Hida, removed his fingers from my hair and grabbed my chin. He urged me forward and forced me to look directly at Korban. "Show us your mark, or you'll watch her die. Do not make us look for it," he warned.

"I'm not marked," Korban growled, his teeth bared. I could see his claws growing as he glared at the wolf touching me.

Hida's scent rolled off of him in aggressive waves as he held my face tight, my jaw clenching from the force. I choked on the air around me as his thick odor filled my nose and throat. Holding my breath, I longed for a single gasp of Korban's sweet scent or a quick breeze of fresh air. Just anything other than the putrid smell coating my lungs.

"A red mark. Circular," Byriel said calmly.

Korban eyed the wolf hard before returning his gaze to me. "Let her go first."

"I promise no harm will come to her," Byriel said.

Hida snorted and pressed himself against my back. I could feel his growing member pressed against my back as he pushed his nose into my hair and inhaled deeply.

"I don't know, Byriel." His voice was loud, right in my ear. "She smells too fucking good just to let go. Maybe he'd be more willing to show us what we want if I just bent her over and fucked her corpse right in front of him."

"Don't you fucking touch her!" Korban roared his fangs on full display. I could see him fighting with his wolf, desperate to shift and attack.

"Show us your mark, and we'll leave her be," Byriel said. "On my honor, she won't be hurt."

Korban looked at him, then gazed back at me. Tears flowed freely down my face and neck, and I struggled to breathe. I wasn't sure how much longer I could remain standing on my shaking legs.

"You know how this is going to end," Byriel said softly to Korban. "Spare your mate. Show us your mark."

Korban smiled brokenly at me, then nodded slowly, keeping his eyes on mine, before raising his arm. He ran a hand over the birthmark next to his ribcage. It was small and circular and had a faded red hue, resembling a crescent Moon.

"Heath!" Byriel roared, making me wince.

Hida grinned and moaned against the side of my neck, my fear feeding into his rage.

The rogue wolves all turned to the tree line as a young beta walked forward. He was short and dirty. At first glance, he appeared to be a child, but the closer he got, the more clearly I could see his age. Bruises and scratches covered his face and arms, and my heart broke for the frightened wolf. The beta stopped and stared at Byriel, awaiting his command.

Byriel pointed a finger at Korban's side. He nodded, then slowly walked over and inspected my mate's mark.

Korban locked eyes with me and nodded again. He looked so defeated. It confused and frightened me, but I wasn't stupid. These wolves weren't going to let us go. Whatever Korban's mark meant to them, it wasn't good.

Again my mind drifted to Sander, and his tortured remains in the tall grass. And I suddenly remembered. He also had a small, red birthmark, but it was on his upper shoulder tucked next to a particularly bold scar that he loved telling wild stories about.

I couldn't keep my body from shaking as the realization of what was about to happen washed over me.

"It's okay, my love," Korban whispered. "It's okay."

The beta turned to Byriel and nodded. Before anyone could speak, the tan wolf behind Korban launched herself at him and sank her teeth deep into his throat.

A horrific scream ripped its way out of me as the tan wolf clamped her jaws down tight and jerked backward, taking a massive chunk of Korban's flesh with her.

Hida slammed my body hard onto the ground and pinned my arms above my head with one hand. "You do smell very good," he grunted in my ear before licking over my neck and up the side of my face.

I screamed and kicked, desperate to escape. I could hear a muffled struggle, gurgling blood, and pained gasps.

I needed to get to my mate. I needed to help Korban.

It's okay, it's okay, it's okay.

I kept repeating his words over and over in my mind as the disgusting wolf above me ran his dirty hand under my shirt and up my side, cupping my breast.

It's okay, it's okay, it's okay.

"Get the fuck off of her." A voice in the distance boomed over the sound of pained growling and tearing flesh.

The evil alpha ignored the voice and thrust forward, pushing against my exposed hips. I shuddered, swallowing convulsively against the rising bile in my throat, and tried to squeeze my legs together.

Hida grunted and thrusted again, but I jerked my hips as hard as I could, forcing him to rut against my thigh. He roared and grabbed me by the hair, slamming my head into the ground.

Pain pounded within my skull, and I was suddenly dizzy and sick, my brain disconnected from my body. I could still see the alpha above me, but I couldn't feel anything. My vision domed to just Hida's twisted, angry face sneering and laughing at me.

A bloody smile split across his face, and his lips moved as if he were speaking, but no sound reached my ears. His body moved backward slightly, and I braced herself, knowing full well he was going to thrust into me. When, suddenly, he disappeared.

Confused, I slowly sat up, my body swayed, and nausea swam in my stomach. I looked behind me. The black wolf, Byriel, was straddling Hida and slamming his fist repeatedly into the alpha's face.

Byriel jerked his head up by his hair and roared long and hard. "I think she's suffered enough, don't you?" he roared.

My senses slowly returned, and my mind cleared a bit. "Korban!" I crawled toward his body.

He was alive. Please be alive. You have to be alive!

My mate laid at an awkward angle against the ground, his feet slightly tucked beneath him, completely motionless on his back.

"Kor, Korban?" My voice cracked when he didn't move.

I ran a shaky hand over the large gash along his stomach as I settled next to his head. His throat was torn wide open. Blood pulsed and seeped over his neck and chest, dripping onto the ground. I could see the muscles in his throat move and jerk as he tried swallowing and speaking, air bubbling out and covering his skin with frothy blood. His wide, frightened eyes darted all around, not seeming to focus on anything.

"It's okay," I whispered, struggling to see through my tears. "It's okay. It's okay." It was the only thing I could think to say. I hovered a shaking hand over the wound, not sure what to do. I wanted to press on it, but it was so massive. *Would it even matter?*

The blood gushing out of his body slowly lessened and then stopped. His labored breath rattled before his face relaxed, and his eyes became dull and unfocused.

"No, no, no, no, no," I sobbed. "Please, no!" I flung myself over his chest, blood smearing over my face and arms.

"Where the fuck is Heath?" someone asked.

"Fuck."

"Let's go. That's an order." There was a pause. "Leave her."

I pushed myself away from Korban's body and watched the alphas retreat into the forest. Rage stole all my fear, and I jumped up, running at full speed toward them. I barreled straight for the nearest wolf and shoved Hida as hard as I could. He barely moved.

He turned, laughing as I launched myself at him again, driving my whole body into his. I bounced off and fell hard onto the ground. Again, he didn't move.

Hida laughed as I pulled myself up. He took a few steps toward me and slapped me once across the face, flinging me back into the dirt.

"Stupid, fucking omega," he laughed, walking off into the trees.

I pushed myself off the ground and began to chase the three as they shifted into their werewolves. I reached the edge of the trees but fell to my knees as a deep, sharp pain lanced my body, radiating from my mating bite. My heart seized in my chest, and I suddenly couldn't breathe. My veins were on fire, and my vision blurred, going fuzzy around the edges.

I clutched my chest, gasping for air.

Then everything went black.

The Edge Of The Meadow

Tzidal

IT WAS ALMOST dawn when I finally opened my eyes. The sky beyond the trees was just turning a soft blue, bleeding into pink and orange as the sun rose. My face was pressed firmly into the grass, and I was cold from being exposed to the night air. I moved my arms and pushed myself up, finding the simple movement made my muscles ache and stomach tense.

A dull ache radiated from my mating bite, and I pressed my hand to it, wincing. The flesh was tender and raw even though I had no actual wound.

Scanning the dark forest in front of me, I squinted into the distance. It was quiet. No footsteps. No voices. Just the wind rustling the leaves.

I looked around the meadow, and my eyes fell to Korban's lifeless body. I had hoped it had been a dream.

I forced my feet forward, my heart constricting with fresh pain. It was like walking through mud, my body fighting every step. I knelt next to my mate's face and cupped his cheek. He was cold, and his skin felt...off. Leaning down, I tried to scent him but only the smell of death hung in the air. I closed my eyes to feel him through our mating bond but felt nothing.

He was gone.

Just gone.

I had never felt so alone.

Hot, silent tears rolled down my cheeks, and I sniffled softly, trying to force myself back on my feet. I wanted my mother. I wanted to be held and loved like a pup again, safe in my mom's arms.

The rustling sound of movement startled me, and I ducked quickly behind Korban's body. Terror flooded my veins, and I trembled as I forced my eyes as wide as they could physically go to take in the meadow around me.

A twig broke, then a soft grunt pulled my attention to a large tree just at the edge of the meadow. I held my breath as the beta from last night dropped down from its branches. He landed hard, smacking his bottom.

"Fuck," he grunted.

He stood and arched his back, stretching his arms and legs. Then he stepped closer to the tree, a slight hitch in his step, and urinated on the ground.

My muscles relaxed a bit and I sat up, just watching him.

The beta moaned loudly and rested his head against the bark.

His behavior was so odd. Like he had no fear of being caught, not by the rogues that attacked us last night nor by my pack, who were undoubtedly looking for my mate and me by now.

The longer I sat there, the angrier I got. While he might not have been the one that killed Korban, he was the reason my alpha was dead. With a simple nod of his head, the tan she-wolf ripped Korban's throat out.

No, this beta was a murderer. He killed my mate.

Rage thrummed through my body as he casually strolled into the forest. I stood tall, my legs stronger and my body firm with purpose, and I quietly followed him.

Allowing myself one more painful glance, I looked back at Korban's face one more time, wishing I could kiss his lips and feel his warmth. I gave myself a brief moment, then I turned away from him and slipped into the trees.

⎯⎯⎯

THE BETA WALKED SO DAMN SLOWLY all day. He'd stop and sit on the rocks, throw stones in puddles, and pick flowers that crossed his path. It was as if he were taking a leisurely stroll with a friend, and it enraged me to no end. Every butterfly he gazed at and every pebble he tossed made me want to pluck his eyes out like berries and force him to eat them.

Staying several paces behind him, I spent all day ducking behind trees and bushes each time he stopped. He was so careless. Not once sniffing the air or scanning for threats. I started to think that he was messing with me. *He had to know I was following him. Otherwise, why would he act in such a purposefully carefree manner?*

I let out a silent yawn, and leaned against a massive rock overlooking a valley. The heat of the day had come and gone, and the beta was enjoying an afternoon of climbing trees and singing to himself. I winced as his pitch got higher and more strained with each branch he climbed.

My fingers grazed over the pearl tied to my wrist as I breathed deeply, struggling to contain my grief. My feet hurt, and I was overly exposed in only a shirt that barely covered my bottom, but I was determined to continue to follow him. My rage demanded it.

Every time I wanted to turn around and run to my

31

parent's house, I'd think of Korban. Of his smile, his scent, his lips. I would never feel those lips on me ever again. The thought consumed me, and instead of crying, I just kept walking. But now, waiting on that damn beta to stop goofing around, I was forced to sit and think of what would become of me. I was a mated omega with no mate. I had no pups to raise, no real skill to offer. To my pack, I had no worth.

I was startled when I realized I could no longer hear the beta. He wasn't singing, and I couldn't hear his loud, lazy footsteps. I slowly turned on my knees and moved to peek over the top of the rock but instantly froze.

The beta suddenly stepped into view only a few feet away from me. His eyes were on the valley, and he seemed oblivious to my presence. I held my breath, too scared to move. While he was somewhat small for a beta, he was still bigger and stronger than me. And I suddenly felt so stupid for following him.

The beta took a deep breath and stretched his arms over his head before turning to leave. His gaze fell to me as he moved, and he jumped in surprise. We both remained completely still, just staring at each other for the longest moment.

Then he ran.

I briefly considered running in the opposite direction, but my feet made the choice for me, sprinting after him.

I ran at full speed, leaves and twigs smacking me in the face and arms. My legs ached, and my lungs pinched at my ribs, but I refused to stop. I had spent all day following the simpleton, and I would be damned if I lost him now. But then suddenly, in the blink of an eye, he was gone. I stopped and stared into the distance where he just was. I held my side, gasping for breath, trying to figure out how he managed to vanish into thin air.

"You've got to be kidding me," I panted.

"Hello?" a strained, breathless voice called out.

I instinctively crouched down, scanning all around me. My wolf let out a weak growl, infuriated with me for putting us in this situation.

"Is someone there?" the voice yelled.

I stood straight up and craned my neck around the wooded area. I could hear grunting and panting as if someone was in a fight, but there was no movement of any kind.

"Hello?" I answered back, still seeing nothing but trees and brush.

"Can you, can you help me?" the voice grunted, out of breath.

I inched forward but stopped short when I came upon a pit wedged between two large spruces. It was only as wide as I was tall, but it was deep. Very deep. The beta stood at the bottom, his head busted and bleeding. He was breathing heavily and trying to claw his way up the slippery walls.

I wanted to scream down at him. Call him a murderer, rip him to pieces, and watch him die. But I took a deep breath, knowing the pathetic wolf wasn't my main target. I wanted those alphas. I wanted Hida.

"You! Omega!" he shouted. "Help me!"

I snorted. "How?"

He huffed, looking at his surroundings. The walls of the hole were packed smooth with red clay, firm and unyielding. There appeared to be no footholds, and none of the surrounding trees had branches that could dip low enough to help him up.

"Just...try to reach for me!" he yelled up, annoyed. He wiped the blood running down the side of his face, then held his hand out as if expecting me to take it.

"Are you simple?" I asked, sitting down at the pit's edge to catch my breath. I looked over the pathetic creature sitting and pouting at the bottom of the hole.

"What?" he scoffed. "Don't you dare speak to me like that,

omega! I may be at a disadvantage here, but I still outrank you to our kind. Now help me up!" he yelled. I was sure he meant it to sound fierce, but his demand came out as just plain whiny.

"So you're not simple?"

"Why the fuck would you ask that?" He looked so angry. I enjoyed it.

"Well, you keep insisting I grab your hand, but there's no possible way that I'd be able to reach you." He fumed at my words, letting out a snort of a growl. "Plus, I've been following you all day, but you haven't noticed. Where are you going?"

"Help me out of here, and I'll tell you."

"Tell me how to find the wolves that killed my mate, and I'll help you out of there."

The beta rocked on the balls of his feet, staring up at me. I could see his anger building. Frustrated, he launched himself at the dirt wall again, clawing at the smooth surface. But he found no purchase and slid back down onto his knees, defeated.

He stood up again, face red and panting hard. "Help me out of here, and I will spare your life, omega. Do nothing, and I will kill you!"

"Well, that's tempting," I said, picking at the blades of grass around me and lazily tossing them into the pit. "How do I find the wolves that killed my mate?"

"What are you going to do? Huh? You look to be just a pup. You're no match for them," he said with a sudden edge of sincerity.

"Let me worry about that." I didn't want to admit that I had no idea what I would do when I found them. "Just tell me where they are."

"Vaesen," he sighed. "They'll be heading back to Vaesen. But that kind of journey is too far for a pup like you. I know you're angry your mate is dead, but let it go. Go home."

"Why did my mate deserve to die?"

"Orders from the King and his eldest, Strayton. She's a horrible, bloodthirsty bitch. Take my words seriously and go home."

I looked around the quiet forest, taking in his words. He must have thought *I* was simple to think I would believe the King of Wolves ordered a lowly Madra Village guard killed. But it was pretty obvious the beta wasn't going to tell me the truth.

"Why have you been acting like this today?" I had to know. He was just so odd.

He cocked his head, brows furrowed.

I raised my voice, annoyed. "You've been smelling flowers and playing in streams. Are you not scared that those wolves will find you again?"

"They'll find me. They always do." He shrugged, seemingly unaffected by the fact. "So I always try to enjoy myself while I can. You never know what day will be your last, so I try to enjoy my freedom until Byriel finds me again."

"He needs you to find the wolves to kill?"

"Kind of. He needs me to tell him if the mark is right."

"How do you know if the mark is right?"

"My mother is a witch. She told me what to look for."

"Does it bother you to kill innocents?"

"Better them than me," he snorted. "Now, will you help me up?"

I paused, eyeing him at the bottom of the pit and thinking it over. I doubted he'd be of any real help to me. He was too clumsy and careless.

"I'll even show you where the break in the border wall is," he whispered loudly as if someone might overhear. "It's just up that way, but it's hard to find. I can show you exactly where it is," he smiled, pointing in the distance.

"Okay," I sighed, standing up and dusting off my bottom.

"Toss me your clothes." He gave me a curious look. "I'm going to tie them together and pull you up."

"Oh! That's actually a good idea," he said as he stripped down.

He balled up both garments and flung them up towards me. It took a few tries, but I was finally able to grab them, immediately stepping away from the mouth of the hole. I quickly stripped out of my blood-soaked top and pulled on the beta's dark pants and dirty, white shirt. They were too big, but they'd do.

"Omega! Where are you?"

I grabbed my shirt off the ground and tore several long strips of fabric off the end, fashioning a belt. Once I was satisfied the pants were secure, I tossed away what was left of the torn cloth and looked down into the hole.

"Help me up!" he yelled, his patience gone.

A piece of me wanted to feel bad for him. It seemed like such an awful way to die: dehydration, starvation, or possibly some unlucky animal that could fall in there with him and rip him to shreds.

I ran my fingers over the pearl tied to my wrist, letting it fuel my anger. "You let my mate die," I said calmly. "Now I'm going to let you die."

I walked off, hoping the break in the border wall wouldn't be too hard to find.

The Madra Village Border

Tzidal

THE BORDER LOOMED tall over the trees in the distance. Just a little further and I could rest my angry feet before trying to find the break in the wall.

My back ached, and my lips were chapped, in desperate need of water. I had never envied an alpha's ability to shift into their wolf at will, more than I did right now. It was a cruel trick of nature to force omegas to be one with their wolf but never able to inhabit them.

I cast my eyes up at the large wall made of thick tree trunks. It was intimidating, easily as tall as three or four alphas standing end to end, and appeared to go on forever. I sighed, looking at my swollen feet, and decided to rest for a moment. Hopefully, I could find the break in the wall before nightfall, but it could take days with how large the border was. And I only had a vague idea of what direction to go.

Spying a downed tree, I made my way to it. I dropped myself onto the forest floor and rested against the trunk, rubbing hard at my eyes and the back of my neck. I just needed a few moments. Then I'd move on.

I twisted the leather bracelet around my wrist, feeling exhausted and hungry. The berries I found along the way were nowhere near enough to fill me.

My fingertips grazed a few pebbles at my side, and I picked one up. Leaning my head back, I looked over the massive border in front of me, ready to toss the rock.

The break in the fucking wall.

It was right there.

Rotting wood near the base of the border had been hacked away, creating a sizable opening that I could easily slip through. I laughed at my good fortune and rushed forward, climbing up into the hole.

I paused, looking at the forest just on the other side. It was the same. I wasn't sure what I expected, but I was a little disappointed.

It was forbidden for omegas to leave their pack villages. It was too dangerous, or at least that's what we were always told. But this looked just like the comforting woods that surrounded my home. The same trees swayed in the wind, the same birds chirped in the distance, and the same sun hung in the sky. No wild beasts or feral monsters. Just quiet woodlands.

I hopped down, placing my feet on the forbidden land. No one attacked me, and no one rang an alarm. It was all very disappointing.

"Okay," I mumbled to myself. "Vaesen is east. I know that much." I paused and looked up. "The sun sets in the west, soooo," I turned my body slightly. "This way."

THE SCENT of death lingered in the air, causing my body to tense with each step. I continuously looked up at the sun, checking my direction as it brought me closer and closer to the putrid scent.

I made my way toward the top of a steep hill, grabbing onto low-hanging branches to pull myself along. I reached the top and took a deep, exhausted breath. Then I froze.

A rotting corpse lay, split open, at the bottom of the hill before me.

I let out a strangled yip and jerked to step backward but lost my footing. I rolled forward down the hill, scraping my arms on rocks along the way, and collapsed headfirst into the dead body.

I screamed and launched myself away from the mangled flesh, pushing my back against the closest tree. I grabbed my chest, panting hard and heavy. Tears blurred my vision momentarily, and I closed my eyes to calm myself.

The body's entire rib cage was cracked open and emptied, one leg was torn off and dragged a few feet away, and its face consisted of only a jaw bone and some bloody chunks of hair.

My wolf whimpered and shivered, my whole body fighting between the urge to sob or run.

A gentle tickle on my hand made my arm jerk. A spider crawled lazily over my skin, and I whipped my hand into the air, flinging it off. Another tickle just beneath my ear made me smack at my neck and spin.

Nimble insects covered the entire tree, both inside and out. A deep crack in the center of the hollowed-out spruce was filled with thick webs, dead bugs, and spiders that rushed out toward me.

I screamed again and shoved myself away from the tree, falling in the dirt next to the corpse.

A frenzy of fear and panic bubbled up in my throat, and I

let out a slow, long whine. I lowered my forehead onto the cool ground and tried to collect myself.

"They're just spiders," I mumbled, trying to will my heart to steady and my breath to calm. "Just spiders." I stood and gently moved to step around the corpse, my legs uneasy and knees suddenly made of soggy twigs.

The bloody handle of a sword caught beneath the body's lower half glistened in the sun, and I paused. I couldn't help but think a weapon might be a good thing to have, especially since I didn't know what kind of creatures I might find here.

I slowly reached out, my hand brushing against the metal, leaving my fingertips red and wet. I winced, snapping my hand back and stepping quickly away from it. I wiped my hand frantically on my pants, a quick gag pushing my tongue out. My wolf begged me to go home, but I ignored her and the tears that glazed my eyes.

"And you're just a dead body," I whispered, my voice high-pitched and shaky. "Just a dead body that's still wet and bleeding and gross. No need to be scared. No need to dwell on the fact that your murderer is probably still out here and probably close. No need to think about how close they might be."

I kept babbling quietly to myself as I walked. Pushing myself further into the forest, away from the smell of blood and the cluster of spiders.

"No need to think," I continued. "Just walk, Tzidal. Just keep walking."

A distant roar of what I could only assume was a violent beast echoed throughout the forest. I stopped and closed my eyes, letting a few tears fall. I hated myself for screaming so loud. *So damn stupid.*

"You're far from home," an alpha said, stepping toward me from the nearby brush. He was massive, tall and broad, and his dark, almond-shaped eyes swept over me as he licked his lips.

My heart thundered in my chest, making me dizzy, and my body flooded with fear. Images of the split open corpse flashed through my mind, and I swallowed hard, wondering what kind of wolf could do such a horrible thing.

Then he edged toward me.

Beyond The Border

Tzidal

"WHAT ARE YOU DOING HERE?" I blurted out, spinning to face the massive alpha.

"I think the real question is, what are *you* doing here?"

He held a shirt in his hand, his broad, tan chest exposed, and his black, shaggy hair hung wet into his dark eyes. "Omegas aren't allowed to leave their villages," he said, glancing around. "Does your mate know where you are?"

"That's none of your business," I said, giving a wide berth as I edged around him. Anxious to escape. He stepped closer, and I stumbled back, smacking into a tree. "I'm warning you. Don't even try to touch me!" I flashed my teeth and snarled. I hoped I looked fierce, but judging from the look on his face, it wasn't as aggressive as I had hoped.

"Okay there, little one," he laughed, holding up his hands. My eyes moved to a scarred claw mark ran the length of one arm. "Let's get you back to your village before you hurt yourself, yeah?" He grabbed my upper arm, yanking me to him.

"Let me go!" I squealed, wanting to sound so much tougher than I did.

"This is no place for an omega," he lectured, pulling me back toward the village. "My name is Joon, but you can call me alpha if you prefer."

He walked calmly, his grip firm, despite my pleas to release me. I twisted around, jerking and flinging my arms out, smacking my fists against his firm, muscular back.

"Let me go!" I screamed, finally slipping from his grasp. I kicked my legs out, scrambling to put as much distance between us as I could. Wrapping my arms tightly around a tree, I glared up at him. If he was determined to take me, there really wasn't anything I could do to stop him, but I could at least try.

He pursed his lips together, his jaw jutting out a bit. His profile was sharp, and his eyes narrowed as he looked me over. "I'm just trying to help," he said, his voice annoyed and loud.

"I don't need your help," I snapped, locking my hands together around the tree's trunk, careful not to take my eyes off of him.

"Clearly," he smirked. "Be careful out there. There are all kinds of vicious creatures that could easily make a snack out of you."

He slipped off his pants, and I tensed. My hackles raised, and I growled high in my throat.

"Calm the fuck down," he said lazily. "I'm getting ready to shift. I wouldn't dare to touch you again. Not after that...warning," he laughed, moving his dark eyes over my face and settling on my battered feet. His cocky grin softened. "Are you sure you're okay? You really should consider going back to your village. This is no place for someone like you."

"I'm fine!" I wished he'd just leave already.

He hesitated for a moment before giving me a quick nod and stuffing his clothes into a satchel secured over his shoulder. Then he shifted quickly. His beast-like form was tall and looming with shaggy, dark hair just like his human. His wolf gave me one more glance then disappeared into the wilderness. I waited until I could no longer hear the heavy thump of his paws before I allowed myself to relax.

I jogged along, anxious to get as far away from the rotting corpse and nosey alpha as I possibly could. The thick stench of death was still stuck in my nose, dulling my senses, and I couldn't pick up anything else in the air. It had me on edge.

I rounded a thicket of trees and jogged toward a river in the distance. The water called to me, my throat longing to slake my thirst. I cupped a hand and dipped it into the cool water. A low growl vibrated through the air, and I froze.

Out of the corner of my eye, an enormous bear jerked its head up. It sniffed the air, baring its teeth, and stalked toward me. I begged my body to move, racking my brain, trying to remember what to do when faced with a bear. The creature tensed and stood up on its hind legs, casting its massive shadow over me. My whole body trembled, and I tried lowering myself to the ground.

I needed to play dead, but my wolf was freaking out. My mind and body were at war with each other, causing my bones to shake and my muscles to tense. No matter how hard I tried to force myself onto my stomach, I struggled to meet the dirt. My wolf was too desperate to run and hide.

The bear let out an ear-piercing roar that vibrated across the ground and into the soles of my feet. My wolf won me over, and I ran.

Sprinting back in the direction I had just come, I could hear the beast's heavy paws as it chased me through the forest.

I pumped my arms and legs, weaving through the narrow trees, but the sound of snapped branches and barreling grunts told me he was nowhere near slowing down.

I stopped abruptly right in front of the dead body, whipping my head around to see the bear throwing its weight into a small cluster of trees. In a panic, I jerked hard on the handle of the sword and shoved myself into the spider-infested tree. Squeezing my eyes shut, I swallowed a whine as bugs rushed over my skin and in my hair. Unable to hold myself together, I cried, forcing myself to stay within the safety of the webbed nest.

The bear slammed its body into the cracked spruce, roaring at me in a blaring rage. The tree around me groaned and creaked, causing the spiders to flood out of the wood.

I swallowed back my tears, and squeezed the sword's handle, suddenly feeling its weight. It pulled at my hands, the tip settling into the ground. I tried lifting it back up, but I didn't have the strength to hold it properly and its sharp end sank even more into the earth.

The bear swiped at me with its long claws, the sharp points inches from my face. Its bulky arms were too big to reach me, and I pressed my back more firmly against the rotting wood.

The horrific beast roared again, spit flying into my face.

"GO AWAY!" I screamed as my whole body convulsed uncontrollably. Spiders crawled over and into my clothes, tickling the inside of my ears and the corners of my mouth.

The bear reared back then jerked forward, swiping and catching my arm. Blood swelled and seeped out of two deep gashes just above my wrist. My eyes widened in shock at the pain that radiated up my neck and flashed down my back.

I eyed the bear in a boiling rage, baring my teeth. I heaved hard on the sword once more, pulling the tip off the ground, then I wedged it forward. I grunted from the weight, then snarled as loudly as I could, and lunged.

I pierced the bear in the center of his gut, just beneath its ribs. The shiny blade stuck firm as thick, red streams gushed around it. I thought briefly about reaching for it, but the beast stumbled forward, and I screamed, racing back into the safety of the heinous spider tree.

The bear jerked its body to stand up on its hind legs, but it faltered and fell forward, impaling itself further onto the blade. It grunted and kicked out its hind legs, scratching at the dirt. A pained snort, then a high-pitched whine left its lips as it twitched.

I waited, arms wrapped tightly around myself as spiders danced all over my skin and hair.

"Please be dead, please be dead, please be dead," I chanted quietly, tears rolling down my face.

The bear let out one last huffed groan then stilled completely.

I bolted from the tree and raced as fast as I could toward the river, not stopping until I hit the water. I flung myself into the rushing stream, smacking at spiders and ripping at my clothes and hair. I sucked in as much air as I could between forced sobs, my body trembling uncontrollably.

Once I could no longer feel the creepy tickle on my skin, I pulled myself to the shore and laid down at the base of a tree, curling myself into its massive roots. I breathed heavily, trying to listen for any sound within the forest around me. Trees swayed, and a few twigs softly snapped in the distance, causing me to jerk and whip around wildly, looking for the source of the noise.

After a few moments of silence, terror finally overtook me, wracking my body. Tears flooded my cheeks as I tried to muffle my painful sobs. I was so stupid. *Why did I think I could do this? What was I even trying to do?*

My body hurt, and my throat burned. I rubbed my fingertips over the pearl tied to my wrist as exhaustion finally consumed me.

The Tree By The River

Tzidal

I SLOWLY OPENED my eyes to find myself curled tightly against the fat roots of a tree. My clothes were mostly dry, and the moon was stamped brightly against the dark sky. I wasn't sure how long I had slept and was somewhat disoriented.

A man's deep laugh drifted in the air from just behind the tree, and I slapped my hands over my mouth to stifle a whimper.

My heart raced as I slowly peeked over the tree's roots, my fingers clutching the rough bark. Careful not to be seen.

A bulky alpha strolled through the forest, walking closely behind a very young man in long elegant-looking robes with a delicate pattern stitched across them. He had a very slight form and looked to be not much taller than me. He was incredibly pale, and his skin seemed to sparkle in the moonlight. His sharp features, paired with his white hair, made the darkness within his eyes startling. He practically glowed.

He was so out of place.

The alpha grasped his tiny hand, pulling the young man to his chest.

"Alpha," the wisp-like boy giggled in a light, feathery tone. "You're trying to get me in trouble, aren't you?"

The alpha pulled the young man's hips against him and growled low in his throat. "You didn't bring me out here to just tease me." The wolf's hand ran down the curve of his bottom, and squeezed. "Stop acting coy."

The young man licked his lips and stepped away. His slender fingers brushed over the bark of a nearby tree, and he pressed his chest against it, swaying his hips at the beast. "Who's teasing who?" he said over his shoulder, biting his bottom lip.

The alpha rushed forward and slammed his body into the glowing boy, pulling his head to the side and sucking hard at his throat.

"You wolves and your obsession with necks," he mused as the alpha dragged his teeth over his flesh. "I just don't get it."

The alpha jerked at the sash around the boy's middle and tugged the robe off in one forceful movement, exposing his flawless skin.

I swallowed hard, unable to look away from the scene before me. I was so frightened for the young man, myself, and, for some reason, the alpha too.

The young man pushed his bottom hard into the alpha's clothed crotch, circling his hips and moaning loudly. The wolf grabbed his chin and jerked his head around, leaning in for a kiss. The boy quickly pulled away. "Not until I get what I want," he smiled, then pushed his hips back again. "Fuck me already."

The alpha ripped his shirt off and jerked his pants down his legs, letting his member spring free. The young man eyed it and hummed in approval. "Come on, alpha. Don't keep me waiting."

The wolf placed his large hands on the young man's hips, pressing his length against his ass. "You aren't an omega. Will this hurt you?" he asked, hesitating for a moment.

"Are you going to fuck me or not?" the young man demanded, loud and angry. He suddenly looked so scary, and I flinched from the edge in his voice.

It was all so confusing. I wanted to run out and pull the glowing boy away. Save him from the threatening wolf. He was far too fragile to be acting in such a brash way with an alpha. Their strength was not something for non-weres to play with.

The alpha grabbed the young man's hips and slammed into him in one hard thrust. The young man opened his mouth in a silent scream and rolled his eyes back into his head.

"Oh, yes!" he moaned. "Harder! Fuck me harder!"

The alpha obliged. He snapped his hips at a brutal pace, shoving the young man's body on and off his cock. Reaching his arm back, the glowing boy clawed at the wolf's side, pulling him into his body.

"Yes! Right there! Keep going!"

The young man grabbed his own member, stroking it in time to the harsh thrusts. The sound of slapping wet skin and broken moans echoed throughout the forest. The young man's body jolted hard in the wolf's hold as he picked up his pace, fucking harder into his small body.

The glowing boy stroked himself faster and faster as he moaned loudly. His body trembled and jerked, and he came onto the forest floor.

"Fuck!!" he gasped, breathing heavy and closing his eyes, still stroking himself. Once he caught his breath, he fussed with his hair for a moment before turning to look over his shoulder at the wolf still pounding into him.

"Are you done?" the young man asked, looking almost bored.

Everything about the scene before me made my skin prickle. It wasn't right, and the desire to flee overwhelmed me again, but I couldn't move. I was held in place by fear and curiosity.

The young man shoved away from the alpha, who stumbled backward, his cock still hard and throbbing. The wolf growled with displeasure.

"Kiss me," the young man moaned, wrapping his arms around the alpha's neck and pulling him down.

The wolf gave him a cocky grin, digging his fingers into the young man's ass before leaning in to press their mouths together. The kiss was quick, but everything changed the second their lips met. The alpha stood motionless as if in a trance, his arms hanging useless at his sides. The young man grabbed his robes, tossing them aside, before turning his attention back to the wolf.

"Lay down," he said softly, his tone almost polite.

The alpha kneeled onto the soft earth and situated himself onto his back. The hair on the back of my neck prickled, and goosebumps scattered across my skin. I ducked down a little lower, careful not to be seen, as fear rose in my gut.

The young man sat down next to the wolf and ran his hands gently over his bare chest. He turned the alpha's head, looking over his features. He caressed the alpha's nose, cheeks, and lips with an almost loving expression. Then he slapped his face hard. The sharp crack startled me, and I hunkered down a little more, unable to tear my eyes away.

The young man giggled, then returned his hand to the alpha's chest. He slowly dragged a single fingernail right between the wolf's pecs. A dark line appeared on the alpha's skin in its wake, and almost immediately, it began to bleed. The thick, red substance poured over his chest like a curtain.

The young man smiled, then flattened his hand and began working his fingers under the wolf's skin. He moved with such ease, it was almost as if he were simply slipping his hand beneath a shirt.

The skin on the alpha's chest peeled away from his body, leaving his raw, pulsing muscle exposed. The young man licked his lips and lowered his head, his sharp teeth flashing white in the moonlight.

I jerked behind the tree and placed both hands firmly over my mouth to keep from screaming. I shouldn't be here. This was one of the monsters the elders of our pack warned pups about. This was why omegas didn't belong outside the village. *This was how I was going to die.*

I pushed my back into the tree's trunk as hard as I could, wishing it would open up and swallow me whole.

The wet sound of tearing flesh and cracking bones filled the air as I tried not to cry. A rush of liquid and the smacking of lips made my throat tighten and my stomach churn. I gagged as quietly as I could, heaving silently into my hands.

As quickly as the rush of sound had consumed me, it was suddenly quiet.

I didn't move. Too terrified to breathe.

Slowly the young man appeared from around the tree. His gaze was squarely on my face as if he was expecting to find me sitting there. He was still naked, his arms and mouth smeared with glistening, red blood that dripped softly down his body.

He smiled sweetly, displaying sharp pointed teeth. His black, wet eyes dragged over my face, and he cocked his head.

"Hello."

The River's Edge

Tzidal

THE YOUNG MAN smiled down at me. His bright, white teeth contrasting wildly against the deep crimson blood that coated his lips and dripped down his chin.

I opened my mouth to speak or scream. I didn't know which. But nothing came out, fear rendering my voice useless. A weak sob worked its way up my throat, and I gasped for air, not realizing I had been holding my breath.

The young man stepped slowly into the water, ignoring my panicked state as hot tears poured down my cheeks. I wanted to run. Through the forest, past the spider nest tree, back through the border, and all the way home. But my body refused to move.

"Did you enjoy the show?" the young man asked sweetly as he dipped his lithe form into the shallow water. He shivered and sucked in a breath through clenched teeth, letting himself settle in the river.

"I'm sorry," I whispered. I had no idea what else to say.

"That's okay," he smiled, washing his face. "I liked it." He gave me a wink, letting his hands glide over the surface of the flowing water. It swept the thick, red blood off his hands, making them pale white once again.

I let out a shaky breath, feeling...off. My body was still wound tight, but my hands were steady, fear slipping away like the blood on the young man's fingers. He leaned toward me and smiled. He exuded such a calming aura, despite the gore. And for the first time since leaving home, I didn't feel scared.

"What are you?" I couldn't help but ask.

"A siren. Scared?" he asked with a teasing lift to his voice.

His features had somehow softened, and he looked almost sweet and childlike. It stopped my bones from shaking and soothed me. It had to be a trick, but I decided to let it calm me. At least for now.

"No," I finally said. "I should be, though. Right?"

He cocked his head, looking me over with his big, dark eyes.

Sirens were known to be terrifying creatures that shape-shifted and hunted mortals, eating their flesh and drinking their blood. I always assumed they were more myth than fact, but here one sat, the blood of his last victim washing away with the current, and for some reason, I felt the need to lean into his inviting smile.

"What are *you*?" he asked.

"I'm a were. An omega-were."

"Ah!" he gasped. "A gentle wolf! I've never met one of you before." He crawled out of the water toward me, stopping right at my feet. I stiffened but didn't move away. "You can't turn into a puppy, can you?"

I shook my head. He was cute.

"That just seems unfair," he pouted. "I have always wanted to meet one of you, though. And I have to tell you," he leaned in, all energy and excitement. "I have met, and fucked, many of your alphas, and while they are delicious and decent in bed, for the most part, they are complete fucking idiots. Well...maybe not all of them. No," he held out his hands, pretending to think. "All of them," he nodded as if coming to a firm decision. "I do not understand how you can stand such fools," he laughed.

I let out a quick puff of a laugh. I still wasn't sure if I should run or just sit and chat, cultivating a strange, new friendship. The pull to be near him was just so consuming.

"Don't sirens live in the ocean?" I asked.

"Only the fat ones," he smirked. "Singing to lure in whole boatloads of men so they can gorge themselves for days. So lazy. So boring. And you never know what you'll get with sailors. Werewolves, vampires, elves, trolls, which are just fucking disgusting. And heaven forbid you get stuck with a boat full of *humans*," he shuddered, the last word oozing out of his mouth. "So gross."

I couldn't help but laugh. I might end up dead by this siren's hands before sunrise, but at least I could allow myself to enjoy his company for now. It was scary being outside my village, and, for now, it felt good to be near someone so...*sweet*?

"No, I don't care for the sea." He leaned against the fat roots of the tree, getting comfortable. "I don't like dark waters. I need to be able to see what's in it. How about you, little wolf? Why are you roaming around the forest all by yourself?"

"I need to go to Vaesen. Can you tell me if I'm going in the right direction?"

"Vaesen? What awaits you in Vaesen?"

"I'm going to kill the alpha that murdered my mate. I'm going to cut him open and watch him die by my hands, and I would greatly appreciate your help if you wouldn't mind."

My confident words caught me off guard just as much as my new friend.

55

"You are very surprising, little wolf," he smiled. "My name is Lex, and I would very much love to help you. I need a little adventure. These woods have started to bore me. There's just nothing exciting left for me here."

He smiled brightly, his teeth no longer sharp but smooth and white, like mine. His sweet face made me want to hug him, pull him close, and snuggle.

"Have you put a spell on me?" I asked, feeling calmer with each passing moment.

"You seemed tired and a little upset," he whispered, leaning closer to rest his head on my shoulder. "Would you like me to stop?"

"Please."

I was too light and soft, like I could cuddle into the grass and sleep forever. But right now, I wanted my anger. It gave me purpose, a reason to keep living. Something I desperately needed.

Lex gently touched my arm with the tips of his fingers. The floating sensation in my head evaporated, and the heavy weight of rage, fear, and pain crashed over me, pressing me into the dirt. I slumped over from the force of it, needing a moment to collect myself.

"Lex?" I asked, my voice low and gruff.

He looked up at me with expectant eyes.

"Are you going to eat me?"

He brushed a strand of my hair out of my face, tucking it behind my ear. "Not today, little wolf."

Into The Shadow Forest

Tzidal

THE JOURNEY WAS MUCH MORE pleasant with Lex. While he promised he wouldn't put any more spells on me, I did wonder if he was true to his word. The all-consuming fear I had felt before was pretty much gone, replaced by a drive I had never known before.

I was still angry. I still wanted to rip Hida's heart out, but the despair was gone.

"So, alphas are just dogs in human suits, betas can only become dogs once a month when the moon gives them permission, and omegas are puppies stuck as people?" Lex asked.

He was fascinated by weres and had asked me a million questions about our status, ranking, and how male omegas worked. I was shocked to learn that apparently, omegas were the only creatures on land where both males and females could birth young. For all other beings, only females were capable. No exceptions. I found it odd and limiting.

"Yes," I nodded. "That's basically it."

"You werewolves are fascinating creatures," he hummed. "I want to cut you open and see what's inside."

"I'm going to politely ask that you find another omega to satisfy your curiosity," I laughed. "I've watched you cut someone open, and I would not care to have any part of that."

Lex giggled, locking his arm around mine.

THE FOREST TERRAIN became rough and jagged as we continued, making it difficult to find comfortable places to camp for the night, but we made it work. I knew this trip would be long and hard, but I wasn't prepared for the abuse my feet would endure. As the days wore on, I longed for my village's lush grass and soft dirt roads.

We had been traveling east for what felt like days on end when a sudden break in the trees caught me off guard. The forest stopped abruptly, cut off by large, shiny red rocks, creating a path into an entirely different-looking forest.

The new land was dense and overly colorful, strikingly different from where we currently stood. The trees had thick bases with large, winding roots that twisted and turned in and out of the earth. The leaves and grass were vibrant and looked fuzzy as if a soft layer of down-hair covered each petal and leaf. And the air sparkled like a thin fog had settled, making the sunlight glisten.

"The shadow forest," Lex sighed. "Do you want to go through or around? We *should* be fine to go through, but..."

"*Should* be fine?"

"This is the Faelands. It holds heavy enchantments. Lots of creatures live here that don't venture out. Fairies, pixies, tree wives, all sorts of things. And they don't take kindly to visitors, but as long as you're gentle, they'll usually let you pass."

I looked into the forest before me. It was so beautiful and calm, but I knew better. Calm things tended to have the most violent reactions when provoked.

"How long to go around?" I asked.

"It'll add days, maybe even weeks, onto the journey. This is the most straightforward way to Vaesen."

"Then we go through," I sighed. I walked across the red stones. The slick surface was surprisingly cool against the souls of my feet.

"Then we go through," Lex mimicked with a quick nod. He marched forward, his robes fluttering behind him. "Just don't touch the trees," he warned. "They don't care for it."

I was careful to step around roots and plants as we pressed on, not wanting to anger the land or its inhabitants. We passed fat flowers with petals so heavy they sagged and fell over as if drunk on amber wine. And when we finally stopped to rest, Lex insisted we sleep on patches of lush moss that grew on top of white, iridescent rocks. I had never slept so well before.

My dreams were filled with my mate's soft touches and sweet words, and I forgot my grief for a moment. At least until morning came. Then I'd wake up confused, my heart breaking all over again.

I sat at the base of a tree and watched the vines slither in and around the branches. Lex had wandered off to dip himself in a stream not far off, leaving me alone to think about Hida and what I needed to do once we got to Vaesen. I longed to see a blade plunge into the alpha's chest and watch the life drain from his eyes. My hands ached to feel his blood pour over them.

At first, I had no idea how I'd lure him to his death, but seeing Lex seduce and eat that alpha, I thought I might be able to do the same. I'd tempt him to a secluded area with the promise of sex and then stab him or cut his throat, whichever opportunity presented itself first. It would be easy, I hoped. I had to try at least, even if it killed me.

Without thinking, I reached my hand up and brushed my palm over the bark of the nearest tree. It felt like any other, but soft vibrations pulsed beneath my fingertips. I jerked my hand back, suddenly remembering Lex's warning.

Holding my breath, I waited for something horrible to happen.

Slowly, a vine worked its way down the length of the tree and swayed, hanging from a branch just in front of me. I eyed it cautiously, watching it twist and turn, dancing in the breeze. Its movements were so enchanting, I didn't notice another vine coil itself around my arm until it constricted, pinching my skin.

I yipped at the burning sensation as the vine moved over my exposed flesh, and tried not to panic or move as it slithered over my shoulder and around my chest. My wolf whimpered, and I slowly placed a hand over my frantic heart, feeling the vine slide across my body under my touch. I closed my eyes, taking several deep breaths, willing myself to stay calm.

"Who are you?" a sweet voice chirped.

I snapped my eyes open.

The most unusual creature hung from the tree in front of me. Its arm was twisted in the vines above, just swinging gently. It had the face of a child, with pale green skin that appeared to have the same texture as the tree bark, and its limbs looked like branches with little sprouts along its wrists and ankles.

"Are you a wolf?" it asked in a musical tone. Its long, dark hair swayed as it rocked in the tree, coiling around its arms like the vines that were snaking around my body,

The creature swung itself forward a bit, its large, wet eyes drinking in my features. It cocked its head to the side and sniffed the air around me.

"Are you a wolf?" it snapped, asking again. A high-pitched chirp pushed from its chest. It sounded like the chatter of a squirrel, but it made the hair on my arms stand on end.

I hesitated to speak. While this small creature looked completely harmless, I had thought the same thing of Lex when I first saw him. The creature narrowed its eyes, and its face pinched when I didn't speak.

"Yes," I finally forced myself to say. "I'm an omega were."

"You're not like those big, angry wolves that rip up the forest floor, are you?"

"No." I tried to keep my voice from shaking as a vine squeezed and coiled down my legs. "I'm not like them at all."

"Why did you touch my tree?" Its pointy teeth flashed momentarily as it spoke.

"It was so beautiful, and I was sad. I like touching the trees and rocks when I'm sad." It was the truth. I just hoped it wasn't offensive.

The creature hung there, swinging slightly, its eyes unblinking.

"Your tree is lovely," I mumbled.

The creature looked around, scanning the area in the distance, before returning its gaze to me. My breath caught as the vines slowly uncoiled themselves from my body. I didn't move, staying completely still.

"Don't touch my tree again!" the creature hissed, teeth bared and eyes blazing.

It leaned forward and grabbed a chunk of my hair and swiped at it, cutting a length of it off with its sharp claws. Then it shot back up into the branches.

I jumped up and pushed myself as far from the tree as possible, slamming my back against the white rocks we had slept on the night before. My heart was pounding, and the skin on my arm stung. The exposed flesh where the vines had slid was now purple and seeping droplets of blood.

"Are you harassing the ashmores?" Lex teased, strolling toward me, his white hair tousled and dripping.

"Ashmores?"

"The tree dwellers," he said as he held out a hand to help me up. "They get very pissy when you touch them."

I rubbed my arm and nodded. "Yes, they do," I said, looking up cautiously at the trees around us.

"Just wait," Lex smiled, wrapping his finger around the end of my snipped chunk of hair. "The trees get even weirder the deeper you go. Just be thankful this one only wanted a locket of hair as penance and not a limb."

"Great," I mumbled as we pressed on, gripping my throbbing arm.

THE FOREST CHANGED several times as we walked through. Shifting from lush greens with angry trees to crystal clear streams where the sun cast rainbow shadows, to a span of trees pressed so firmly together with branches so thick they practically blocked out the sun.

I was worried we'd have to extend our journey by walking around this part of the forest, but Lex insisted it was okay to step on these trees, just not to sit or stand near one for too long. The roots liked to suck sleeping travelers into the hollows of the earth and digest them for weeks.

"Why do all the trees here want to kill everyone?" I groaned as we walked further into the dark, crowded woods. My body begged for a break. "I miss the trees back home. They didn't threaten to kill me or try to strangle me because I stepped on it or touched its branches."

"Well, maybe they would love to kill you." Lex stared at me

pointedly. His usual cheerful demeanor was completely gone. "Have you ever bothered to ask them?"

"No," I mumbled, not wanting to upset him further. We had been traveling together for a while now, and he had been so pleasant. His sharp tone caught me off guard.

"The attitude of wolves." He shook his head. "So ungrateful."

I opened my mouth to argue, but I was worried he'd abandon me in the gloomy thicket of trees. Plus, I was sure his feet hurt as badly as mine, and I hadn't seen him eat since that alpha. I didn't know how frequently sirens needed food, but I would have been long dead if I had to wait as long as he had.

"You're right," I sighed. "I'm sorry."

Lex stopped in his tracks and spun around to face me. "What?"

"I'm sorry," I repeated, eyeing the trees around me for any movement as we stood in the center of several coiled roots. "It was rude of me to assume that just because something can't complain doesn't mean it doesn't want to."

Lex raised his brow in surprise. Then his expression fell into sadness.

"What?" I asked.

Lex hesitated for a moment before finally speaking. "I sincerely hope that you are happy with your story at the end of this journey, little wolf," he smiled sweetly.

"What does that mean?"

Before he could answer, both our heads snapped around as a horrifying roar ripped through the forest. It was hard to understand, but I heard it. A single word. *Help.*

Beneath The Trees

Joon

THE ROOTS CONSTRICTED around my chest, locking my arms to my sides as the tree slowly pulled me across the forest floor.

I coughed and gasped. It was getting difficult to breathe, and I wasn't sure how much longer I'd be able to stay conscious. I had used my last breath when I thought I heard voices, but other than the crack of the wood twisting around me, it was quiet.

My wolf snarled and struggled within me, desperate to shift, but the tree held me too tightly. I was livid. A whole year of tracking and hunting, so close to exacting my revenge, only to be done in by a fucking tree.

The soft patter of feet pulled me from my thoughts, and I tried like hell to move my head toward the sound.

The little omega I had met along the border of Madra Village ran toward me, a pale boy following not far behind. I

64

tried calling out, but I had no air left in my lungs. I just prayed they would see me.

The two paused and looked around. The tree's roots cracked as it spun itself around my hips, and the omega jerked her head in my direction, letting out a shocked gasp.

"It's you," the omega said as she knelt, placing her hands on the ground next to my face. Her dark hair fell over her shoulder as she inspected my bound body.

"Do you know him?" the pale boy asked.

"Not really," she said, turning her attention back to me. "Can you move at all?"

"No," I rasped.

"Is there a trick or a spell to get him out?" she asked the pale boy.

"No," he shook his head. "These aren't creatures so much as just predators. They react on instinct, not thought. I can't affect this."

The boy grabbed her arm and pulled her away for a moment, speaking to her in a hushed tone. I tried to talk or move, but I could do neither, and despair started to settle within me. I was completely immobile and very lightheaded.

"We have to try at least," she shouted, jerking her arm away and returning to my side.

She let out a puff of air and plopped back down next to my head. Looking over the tangle of roots and branches, she clicked her tongue.

The omega leaned closer to me and ran her hands over the twisting bark, deep in thought. The tree's movements slowed. She noticed as well and brought her wide eyes to mine. They were light, almost golden in color, and had a deep sadness that caught me off guard.

She continued to run her hands up and down the thick roots as their movement completely stopped, still holding me firmly but no longer tightening. I was too dizzy, and my throat burned as I fought to pull air into my lungs.

"Lex," she said to the pale boy. "I think this is working! Pet it!"

"Pet it?" he snorted, watching her work with a look of disbelief on his face.

"Yes!" she snapped. "Get down here and pet the damn thing!"

The pale boy huffed and knelt next to her, running his long, slender fingers over every surface. The roots slowly uncoiled, and my eyes went wide. I nodded the best I could at the omega, urging her not to stop.

The tree shot out toward her and twisted itself around her wrist. She yanked her hand away, then returned to stroke the bark as vigorously as she could. There was a loud crack, and my body jerked as the roots uncoiled faster. I sucked in a gust of air, filling my lungs and coughing repeatedly.

The roots whipped like coiled snakes toward the pair with more force as they abandoned my body in favor of new prey. It rushed across the forest floor, twisting over rocks, and curled around the pair's ankles and legs. The pale boy jumped back as the aggressive tree shot up his robes.

"Fuck!" he yelled, smacking the garment back down and frantically running his hands over his legs and torso. "Tzidal, this thing is getting angrier!" he yelled at the omega.

"Can you move?" she asked me, her voice shaking with fear as her hands moved in a blur over the bark. Her body jerked as she dodged another winding branch.

I was able to finally pull one of my arms free, reaching it over my head. I kicked out hard and stretched my hand out to grab anything within reach. The omega jumped up and took hold of my hand. She planted her feet then heaved, a small grunt leaving her lips. I pushed against any surface my feet could find, desperate to work my way free.

The tree let out a loud snap as it stopped moving toward the pale boy, then immediately reversed direction, tightening around me again.

"Fuck!" I yelled, over the deep, hollow groan that vibrated out of the bark around me.

I jerked and squirmed as the pale boy rushed over to help pull on my arm. I kicked out once more as hard as I could, launching myself forward and on top of the stumbling omega. I looked down at her big, brown eyes and took a deep, shuddering breath. Her sweet, floral scent rushed through my body, shocking my senses. My wolf let out a nervous growl as the tree cracked once again behind me.

"Move it!" the pale boy screamed.

I jumped, snatching the omega up with me, and ran. The pale boy startled and scurried after us, yelling out in our wake. I rushed through the thicket of trees, dodging branches and rocks, the omega firmly in my hold. She tightened her grip around my neck and pushed her face into my chest.

My wolf roared with a possessive edge as my senses went into overdrive. I was suddenly keenly aware of every sound and shift of the wind around me as I struggled to remain human, my wolf lusting to break free.

I spotted a clearing ahead and picked up my pace, not slowing until I reached it. Once we were on safe ground, I stopped and took several long, deep breaths. The pale boy screamed from inside the tree line, his blonde hair catching the sun and bouncing toward us.

"You can put me down," the omega said firmly.

I immediately placed her on her feet. She looked flushed and a little frightened despite her stern expression. She had two healed claw marks on one arm and purple burns that twisted around the other.

"You've seen some of those creatures I warned you about," I said, looking pointedly at her old wounds.

She nodded and ran her fingertips over her marked skin, stepping away from me. "Yeah, but I didn't need anyone to save *me*."

My smile dimmed, and I nodded, my pride taking a bit of a blow.

"What the fuck?" the pale boy yelled as he finally reached us. "That was a fantastic *'thank you for saving me'*!" he screamed at me. "You fucking abandoned me with murder trees!"

"I'm sorry," I said. "I saw an omega in danger, and my instincts kicked in."

"Yeah, well, there was a siren in danger too, asshole. Next time maybe your instincts could be a little more considerate of everyone that helped save your ungrateful ass."

"I am grateful." I struggled to remain calm, hating the pale boy's tone. It was aggressive and demanding, and I wanted to smack his mouth. "Thank you both for helping me."

"Fuck you," the pale boy sneered. "I have to eat something," he said, turning to the omega. "And if I spend one more minute with this one," he jabbed a finger into my chest, forcing me to swallow a growl, "I'll end up cutting *him* open."

The pale boy turned on his heel and stalked off into the woods.

"Don't mind him," the omega said. "He's just hungry."

"Seonjoon." I bowed my head. "But everyone calls me Joon."

"Tzidal," the omega responded. "So, are these trees one of the vicious creatures you warned would want to eat *me* as a snack?" she smirked, looking a little more relaxed. Her eyes were hard, but her pink lips pulled up in one corner, making her look soft and sweet, despite her shitty comment.

"Enchanted trees are much more dangerous than they are given credit."

She snorted. "Clearly."

The Edge of The Forest

Tzidal

JOON WALKED with us through the rest of the Shadow Forest. He claimed it was to help protect us, but Lex was quick to point out that we had, in fact, saved him.

The siren clicked his tongue, savoring the look on Joon's face as he told the alpha that he needed us more than we needed him. Joon puffed his chest out in annoyance, obviously not caring for Lex's snarky comments, but he didn't say anything. The alpha simply shifted his glare into the distance and huffed. But he needed the reminder.

When I first met the alpha, he had the gall to mock me and treat me like a child, warning me about creatures I didn't have the strength to fight. But here he was, alive because of our kindness. I hoped his pride was slow to recover.

"Once we reach the other side, we'll have to trek over the barren lands to get to Gygax," Lex said. "I will need a fat, juicy meal before we cross. I'm not eating desert trash. My system is far too delicate to be forced to settle for lizards," he groaned, pretending to gag.

He was much more pleasant since having a proper meal, and while I was curious as to who he was able to find wandering around the enchanted forest, I thought it best not to ask. However, the siren still had an edge in his tone every time he spoke to Joon, but the wolf didn't meet his challenge.

It made me smile to see the massive alpha bite his tongue around such a slight and delicate creature as Lex.

"Gygax?" I asked, fanning myself with a palm leaf. The day was hot, too hot, and the trees were thinning, providing less shade with each step.

"The Stone City," Joon said, pulling his shirt off.

The alpha looked just as I remembered. His skin was a beautiful tan color, and his muscles flexed, defined and firm. Scars covered his chest and back, giving a glimpse of his violent past.

The wind shifted as we walked and, more than once, his thick masculine scent drifted toward me. It was sweet and smokey, making my nose tingle and my eyes flutter.

He paused every few feet or so, glancing over his shoulder as he walked ahead, making sure we were safely behind him. His eyes were deep and serious, and I looked over the long claw mark down his arm, wondering what it would feel like to run my fingers over it. My wolf thrilled at the idea.

I shook my head at the odd thought and eyed Lex. He glanced at me out of the corner of his eye, shooting me a quick smile, and I grabbed his arm. Pulling him back, away from the alpha, I was suddenly irrationally annoyed with the siren.

"Are you doing something to me?" I asked in a hushed tone. Lex gave me a confused look, his brows knitted together. "A spell. Did you put a spell on me?" My eyes flickered to Joon's back, causing Lex to crack a wide grin.

"Why?" he teased. "Is he doing something to you?" He motioned to the alpha, his tone playful and excited.

"You promised you wouldn't put any more spells on me," I gritted out in a harsh whisper.

"I'd like to put a spell on him," Lex hummed, eyeing the alpha's broad shoulders. "Make him do something to me."

"Seriously, Lex. Stop it." I pulled at his arm, forcing him to face me properly. "I don't like it, and I have a mate."

"I'm not doing anything to you, little wolf. I said no spells, and I meant it." All humor was gone from his voice. "And I don't want to upset you, but you don't have a mate anymore. And this alpha is alive and well and looks *very* good. Maybe you should —"

"Stop it," I repeated, my face heating up. I didn't want to think about touching another alpha like that. The thoughts the rushed through my head were embarrassing and inappropriate, and I barely knew Joon. "It's not funny, and I have no interest in him. So please, quit."

"Well, if you aren't going to enjoy his company, mind if I have a bite?" He licked his lips, his teeth angling into sharp points for the briefest of moments.

"No!" I yelled louder than intended.

Joon spun around. "What's wrong?" he yelled back.

"Just admiring the view," Lex smirked, eyeing the alpha's half-naked body. Joon frowned before turning back and pressing on. "Just look at his jawbone," Lex hummed. "It's so sharp. I just want to cut my lips on it."

"You don't even like him," I mumbled.

"Just because I don't like him doesn't mean I don't want to eat him."

I huffed and walked on, leaving Lex to eye Joon like a tempting delicacy. My wolf agreed, wagging her tail.

WE SET up camp not far from a stream of water, wanting to rest as much as we could before crossing into the barren lands. The deadly creatures that lived in the enchanted forest mostly kept to the center, leaving the occasional playful wisp or fluttering pixie as our only companions.

A few tiny wisps danced in the breeze, taunting each other and making me laugh as I searched for firewood. I had never seen one so close before. I had spied them outside the village gates many times, but they never ventured inside the border walls.

I followed the smoke-like creatures, laughing as they spun and flipped through my hair. For the first time in a while, I didn't feel like I might be attacked at any moment, and I allowed myself to enjoy it.

I paused and reached for another stick, adding to the growing bundle in my arms. The wisps swirled around me once more before catching in a swift gust of wind and drifting into the forest. I waited until they disappeared before heading back toward our camp.

I dropped the sticks into the make-shift fire pit and froze when I caught Joon's eyes on me. The alpha stiffened and looked away. More than once, I saw him watching me, and it made me a little uncomfortable. I wondered if he found me as ridiculous as I sometimes felt. He was a fierce predator, and I was just a weak omega, made to provide young and care for my family, not exact revenge.

I couldn't help but wonder if he and Lex took me seriously at all. Joon's lingering gaze and Lex's overly playful attitude occasionally cut through my exhaustion, making me wish I hadn't left home.

"What are you looking at?" Lex practically yelled at Joon. I looked up to see the alpha's eyes pull away from me once again.

Joon growled low in his throat at the siren. "I was scanning the tree line. Just because we aren't in immediate danger doesn't mean it won't find us."

Lex looked him over and snorted. "The trees. Right," he scoffed.

"Why are you here?" Joon demanded, his voice deep and suddenly angry. "What are you doing with this omega?" He motioned to me.

"He's my guide," I said, confused by his sudden aggressive attitude. What did it matter *why* Lex was here? I enjoyed his company, and I didn't need Joon's temper running him off.

"Yes, but *why*?" the alpha asked again, his words slow and deliberate.

"I want to see how this story ends," Lex answered, unfazed by Joon's hostile stare.

"What story?"

"This little omega is absolutely determined to kill the alpha that murdered her mate. She might be the angriest wolf I've ever encountered. I can feel the rage pouring off of her when she talks about it, and it's positively mouthwatering. But more than anything, I love a good story, and it would be wild if she actually pulled it off. I mean, she won't. But it would be so great if she did."

"What do you mean I won't pull it off?" I asked, defensive and tense.

"Tzidal," Lex sighed. "You are too small and sweet. As angry as you are, and as bad as you want it, that alpha will rip you to pieces. And if he doesn't, you won't have it in you to kill him. You're too kind."

"Kind people can still kill. In fact, we may do it better than you. No one ever expects us," I said, my voice loud and firm. I locked my eyes on his, holding Lex with barely contained outrage. "I will kill Hida, I will feel his blood on my hands, and I will release my mate from the torment of an unjust death. That alpha is as good as dead."

"I do adore your passion, little one," Joon laughed, a dimple displaying deep in his cheek. I instantly hated it.

I swallowed hard and tried like hell not to cry. I didn't want to look weak. Not right now. Not when they were confirming all my worst fears; they thought I was a joke.

"See what I mean? How could you not want to see what will happen?" Lex said, turning to Joon.

I growled high in my throat at how quickly they dismissed me. I knew they didn't believe me, but I didn't need them to. I just needed a guide and a blade. The rest was up to fate.

"This seems like a lot of trouble to put yourself through just because you're bored," Joon scoffed, looking at Lex as he settled himself on the forest floor.

"I'm over four hundred years old. Nothing amuses me anymore. I'm always bored. At least until recently." He winked at me.

"Why did this wolf kill your mate?" Joon asked.

"I don't know." I deflated a bit and shook my head, hating the memories that flashed through my mind. "They asked to see a mark that he's had since birth." I grazed my fingers over my ribcage, remembering exactly where the small crescent Moon once graced his skin. *How I had loved to trace it with my fingers...*

I pulled myself away from my thoughts, folding my hands in my lap. "Then they killed him."

Joon sat stiff, with wide eyes. "Fuck."

Camp

Joon

My breath caught at the realization that I might share more in common with the small omega than just a need to get through the forest.

I hesitated, reluctant to speak. "Were there," I cleared my throat, "any other wolves with this alpha, Hida? Or did he act alone?"

"Two others," she said, watching me with narrowed eyes as my scent shifted. I was on edge, and it was clear she could sense it.

"Byna. Was that one of them?"

"No." She shook her head, thinking. "Well, I don't know. I only know two of their names. Hida and Byriel."

I jumped up. "Byriel? A black wolf when shifted?"

She nodded.

"Was one of the other wolves tan in color?"

She nodded again.

I rubbed my face hard, then laughed. It was horrible, but I couldn't help it.

"You and I have a common enemy, little one," I sighed. "The same alphas killed my mate. All because of a mark on her skin. I wasn't there when it happened, but I was able to catch up to them before they could slip my village borders. Byna, the tan wolf, still had my mate's blood on her muzzle. The three of them overpowered me, though." I gestured to the ugly scar down my arm. "I've spent almost a year tracking them. I was close at your village, but they managed to escape me again."

"It just keeps getting better," Lex whispered, his eyes wide with excitement.

The omega looked at me with an onslaught of emotion. Sad, but so much more. Rage, sorrow, uncertainty, and exhaustion poured out of her big, bright eyes. I hated how much comfort I found in our shared grief.

"I'm sorry about your mate," she mumbled. "The tan wolf, Byna, she was the one that ripped my mate's throat out."

I paused, confused. "Why do you want to kill Hida and not the one that actually killed your mate?"

"Hida mocked Korban and tortured him by threatening to hurt me. He held me down and forced me to watch my mate die. That wolf has no honor and made Korban's last moments before his death as horrible as he could. He tormented both of us for his own pleasure. No," she said with a set resolution in her voice, "he deserves to die, and I deserve to be the one to do it."

The fire blazed in her eyes as she spoke. Even though she was so small, she carried her anger well, and for a moment, I truly felt she would be able to exact her revenge. She had an alpha's determination.

"I look forward to killing beside you," I nodded.

I could feel it deep within my bones. This was the path the Moon had chosen for me. This was our shared destiny, and I would help her see it through. I would help her and protect her, and we would both get the blood owed to us.

Tzidal nodded in return, her expression hard. Tears clung to the corners of her eyes, but she didn't let them fall. She was an impressive omega. *She was an impressive wolf.*

"I am sorry about your mates," Lex said. His signature smirk was gone, and he seemed almost sincere, but I knew better. sirens weren't sincere. They were too cunning. "Your mate," Lex asked me, "did she suffer?"

"No, she didn't. I was told it was quick." I kept my head up, refusing to allow either one of them to see my grief. "That was the only luck she had that day. My brother's mate was with her in her last moments, and he said it was quick."

"Your brother's mate is a boy?" Lex asked, a curious expression on his face.

"Yes," I said, not understanding his confusion.

"Why do so many werewolves have male mates?" the siren asked, turning to Tzidal. "More than any other species, the wolves I hunt seem to prefer males. Why is that?"

Tzidal shrugged. "You don't know anything about the images you pull from someone's mind?"

"Nope. Just that rogue wolves crave dick."

"That's not how wolves work, Lex," Tzidal laughed. "We aren't attracted to others like that. It's more about scent and instinct, not male or female. We fall in love with someone's wolf, not their body. I'm sure it's just a coincidence the wolves you've met all loved males at some point."

"I highly doubt any of those alphas were capable of such an emotion. Trust me," Lex snorted.

"I just don't understand creatures that pick mates based solely on such meaningless physical attributes. Does nothing else matter?" I leered at Lex.

"You're asking the wrong person," he laughed. "Sirens don't have mates. We have dinner."

Before the Barren Lands

Tzidal

JOON SHIFTED into his wolf and hunted along the outskirts of the forest, hoping to find a decent meal. I had been living off berries and bird eggs for too long and was desperate for the taste of meat. My wolf purred in approval when the alpha returned with a sizable boar or at least something that resembled one. Either way, it tasted good.

Lex sauntered off as the sun started to set, saying he wanted to find something proper to eat before we left the forest, and trolls and cave dwellers were all he'd have access to. According to him, sex with a troll was just as bad as eating one.

"Do sirens have to mate with their prey?" I asked Joon as I finished my meal.

"I think they just like to," he smirked. "I've met a few sirens in my time, and it's my understanding they get drunk on emotion. I bet their prey's excitement for sex, right before the fear of death, feels good to them."

"They feed off our feelings?" I wracked my brain, trying to figure out how such a thing could even work.

"I don't know if they *feed* off of them, but they do feel them. I think it helps to know what to shift into to lure people to their deaths," Joon mused as he arranged a small pile of sticks and logs in the makeshift fire pit. "Why does Lex look like that? Does he look like someone you know?"

"I saw him...eating, and he looked like that already," I said, forgetting that wasn't Lex's actual appearance. I wondered if anyone had ever seen a siren's true form before.

"Ah, so we've been befriending someone else's fantasy?" he smiled.

"I guess so," I shrugged, watching him struggle to spark a fire. "You're doing that wrong."

"I am not," he snapped, his wolf on edge at being challenged. I pressed my lips together to keep from smiling.

"Of course not. My apologies, please continue," I said, a smirk lurking behind my blank expression.

Joon sat motionless for a moment, crouched next to the fire pit with a stone in each hand. He flicked them together several more times before sighing hard and silently holding them out to me. I smiled and settled next to him.

I adjusted the rocks in his hands, then cupped them, moving his arms to just the right angle. His hands were warm and surprisingly soft for the most part. My fingertips brushed over the callouses along his knuckles, and a shiver ran up my spine. My wolf edged closer, wanting to feel his hands elsewhere.

I swallowed hard, trying to ignore the feeling of his eyes on the side of my face. My cheeks warmed, and I could only imagine how flushed I must look. My wolf preened at his undivided attention, making me want to smack myself in the nose, hard.

Pushing back my flustered wolf, I showed the alpha the quick movement needed a few times, then let him take over. He sparked a small flame immediately and laughed. His breath fanned over my neck, causing my skin to tingle. I jumped up and rubbed my throat hard, trying to quiet the sensation.

"You okay?" he asked.

"Yup. It looks like you've got it," I smiled, moving back to my spot.

He nodded in thanks, adding some dried grass and adjusting the wood until a decent fire flickered away.

"I've never been great at starting fires and tend to sleep without them." He watched the flames dance. "Thanks."

A loud, rough screech echoed toward us from somewhere in the distance. I looked out in the direction of the barren lands trying not to think too hard about what was out there. We were so close, and by tomorrow morning, we'd be in the thick of the desert. There'd be no turning back.

"Were-wrack," Joon said. "Mutated shorebirds that feast on the dead and dying in the drylands. Don't worry. They won't venture into the woods. But it might be a good idea if we slept near one another. Just in case."

"Why?" I asked, hating how desperately my wolf wanted to press up against him. "If they come this way, won't they just kill us no matter how we're sleeping? Would it matter if we're laying close?"

"I'm just trying to be safe," he said, a strand of dark, wavy hair falling into his eyes. "I'm not trying to be inappropriate if that's what you're worried about."

"No!" I said quicker than I intended. "I wasn't trying to say you would...I didn't...I wouldn't..." I sighed hard, not sure what I was trying to say. "I'm just tired."

Joon scooted back, leaning against a fallen log, and patted

the space next to him. I rubbed the soft pearl on my wrist and stared at his muscular, sun-kissed arms. He held them open to me, so inviting and warm. Lex's words repeated in my mind. '*You don't have a mate anymore. And he does look delicious.*'

"I'm fine, thank you," I said firmly, much to my wolf's disapproval.

"I just want to make sure you're safe," he said, crossing his arms over his chest. "A little thing like you would be snatched up before you even woke."

"I've made it this far by myself," I shot, trying not to look too offended. "I'm sure I'll be fine for one more night."

"Everyone thinks they're safe right before they're killed," he smirked. "But if you think you have the strength to fight off one of those wracks, then, please, sleep where you like."

He was starting to annoy me with his smug face and stupid muscles.

"Strength doesn't automatically mean you'll be safe," I said, feeling anger rise in my chest. "If that were the case, I wouldn't have been forced to pull you out of a tree."

His grin fell. "You didn't pull me out of a tree. This is an enchanted forest with a strength no man or beast could challenge. There is no winning a fight against a creature like that."

"*I* won a fight against a creature like that," I said, staring at him hard. "I got that tree to let you go. *I did*. Not you."

"And I said thank you," he growled low through clenched teeth.

"I don't want you to thank me. Just don't forget that I don't need you to keep me safe. I'm not a child."

He sucked a hard breath in through his nose, letting it out slowly. "Understood."

Into The Barren Lands

Joon

THE SUN PEEKED over the horizon, rousing me before the others. I turned to sit up but stopped when I noticed Tzidal tucked securely at my side. It surprised me after she had repeatedly declined my offer to lay together.

I couldn't help but be so insistent last night. My wolf was nervous for the omega to be too far away, and I was well aware of how desperate I had sounded, but the compulsion to have her near was difficult to fight. I needed to have her next to me, touching me.

I needed to know she was safe.

I looked over Tzidal's delicate features as she slept. She looked tired, almost worn, like the emotions she held within her had aged her more than the journey. But she was still so lovely. Her innocent eyes and delicate mannerisms called to my wolf to protect and dominate.

The urge to lean into her neck and inhale her sweet floral scent was overpowering.

"And what are you thinking about?" Lex asked, a wide grin on his face. He was lying on the other side of the dying fire, with his head propped up in one hand.

"I guess it was too much to hope your meal would end up eating you last night instead," I groaned, standing up to kick dirt over the smoldering logs.

"Oh, she did," he winked.

"You wink an awful fucking lot."

"You love it," Lex whispered, blowing me a kiss and winking again.

I frowned, then turned to wake Tzidal.

"Omega," I said in a quiet tone, placing a hand on her shoulder and shaking her gently. My eyes lingered at her exposed collarbone. Her skin was soft and dewy in the early morning light. For a moment, I lost myself in the desire to drag my fingers over her warm body, but I jumped up before I could act, all too aware of Lex's eyes on me.

"Tzidal," I said loudly, standing stiff over her petite body. She jerked awake and looked up. She held a hand up to block out the early morning rays and rubbed the sleep out of her eyes. "Time to go?" she asked, her voice rough.

"Yes. We should fill up on water. Carry what we can." I grabbed my satchel, walking off into the woods toward the stream, hoping they'd get a move on. We needed to start our trek into the barren lands before the sun got too hot. It would take several days to make it to Stone City, and I was hoping I'd catch Byna there.

I reached into my bag, pulling out my water canister, causing the silver necklace I carried with me to fall onto the ground. It was a circular medallion with our pack's seal pressed on one side. I had traded it for a dagger my father had left me, so I could present my mate with something beautiful when I asked her to be mine. It was the only thing I had left of her.

Tzidal's musical laugher drifted toward me, and my wolf purred at the sound. I tightened my hand around the medallion as my stomach twisted with thick guilt.

My mate wouldn't have expected me to remain celibate for the remainder of my days, I was an alpha, after all, but my pull to Tzidal wasn't just one of lust. My wolf had laid a deep-rooted claim on the omega the second I scented her, and everything about her intrigued me. It was like the first time I met Fennah, and it was ripping me apart.

She was the love of my life, a wolf that no one else could ever compare. And it felt like a deep betrayal to think of Tzidal, an omega I hadn't known very long, in the same vein as her.

Fennah was a fierce beta who worked tirelessly, training and studying to meet the requirements to patrol our village's borders. Very few betas had ever had the honor, as they rarely met the physical requirements, but she was determined and strong. When she set her mind to something, she did it. It was a quality that always impressed me. The fact that Fennah was able to will herself to be better than what she was born to be made me want to take her, love her, mark her.

My wolf preened with pride when she finally agreed to be my mate. Having such a strong, capable partner that would submit to me, and only me, was thrilling. But it also made for many passionate arguments, neither one of us wanting to yield easily. She was wild and unpredictable, and I missed her dearly.

"This is freezing!" Tzidal squealed as she dipped her toe into the water.

"Well, push through it, pretty puppy," Lex laughed as he tossed away his robes and sank into the water. "This might be the last bath you get in a while."

"Lex is right," I said.

"I'm convinced you are incapable of feeling anything," she said to the siren as she eased her clothes off and joined him.

I turned my back, trying to respect Tzidal's privacy, but my eyes kept pulling to her. She sat with the cold water up to her shoulders, shivering. Her long, dark hair draped over her back like a curtain as she splashed the very unamused siren.

"I swear, I will eat you right now," he said in a serious tone, his finger pointing at her and jerking as he spoke. "I'll do it. I'll kill you, eat you, then save Joon as a snack for later."

"If you killed me, you'd have no one to entertain you," she giggled.

"It's a risk I'm willing to take, you dirty mutt."

"So mean," she pouted, her bottom lip poking out. I stared at it. It looked so soft, so pink, so fucking —

"You okay?" Tzidal asked, looking right at me.

"Get out," I ordered, trying to hide my embarrassment at being caught staring at her. Again. "We need to go."

I quickly finished filling as many containers as possible with water before stuffing them in my satchel and stomping off back toward the camp. I needed to focus on Byna. I needed to kill her for Fennah, and that was my priority.

I only hoped the intense heat and severe dehydration we were about to endure would help relieve me of my infatuation with the little omega, and fast. I had never longed for a harsh journey through a volatile desert more in my life.

The Barren Lands

Tzidal

THE FLAT EARTH stretched out for what felt like forever. A few jagged plants decorated the lands with thorns and barbs as brutal and unforgiving as the desert around us. My feet sizzled against the hot, dry dirt. I had wrapped large palm leaves around them before leaving the forest, but the rough terrain wore them down quickly.

Joon regularly shifted, letting me and Lex take turns clinging to his back. I felt terrible for tiring the alpha out so quickly, but we needed to press through to the city as fast as possible, and he was the most resilient.

The days were hot and dry, and the nights were freezing, the harsh ground giving no comfort or warmth as I shivered in my sleep. It felt like our destination was more of a distant dream and not a real place in the middle of this barren hell.

"Ugghhhh!" Lex groaned for the millionth time. "This is

86

nowhere near as fun as you said it would be," he whined, pointing an accusing finger at me.

"I never once said this would be fun," I mumbled, too hot and tired to put up with his shit. Sweat rolled down my back and over my buttocks and thighs, making my clothes cling to my hot skin. I wanted nothing more than to remove all of them and run headfirst into a freezing river. Everything was sticky, and everything hurt.

"Revenge is always fun. This feels like...work," he gagged.

"Quiet," Joon demanded. My wolf trembled at his harsh tone.

He stepped forward carefully, his stance low and alert. I slipped behind him without prompting, knowing the safest place for an omega in a dangerous situation. Joon's shoulders rolled as he prepared his body to shift, a dark figure in the distance slowly coming into focus. He paused and sniffed the air, narrowing his eyes.

"Dead body," he said, standing back up and pressing forward.

I relaxed and begrudgingly followed, my feet hating me with each step.

The sun was starting to set as we finally approached three corpses sprawled out in the sun. I could almost taste the thick, bitter scent that filled the air around them. The stench was horrid, sticking to the inside of my nose and throat, making me dizzy.

"They look elvish," Lex said, examining their faces. "What killed them?"

I leaned over a rotting body. The earth had sucked up all the spilled blood and dried all its exposed skin, but the parts wrapped in clothing cooked, hot and wet, all day in the sun. I covered my nose with my shirt, trying to block out the putrid air.

"Doesn't matter," Joon said, pressing on.

I moved my feet, my eyes catching sight of something gleaming brightly in the last rays of the sun. It was a sword. It was thinner and longer than the last one I had tried to wield, and this one wasn't coated in a sticky layer of blood. I leaned down and grabbed it, dragging the blade on the ground as I walked. I was too tired to hoist it up any higher.

"Are you seriously taking that with you?" Joon asked.

"Yes. The last time I passed up a sword, I ended up needing it. This is a gift, and I won't ignore it this time."

"You aren't strong enough to use a sword," he said flatly. "You're barely strong enough to carry it. One good swing and you'd topple over."

"If you aim right, one good swing is all you need," I challenged, one eyebrow cocked.

He laughed, his dimple gracing his face for the first time in days.

"Fair enough," he said, stepping toward me. "But at least secure it at your hip."

He grabbed the blade from my hand and reached for my belt. His fingers brushed against my waist, making my skin tingle. My wolf simpered at his gentle touch as something deep inside began to twist. I hadn't felt the familiar ache of desire in a very long time.

I glanced over at Lex, and he raised his eyebrows suggestively at me. I scowled, too gross and cranky to find him amusing. I wondered if the siren could recognize the arousal in my flushed cheeks. I glanced away, trying to pretend it was because of the sweltering heat and not the massive alpha tugging at my clothes.

Joon leaned away from me, confusion lining his brow. I didn't move, too embarrassed at my body's reaction to a few swift grazes to my waist.

"What are you doing?" I asked, feeling very self-conscious

as he tugged at my waistband again, my core starting to throb with each movement of his large, strong hands.

"Is your belt made of fabric, like a shirt?" he asked, running his thumb and finger over the material. His skin brushed against mine in the process. "There's no way this will hold the weight of a sword."

Before I could argue, a deafening screech ripped through the silence. My eyes went wide as I frantically scanned the quickly darkening sky, but I couldn't see anything.

A deep rushing sound above us caused the air to pulse in my ears, then another screech.

"There!" Joon pointed.

Camouflaged by the darkening sky, a bird-like creature hung in the air. Its grey, leathery skin stretched across its bones, and its large, bulbous eyes glowed yellow and red at the top of a long pointed beak. The talons on its feet hung heavy and sharp as it swooped down.

Lex wrapped his arms around me and jerked backward, causing the creature's claws to pierce the ground, kicking up a cloud of dirt.

Joon shifted, his dark, shaggy wolf, tall and angry. He reared back and roared at the beast that hung in the sky. The creature screeched and swooped toward me again. Joon lunged for it, landing on its back. He sunk his teeth deep into the base of a wing and jerked, rolling the two of them over the ground.

"Fucking were-wrack," Lex shouted, looking around frantically. "We need to find cover."

I scanned the area, but it was empty, flat, and dark as the last rays of the sun died for the day.

There was nowhere to run or hide.

The edge of a thick wing smacked Lex hard on the back as another creature swooped down. My eyes shot toward Joon. He was rolling in the dirt with the other wrack, both biting and scratching wildly at one another, in a flurry of claws, teeth, and talons. I couldn't wait for him to save us.

I planted my feet and tried holding the sword out, but it was too heavy, and the tip fell hard into the earth. I let it settle there as I tightened my grip, waiting for the wrack to attack again. It hung in the air as if teasing me, dropping several feet suddenly before raising back up again. It swayed and circled us from the sky, forcing me to spin, dragging the blade as I moved.

It let out a sharp, ripping scream then darted right for me. I closed my eyes and swung the sword as hard as I could. The weight of it sent me toppling over, and I opened my eyes to see the wrack circling us again. It angled its beak and swooped down fast. I scrambled to my feet, slicing into the air as hard as I could. Again, I smacked into the ground, dropping the sword as my hands scraped across the hard earth.

Another piercing cry and the pulsing flap of wings told me the beast was diving again. I pushed myself up and spun just in time to see the wrack's pointed beak, filled with razor-like teeth, flying straight toward me.

In The Desert

Joon

I CLAMPED my teeth deep into the wrack's neck and jerked again, forcing it on its side. It let out a rasp of a screech as blood filled my mouth. Quickly, I kicked my back paws out over the creature's back and side, shredding it with my claws until it went completely limp in my hold. Once I was sure it was down for good, I unclenched my jaw and spun around.

Tzidal was pulling herself off the ground, sword in hand. Lex sunk into the dirt behind her as a wrack circled above them. But before I could move, the creature launched itself, hard and fast, toward the pair.

Tzidal steadied her feet and heaved the blade, slicing it forcefully through the air. It looked as if she made contact as the wrack's wings faltered slightly, but it pushed itself up and away from her. It awkwardly jerked as it hung in the sky, its wings beating in a halting manner. Then it let out a garbled sound as its belly split open and its guts spilled out onto the desert floor. Its body followed moments after, smacking the ground with a heavy, wet splatter.

I walked over to Tzidal, still in my wolf form, and licked her hands. They were bloody and shaking. She dropped the sword and stood for a moment, letting me care for her. She let out a soft whine and pushed herself into my neck. Her body trembled as she cried, but she made no sound. She simply clung to me, my fur absorbing her tears. I wanted to shift and hold her, but she seemed to find comfort in twisting her fingers in my fur, fear and adrenaline still pulsing off her in thick waves.

I dropped my head over her shoulder and sniffed her hair, the air around her smelling of sweet flowers, death, and acute distress. My wolf let out a soft whine, wanting to acknowledge her suffering.

"We should sleep while we can," Lex said softly, still sitting in the dirt.

The siren's pale skin was shiny, covered in a thin layer of sweat, but his complexion was still very white. No hint of red in his cheeks. The Moon illuminated his face, giving off a soft sparkle that made him look so out of place in the dark desert surrounded by rotting corpses.

Tzidal pushed herself away from me and walked silently toward Lex. "Are you okay?" she asked, holding out a hand.

"Yes," he sighed, allowing her to help him up. His robes were grimy and covered in dirt with a small spatter of blood along the hem.

I shifted into my human and craned my neck around. A jutting hill made of rocks was situated in the distance.

"There," I said, pointing. "There might be a cave or crack in the surface that we can crawl into for the night, just in case there are any more were-wrack around."

I wasn't worried about Lex. He tricked and killed beings for food and, possibly, just for fun. He could take care of himself, but Tzidal...she had a much softer feel to her. She did have a few scars on one arm as if something had clawed at her and a purple twisting mark on the other that I had thought was a bruise, but it had been weeks, and it had yet to fade. Other than that, she was unscathed, free of the kind of violence that marked one's body and soul. And the last thing I wanted was for her to get hurt.

Tzidal looked rattled, but she held her head high as she padded over the small hill of rocks. Other than those few tears, she hadn't panicked or cried when the wrack attacked. She was calm. But I kept my eyes on her just in case. Omegas were fragile by nature, and I didn't want to neglect her should she fall apart.

"This is small, but you should fit," I said to Tzidal as I looked over a tight break inside the rock's surface.

"No, thank you," she said softly as she laid down, out in the open. "If under the stars is good for you, it's good for me."

"Omega." My voice was firm. "This isn't an offer. You need to sleep in here. It'll be safer."

"Then you sleep in there," she snipped. "I'm staying right here." She pushed her side into Lex's back, making him hum in approval.

"This isn't a request. Get your ass in there now!" I was exhausted, thirsty, and over the fucking attitude. I wanted a good night's sleep without worrying that she'd be carried off by a fucking wrack in the middle of the night. I didn't feel like I was asking for too much.

"No."

"No?" I was shocked. Many alphas had challenged me in my life, and I always won the better of them, but no beta or omega had ever dared to speak against me like this. I was convinced omegas weren't capable of such behavior. "You can't defy an order from an alpha."

"Why not?" She sat up and glared at me hard.

"It goes against your nature," I said, trying so fucking hard to stay calm.

"My nature?" She gave a bitter laugh, her eyes blazing. "We can absolutely defy you. We just choose not to."

"Why?" Lex asked as he propped himself up, his dark eyes wandering between us.

"Because alphas are all a bunch of unhinged children, and omegas aren't dumb enough to put ourselves in a situation where we might get killed for simply saying 'No'. But I'm too hot and tired to put up with your alpha-knows-best bullshit. I'm sleeping out here next to Lex and not in that snake hole. This discussion is over."

I could smell the faint scent of fear drifting off her and could hear her heart pounding hard in her chest from the effort she was using to disobey me. I wanted to pick her up, smack her ass, and fling her into the tiny cave.

Taking a step back, I tried to settle my wolf. "That's fine," I growled. "I hope a wrack comes and fucking takes you in the middle of the night."

"Me too," she spat.

"I hope it rips you to pieces and drops your corpse on the desert floor."

"As long as I don't have to hear you bitch anymore, that's fine by me."

A splintering roar ripped from my throat, and I jerked forward but stopped myself almost immediately. I instantly felt awful. I didn't mean to react like that, but I was too wound up. Tzidal's body shook at the sound, and I could practically see her wolf cowering to me. She slowly moved to bow her head, showing the back of her neck in an act of submission, but she stopped herself and, with obvious effort, pulled her head back up, looking me square in the eye.

"No," she whispered, her body trembling.

"Okay," Lex said, moving so he was between us. "Let's

focus here. I know we're all tired and hungry, and we almost died, but let's not kill each other. There's no need to lash out." He spoke as if addressing both of us, but he kept his eyes on me. "Let's just get some sleep and move on in the morning. She can sleep between us. I'm sure it'll be fine."

Tzidal opened her mouth, but Lex held his hand up, stopping her.

"Things have to be pretty bad for me to be the voice of reason, puppy. Please let this go," he said in a hushed tone.

"Fine," Tzidal huffed, getting up and pulling Lex with her. She settled both of them right against several jagged rocks.

"I can't sleep there," I huffed.

"That's your problem. Not mine."

I had hoped the desert would cure my wolf's infatuation with the omega, refocus me on my task and keep me from wanting to scent her, touch her, and feel her. But I was wrong.

I still wanted to touch her.

I wanted to throttle her fucking neck.

Stone City

Tzidal

THE NEXT DAY was pretty quiet as we trudged further into the desert. Joon woke up sulking like a big baby, and hadn't said more than two words to me all day. I was fine with it. I didn't need him ordering me around when I was capable of taking care of myself.

Just past mid-day, Stone City came into view, and Lex started squealing like an excited pup. Joon quickly squashed his excitement by stating that it was still many miles away, and we probably wouldn't reach the gates before sunset.

I wanted to ask the alpha how he planned to find the three wolves once we entered the city, but I didn't want to give him the satisfaction of being the first to break our game of aggressive silence. His hostile display the night before, practically demanding my submission, still didn't sit well with me.

Many alphas had flexed their muscles and ordered me around in the past, but this was different. I was Joon's equal in this. We had a common goal. I had also saved his life in the Shadow Forest and managed to hold my own more than once. But, the way he acted last night...it was like he saw me as a pup. A burden in need of supervision and discipline. It was insulting.

We stepped onto a properly paved road just as the sun kissed the edge of the desert in the distance.

"Oh, praise the Gods!" Lex groaned loudly.

The smooth path blended in with the surrounding dirt, only standing out by its texture. It led right through an arch into a large, bustling city. The silence of the desert was quickly overthrown by the overlapping chatter and shouting of creatures, various beings, and even a few humans.

The buildings were all made of the same beige stone as the street, giving everything a gritty and monotone feel. After walking for days on end through the harsh desert, I was worried our appearance would draw attention. But most everyone looked as rough as we did: dirty, tired, and in need of a good, strong drink.

"Come," Joon snapped, cutting through an alleyway.

He moved quickly across the congested streets and down narrow passages that hid easily amongst the crowd. We passed a particularly hard-looking group of trolls, causing Joon to motion for us to pick up our pace. They were arguing loudly about gambling debts and unpaid bar tabs. Their aggressive mannerisms made my wolf very nervous, and I edged closer to the alpha.

"Here," Joon said, grabbing a thick blanket hanging from a wall and pulling it aside to reveal a doorway.

Drunkards yelled and laughed in the dark space as music played and glasses clinked. It was cramped, and the dirt from outside seemed to have settled in the air, making everything hazy.

Joon walked straight up to the bar as Lex smiled sweetly at

a pair of scary-looking Targon elves. They licked their lips and smiled back at him. It was odd seeing the fierce creatures so far from their territory. They were rarely seen outside of Targon, and when they did leave, it was never a good thing.

"I'm starving," Lex whispered in my ear. "I'll definitely find something good here, though." He scanned the room before walking quickly over to the elves.

An alpha at the end of the bar leered at me, running his tongue over his teeth. I thought about pushing my hair back to show my mating bite, but I doubted it mattered to a wolf like that in a place like this. He flexed his muscles and narrowed his eyes, sniffing the air in my direction.

I rushed after Joon, not caring for the feel of the alpha's eyes on me. His glare had a violence to it that caused my wolf to tremble. I hopped into the seat next to Joon and wrapped my arms around his middle. I eyed the scary alpha hard, trying to make it clear I was taken.

Joon looked down at me, eyes wide and his hand hovering just over my back. It was as if he was scared to touch me. "You okay?" he whispered. He seemed caught off guard by my behavior, which was understandable since we hadn't spoken to each other all day.

"I'm fine," I said, not wanting to draw attention to the alpha at the end of the bar. The last thing I needed was for Joon to feel validated about the way he acted last night. I did not need his protection, and I refused to acknowledge how ridiculous that thought was as I tightened my grip around his waist.

I flicked my eyes back to the scary alpha, hoping he had turned his attention back to his drink, but he was still looking at me. His glassy eyes were bright at the challenge I was presenting him.

Joon followed my gaze, turning to see the drunk alpha snarl at him. He jumped up, forcing my hands free from his body, and crossed the bar in three quick steps. Then, before I could register any movement, he punched the wolf square in the jaw.

Unable to stop myself, I let out a sharp scream, then ducked behind my barstool. The drunk alpha reared his fist to return a blow but swung too slow and too broad. Joon leaned back, easily dodging it.

I slapped my hands over my mouth to suppress another scream, and my wolf let out an excited trill as Joon defended me. I hated how much I loved it.

Joon held the alpha's collar and punched him repeatedly in the face. No one in the bar moved, the fight not phasing anyone but me. Their lack of response scared me even more. Wolves and elves continued to chat and drink as Joon pounded his fist into the bloody wolf.

The alpha grunted and held his hands up in surrender. "What's your fucking problem?" the drunkard yelled, his words slurred.

"Don't fucking look at her," Joon growled, jerking the alpha off his stool and flinging him onto the floor. "Get the fuck out of here before I rip out your throat."

I pressed my thighs together, loathing my body's betrayal to Joon's display of dominance.

The alpha slowly pulled himself up and reached for his drink. Joon grabbed it first and downed it in one go, slamming the glass back on the counter. "Get the fuck out," he growled.

The drunkard swayed, then turned, mumbling under his breath as he stumbled out the door.

"Joon!" A beta behind the counter gave him a wide smile. "Good to see you."

Joon nodded. "Is Patthar here?"

"Of course." The beta turned and disappeared through a small door behind the bar.

"Stay with me," Joon snapped, looking me hard in the eye.

His knuckles still had a trace of blood on them. "Do not leave my side."

"I'm fine," I huffed, feeling defiant for some reason. "You didn't have to —"

"I would not drink a vat of poison, knowing full well it would kill me, just to prove my strength," he said. "Know your limits and respect them. It doesn't make you weak. It makes you smart. This isn't the kind of place where *you* could win a fight."

I had to agree but wasn't about to say it out loud. I simply gave him a curt nod and looked around for Lex. He sat uncomfortably close to one of the elves, who was now licking his fingers. The beta returned and gestured for Joon to follow.

"He's fine," Joon said, noticing my eyes on the siren. "Come."

We entered a much quieter room near the back of the building. The air was cleaner, and, except for some Faeland music, almost all the sound was drowned out.

"I fucking hate that fairy shit!" a jutting rock creature bellowed.

I had heard of the mountain men of Gygax Ridge when I was young, but I never thought I'd get to see one. The story was when the humans declared war on the werewolves, attempting to kill all omegas, the witches and Fae bewitched the mountains to fight on their behalf. I assumed it was mostly legend and, now that one sat in front of me, I couldn't help but stare.

He was oddly small in height, barely taller than me. His body appeared to be stacked and pressed sandstone, with a rough texture covered in a thin layer of loose dirt that fell and kicked up in the air every time he moved or spoke.

"Seonjoon!" he yelled, reaching a thick hand out to shake Joon's. His body moved slowly and with purpose, the rocks sliding over each other, clicking and grinding together. "How's Fennah?"

"Dead," Joon shouted. He looked angry. I took half a step away from the alpha. I was already on edge and, if he became any more provoked, the scent would surely spiral my wolf into a panic.

"Fuck, Joon," the rock man sighed loudly. "I'm very sorry. She was a good beta. A good wolf!"

"Thank you, but I need a favor, Patthar."

"For Fennah, anything. Well, almost anything. Don't ask me for money."

I smiled briefly but quickly stopped when it was clear he wasn't joking in the least. His expression was as hard as his skin.

AT FIRST, it was all business. Joon told him of the alphas we were hunting and the information he needed. But after a few hours and several foul-smelling drinks, both wolf and rock were laughing and yelling loudly about past adventures and lamenting lost loves. As time dragged on, I became incredibly bored. Neither one of them acknowledged me and, after a few failed attempts at speaking, I finally went silent.

Joon finally peeled himself away from his friend, promising future visits and gifts of hard found wine from the north. He grabbed my arm and pulled me out into the bar.

The beta from earlier walked up to Joon and handed him a small slip of paper. The alpha nodded, then caught the attention of a very relaxed-looking Lex, who was practically straddling the elf. Joon pushed me out the door and into the open night air.

"You could have at least acknowledged me in there," I said, trying not to sound whiny.

"Rock men are enchanted creatures made by witches and fairy folk. They respect women deeply and refuse to speak to them unless spoken to. He was being polite to you by letting you decide if you wanted to speak to him. He would have seen it as rude if I had pulled you into the conversation without your permission."

"I tried to speak but —"

"He has ears made of stone, Tzidal," Joon said, looking over the paper in his hand. "You literally have to yell for them to hear you, and you speak barely above a whisper most of the time."

"I do not!" I spat.

"Why are you yelling?" Lex asked as he appeared next to me.

"I'm not," I mumbled.

"What did you find out?" Joon asked.

"Three alphas came in two days ago asking around about wolves with marked skin. My friend," Lex smirked, pointing at the doorway behind him, "says that one of them is the Were King's son."

"Really?" I asked, a little shocked.

"That changes nothing," Joon said firmly.

I nodded in agreement but still couldn't help the uneasy feeling in my gut. No one batted an eye when wolves settled a score or grudge that ended in bloodshed or death, but to kill a noble would mean a bounty on all our heads.

"Anything else?"

Lex shook his head, then adjusted his robes. He seemed to have just realized how dirty he was, a pout firmly on his face. "Once we settle somewhere, I need a meal and to phase," he said flatly. "I'm sick of this face."

"Come," Joon said. "We're going to the Kaska Inn."

"What's there?" I asked.

Joon pocketed the scrap of paper.

"Our prey."

Kaska Inn

Joon

I HADN'T STEPPED foot in the Kaska Inn since before I met Fennah. It was the kind of place young alphas sought out a cheap drink and an even cheaper fuck. Betas, elves, and even a few blood-drinkers worked the customers over every night, bringing them pleasure and occasionally death if they didn't pay their bar tab.

I was worried about dragging Tzidal there, but I didn't want to say it out loud. It was as if she had something to prove lately, and I didn't want her acting irrational just to make a point.

"Okaaay," Lex nodded in approval, looking around the smoky parlor filled with loud, horny beasts of all kinds. "This is my kind of place."

He stepped forward, looking eager to get lost in the crowd, but I grabbed his arm and pulled him back. "I need you," I said.

"I love it when big, sexy men say that to me," Lex smiled.

I groaned and walked to the bar to purchase a room for the night, leaving the siren to watch Tzidal.

Patthar's men believed the alphas were still here, and my plan was simple enough. First, I needed to track them down. Which, admittedly, was the hard part, but we'd start here at the bar and work our way through the city. Once we found them, I'd return to the Inn and wait. Lex would seduce one of them and bring them up to the room. Then I'd take it from there.

It was simple and bound to go fuck-all wrong. I just hoped we could find at least one of the three alphas soon. They clearly had more wolves to hunt down, and I had no intention of letting them live long enough to carry out their plans.

I returned with a key in my pocket, noticing a drink in Tzidal's hand. "Where did you get that?"

"That beta over there bought it for me," she motioned to a short, eager-looking wolf.

"Did you drink any of it?"

"Not yet," she said, eyeing the glass.

I grabbed it, looked directly at the beta, and threw it down, glass shards spraying all over the floor. The sound could barely be heard over the rowdy customers and jarring music, but I made my point. The beta's expression went sour as he turned back to his drink.

Tzidal pulled her lips into a tight line, and her nose scrunched up. I was ready for the little beast to give me a fight, but her face fell, looking just past me. She gasped softly, tugging at my arm. "Look!" She gestured to the other side of the room.

Son of a bitch.

Byna and Byriel stood at the end of the bar. The female laughed and slammed down an impressive number of shots. She joked loudly with a few nearby drunks, making a spectacle of herself. Byriel looked solemn, staring off into the distance. My blood boiled, and my breath quickened. I desperately wanted to rush across the room and crack both their heads open onto the bar.

A feather-light touch rested on my forearm, and I glanced down to see Tzidal looking at me with determined, quiet eyes.

"Not yet," she said. "Soon."

I nodded and pulled Lex over to make sure he knew exactly who his target was. Then I grabbed Tzidal's hand and ushered her up the stairs toward the room. It was a decent size space with a large bed, washbasin, wardrobe, and a few lanterns giving off a soft glow. But most importantly, it was at the far end of the lodge, meaning we weren't very likely to be bothered, no matter how much noise we made.

"Will you shift now or wait?" Tzidal asked. She seemed calm. Very calm.

"No shifting here," I said, pointing to a bundle of lavender colored flowers hung above the door. It was wolfsbane. "They don't exactly mind a rowdy crowd, but an old-fashioned fist-fight causes a lot less damage than a couple of werewolves going at it."

"Would it be better to try to get them outside?" she asked, opening the wardrobe and looking it over.

"They'll be more guarded out there. This is better." She grabbed a few blankets stacked at the bottom of the wardrobe and tucked them under the bed. "What are you doing?"

"I'm making room so we can hide in here."

"I'm not hiding," I scoffed.

"Yeah? And what happens if Lex gets Byriel up here and he sees you before they even reach the doorway, and he decides to run? Then what?" she asked with a hand on her hip. "Are you going to chase him through the city? Hope he doesn't disappear? Warn his friends?" She paused, looking as if she was ready for a fight. "This way, you can make sure he's in the room and cornered before you make your move."

"Fair point," I nodded. "It's smart. But why are we both hiding in there? I don't think you should be here when —"

"Then where should I be?" she snapped. "Out in the streets making new friends? Or how about down in the parlor with that drunk beta? Maybe he'll buy me another drink," she said with an annoyed lift to her voice.

"I got it," I huffed. "Just...stay in there, okay? I don't want you to get hurt."

She nodded.

The sound of voices drifted from just down the hallway. Tzidal startled, and I guided her into the wardrobe, tucking myself in with her before shutting the doors.

It was a tight fit. I had to lean down a bit, pushing my face into her hair. She squirmed for a moment, then placed her hands on my forearms, steadying herself. A small amount of light from the crack in the doors illuminated her profile perfectly. Her breath was even, and she looked almost serene. I could feel her quickening heartbeat from our proximity, but her presence was still so comforting.

Her sweet, floral scent lingered around me, and I inhaled deeply, letting it fill my lungs. It made my blood crackle and skin hum.

Tzidal slowly brought her gaze up my body to my eyes. I was staring, but I couldn't stop myself. She was so damn close with those bright eyes filled with so much fire. She licked her soft lips, and my wolf growled. Her pink mouth was just waiting for me to claim it, nip it, make soft moans fall from it.

I leaned down, just wanting to inhale her sweet breath when a loud bang reverberated throughout the room. I angled my head to peer through the crack in the door the best I could.

The bedroom door swung hard, slamming against the wall

as two figures stumbled in. I recognized the pattern and color of the robes on one of the creatures. It was Lex, but he was wearing a different face. And a different body. Cleavage, and lots of it, flashed briefly in my eye line before disappearing with the other figure as they both fell hard onto the bed.

My heart hammered in my chest, and I closed my eyes, preparing myself. I wanted this to be over so fucking bad, but I also wanted to savor it. I wanted to inflict the same pain they had forced so many others to endure.

Small hands cupped my face, and I opened my eyes to see Tzidal looking at me hard. Her posture was tense and resolute. She simply nodded.

It was all I needed.

The Corner Room

Tzidal

I RELEASED JOON'S FACE. He gave me a small smile then slammed his body into the wardrobe doors, busting one of them clean off its hinges.

A beautiful, golden-haired elvish woman with pointed features straddled a female alpha on the bed. She screamed and grabbed the front of her robes, Lex's robes, then flung herself across the room. My eyes moved over Lex's elvish face, and she jerked to reach for me. But Joon's body flew through the air, hitting the opposite wall, startling both of us.

He jumped up and launched himself back at Byna.

Lex hesitated, her eyes darting between me and the two alphas ripping into each other on the bed. A crack of a growl cut through the room, and I hunkered down in the closet, trying to make myself as small as possible.

"Go!" I mouthed to Lex in a rough whisper, trying not to draw attention to myself. "I'm fine. Go!"

Lex hesitated for a few moments, but another piercing roar caused her elvish form to jump, and she ran out of the room. The door slammed shut behind her.

Joon pinned Byna beneath his massive body and wrapped his hands around her neck.

Byna delivered a punch to his ribs.

To his gut.

To his jaw.

The scent of blood and rage choked my wolf and stung my eyes. I glanced at the door, wanting to make a run for it but thought better of it. The room was so cramped, and Byna didn't seem to realize I was here. The last thing I wanted was to move and somehow get stuck between them.

Joon grunted hard as Byna kicked her foot out into his stomach and shoved him across the room. His broad back crashed into the window, the sharp crack of splintering glass echoing around the room. He jumped up and steadied his feet, rolling back his shoulders to attack again.

"You fucking dog!" Byna yelled, her blonde ponytail askew. Her hair swung forward and fell into her face as she jumped up. "What the fuck do you want?" She stood to her full height, her figure tall and muscular.

"You killed my mate," Joon growled, standing up and matching her movements. His eyes were burning red, his wolf clearly wanting to break free. "And now I'm going to kill you."

Byna smirked. "Yeah? Which one was yours? The redhead that pleaded for her life and the life of her unborn pup? Or the alpha that cried when I threatened to track down his mate? Or the beta caught off guard patrolling her village?"

Joon stiffened, and she smiled.

"The beta. Hm?" Her mouth twisted into a wicked grin, displaying her pointed teeth. "What kind of village gives a fucking beta so much power? She couldn't sniff out three alphas closing in, but you thought she could protect a whole village?" Joon's jaw clenched, and the vein in his neck pulsed. Byna shook her head, clicking her tongue mockingly. "More's the pity. Still, she went quickly, though she cowered as she sensed death approaching."

Joon said nothing, but his muscular shoulders rose and fell with each harsh breath, betraying his anger. The power behind his dark scowl made my breath hitch, and the small sound pulled Byna's attention.

"What's this?" Byna laughed, baring her teeth and looking me over. "Having one mate killed wasn't enough? You brought me another?"

Joon let out a strangled growl and rushed Byna. He grabbed her arms and shoved her body hard into the wall, sinking his teeth into her shoulder. Byna roared and kicked out, dragging her claws over his back, blood blooming through his shirt.

Joon punched her in the jaw.

Punched her in the ribs.

Raised his fist to deliver another blow.

Byna head-butted him.

The crack to his skull clunked in my ears and knocked him backward.

The she-wolf rushed to me, her hair sticking to her sweaty face. Her eyes were wild and savage, and pulsing red. I froze in complete terror. She grabbed my arm, jerking me out into the open.

"Let her go!" Joon roared, flexing his muscles and angling his body forward.

Byna's grip was tight as she yanked me to her powerful body, using my slight frame like a shield. "Do you want to watch your alpha die?" she whispered low in my ear, running her nose along my neck. I swallowed down a whimper, fighting my tears. "Such a sweet, little omega. How about I force her to sit like a good pup and watch while I rip your guts out?" she clicked her tongue, mocking Joon.

He jerked forward but stopped when Byna's clawed hand wrapped around my throat, wrenching my head up. "Stop!" she ordered in a firm voice, her brown eyes boring into Joon's. His muscles tightened and flexed, violence boiling within him. The she-wolf seemed to enjoy his rage flooding the room.

"Before your mate died, she begged for her life," Byna whispered, her lips caressing my ear. "She cried and begged at my feet like a coward," she laughed. "Who would want to be bound to something so weak? I did you a fucking favor."

Joon bared his teeth and let out a sharp growl as he slowly circled his prey.

Byna mimicked his movements as she again turned her attention to me. I wanted to look away, to submit and cower, but the wrath pouring off Joon was feeding into me. It made me feel stronger and braver than I had ever felt before.

"Beg him to save you," Byna whispered low in my ear. Her claws twisted around my throat, piercing my flesh ever so slightly. "Beg him while I rip your tongue out."

My wolf whined at the authority in her voice, and I struggled to look at her face. Byna's glassy eyes were narrowed and filled with a disturbing exhilaration. I shuddered, then lifted my head, bearing my throat in submission at the feral woman. I couldn't help it.

"Tell your alpha he's weak," Byna ordered loudly.

"Joon," I whispered, my voice strained and my wolf bellowing, making tears drip out of the corners of my eyes. Byna grinned, running her tongue over her teeth.

I sucked in a shuttering breath and spoke as loudly as I could. "Kill her."

Byna's face fell into shock at my pointed defiance, and I went dead weight, falling to the floor. I kicked out my feet and pushed myself against the wall, out of the way.

Joon was on top of the she-wolf before I could even look up. He clawed, bit, scratched, and punched. His movements were wild and frenzied. He might not have been able to shift, but, at the moment, he was more beast than man.

Byna tried to meet his fury, but she struggled. Joon lashed out at every piece of flesh he could reach. Eventually, she was able to dig her nails into his side, forcing him beneath her. Joon kicked out hard, but she didn't move. She simply shoved harder into him, and his breath caught.

In a rush of adrenaline and panic, I ran toward the window and grabbed the biggest shard of glass I could find. I hurled myself as hard as I could into Byna and sank the sharp object into her back right between her ribs. It slipped into her easily, blood pulsing out in quick spurts around the glass.

The alpha stiffened and gasped, gulping for air. My eyes met Joon's briefly before I raced to the other side of the room, leaving him to finish her off.

Joon pulled Byna's wheezing body to him and sank his teeth deep into her throat. He stilled for the briefest moment, then kicked out and flung her across the room, a chunk of her flesh still secure in his mouth.

Byna stumbled backward, blood gushing out of her throat and down her body. Her breath came out in wet, stunted pants. Joon stood up and narrowed his dark eyes. Without a word, he let out a vicious snarl and barreled into her, shoving his shoulder right into Byna's gut. She let out a quick, pained grunt before flying out the open window.

With weak knees, I made my way over and looked outside. Byna's body twitched in a thick pool of blood, her blonde hair soaking red in the moonlight. A pair of drunk trolls pointed and laughed at her mangled corpse before stumbling off.

I turned to Joon. He had ripped off his shirt and was washing the blood off his face and chest in the washbasin. How it had managed not to get destroyed, I didn't know.

Crossing the room quickly, I grabbed his face, relief washing over me. I looked into his rich brown eyes wanting to tell him how strong he was, so brave and fierce, but the words wouldn't leave my mouth.

His eyes were dark and wild as they darted over every inch of my face. He looked unhinged and possessive, and it sparked something deep within me. Without thinking, I tangled my fingers in his hair and pulled him to me, kissing him deeply.

The alpha instantly responded, pulling my body flush with his. Joon growled low in his throat as he forced my lips open, dipping his wet tongue into my mouth.

His hands moved down my back, stopping to squeeze my ass before grabbing my thighs to pick me up. He stumbled across the wrecked room and fell forward onto the bed, my body still tangled in his arms.

Adrenaline and fear melted into an all-consuming lust, making my core clench with a desperate heat.

Joon moved down my jaw to my neck, sucking long and hard. He pressed his lips to the pulsing vein in my throat, letting out a deep moan that radiated through my whole body. His mouth felt so damn good on my skin.

Joon rolled his hips forward, and I could feel his long, hard girth against my hip, making the ache in my belly twist. I was so wet and ready for him.

"Fuck," he rumbled deep in his throat. "You're mine," he growled as he grazed his teeth over my sensitive skin, making my pussy clench. "All mine."

I could do nothing but nod. At that moment, I was his.

The Bed

Joon

I LICKED the sweat off the soft curve of Tzidal's neck, letting her scent flood my senses. Her sweet moans spurred me on, making me rock hard. I sucked and licked all along her neck, collarbone, and shoulders, pulling her shirt down to get to more of her sweet skin as she pushed her hips up in a desperate hunt for friction.

My cock strained in my pants, need intensifying with each flick of my tongue. *Fuck! She smelled so good, and she tasted even better.*

I leaned up and pulled her shirt off, exposing her perfect breasts. Soft mounds of flesh with pert, pink nipples begging for my tongue. I looked up at her face, making sure she was okay before pressing on. Her blissed-out expression and soft whimpers gave me all the permission I needed.

I leaned down, taking her sensitive nipple into my mouth, sucking and swirling the hard bud between my lips. Tzidal moaned and pushed her hips up into mine, making me hiss. I moved my attention to her other breast, gently tugging and kneading the delicate flesh.

Moans rolled off her tongue as I dipped my head lower, running my hands down her sides and sucking at her stomach and hips, leaving faint love bites as I went.

I pulled at her pants, stripping her completely naked, before reaching for my waistband, desperate to free my straining cock from my painfully tight pants. My member bobbed heavy and ready as she looked at me with hungry eyes. Tzidal licked her lips, making me desperate to see my cock between them.

I settled between her legs and grabbed her thighs, spreading her wide. Her pussy dripped, and I inhaled deeply at the delicious sight.

"Fuck," I moaned, dropping between her legs.

I nuzzled my face against her inner thigh, kissing and sucking at the skin as I worked my way closer to her core. I swiped my tongue through her folds, pressing a little harder right over her swollen clit. She yelled out and jerked up.

"Wuh, what..." she stuttered. "What are you..."

"Shhh," I placed a hand on her chest, easing her back down. "Let me taste you."

Had her mate never forced her to come with his mouth? It was shocking for me to think an alpha had possessed such an exquisite creature and had not licked every fucking inch of her.

I swiped my tongue over her wet clit again, flicking it back and forth. Her breath quickened, and she moaned louder and longer, threading her fingers through my hair. I thrust my tongue into her as far as it would go, swirling it around, sucking and tasting her. Her sweet slick coated my mouth, and I moaned loudly, forcing the vibrations over her pussy. Her thighs trembled, and her grip on my hair tightened almost painfully. I reveled in it, puckering my lips and sucking hard as she came into my mouth.

"Ngh...alpha!" she gasped, squeezing her thighs against my head while her body trembled uncontrollably from her orgasm.

I didn't give her time to recover. I crawled over her still-shaking body and took hold of the base of my cock. I pressed against her pulsing slit, sinking slowly into her tight, wet heat. Her mouth dropped open in a silent scream as I stretched her open. It was agony not to slam into her, taking her hard and fast, but I wanted to feel her. To taste her. To fucking bathe in her moans.

I waited, holding myself over her, letting her adjust to the intrusion. Her eyes were blown out, and her hair was wild, already looking thoroughly fucked. She gulped, panting, before giving me a quick nod. I rolled my hips, and her eyes rolled into the back of her head. She grabbed my shoulders, fingers curling into my flesh, as I quickened my pace.

Thrusting longer, harder, faster.

Plunging into hot, sloppy kisses.

Groping soft, sweet flesh.

"*Fuck*, you feel so good," I growled against her mouth, not slowing the pace of my hips as I breathed in her sweet scent. "So fucking tight."

I nipped at her jaw and neck as I continued pumping into her. Pulling all the way out before plunging back in again. My instincts quickly took over, and my hips pistoned faster and harder. Fucking into her wildly, ultimately yielding to my wolf.

Tzidal moaned and shuddered beneath me, her body tensing as her pussy clenched around my cock.

"Fuck, yes. Let go, baby," I growled. "Come for me!"

"Ah...alpha!" she called out, dragging her nails over my skin. "Don't stop! Please...nnngh!"

I was unable to hold back the growl that ripped from my throat as I took her body, feeling her tremble and throb, completely unraveling beneath me.

I snapped my hips a few more times, feeling my end approaching. Then I stilled briefly as my cock pulsed, and cum drenched her inner walls, seeping out around my shaft. I slowly rolled my hips forward, letting both of us ride out our high. Tzidal's eyes fluttered as I continued to push into her gently.

I stopped my movements, then leaned in and softly kissed her lips. Inhaling her soft scent, I moved my mouth over hers, savoring the feel of the omega in my arms. Tzidal's puffy, pink lips moved perfectly against mine, and I dipped my tongue in, tasting everything she had to offer.

She smelled like jasmine, but she tasted like honey.

So soft, so sweet.

The Throne Room

Byriel

I WALKED down the long castle corridor. The stones beneath my feet slid and rolled with each step like the scales on a snake. Guards flanked each side of me, standing single file along the walls. Their motionless presence made my wolf uneasy and restless.

I quickened my pace, the stones moving faster. The guards snapped their heads toward me as I passed, their eyes hollow and menacing. My heart quickened, and I ran. My footsteps echoed loudly in my ears. The walls pushed down, and the guards crowded me.

I could feel my heart thumping wildly in my throat, and my ears buzzed with a rushing silence that caused my head to pulse. Just when I thought my heart would seize from its thundering movements, I burst out of the corridor and into the massive throne room.

It was quiet and still. My breath hitched as my eyes swept

across the room. A chill in the air made me shiver, scattering goosebumps all over my clammy skin.

My father, sitting on his throne, and my sister, tense at his side, stared at me calmly from the front of the room.

"Come and bow to the King of Wolves," my sister commanded, her voice echoing off the dark, stone walls.

My body moved even though I didn't want to. I quickly approached my King and bowed low at his feet. My nose hovered just above the floor.

"You must prove your worth to him," Strayton smiled, placing her thin hand on our father's shoulder. "Prove what your King means to you."

A baby's cries filled the hall, echoing off the walls and reverberating through my bones. One of my father's stewards stepped toward me with a tiny pup in his hands. The child's arms and legs kicked out, and it cried louder as the thin blanket covering it slipped off, leaving the poor thing naked and shivering.

Strayton stepped forward and placed a dagger in my hand.

"Prove it," she said, her wicked grin displaying pointed teeth.

My fingers curled around the cold handle as I stepped toward the pup. A red, crescent-shaped mark shone brightly on its belly. I raised the blade and swallowed back a thick sob, then took a deep breath allowing silent tears to roll down my face.

"Do it!" My father roared.

I let a sob rip from my throat as I plunged the knife down.

I JERKED awake in a cold sweat.

My breath was ragged as I wiped at the tears running down my face and neck. I couldn't remember the last time I had slept soundly. Every night the souls of those I had murdered haunted my dreams. I had taken their lives, and now they were slowly taking my sanity.

I was a warrior. I had fought so many magical beings and beasts. Killing for honor, love, and pride. But I had never killed a child before, and I feared my soul would never recover.

I stood up and looked up at the Moon. She hung brightly in the night's sky, bringing me the smallest amount of comfort. I took a heavy breath, then moved my feet. I needed to keep going. I needed to make it to Vaesen as quickly as possible.

It had only been a few hours since Byna's lifeless body lay at my feet, and I didn't know who might be on my heels.

I had stepped out of the Inn, needing a break from the rowdy crowd and stale air, when Byna's body flew out of a window, splattering onto the road in front of me. The shock of seeing her broken, bloody corpse made me freeze momentarily before my senses returned. I looked up at the broken window she had fallen from to see an omega leaning out. I recognized her almost immediately.

She was the mate of an alpha we killed at Madra. Hida tried attacking her, and now this was our penance, being done in by a simple omega. The stars were so clearly angry with me, they sent the weakest creature in our lands to deliver me to my end.

But if I could get to Vaesen, perhaps I could escape my fate...I hoped.

Death was coming for me, as it should. I just prayed it would be quick. Not that I deserved it.

The Next Morning

Tzidal

THE SUN POURED through the broken window, casting golden streaks of light across the floorboards.

I straddled Joon, rolling my hips at a lustful, sloppy pace. My body tensed, and I called out as a wave of pleasure ripped through me. Joon's large hands gripped my ass as he thrust up into my spent body, causing me to jerk with each rough movement.

"Don't stop, baby," he growled through gritted teeth. "Just like that."

My body went limp, and I struggled to stay upright, exhaustion consuming me. Joon grabbed my hips, helping me move over him. He swelled and hardened within me, on the verge of coming. He pulled my head down by my hair and latched his lips onto my throat. His hips stilled, and his body stiffened as he spilled his orgasm into me, dragging his teeth over my flesh.

Panic flashed through my body, and I went rigid, jerking out of his hold. I clamped my hand over my old mating bite, where his teeth just grazed, unsure of what to say or do.

"I wasn't going to mark you," Joon said softly through heavy pants. His cock still pulsing within me.

"I know," I whispered, keeping my eyes cast down. The apples of my cheeks going bright red.

"Baby, are you okay?" His voice was tender and concerned, making me feel even worse.

Joon cupped my cheek briefly before running his fingers through my hair. I nodded quickly, suddenly consumed with an urge to cry. I swallowed it down and smiled as brightly as I could, but I could tell he didn't believe it.

An awkward silence settled between us. Joon looked like he wanted to say something, but instead, he turned his attention to rubbing small circles over my thighs with his thumbs. It was so comforting.

I opened my mouth to apologize, but I didn't want to say out loud that I didn't want him to mark me, so I kept quiet. The scar from my mating bite was the only piece of Korban I had left, and I wasn't willing to let it go just yet.

"We have to leave soon," he said quietly, his voice laced with a hint of sadness.

I laid my head over his chest and tried to relax. I felt so guilty, even as my body continued to thrum in the aftermath of our indescribable night together. It was all very overwhelming.

He shifted his hips, and I moaned brokenly as his cock slipped out of me. Our fluids dripped out down my thighs and onto his hips, and Joon groaned deep in his throat.

I propped my head on his chest and looked over his still flushed face. He was so handsome.

"Okay, my puppies!" Lex sang as she burst into the room. She gasped dramatically, placing a hand on her heart. "Oh!

And what do we have here?" She moved her eyes over our very naked and sweaty bodies.

"What the fuck?" Joon yelled, quickly moving me behind him and shielding me from the siren's view. A loud growl ripped through him, and he bared his teeth.

I placed my hand on his shoulder and laughed. "That's Lex," I said.

Lex still wore the same body as the previous night, elvish features with long, golden hair and a striking figure. She smiled at the alpha and swished her robes at him. Joon narrowed his eyes, then his muscles relaxed.

"I'm sorry," he said. "I forgot what you looked like."

"Well, I came to yell at you. But after catching the two of you like this, I don't know if I have the heart to ruin such an *interesting* morning," Lex said, practically dancing across the room and snuggling up to my still very naked body. I giggled and threw my arms over the siren's slight shoulders despite feeling awkward wrapped in only a blanket.

Joon groaned and got up, pulling on his pants.

"Why were you going to yell at us?" I asked.

"Not you, silly. Him," Lex said, pointing a long finger at the alpha. "I had a plan last night, you know! I was going to kiss your wolf friend and knock her out so Tzidal and I could get to safety before you went all feral on her. You scared the shit out of me jumping out of the closet like that, you asshole."

"I'm sorry, but can you put the old face back on?" Joon asked. "It's hard to talk to you like a friend when you look like a stranger." Lex huffed, a gentle pout on her perfect lips. "You don't have to," Joon groaned. "I just find comfort in familiar faces, and this is...different."

Lex smiled sweetly and stood up, her appearance melting away like rain down a windowpane. Her face drifted back into the young man I had met in the forest. Lex stepped toward the alpha and placed a quick kiss on his cheek.

"We don't want to upset our big, bad wolf. Do we?" he cooed, turning to look at me. "He finds comfort in my beautiful face."

"That's not what I said," Joon mumbled.

Lex was already dancing his way out the door, purposefully ignoring the alpha. Joon swung it shut behind him, then moved toward me, nervous lines etched between his eyes.

"Omega," he said in a loud, firm voice. He paused, then pushed out a deep sigh, letting his shoulders relax and slump a bit. "Tzidal," he said softly, his dark eyes dancing all over my face.

My heart fluttered at the way his mouth held my name.

He stood at the foot of the bed, not quite meeting my eyes. He opened his mouth to speak but quickly closed it. I was suddenly nervous, my mind working over several possibilities as silence reigned between us.

Maybe he regretted our night together.

Maybe he wanted to talk about my hasty reaction to him marking me.

Or maybe he wanted to pretend none of this had happened.

Either way, my stomach filled with dread. I wrapped the blanket tighter around my shoulders, feeling vulnerable and stupid, waiting for him to speak.

Joon's eyes flashed up to mine for a quick moment, then he bent down and grabbed my clothes, handing them to me. "We should get going," he said, clearing his throat. "We have a long way to go before the cursed land, and we need to get supplies to prepare."

I pulled my shirt on, watching as he walked out the door.

Regret lanced my chest. I wondered if he hated me for so clearly rejecting him. I hadn't meant to react so strongly. After all, he had sucked and licked at my neck all night. But for some reason, in the light of day, it felt different. It was like all the passion had melted away, and I was stuck with the realization that I had laid with an alpha that wasn't my mate.

Thick, sour guilt flooded my mouth.

I felt guilty for betraying Korban.

For rejecting Joon.

But most of all, I felt guilty for how badly I craved for Joon to sink his teeth deep into my flesh.

The Barren Lands...Again

Joon

WE STOOD on a precipice just outside Gygax overlooking the span of desert before us. It stretched on forever, a reminder of the daunting journey ahead. This side of the desert would take twice as long to cross, and we didn't have the comforts of a friendly city waiting for us on the other side. But we were lucky this time, our journey being much less eventful and bloody. We only encountered a few snakes and the occasional troll that simply grunted at our presence then stalked off.

After several days, a storm came into view far off in the distance, hanging over the cursed lands. It looked inviting as we traveled across the scorching dirt, the sun's rays burning into my skin. I couldn't help but look forward to the promise of shade, no matter how painful the acid-like rain would be.

The dark clouds got larger the longer we walked, and I could hear the muffled sound of thunder at night. We were starting to run out of water when I woke one morning to feel a wisp of a cool breeze coming from the rain-drenched land.

I stared at Tzidal as she watched the lightning dance in the thick, black clouds just a few paces away. We decided to rest for the day, then breach the barrier first thing in the morning. The storm would be very hard on our bodies, and it was essential to be at full strength before moving on.

"It's not normal rain, is it?" Tzidal asked.

"Will it hurt?" Lex turned to me.

"Yes. It will."

"Of course it will," Tzidal mumbled. "Why can't anything be normal out here?"

"It is normal for out here," Lex replied, poking her side. "Everything out here is looking for its next meal, including the rain." He gave her a menacing laugh.

"And how exactly do you fight the rain?" she snorted.

"With a couple of fat palm leaves tied to your head."

"Are you saying I just need one good coat to win a war against the clouds?"

They continued laughing and teasing each other, but I couldn't enjoy it. We'd be in the thick of it by mid-morning, and we needed to prepare if we were to get to Vaesen in one piece.

The city had been a haven for humans during the war. They had captured it then forced witches and Fae to curse the land around it, flooding it with rain that stripped anyone of their enchantments. Heavily magicked creatures, like rock men and Fae, almost immediately died. Others simply couldn't bear the pain of having a portion of themselves burned away and eventually succumbed to the torture before making it out. This left the land riddled with corpses for scavengers and wayward beasts to rip apart.

I was worried, not fully knowing what to expect. I had never been forced to walk over the cursed lands before, always getting to Vaesen by boat. But the ports were heavily guarded, and stowaways were thrown overboard or killed on sight. I knew I'd be able to hide on a ship easily, but three of us was just too risky.

When morning came, I sat watching the rain in the distance and glancing at Tzidal as she slept. She seemed to have rested well on this half of the trip. Before we arrived in Stone City, she had been much more prone to bad dreams and restless nights. But now, the omega appeared to be a little more at peace, or at least I hoped she was.

My wolf and body craved her in a way that weakened me, stripping my most basic instincts down to a possessive yearning to mate and settle down. It was jarring, but I wanted to embrace it. Embrace her.

I wanted to carry her away from all this pain and violence, but I couldn't. This was her fight as well. Not just mine.

I brushed a strand of hair from Tzidal's face and tucked it behind her ear. She was just so lovely.

I wanted to tell her how special she was, that she had awoken something in me I thought had died with my mate. I tried to tell her how much I did want to mark her that blissful morning in the lodge. But I couldn't, not after seeing the panic in her eyes when she slapped her hand over her throat.

I could see the love she still carried for her mate, and it made me jealous. It made my wolf snarl possessively, knowing I could never fight the dead for her affections. I would have to be patient. Something I wasn't great at. But when her heart was ready for me, I'd take her. I'd take her and keep her and make her mine. But until then, I'd wait.

I just hoped we lived long enough for me to claim her properly. Assuming she even wanted me.

"I'm so thirsty," Lex said, rolling over. His voice still groggy with sleep. "And being forced to look at all that poison water pour from the sky is just cruel."

"Maybe we'll get lucky, and it'll immediately kill you," I smirked.

"If I weren't so tired, I'd slap your gorgeous face."

"Is it time?" Tzidal asked, pulling herself up and rubbing her eyes with little fists.

"Yes," I sighed. "There's no sense putting this off."

I reached into my satchel and handed out thick, shiny capes. They were made of animal hides covered in a heavy layer of tree sap. Somewhat water-resistant, but better than nothing. I had spent the last of my gold in Stone City getting them. The merchant, sensing my desperation, marked the price up to a laughable rate until I threatened to rip his throat out.

I secured the cape around my shoulders and pulled up the hood. Then I stepped up to the wall of pouring water. It was as if an invisible barrier separated the two lands, keeping the water from spilling into the barren land. My feet still planted firmly in the desert, I held out a hand and breached the unseeable wall. The moment my fingers touched the rain, I jerked them back. A piercing pain ripped up my arm and settled inside my joints.

I hissed, examining my skin. I expected to see it burned or bleeding from the stabbing sensation that radiated up my arm, but my hand looked no different. I turned to Lex and gave him a sympathetic look. *This was not going to be easy.*

"Tzidal," I said. "Remember, the rain might not affect you as badly as us, if at all. You will need to be prepared to protect or even abandon us should things get too hard or dangerous."

"I understand," she nodded, calm as ever. A fucking mountain in a sea of chaos and uncertainty. *Fuck, I adored her.*

My brave omega. Even if she didn't belong to me. Not yet, at least.

Into The Cursed Lands

Tzidal

I HELD OUT MY HAND, breeching the invisible wall of water, and waited. A slow, uncomfortable burn radiated up my arm, but I could bear it. I didn't have a choice. I nodded at Joon and Lex before stepping from the cracked, thirsty desert onto the sopping wet grass.

My cape protected my head and most of my body, but my bare feet couldn't be helped. Pain stabbed into my legs, where the rain fell against the earth then splashed up, hitting my skin.

Lex crossed the threshold and almost immediately doubled over. He caught himself before he fell, but his body stayed slumped over as he pushed forward. I eyed the siren hard as he slowly passed me, not confident he wouldn't topple over.

Joon wasn't much better. His tan complexion was already washed out and sickly, and his chest heaved as he followed Lex.

I shoved my fear aside and stepped inline behind them, scanning the distance the best I could through the hammering rain.

As we walked, the vegetation around us became thicker and bigger. We passed mushrooms, fat and red. Tall enough to be used as comfortable seats. And flowers shaped like bells leaned upward as if trying to kiss the sky, falling over when they became too heavy with rain, then bouncing back up once all the water spilled out.

I stumbled many times as we moved. Vines were so thick, stretching lazily over the ground, that there were many places where I couldn't even see the grass because of them. It felt like they were trying to coil themselves around me and suck me beneath the soil.

It was hard to believe how colorful everything was. It stormed so hard, pulling at my skin and cape as if it were trying to force me to the ground. It felt as if the pummeling rain could have stripped the color off of anything it touched. There was also no sun. The light grey sky offered nothing but an onslaught of water and the occasional rumble of thunder. How anything grew here, I just didn't understand.

As the day wore on and night approached, I had no idea what to do about food. Lex ate during our last night in the desert, but Joon needed something soon. I walked over to a heavy, yellow plant hanging low on a tree. It looked harmless enough, but so did the rain. The second I plucked it, the tree branch snapped upward, making me jump. I cradled the heavy melon-like plant and walked toward Joon.

I asked the alpha if we could eat it, but it was as if no words left my mouth. All sound sucked into the pounding of water on grass, trees, and plants. I frowned, my ears giving up on ever hearing another sound again.

Slowly, I grabbed Lex's upper arm and guided him to a cluster of trees. They would provide a decent amount of cover for the night. The siren, wrapped tightly in his cape, looked smaller somehow. He was a thin creature to begin with and only a little taller than me, but he walked as if he had shriveled into himself. I tried leaning down to look up into his hood, but he bowed his head further, avoiding my eyes.

I guided him onto the ground and sat the melon next to him. Then I turned to retrieve Joon. He was walking toward me as if in a haze. His steps were unsteady and his direction a little jolting. He looked...confused.

Once I had them both sitting under the trees, I pulled off my cape, becoming instantly drenched. Pain burrowed into my skin, and I hissed at the sensation, every breath pinching my ribs.

I draped the waxy fabric over the ground then heaved Joon on top of it. I hoped it would provide at least a little protection against the wet grass. I shoved Lex into Joon's arms and situated their capes to better shield them from the water dripping between the branches.

My whole body shook with a deep, dull ache that pulled at my muscles and twisted my bones. It made me dizzy and queasy.

I grabbed the melon and tried pushing my nails into the flesh, but it wouldn't break. I snuck over to Joon and pulled his hand free. A broken moan drifted from the alpha, but I ignored it, too hungry. The alpha's claws slipped into the fruit and I laughed when it tore open quickly. I tucked his hand back in the safety of the cape, then ripped off a chunk of the fruit's flesh. It was orange in color, like the sunset back home, and it looked innocent but terrifying at the same time. *It looked delicious.*

I popped it into my mouth and held it there, waiting. No pain spread across my tongue. I chewed and swallowed. No pain ran down my throat. I paused, wondering if I'd simply fall over dead or if the stars would be kind enough to let me finish the whole thing before it killed me.

Fuck it, I thought.

I took a huge bite, feasting wildly. Sticky juices ran down my chin, and I was thankful for a liquid that didn't burn my skin. I finished almost half of it in no time before moving back to Joon.

I adjusted his hood to better see his face then placed a small piece of fruit in his mouth. I patted his cheek, trying to wake him enough to get him to eat. He slowly chewed and swallowed, not appearing to be in any more pain than before. It was pitch black by the time I finished feeding him, but he would need as much strength as possible come morning.

I had no idea how long it would take to get out of these lands, and I had every intention of all three of us making it to Vaesen safely. No matter what I had told Joon, there was no way I would abandon them.

I leaned back and had only just closed my eyes when heavy, thumping footsteps made me jerk awake. I couldn't see anything in the black, wet night around me. The clouds offered no reprieve for the Moon, and the rain made everything in the distance grey and hazy.

I jumped up and grabbed a thick, fallen branch. I held it out defensively as I crouched near Joon and Lex's limp bodies.

The thumping footsteps returned, closer this time, shaking the ground. I glared out into the night as a guttural bellow overpowered the sound of the rain.

Something darted out of the darkness toward me, and I swung.

Under The Trees

Joon

A BOOMING ROAR rang in my ears and heavy footsteps vibrated against my cheek. I begged my body to open my eyes, but it refused, fighting hard against me. I was so exhausted. My body pulsed with a sharp pain that ripped through me, leaving me unable to make even the simplest movement.

Tzidal grunted and yelled out, forcing my eyes to finally snap open. I could see the omega swinging a stick at a pair of flat, fat lizards. They were massive, almost the same size as the omega. They lunged hard and fast at her, baring their teeth and whipping their long tongues at her feet. The reptiles swung their heavy tails, hissing and roaring. The sharp talons on their saucer-like feet dug into the soft earth, and their eyes shone like mirrors, putting off a pinkish glow in the otherwise black night.

I tried pulling myself up, desperate to help, but my flesh hung on my bones like dead meat, unwilling to move. I begged my wolf for strength, but he was utterly silent within me. I was so empty and weak. A few tears fell from my eyes as I watched helplessly.

Tzidal snarled and swung at the horrid beasts, moving quickly in the heavy rain. Her soft body drenched and panting.

I did nothing to protect Fennah from death, I did nothing as Byna dragged her hands over Tzidal's trembling body, and now I did nothing as she was attacked mere feet from me by wild creatures. I was a horrible alpha, not fit to protect. This was why the Moon had ripped my mate from me and why Tzidal was so quick to reject me.

I didn't have the right to lay claim to anyone.

I let out a desperate moan, letting my despair consume me. I hoped, come morning, Tzidal would leave my body here to rot, saving herself and Lex. I wanted her to get to Vaesen and take the life she was owed. She deserved a happy ending to her story. She deserved so much better than I could ever give her.

My eyes pulled themselves closed, too weak to stay open anymore. And I slipped back into a black fog, listening to the sounds of Tzidal yelling and grunting, her voice becoming smaller and softer as she drifted away.

Into The Cave

Tzidal

THE SKY slowly turned from black to a dull grey as the morning set in. I clung to the branch, still clutched tightly in my fist. My torso was draped over Joon and Lex's bodies, sweat and rain dripping down the side of my face.

My eyes darted around, terrified the lizard-like monsters might return. The creatures spent almost the entire night trying to get to Joon and Lex, eventually abandoning their attempt just a few hours before dawn. Or at least it felt like a few hours. I tried to sleep the best I could, but every little sound that managed to cut through the pounding of the rain caused me to jerk awake. I glared long and hard into the storm, looking for any movement, before allowing my body to relax again.

Staring up at the heavy clouds, I understood why people just laid down and died here. It was so tempting just to let my exhaustion and the relentless water push my body deep into the soggy earth, never to get up again.

Groaning, I forced myself to my feet.

I heaved at Joon's arms and shoved hard at his back, pushing his body upright. He finally stood, his face blank of all emotion except the pain etched around his eyes. He swayed for a moment, but his legs appeared to be steady enough. I eyed a small cut on his arm. One of the lizards was able to get close enough to scratch him before I fought it off, but, thankfully, it was barely skin deep.

I turned my attention to Lex, quickly lifting him to his feet. His body curled tight in on itself, and he fell over quickly.

I pulled my cape off the ground and secured it before leaning down and hoisting Lex over my shoulder. It was shocking how light he was, but I knew I'd feel his weight before mid-morning. I was concerned, though. He looked even smaller than yesterday, and I wondered if it were possible that he could melt into himself and disappear altogether before we made it to safer ground.

My head hurt from the rain beating the trees and ground, and my shoulders ached from the weight of Lex's stiff body. Joon dragged his feet in front of me, his cape softly swaying at his knees. I was careful to keep him within my eyesight, too terrified he'd keel over and I wouldn't notice.

The day slipped by so quickly, and it felt as if we had barely moved more than a few feet. I glanced around, looking for a decent spot to put Lex down, when I saw a slumped-over corpse wedged under a huge, wine-capped mushroom. The waxy skin of the long-dead creature hung to its bones. Vines tangled around its limbs and wove through what used to be its mouth, and a tight grouping of fungus bloomed out of an otherwise empty eye socket.

I swallowed convulsively, trying to push back the nausea

that rose up my throat. A low whine forced its way out of my chest, and hot tears ran down my cheeks, mixing with the cool rain. Lex's stiff form pulled hard at my body, making my back and knees ache.

We might die here.

I softly placed Lex on the wet grass and gave myself a moment to cry. I tilted my head to the sky, allowing fat raindrops to lance my cheeks, lips, and eyes. Pain melted into my skull and I hissed at the sensation. Joon shuffled forward in the distance. I needed to get his attention, but I was sure there was no way he'd hear me over the deafening storm.

"Joon," I said, my voice holding no strength. "Joon, wait."

My eyes flickered just beyond him, and I jerked when I saw it, praying my eyes weren't playing tricks. A cave.

Please, let it be a cave, I said in a silent prayer.

Set off to the side of our path was a blunt cluster of rocks along the side of a hill. A dark crack in the rockface looked like it led somewhere...somewhere the rain might not be able to touch us.

I hoisted Lex back over my shoulder as adrenaline pulsed through my veins. My feet moved with renewed purpose, and I rushed past Joon toward the rocks as fast as I could, Lex still firmly in my hold.

I hesitated for a brief moment before stepping inside the cave. It was deep enough, but it was so hard to see. I set Lex down then raced back out to retrieve Joon.

Once I had them both situated inside, I moved my hands around the stone floor, thankful to feel the remnants of a fire pit. Pulling the flint rocks out of Joon's satchel, I immediately set to work lighting a fire. Within moments the leftover firewood came to life, casting a dim glow over the space. I thanked the Moon when I found a small stack of dried sticks that someone had left behind. It wouldn't be enough to last us more than one night, maybe two, if I was careful, but even the thought of a few moments of warmth filled me with excitement.

I dragged Lex's tiny body toward the fire by the hem of his cape, then slipped the hood off his head. I gasped and jerked away from the shriveled creature. Its sickly grey skin was wrinkled and hairless, without any real features other than a slit for a mouth and white, cloudy orbs for eyes.

"It's just Lex, it's just Lex," I chanted.

I pulled the cape away with shaking hands, wanting to strip off his robes to allow them to dry, but he wore nothing underneath. He was completely naked. *Were his clothes a part of the fantasy he projected? Was he always truly naked?*

His hands and feet held three digits each and spread out like a bird's talons at the end of his stick-like arms and legs. He trembled, and I gently ran a hand over his back, humming softly. My fingers brushed over tiny little feathers embedded in the withered skin along his spine. It was terrifying to see his true form, but it also somehow brought me comfort. I could feel my friend deep within the creature under my fingertips.

Once Lex stopped shaking and relaxed into the glow of the fire, I turned my attention to Joon. The massive alpha was a whole other beast to strip down, and I prayed to the Moon for strength.

I made quick work of his cape and pants, grounding my feet into the stone floor and heaving backward to get them off. But the shirt was another battle altogether. I had to wedge myself under and around him, shoving his body every which way to navigate the wet garment off his arms and finally over his head. I sat for a moment, panting and sipping slowly at our water supply.

Once I had him situated closer to the fire, I turned his head to look over his face. He was pale with deep frown lines around his eyes and mouth, even though he was out cold. To see such a strong and imposing wolf so broken and weak made my heart ache. I wanted to pour what little strength I had left into him. I wanted to see the fire in his eyes, hear his roaring laugh, and poke his adorable dimple.

I ran my fingers over his eyebrows and down the bridge of his nose, hoping to soothe him. He was so beautiful. While he made no sound, his breathing did eventually even out. I didn't know whether it was from the fire or my ministrations, but a part of me hoped it was the latter. I wanted him to find comfort in me. I wanted a part of him to need me.

I placed a soft, lingering kiss on his lips, inhaling his smokey, sweet scent.

I needed him awake. I didn't want to do this without him. I needed the alpha to hold me and run his hands through my hair. Exhausted, I pushed my nose into his chest and closed my eyes.

And for the first time since I left home, I didn't dream of Korban.

The Cave

Joon

THUNDER RUMBLED and water tapped on stone. The scent of wet rock filled my nose...*and fire*. I could smell the wonderful, musky scent of ash. *Was I dead?*

I moved my hands over the ground beneath me. It was cool but dry. Slowly, I opened my eyes, looking around. I was in a small, dark cave.

My eyes fell to the fire blazing next to me and I let out a grateful groan of relief. Thankful to have a break from the wicked rain. The air in the cave was still heavy and wet, leaving a thin layer of moisture all over my body and hair, but it was still a welcome change.

I moved to stand, and my head spun making me sit back down quickly. Trying to center myself, I sucked in several deep breaths. The sharp ache that clung to my bones wasn't near as bad as before. It was bearable.

I scooted closer to the fire, absorbing as much of the dry

heat as I could. I had never missed the desert so much. My clothes were laid out on the ground around me, and I glanced down, noticing for the first time that I was naked.

A small, pale body laid on the other side of the fire, and I crawled to it, bending down to check on Lex. He looked awful. His smooth skin was grey and dull, his normal glittering complexion gone. His face was smooth with the faint outline of lips and a nose, and he had no hair to speak of. It was as if he was molded poorly out of clay, the features were there but not completely drawn out. I leaned down to scent the siren, but the rain had washed out my nose. All I could smell was wet stone and burning wood.

"You're awake," Tzidal said as she entered the cave. She held two fat, yellow melons and a bundle of soaking wet sticks.

"I don't think those will burn," I said, my throat strained and raw.

"They're not for us," she smiled, setting the wood down. "I thought it would be kind to leave them here to dry for the next travelers. Whoever left this saved us," she motioned to the fire pit.

She handed me one of the melons and pulled off her cape, revealing her small body in only her shirt.

"I didn't want to risk getting my pants wet until I had to," she said, noticing the look on my face.

She settled next to me in front of the fire, drying her wet feet. We ate quickly, fashioning a plan for once we left. We had lasted almost two days before Tzidal truly felt she couldn't go any further. So if we couldn't make our way out of the cursed lands in that amount of time, we might truly be fucked. Luck was on our side at the moment, but who knew what tomorrow would bring.

"I think instead of taking the most direct route, we should walk mostly under the trees," she said, moving her fingers over the flames. "It might add some time, but it'll give us a little more protection from the rain. Maybe let us travel for longer."

"Then that's what we'll do."

"You don't think there's a better way?"

"I trust you," I smiled, loving the blush that dusted her cheeks as the fire warmed her skin. "You've gotten us this far by yourself. You'll get us the rest of the way."

She smiled, averting her eyes and turning her attention to the flames.

It was true. There weren't many beings in this land that I'd so willingly trust my life to, but this omega was one of them. My overwhelming sense of despair that consumed me the night before had dimmed considerably. My pride was still deeply wounded at my inability to protect Tzidal, but I had to get over it. This land was built to eat beasts like me alive, and it made me want to laugh. The strongest creatures in Havre were made to die here, but a simple omega could conquer the rain without even trying.

"I can't feel my wolf," Tzidal said softly. "It's weird. I never realized how heavily I relied on her to tell me how to react. What to do, where to go, when to run. I feel lonely without her."

I nodded.

I didn't feel lonely, though. I felt empty. I was my wolf, and my wolf was me. An alpha's dynamic with their beast was so drastically different than betas and omegas. We inhabited each other, thinking together, acting as one. I just hoped my wolf would come back. He had to come back. But I couldn't help the feeling that he might never return, that I was abandoned. A husk of a were with no beast to guide me.

"It'll be okay." I forced myself to smile. "Your wolf will return once we get to Vaesen."

Tzidal brought her finger up and poked my dimple gently,

giving me a teasing smile. Then she slapped my cheek. "Don't lie to me, you jerk. It doesn't make me feel any better."

I laughed. I couldn't help it.

She laughed with me, and we both fell into a happy moment, something neither one of us head felt in awhile. Our pain and exhaustion completely forgotten for a moment.

She nuzzled her head into my shoulder. "I'm so glad you're awake," she sighed. "It's been very scary out there without you."

I looked down into her wide, golden eyes, wanting to say something comforting, but I was caught off guard by her sweet expression and delicate features; long lashes, soft cheeks, and her nose rounded at the end like the bud of a bellflower. She looked tired and hungry and scared. She was the most beautiful thing I had ever seen.

Placing my hand under her chin, I tilted her head up. The world faded away as I looked at the soft curve of her lips. I leaned down, pressing my mouth gently against hers, before fully leaning into her and kissing her long and deep.

Fireside

Tzidal

I THOUGHT I would never again feel anything other than the itch of water crawling across my skin. The last few days had deadened and washed away my senses, leaving me numb to all sensation. But right now, I was on fire. Alive with lust and desire so intense, I felt like I could burst into flame at any moment.

Joon ran his hands down the curve of my back, holding me tight as his tongue explored my mouth with a rough, possessive intensity. My eyes drifted to the unconscious siren right next to us, and I pulled away.

"Lex," I whispered.

Nodding, Joon quickly stood. Holding me in his arms, he moved to the far end of the cave and laid me on the cool stone, pulling my shirt quickly over my head. I shivered as the cold air hit my sensitive skin.

The alpha's hooded eyes moved over my exposed flesh, his

member already hard and leaking. He cupped my breasts with his large hands and pulled a nipple into his mouth. I whimpered as his hot tongue swiped and flicked at my pert buds. I needed more. More of his touch, his taste, his scent.

He switched between soft, delicate kisses and lust-filled nips, intensifying the tingle in my core. I could feel myself growing wet and ready for him, my thighs rubbing together with each swipe of his tongue.

"Joon?" I whispered, my cheeks flushed as I gathered my courage.

"Yes?" he asked with a deep, husky voice. His almond-shaped eyes drifted up to my face.

"Will you...will you..." I looked away, feeling overly self-conscious.

"What do you want, baby?" he asked, dragging his lips over the swell of my breasts and up my neck. "Tell your alpha what you need." His mouth lingered just beneath my ear, making me shiver.

"Will you...lick me?" My voice was so small I was scared he hadn't heard me, but he smiled wide. A deep rumble rolled off his chest and vibrated against my skin, making my core clench.

"Of course." He licked his lips.

The alpha pushed himself down my body, settling between my legs. He gave me a sexy smirk, his eyes flashing with a mischievous glint. I hid behind my hands, feeling so stupid for how indescribably shy I was at the moment. I had never asked an alpha to do something that wouldn't bring him pleasure as well. It made me feel a little selfish but also powerful and sexy.

"You're so fucking soft," Joon mumbled against the delicate skin of my inner thigh. He sucked hard, not pulling away until a deep bruise bloomed just next to my dripping center.

"And you taste so fucking good," he moaned, swiping his tongue up between my folds.

I moaned loudly and grabbed my knees to hold myself open for him. He plunged into my desperate body and devoured me from the inside out. He rolled the end of his tongue over and around my throbbing clit, sucking long and slow. Humming in pleasure every time I whimpered or moaned. My body flushed, and my thighs trembled as fierce pressure built and twisted inside me.

Joon moved his hands up over my body and squeezed my breasts firmly, his thumbs grazing across my hard nipples. He clamped his lips over my clit and sucked, flicking his tongue wildly back and forth, over and over.

I tried to muffle a wild moan, sobbing with pleasure into the back of my hand, as the alpha grabbed my hips, helping me fuck myself on his tongue. I arched my back as far as my body would allow and yelled out as the ricochet of my orgasm devastated my body.

My thighs pressed against the sides of Joon's face as he kept sucking and flicking, letting me feel every pulse of my climax for as long as possible. Finally, my body relented, and my legs fell open. I covered my face and laughed softly at the exhilarating sensations Joon pulled out of me.

"Feel good, baby?" he asked from between my thighs, his lips swollen and wet. Giving him a small smile, I hid behind my hands and nodded.

Joon placed soft kisses over my hips and between my breasts, moving up to capture my lips again. He sucked at my tongue, pulling it slowly out of my mouth. I could taste myself on his lips, and it sent a thrill through me.

"I want to fuck you," he moaned in a rough whisper. He pressed lingering kisses across my jaw and neck, running his thumb down the hollow of my throat. "I want to fuck you long and hard and slow and soft. I want to taste every fucking inch of you."

"Please," I whispered, desperate to feel him inside me.

Joon moved onto his knees and dragged his gaze down my flushed body. I felt so vulnerable under his savage eyes. He knocked my legs open, looking at my dripping center with wild hunger. I felt like his prey, and my pussy throbbed once again with anticipation.

He grabbed his beautiful, heavy cock and pumped himself a few times, looking at me such intensity it made me shiver. Goosebumps flashed over my skin at the thought of his thick member filling me once again.

"Ready for me, baby?" he growled softly.

I nodded, too desperate to speak.

Holding my gaze, he slowly pushed his considerable length inside me. The feel of his cock moving deep into my core satisfied every inch of my aching body. I gasped loudly and shivered as he stretched me out in the best possible way.

Joon growled deep in his throat as he pressed his hips firmly against me. Holding me in place, he thrust forward. My pussy throbbed, still so sensitive, as his heavy cock glided in and out of me. His member hit that blissful spot deep inside, and I let out an intense scream of pleasure.

His control instantly snapped.

Suddenly, he pulled completely out and flipped me over in one swift movement, lifting my ass into the air. I couldn't help but gasp at his strength. Joon slammed himself back into me in one quick movement, circling his hips. My body, spread and sated, brimmed with his fullness.

He pounded into me with sloppy, wild thrusts.

I let out a strangled cry of pleasure.

I gasped.

And panted.

And moaned.

The alpha inside me owning every pulse of pleasure ripping through my veins.

"You're mine," he growled, leaning over my body and

KITT LYNN

sucking long and hard at my neck. His hips continued to frantically piston into me, and I moaned out. My body wound so tight, on the edge of coming again.

"You look so pretty with my cock inside you." His voice was husky and strained as he sucked just beneath my ear and palmed my breasts. His enormous hands, cupping and kneading my flesh. "You're so good for me. So fucking wet and tight."

I blushed, but my body hummed with excitement at the dirty words he rained down on me. I was so powerless beneath the possessive wolf, and it thrilled me.

"Come for me, baby," he moaned, leaning back and pulling my hips on and off his pulsing girth. "Let me feel it on my cock."

I could feel his member throb and swell within me, pushing me over the edge. The coil in my belly snapped, and my body burst apart. Wave after indescribable wave of pleasure radiated from my core, up to my nipples, and down to my toes.

Joon stilled inside me for a brief moment as he came long and deep. A restrained growl pushed its way out of his throat, as he rolled his hips forward, milking his orgasm and running his hands up and down my back softly. I could feel his cum leaking out around his cock, and I hummed at the sensation.

Joon slipped out of my sore entrance, and slumped next to me, pulling my wrecked body into his strong arms. I was dizzy and tired and filled with an electric energy.

He let out a soft moan as I lazily brushed my fingers down the side of his arm, trailing over his deep scars. He cupped my face and kissed me slowly, letting me savor his lips.

"Do you two want me to leave?" Lex mumbled weakly, his body still motionless next to the fire.

I startled and let out a short, distressed whine. Joon chuckled. The ass. I curled hard into the alpha's side, horrified the siren saw us mating.

"Lex," I squeaked softly into my hands. "I'm so sorry."

"I'm not." Joon gave a contented hum. "I haven't felt this good in a very long time."

"Yeah?" Lex asked, "Does someone want to fuck me? Cuz I feel like complete shit at the moment."

Joon let out a bark of a laugh, and I smacked his chest. Grabbing my shirt, I moved over to Lex, trying to look the siren in the eyes.

"I don't think I'm your type," I said, pulling on my clothes and looking over his fragile form. His features were a little more defined, and his eyes were no longer a milky white but were filled with wide, black pupils.

"But Joon is." He gave a very weak smirk. "I'd wink, but it might kill me."

"I haven't come this far just to end up skinned and eaten alive by a half-dead siren," the alpha's voice boomed, strong and loud.

"You're so mean," Lex huffed. "I just need a quick bite."

"I think I'd rather take my chances in the rain," Joon smiled.

The Border

Lex

AFTER SPENDING a few days in the cave, I was finally feeling back to normal. But I was sick of watching the two wolves exchange knowing glances and intimate whispers. I was desperate to return to the searing pain the clouds provided just to get away from them.

After finding them going at it in the Inn, I had been worried that Joon would get all possessive and alpha on Tzidal's ass, but I was pleased to find that the pair acted some-what normal as we made our way through the barren lands. However, now that we were stuck in a cave with nothing else to distract them, their behavior was worse than I could have ever imagined.

They were giggly.

Well, maybe they weren't actually giggling, but they were pretty damn close.

They were all doe-eyed and with soft emotions that caught

in my nose and made me want to sneeze. Their fingers brushed together as they did the simplest tasks, and they spoke softer than needed, forcing the other to lean in to hear them.

It was disgusting.

I was prepared to sacrifice myself to the onslaught of the poison downpour when Joon finally announced it was time we moved on.

The intricate pattern that usually adorned my robes could be seen in faint traces over my skin, and I was almost back to full strength, finally able to project the young man Tzidal had grown accustomed to. She liked his face for some reason. I never understood woodland creatures and their ridiculous comfort in the mundane.

I wasn't looking forward to having my body dominated and stripped down by the rain, but there was no putting it off. Instead, I just tried looking forward to a strong alpha or powerful elf I'd find to dominate me properly once we were out of this hell. *How I longed for the feel of a sex-crazed monster to feed my soul and fill my belly.*

We stepped out into the violent storm, and almost immediately, my skin shriveled at the intense, piercing pain that burrowed into my body and settled in my lungs. I moved my feet, following Joon, who already looked stiff and pale.

As we pushed forward, I glanced under my hood at the omega at my side. I was so proud of my little wolf. She had been through so much, but I could still feel her determination and desire for revenge hanging in the air.

Interestingly, her rage was slowly being overpowered by a growing warmth every time she glanced at Joon.

I could feel the omega's love, rage, confusion, and fear all dancing around her. Her intense, mixed emotions focused my mind and gave me an indescribable amount of energy. Joon, on the other hand, like most alphas, felt one fucking thing at a time. The beasts were so easily consumed by whatever entered their hearts or heads at the moment. They felt it so intensely I wondered how they were capable of getting anything done. The second Joon set eyes on Tzidal after we saved him in the Shadow Forest, I could feel it. The beast was practically obsessed with the little wolf. Joon's body was constantly switching between searing guilt, overwhelming infatuation, and an indecent, carnal lust that the alpha did a shit job of hiding.

I could survive for years without a proper meal, just being near them. Feasting and gorging on the sensations pulsing off the wolves. It was exquisite.

As the day quickly fell into night, Tzidal grabbed my elbow and helped guide me. I was struggling. Each step was more difficult than the last. We had agreed to keep moving for as long as possible, not resting until we absolutely had to. I was worried I'd shrivel back into my base form if I laid on the soggy ground again. And I didn't want to admit how close to the end I had been. I could feel death's steely breath on my neck, waiting to collect my soul as I clung to life in that cave. But I had no interest in crossing death's gates just yet.

I was mortified Tzidal had seen me so vulnerable and ugly, but she was so tender. Touching me and soothing me when I knew for a fact anyone else would have run from the cave screaming at the top of their lungs.

The little wolf was also kind enough not to mention it once I regained my power, not asking any questions or mocking my withered form. No one had ever seen me like that before, but I had known other sirens that were forced into a weakness so great they lost their ability to project themselves. They were almost always beaten or killed for their unnatural appearance.

Tzidal was good, though, maybe even too good for her desired revenge. I had never met someone that crossed the line from kindness to killer, and I wondered if the air around her would taste different after she took Hida's life. Assuming she was actually capable of doing it.

IT WAS mid-morning the next day when the exhaustion and pain started to rob me of my ability to walk straight. I curled tightly into myself, my spine arching and muscles pulling hard within my arms and legs. Each step took such strength, feeling like it might be my last.

Tzidal gasped and froze. I straightened as far as my body would allow and peered under my hood.

The sun.

I could see the sun's rays dancing over the tops of the trees in the distance. We were near the border.

We were almost free of this tyrannical hell, and its stupid, fucking rain. I moved my feet faster. My comical, galloping shuffle made Tzidal laugh, and she quickened her pace to run next to me. My eyes stayed trained on the clear skies ahead as I pushed my body harder and faster, desperate for warmth and a nice, lively meal.

The Vaesen Forest

Joon

THE SECOND I stepped over the invisible barrier, I ripped off my cape and shirt, allowing the hot sun to pour over my damp skin. My body hurt, and I yearned for sleep, but right now, I felt fucking alive.

We made it through.

I looked at Tzidal with a wide grin. She turned her face up, bathing in the warmth of the blessed sun. Lex slumped over on the ground, a chittering groan pushing from the lump within the cape. I rushed over and helped him up, pulling off the wet fabric.

"What the fuck?" I gasped, jerking back.

Lex looked much more fucked up than he had back at the cave. He had returned to the odd greenish-grey color, but unlike before, when he just looked like a smooth human-like being, this time his hands and feet were mangled. His fingers and toes were fused, giving them a claw-like appearance. He looked like something a warrior might trap and eat along the Northern Border.

"He's okay," Tzidal said, coming over to run her hands over the siren's exposed, leathery skin. "He just needs to rest, and he'll be back to normal."

We rolled up our capes and shoved them into my satchel. Then I pulled Lex into my arms. Thankfully, he was barely conscious, so I didn't have to suffer his fussy remarks.

I was looking forward to making camp. Even though it was still early in the day, and we could cover a lot of ground, we needed to rest, sleep, and eat.

My mouth watered at the thought of a large buck or a small bear, but I wouldn't be able to manage one of those in my current form. I would need to shift, but my wolf was still silent within me. I tried not to dwell on it and instead set off to make a few traps for some small game. A few rabbits or squirrels would do nicely.

I left Tzidal to tend to Lex and start a fire as I wandered out into the quiet forest. My senses were still dull. My ears were ringing from being forced to listen to the hammering of rain for days on end, and everything I sniffed was dim like my nose was stuffed full of cotton. All scent washed out and weak.

I made a few traps around some shrubs and thickets before heading toward a steep hill in the distance, wanting to get my bearings. Stepping over the crest, I looked out over the comforting forest. I had longed for familiar trees that grew upright and calm, blue skies, and wildlife that respected my kind as the superior beast.

Even without my wolf, I felt more like myself here than I had in weeks.

A grunt brought my attention to a dark figure at the base of the hill. I crouched down and narrowed my eyes. An alpha in all black stumbled forward, tripping and falling over. He looked drunk. I smiled to myself and watched as he moved toward the city on the horizon.

In any other circumstance, I would have raced out and cornered him, fighting him off if he proved to be a threat. But my body was still weak, and the alpha seemed worse off than I was, so I let him go. I patiently waited as he disappeared into the trees.

My mind wandered to Tzidal as I walked through the forest, checking over the area around us. She had done so well. She brought us through the cursed lands safely, and I couldn't help but be impressed by her strength and resilience. Even so, I was still worried about the omega.

She was lucky we hadn't encountered anything bigger or more aggressive than a few fat lizards. Her small form wouldn't have lasted long against a real predator, but I could protect her now that we were on normal land.

My heart swelled at the realization that I did still want her. I thought perhaps my pull to her was pure instinct, my wolf feeling the natural urge to claim and keep an omega. But my wolf was gone, and she still dominated my thoughts. I smiled as my mind drifted to the feel of her soft skin and sweet lips.

When this was all over, I hoped she'd be willing to let me take her completely. Mate her and love her. Spend our lives together the way we should have with our mates.

I stopped and leaned against a large spruce. I bowed my head, Fennah's beautiful face suddenly obscuring my view of a future with Tzidal. Guilt pierced my gut, and I let out a long, deep sigh.

A future with Tzidal...one I should have had with Fennah.

I spent the last year refusing to allow myself to think about the things Byna had robbed from me. Fennah's laugh, her smile, her stories, and our longing to one day start a family. It was all gone.

I had clung to my rage for so long, letting it overshadow

my grief, and cloud my memories while I chased revenge. But now, my weak body, coupled with my faltering heart...it all overtook me. I slumped down to the forest floor and cried as quietly as I could, clutching my chest as the dirt soaked up my tears.

My heart twisted and ached from the undying love I held for Fennah clashed with a new, consuming love for Tzidal.

Losing Fennah had crushed me. It ripped my soul out and killed the alpha I once was. But Tzidal was my rebirth, and I couldn't lose her. I'd make sure of it.

The Vaesen Forest River

Byriel

I STUMBLED DOWN THE HILL, hitting the ground with a choked grunt. I was so stupid for not taking a boat to Vaesen but instead traveling through the cursed lands. It seemed safer than taking a more direct route that someone could easily follow. And I was being hunted. I could feel it.

For the most part, I had been lucky in my journey. I was able to find several giant mushrooms in the cursed lands that were reasonably easy to hollow out and take shelter in when the pain became too much. And at one point, I was even fortunate enough to find a small cave, but my luck didn't last long, and the lands eventually beat me down.

I pushed myself back up and forced my feet forward, not allowing my body to stop. A twig snapped somewhere behind me, and I spun around, glaring into the trees.

My mind swirled with images of Byna's body and the look on that omega's face as she stared down from the window. The small wolf looked frightened but also relieved. She was happy to see Byna's mangled, bloody corpse cracked open on the paved road.

I also saw a shadow of a much larger creature in the room with her, but I couldn't be sure. It was a safe bet, though. The omega was tiny, and such a creature couldn't have won a fight against Byna alone.

No. More than one wolf was hunting me.

I had killed innocent members of my father's kingdom, wolves that I had sworn to protect. And now, I was the prey and would most definitely die for my sins, sins that could only be repaid with my blood. The Moon and stars demanded it. I could feel it in my bones.

The sun began to set when I fell once again, unable to get up this time. I was exhausted, my breathing heavy and sweat pouring down my face. I crawled to a large tree and propped myself up, watching orange and pink streaks paint the sky.

A soft giggle pulled my attention, and I jerked, my whole body lighting up with pain and heat.

In the distance, a young pup, maybe four or five years of age, danced around the forest floor. Her father trailed behind her, a few fish hanging from a rope in his hand. The little girl twirled and skipped, jumping toward every flower she could find to sniff and touch.

"Don't go too far, love," he warned. Though his voice was firm, the alpha smiled as he walked slower to allow the pup a chance to stroke every petal her heart desired.

I smiled briefly at her whimsical laughter, enjoying the bliss that floated around her. But my happiness faded when I caught myself wondering if she held the red mark of the Moon somewhere on her skin. Shame filled me, and I looked down at my shaking hands.

I had murdered children. Three now, to be exact. One not

even born yet. They visited me every night in my dreams, taunting me before screaming and begging for their lives.

I swallowed hard, fighting the tears that threatened to fall.

The pup's father, catching my scent, narrowed his eyes at me, a low growl pushing off his chest in warning. I bowed my head, displaying the back of my neck in submission. I wasn't a threat and had no intention of challenging anyone. A year ago, I would have never imagined behaving in such a way to another alpha, but the person I once was, was gone. Dead. My body was just waiting to catch up with that fact.

I let out a pained groan and let my mind drift to the last wolf I needed to find.

There were eight children of the blushing Moon. But I had only found seven, and with my last victim still out there alive, my father's life was still in danger.

Again, I couldn't help but wonder about the little girl and if she carried the mark. *If she did, would I be willing to kill her? Could I destroy the last bit of my soul to protect my father and his reign?*

I closed my eyes, and silently prayed for death.

The River

Tzidal

WE DECIDED to wait another day before starting the trek to Vaesen. Lex was still struggling to project himself and needed more time to recover. He had managed to change his black irises to something a little softer, a gentle grey, but still couldn't create his robes or manipulate his facial features. His body was smooth, stark white, and without any actual definition. He was a canvas on which to paint. He looked lovely.

"Why don't you have a dick?" Joon asked as we washed ourselves in the calm water.

Lex let out a heavy sigh, then turned to face the alpha. "I have every part I'm supposed to have, thank you very much."

"But this is you, before changing, right?" he asked, motioning to Lex's soft form. "To your people, are you a man or a woman?"

"To my people, I am Lex," he smiled, keeping his annoyance in check, but I could still see it in his eyes. "Sirens are not male, and we are not female. We are what others need us to be."

"You mean what your prey needs to trust you." Joon raised an eyebrow.

"Does it bother you that I think of you as a boy?" I asked, suddenly concerned he might not like it.

"It bothers me that Joon won't stop thinking about my dick," he deadpanned. "But you know, alpha, if you ever want to see what I can offer you —"

"I'm good," Joon cut him off, returning to the shore to get dressed.

"Are you sure?" Lex teased. "I could put a few alphas to shame with a little amber wine and some inspiration."

I laughed, scrubbing my hair. I hadn't bathed properly since before the barren lands. And while I did spend the entire time walking through a torrential downpour, I was never clean there. Always covered in a thin layer of sweat and surrounded by fungus. I couldn't help but think that certain unexposed parts of my body might be prone to sprout spores or mold. Thankfully that hadn't been the case.

"I am starving," Lex moaned. "I need to find someone, and soon."

"Do you think that's why you can't change? You need to eat?"

"Maybe," he frowned. "Right now, I'd be willing to settle for a human. I'm going to walk up the river and see if I can snag a fisherman."

"Okay. Happy hunting," I smiled.

I wanted to ask him not to kill anyone that looked nice, but it was a stupid thought. Lex just needed food, and he probably didn't care if it was the Moon Goddess herself walking along the river bank as long as he got his fill.

I made my way out of the water and into the trees to find Joon. He was shirtless, his tan skin and hard muscles on full display, as he scanned the forest.

"See anything good out there?" I asked as I pulled on my shirt and pants.

"I'm just looking," he said, his eyes moving slowly all around us. "It should only take us a few days at most to get to Vaesen, and the land here should be pretty easy on us."

"No blood-thirsty trees on this side of the barren lands?" I smiled.

"None that I know of." He hitched an eyebrow.

Looking over the land, his eyes narrowed, taking in every movement. Even though this part of the journey would be much easier than any other we had encountered so far, he looked alert and ready for anything.

"My senses are going back to normal," he said. "I can smell properly and...." He pressed his lips together, a hint of something exciting in his eyes.

"And?" I asked, intrigued by the smile pulling at the corners of his lips.

"I think I felt my wolf." He turned slightly, giving me that adorable dimple.

"Yeah?!" I squealed, clapping my hands together. "When? Did it only happen once? How long did it last?"

I needed to know everything so I could get my wolf to return. Now that my body wasn't filled with unbearable pain, distracting my every thought, I could feel how truly hollow I was. My instincts were out of whack, and nothing smelled or tasted quite right. I needed my wolf to come home.

"It happened just a few minutes ago," he smiled. He hesitated before speaking again, bringing his hand up to rub the back of his neck and avoiding my eyes. "I felt him when you were...when you...got into the water."

"Oh," I smiled, my heart fluttering. "Was he happy to see me?" I stepped closer and pressed myself gently against Joon's chest, excited that the mere sight of me was enough to pull at the beast within him. His hands settled on my waist, and he gave me a sweet, shy smile. It was not the look of a fierce alpha but a slightly embarrassed pup. It was adorable.

"I think he was," he laughed, quick and low.

I leaned up onto my toes and kissed his perfect lips. "Maybe we can get him to come out and play," I hummed.

Joon growled low and long, pressing his forehead to mine. "You want me to take you right here, little omega?" he whispered, his voice dark and sexy.

I ran my hands up his strong arms and over his chest. "Please, alpha," I whispered as I ghosted my lips over his, my body stirring for his touch. "Take me."

Joon moved quickly, pushing my back against the nearest tree and lifting one of my legs up over his hip. He thrusted against me impatiently and pulled my face to his, taking my lips. I opened up, allowing the alpha to dominate my mouth, sucking and nipping roughly at my lips and tongue. I felt so small in his hold, his strong hands cupping my face as his powerful body rutted against me. It was exhilarating.

He moved his head down and pushed his nose into my throat, nuzzling and inhaling me deeply. His chest rumbled with pleasure as he scented me, sucking my mating bite long and hard. I gasped and rolled my hips up, feeling his hard length against my core.

My wolf purred.

I jumped and squealed, my mouth hung open in shock.

Joon startled at my sudden movement. "What's wrong?"

I laughed. "I felt her! I felt my wolf!"

Excitement coursed through me, and I tangled my hands in his hair and tugged him to me, demanding and needy. He obliged quickly, kissing me back with just as much passion.

Without warning, he pulled away and spun me hard, forcing my hands and chest onto the trunk of the nearest tree.

I panted, confused for a moment.

He whispered low in my ear. "Let's see if we can't wake her all the way up."

The Forest

Joon

I SLIPPED my hand up Tzidal's shirt and palmed her perfect breasts. She pushed her plush ass back into my hardening cock as I tugged at her pert nipples, caressing and squeezing. My wolf peeked his head up, inching forward.

Tzidal let out a soft whimper as I moved my hands down her stomach and into the front of her pants. Sliding my fingers through her wet folds, I glided over her sweet core. She was so fucking wet.

"You're dripping for me, baby," I moaned in her ear.

"Yes, alpha," she gasped, nodding quickly.

I pushed my aching cock into the curve of her ass as I slid two fingers deep inside her. Her pussy tightened around my digits, making me rock hard. I circled her swollen clit then dipped into her again, curling my fingers as I thrust them into her hot, wet body. Tzidal rolled her hips against my palm, edging closer to her orgasm.

I moved my hand up quickly. Rubbing her swollen nub and thrusting back into her. Over and over again.

"Ugh...alpha...I..." she moaned, her body trembling around my digits. "Please..." her voice was strained and shook slightly, making my wolf surge with a need to bury myself deep into her sopping wet cunt. But I held back, wanting to feel her come first, wanting to taste her sweet slick on my skin.

I placed my other hand around her neck and squeezed gently, feeling her gasp and pant harder. Her pussy clenched, and her body trembled violently. I quickly wrapped my arm tightly around her waist as her knees gave out, still thrusting my hand into her. Her heat fluttered as she continued to moan and pant, going completely limp in my arms.

When I finally pulled out of her, my fingers were drenched. I brought my hand up to my mouth and sucked. *Fuck, she tasted so good.*

After a moment, Tzidal steadied her feet and looked over her shoulder at me. Her face was flushed with sweat and her still wet hair clung to her dewy skin. She looked at me with dark, hooded eyes, biting that plump, bottom lip.

"Fuck me," she demanded, her voice breathless and firm.

I immediately jerked down her pants, exposing the sweet curve of her ass and her smooth legs. I smacked her cheek hard, loving the way it jiggled slightly beneath my hand. Unable to wait even one more moment, I undid the front of my trousers and pulled out my cock, pumping it a few times.

My omega hummed and licked her lips as she watched me move my hand over my length. *She was so fucking sexy.*

I lined up my throbbing shaft against her slit and slid into her tight, velvety entrance. Stretching and filling her completely.

Tzidal threw her head back and moaned deeply, exposing her beautiful throat. She pushed her ass back and forth onto my cock, and I hissed at the sight, letting her take control...for now.

"Just like that, baby," I growled. "Keep going." I grabbed her ass and spread her open, watching as my cock repeatedly disappear into her tight, wet cunt. "Fuck, you take me so well."

"Ugh! alpha...I...can't...please!" she stuttered through harsh pants. Her thighs shook as she struggled to keep herself up.

I grabbed her hips, curling my fingers into her flesh, and fucked into her with everything I had. She gasped and babbled a string of broken moans and whimpers as my cock swelled and throbbed, desperate to come. My wolf took complete control as my hips snapped in a crazed frenzy of lust and desire.

"You like being fucked out in the open where anyone can see?" I asked, my voice hard and deep.

"Yes," she moaned, arching her back and gasping for air. "I...ugh...I love it."

I grabbed a fistful of her hair and jerked her head to the side to give me free rein over her throat. The vein in her neck pulsed as her heart quickened and her thighs shook. I could feel her swallow hard as I dragged my teeth over the juncture of her neck and shoulder, away from her mating bite.

"You want everyone to see how I take you?" I growled against her skin. "You like that?"

"Yuh, yes!"

I slammed my hips forward into her drenched pussy. She tensed and clenched around my member on the edge of another climax. "You want to cum so fucking bad, don't you, baby?"

Tzidal nodded frantically.

"Come for me. Come for your alpha." I dragged my fangs over the delicate skin of her shoulder, licking and sucking the sweet sweat off her body.

Tzidal's cunt clenched around my cock as she came hard, and I sank my teeth into her shoulder. She cried out as she shook and gasped, her body trembling with her orgasm.

I sucked at her skin, my eyes rolling into the back of my head at her taste. The metallic tang of blood immediately faded into a rush of her sweet honey scent that flooded my entire body.

My orgasm barreled through me with an unimaginable force, and I let out a rip of a roar, filling my omega up to bursting with my cum. I lapped and sucked at the bite on Tzidal's shoulder to soothe the abused skin as my cock continued to pulse inside her.

Tzidal's body softened in my arms, and I laid my sweaty forehead against her back. My chest heaved, still holding her tightly to me, as I tried to regain control of myself.

My wolf was awake and ready to fight, fuck, and run like a wild, uncaged beast.

The River's Edge

Tzidal

"YOU LOOK...DIFFERENT," Lex said as he walked toward me. His long robes flowed behind him, and his white hair bounced on top of his head. He was the young man again, except his eyes were still a light grey.

"I can't quite get the eyes how I want them yet, so I figured I'd leave them like this," he said, sensing my hesitation as I stared deeply into them.

"I think both dark and light are lovely on you," I smiled.

"Where's Joon?"

"Our wolves are back, so he shifted to let him out. Run around for a bit."

"Okay, well..." He bit his bottom lip, pausing.

"What?"

"I found something," he said with a trace of excitement, his hands clasped together under his chin. He looked like a pup on Solstice Eve. "I don't know if we should wait for Joon or not, but I think you should see it."

"What is it?"

"Just...come," he said, turning back toward the water.

I nodded and followed after him, not sure if the cryptic language was entirely necessary, but he seemed to find comfort in dramatics, so I let him keep me in suspense.

"You know you smell like sex, right?" Lex said, glancing at me sideways.

I snapped my head to him, unsure of what to say. "I do not!"

My body flushed, and my hands began to sweat. I quickened my pace, hoping he wouldn't say anything else about it. In the heat of the moment, it was exhilarating having Joon take me in such an open and wild manner, but now, it just mortified me.

"Tell me the truth. Did you two fuck yourselves back to normal? Did you use dirty sex to call your wolves home?" Lex teased. I didn't answer, but I was sure he could tell from the deep blush in my cheeks. "You're such a tramp," he snorted.

"Isn't that what you just did?" I yelled defensively. "Out here hunting and...doing...things."

"No, you beast. I did not fuck anyone," he said, meeting my tone. "I may be considered a harlot to your kind, but I have standards, and I draw the line at Vaesen Sea-Dogs. Just a bunch of dirty, old fishermen covered in sea slime and saltwater. No, thank you."

"This is a freshwater river."

"Doesn't matter. Still gross," he said in a loud musical tone. It was good to have him back. I missed his energy.

A winding section of the river came into view, as did the remnants of Lex's last meal. The corpse was sprawled out and split open on the other side of the riverbank, his fishing pole still in his dismembered hand. I averted my eyes, not wanting to think too hard on whether the poor thing had a family or pups.

Lex pulled me a little bit away from the water and near a cluster of trees. "I found this," he said, stopping abruptly and looking down.

An unconscious alpha leaned against the base of the tree, his head slumped over, making his face difficult to see. From what I could tell, he appeared to be alive, but he looked sickly. His dark skin was washed out, almost ashen.

"Why do I need to see this?" I asked, waiting for Lex's punchline.

"Look at his feet," the siren clicked his tongue.

I pulled my gaze down his mostly black attire; a black shirt and pants with an ugly, brown belt and matching sheath for his dagger. My eyes settled on his feet. The alpha wore big, black boots, which was a little odd for a wolf out here. Most went barefoot to make it easier for when they needed to shift. Only palace guards wore boots all the time, and mainly as a symbolic reminder that they obeyed the King, not their wolf. My suspicion was confirmed when my eyes fell on the King's seal on the top edge of one boot, a bright green vine twisting around his leg above it. It resembled the plants all over the cursed lands.

The pit of my stomach grew heavy as I leaned down and looked up into the wolf's face.

Byriel.

"Remember what that elf told me in the bar?" Lex asked.

"Yeah," I sighed. "One of the alphas is the Were King's son..." I looked over the pathetic alpha. He'd be so easy to kill right now, but my fight wasn't with this wolf. This one meant nothing to me. I wanted Hida. "We need Joon before we do anything."

"How the hell are we supposed to find him?" Lex huffed,

holding out his hands and motioning to the vast forest around us.

"He knows to come," I said. "He'll catch our scent and find us."

"And how the fuck do you know that?"

I tugged at the collar of my shirt, exposing the bite Joon left on my shoulder. It was tender but clean and already healing. It felt so good on my skin.

"Holy fuck!" Lex yelled, jerking my shirt down more to better see it. "Does this mean you're...mated or bonded? Like forever?" His excitement was endearing. He was so giddy, and it surprised me.

"No," I laughed. "To be truly bound, he'd have to bite me here." I tapped at my old mating bite positioned perfectly over the one vein an alpha had to puncture to create a permanent connection. "This is just a love bite. It'll fade quickly, and it only provides a faint connection for a little while."

"Love, huh?" Lex cooed, pushing his nose into my cheek. "That alpha has it so bad for you. And I don't blame him. You are a delicious, little snack." He raised his eyebrows suggestively.

"That's just what it's called," I huffed, smacking his shoulder. "You are out of control today."

"I feel good," he said, kicking at the unconscious alpha's boots. The wolf's body jerked at the motion, but he didn't stir.

"What's the problem?" Joon said as he stepped around a tree. He was breathing hard, and his muscles flexed under his sweaty, tan skin. My thighs tensed at the sight.

I pointed a finger down at the alpha. Joon stared at him for a moment as if bored, then his eyes went wide. He rushed to the wolf and fisted his tight black curls, jerking his head up to see his face.

The dark alpha had changed a lot since I last saw him in Madra. His clothes were dirty and loose, as if he had lost a decent amount of weight, and his once very short hair was grown out and twisted at the ends. It looked matted and dirty.

"Fuck," Joon said, looking up at me in complete disbelief. "How did you find him?"

"Lex," I said, hitching a thumb in the siren's direction.

"He was just here," Lex said, reaching down and pulling the unconscious alpha's dagger out of his belt. "Here." He held it out to Joon. "One more down, one to go."

Joon shook his head firmly. "No. I can't kill him like this."

"Fine," Lex said, raising the blade high into the air. He brought his hand down quickly, but Joon caught him around the waist and yanked him away before he could stab the alpha.

"What the hell?" Lex yelled.

I moved away from them, my wolf anxious and on high alert. The sudden movement made me surprisingly nervous.

"You can't attack someone unarmed and unconscious," Joon yelled, ripping the dagger out of Lex's hand and throwing it on the ground. "There's no honor in it."

Lex rolled his eyes. "Fucking werewolves and your fucking honor. I just don't get it. He killed your mate. Now you kill him. It's that simple."

"I will not anger the Moon by robbing her right to decide my fate. If she wishes for this alpha to be able to defeat me, then that's the way it is. But I have to fight him while he's awake!"

"Ah, yes," Lex snapped. "The stars and the moon. We can't forget what they want, can we?" he mocked. "Just remember that your gods up there wanted both your mates dead. The moon wanted to torture you and hurt you and force you to walk across hell and creation just to hand you the asshole that killed someone you fucking loved! But you can't even appreciate that, can you? No! Instead, you just stand here like a bitch and spout —"

Joon grabbed him by the throat and slammed him against

a tree. "Watch it, Siren," he growled, his muscles twitching with razor-thin restraint.

Lex struggled to get a proper hold of Joon's hands, but his face remained relaxed and calm. "Careful there, Wolf," he smiled, narrowing his eyes. "Don't start something you might not be able to finish."

Lex's pointed nails slid easily into Joon's flesh, but the alpha didn't even blink as he held the siren's throat firmly in his hands.

"You have got to be kidding me!" I yelled. "We are moments away from Vaesen, with one of the alphas at our feet, and you two are acting like this?" I snatched the dagger off the ground and threw it at Joon's feet, piercing the earth. "If you're going to insist on acting like fucking children, then do me a favor and kill each other already because I'm too tired for this shit!"

I turned my attention to Byriel, jerking the alpha's head up by the hair and slapping him hard across the face.

He stirred. I slapped him again. Harder.

The alpha blinked then rolled his head back, his eyes taking forever to focus. Finally, he cocked his head, taking me in, a glint of recognition in his eyes. Then he laughed. He sounded weak and rough, but the crazy bastard laughed.

The Alpha By The River

Joon

I LOOSENED my grip from around Lex's neck and let him down. My wolf's displeasure with how upset our omega was overpowered my need to put the siren in his place. I shoved down my frustration and focused on Byriel. I'd tend to Tzidal's feelings later.

"Do you know who I am?" Tzidal asked, crouched right in front of the alpha.

I didn't like how close she was. One swift movement and Byriel could snap her neck before I could blink. But I kept quiet, fighting every instinct in my body. I could tell my omega needed this. She needed to look the alpha in the eye and talk to him. But I still angled my shoulders forward, ready to rush the fucker and make his death as painful as possible should he lay a finger on her.

"The omega from the Madra Village." His voice was raspy

and dry. His eyes drooped, and his head swayed a bit as he struggled to keep himself upright.

"Are you drunk?" Lex asked, eyeing the wolf with disgust.

"No," he sighed heavily. "Bit."

He moved slowly, pulling up the side of his shirt to reveal a nasty mark just above his hip. The skin was shiny, tight, and an angry shade of red. It looked painful.

I smiled.

"Fucking snake, or something like that, got to me in the cursed lands," the alpha moaned, sweat blooming across his forehead.

"Why did you kill my mate?" Tzidal asked, her voice serene and soft.

"I didn't," he grunted as he shifted slightly.

Tzidal flung her hand forward and smacked his side, right over his wound. The alpha curled over, a strangled yell leaving his lips as he gagged.

"Why did you kill my mate?" she asked again, a little louder but still calm. I could smell the anger flowing off her in waves as she kept her eyes on Byriel, waiting patiently for him to stop heaving. She looked fierce. I was so fucking proud of her.

With great effort, Byriel pushed himself back up, leaning his head back against the tree. Sweat beaded and rolled down the sides of his face, dripping off his chin, and his chest rose and fell quickly with each gasping breath.

"I will not ask you again," she warned.

"Because I had no choice," the alpha finally gritted out, blinking back tears. "He held the mark. He had to die. I...I had no choice."

"The red mark on his skin?" Tzidal asked.

"Yes," he gasped. "The prophecy said the eight wolves that held the mark of the," he sucked in a harsh breath, "of the moon had to be killed...otherwise..." he swallowed hard as he continued to clutch his side protectively.

"Otherwise?"

Byriel took a deep breath then burst into broken sobs. His chest heaved as tears and snot poured down his blotchy, shiny face. I winced in disgust and Lex took a few steps back. Tzidal leaned in, not letting him break eye contact.

I looked over the alpha's slumped form wanting to pity the creature, but my anger wouldn't let me. *What kind of alpha so willingly showed this kind of weakness?*

"My father," he gasped. "If they lived, my father would die. It was foretold and read by the witches. They had to die. The prophecy and my King demanded it."

Byriel swayed and fell onto his side, pouring his tears into the earth. "I'm so sorry," he sobbed, curling his fists around tufts of grass. "I'm so sorry for what I've done. I've killed so many innocents undeserving of death. And the Moon hates me for it, and the stars demand revenge. Please," he looked up into Tzidal's face, pleading. "Please, just do it. Kill me. Release me from this hell."

The dagger bounced and rolled, coming to a stop just at my feet. I looked up to see Lex giving me a cocky grin. I snorted, unable to help myself from smiling in return.

"I don't think you've earned the right to have your suffering end," Tzidal said.

"I deserve to die," Byriel coughed out, his voice a little stronger. "You have to kill me."

"No," she said, standing up. "I don't."

She turned to leave, thoroughly confusing me. This was an easy end. *How could she not take it?*

"I've killed more than men!" he yelled at her. "A young pup, not fully crawling yet."

Tzidal froze, turning her head to listen.

"I serve my King and defend my land, but this was evil. I am evil. I deserve to die." Tears rolled freely down his face. "I've killed children, and it's put a black mark on my body that I can never scrub clean. And, and when I begged my father not to kill the child, he laughed and told me to do it or die a traitor...so...I...I did it."

He lowered his head and sobbed. Continuing to speak as if unable to help himself. "I killed that pup out of love and loyalty to my King, my father. And in turn, I killed myself. Please, please just do it. Just kill me!" the alpha cried harder, choking on his words.

Tzidal looked over the broken wolf as he pressed himself into the dirt at her feet. I desperately wanted to ask her why she was waiting, why she hadn't plunged the dagger into his heart. But I kept quiet. This was her kill. Not mine.

"Has serving the King done you well?" she finally asked.

Byriel looked up confused, and shook his head. "What do you mean?"

"You are undeserving of the title of alpha," she snorted as Byriel stiffened at her words. "If I kill you now, you will rot with the taunts of your victims forever in your ears. Or..."

Byriel looked up into her face, holding his breath and waiting. "Or?" he asked, his voice barely a whisper.

"Or you can sever your ties to the King that has killed you with his commands. And help us. Then die peacefully, some of your debt repaid."

My whole body went tight, and I snapped my head towards her, glaring much harder than I meant to. A soft rumble of a growl pushed out of my chest, but Tzidal ignored it, still looking firmly at the broken alpha.

"Peacefully?" Byriel asked softly. "How?"

I stepped in. I couldn't help it anymore. I placed a hand on Tzidal's waist and gently guided her away from the alpha. Lex followed.

"Help us?" I asked, trying to keep my voice even. "We don't need help. We need to finish the task at hand and just fucking kill him."

"No," she said firmly. "Think about it, Joon. We spoke to so many in Stone City to find these alphas, and more than one person saw us with Byna. Killing her was inconsequential. No one will track us down for that. But killing a nobleman and the King's son...they will know it was us, and we will be hanged long before we find Hida. But if he helps us..."

"We can find Hida faster," Lex sighed.

"Yes. And," Tzidal paused before speaking again, her voice strained. "And Hida attacked me right after they killed Korban. He tried..." she swallowed thickly, the words struggling to come out.

I stepped toward her, a twinge in my heart at the look on her face.

"He tried to hurt me, but Byriel wouldn't let him," she whispered. "That alpha attacked another member of his pack to save me from the humiliation and pain of being taken by force. He has good in him, and I want to use it. I want to use him to get what I want, which is Hida's head."

I pulled my eyes away from my distressed omega and looked at Byriel's weak, pathetic form. I was so conflicted. This alpha had a hand in killing so many but had also helped protect Tzidal in a situation most would have simply walked away from.

Her idea wasn't stupid, but I didn't know if it was smart.

No one just severs their allegiance to their King so easily. If Byriel agreed to this, it could be a trick. The temptation to sink my teeth into the sniveling alpha's throat, and end the whole conversation was almost overpowering.

"Look at him, Joon," Tzidal whispered. "He's as good as dead anyway. He might not survive his injuries, and if he does, the King won't let him live. Especially if he helps us. We might as well use him while we can."

"Fine," I relented, not happy with a single aspect of this

plan. "But if at any point he proves himself in any way untrustworthy, Lex will eat him."

"Yes!" Lex hissed, his eyes flashing with excitement.

Tzidal nodded. "We agree then?"

"If I help you," Byriel leaned forward, listening to our every word, "will you release me from my torment?"

"Yes," I said without hesitation. "And I look forward to it."

The River's Edge

Tzidal

I ASKED Byriel to wash in the river so I could dress his wound. I could see an infection setting in and was worried he'd be dead in a few days if it wasn't properly cleaned. I needed him better to guide us through Vaesen. He knew where Hida was, and I couldn't risk losing the alpha when I was so close.

Byriel sat in the river bed, breathing heavily and grunting hard at every little movement. I could see a thin layer of sweat over his brow from where I sat in the tree line. He was moving so slowly, and with so much effort, I was amazed he hadn't passed out from exhaustion.

"This is just sad," Lex said, sitting cross-legged on a nearby rock, watching the alpha struggle.

"At this rate, winter will arrive in Vaesen before we do," Joon frowned.

"Do you need help?" I called out to Byriel.

Joon jumped up. "No, he does not!" he yelled loud enough for the alpha to hear. Byriel simply turned away from us, still trying to pry his wet shirt off.

I took in Joon's tense stance, knowing better than to challenge an agitated alpha. "I'm hungry," I said, looking up into his eyes and giving him the saddest pout I could muster.

Joon rocked on the balls of his feet, eyeing my sudden change in subject. He glanced at Byriel, then me, probably sensing what I was up to. I smiled sweetly at him, rubbing my stomach.

"Fine." He took a deep breath then pushed his alpha into every word he spoke. "But you are in no way allowed to help him. Do you understand? Do not go near him, omega. I mean it." He pointed his finger at me as if it made his point clearer. I wanted to bite it.

"I heard you," I said, holding my hands out in surrender. He had no right to command me in any way, but it would be easier to let him think he had the upper hand rather than argue. So I pretended to relent and gave him my most adoring smile, but I had spent my life with too many alphas for his bossy voice to affect me.

"Okay," Joon nodded, moving slowly away. He turned to Lex. "Watch her," he ordered.

Lex nodded lazily, playing with the hem of his robes.

Within moments, Joon shifted and was gone, his massive wolf cutting through the trees and into the distance.

"Okay," I huffed, walking over to Byriel.

"I don't suppose I can convince you to stop?" Lex asked as I stepped foot in the water, edging closer to the weak alpha.

"No," I said firmly.

"Well, I tried." Lex draped himself over the flat rock and bathed in the warmth of the sun.

Byriel's dark skin looked even paler, almost grey, if that was even possible. He had one arm out of his shirt but was struggling with the other. Every time he moved, he hissed as the skin around his wound pulled and oozed pus around thick, crusty puncture marks.

I quietly pulled at the garment, gently rolling the wet fabric up and over his head. I threw it towards the shore before turning back to him.

"Loosen your pants, but do *not* take them off," I said, giving him a firm glare. "The bite is right on your waistband, and I need to make sure the whole thing is clean. Don't try anything. Got it?"

The alpha nodded, unbuttoning his pants and pulling at his waist. He leaned back a bit so I could examine it more clearly.

"Thank you," he mumbled.

I gave a curt nod. I hated that I felt sorry for him, and wanted to help. I hated that I felt anything but disgust for him. But he was so broken. The murdering of the wolves bearing the birthmarks had marked him as well, as it should have.

"Omega?" he whispered.

"There's no need to address me formally," I said firmly, washing away as much of the infection as I could. "Because I will not be calling you alpha."

He nodded. "I understand. Can I ask...what was your mate's name?"

My eyes snapped to his. I couldn't tell if he was mocking me or plotting something. But the desire to answer the alpha's question was a bit overwhelming at the moment. There were too many emotions in the air, and my wolf was still sensitive and overworked.

"Korban."

"Korban," he whispered, leaning his head back and closing his eyes.

I worked quickly and had him out of the water and his wound dressed, applying a thick paste of a few familiar herbs before Joon returned. I hoped with a decent amount of rest and plenty of water, Byriel would be back on his feet in a day or two, and then we'd really see what kind of alpha he was. It was easy to be agreeable on death's door, but it's quite another for a strong, capable alpha to throw away his entire life for three beings he didn't know, especially ones that wanted to kill him and one of his friends.

Joon returned, dragging a buck just off the side of the river's edge, then shifted into his human. He dipped into the water, washing the blood off his face and arms. He eyed Byriel's sleeping form as he pulled on his pants and settled next to me, taking in my wet clothes.

"You helped him, didn't you?" His voice was deep and laced with anger already.

"Yes," I said simply, arranging some rocks to make a fire pit.

"I told you —"

I cut him off with a stern look, glaring at him with blazing eyes. I did not belong to him, and I didn't want to be forced to say it, but I would if I had to. He had no right to command me to do anything. Silence hung in the air for a moment as we glowered at one another.

"We should eat," Joon said stiffly, clearly angry but willing to let it go...for now at least. He stalked off towards the deer without another word.

"Do all alphas eventually submit to their omegas?" Lex asked as he rolled himself on the rock to face me properly.

"Don't let him hear you talk like that," I said pointedly. "I just patched one wolf. I don't need to worry about you two as well."

"Do you think he'll kill us?" Lex asked, motioning to Byriel.

I looked over at the sleeping alpha. This was dangerous. Once he got us within the city boundaries, he could ditch, kill, or double-cross us. I just didn't know for sure. But for some reason, I felt he was honest in his regret. His grief seemed real.

"Maybe."

Camp At The River's Edge

Joon

NIGHT CAME QUICKLY, bringing with it the gentle chatter of crickets and tree frogs. The air was getting chilly, and the breeze rustled the leaves in an almost rhythmic manner.

Byriel was still passed out, having not moved or made a single noise all evening, and Lex had skipped away to find something to eat, claiming the fisherman he had that morning had left a bad taste in his mouth.

I watched Tzidal fiddle with the fire, carefully placing a sizable log into the flames. My wolf wasn't pleased with her willful disobedience, and I kept having to remind myself she wasn't my mate. But it didn't excuse her for challenging me or change how angry my wolf was. She was just being so reckless. She was going to get seriously hurt, and the thought killed me.

"Omega," I said softly.

Tzidal looked up, the fire illuminating her beautiful eyes.

I intended to apologize, but the words wouldn't leave my mouth. I didn't want to look weak, willing to bend and break at her slightest whim. Suddenly my pride overpowered my feelings for her, and I shut my mouth, feeling overly frustrated. Since returning, my wolf had been more aggressive and territorial, and it was getting hard to push down the desire to put the omega in her place.

"Nothing," I mumbled, giving her an awkward smile and turning my attention back to the fire.

She moved closer and snuggled into my arms. I pressed my nose into her hair and inhaled. My muscles relaxed a bit, even as my mind continued to spin.

"What's wrong?" she asked. I was sure she could smell the edge of stress in my scent.

"Nothing," I lied. "Just thinking about...everything."

"It'll be okay, alpha," she sighed. "You'll see."

"I'm glad you think so," I snorted. I tried not to stiffen at her words, but I couldn't help it. I was too worked up.

"What does that mean?" she asked.

"I just..." I sighed. "You need to listen to me when I tell you to stay away from dangerous wolves. Helping Byriel was incredibly stupid. We don't know this alpha or his real intentions, and I don't want anything bad to happen to you."

I tried to keep my anger from bubbling over, but I couldn't seem to reign myself in. And the look on Tzidal's face was not one of understanding.

"I can take care of myself," she said in a loud, firm tone, leaning away from me. "If I get hurt, it's on me, not you. It's my choice. And I don't belong to you. You don't get to tell me what to do."

I tensed and crossed my arms. She *was* mine. Whether she was willing to admit it or not, our wolves had laid claim to one another and belonged to each other, even if I hadn't marked her yet. But I was sick of her attitude, and I'd be damned if I let an omega talk to me in such a disrespectful way.

"No, I guess you're technically not mine, are you?" I snapped through gritted teeth. "Because if you were, there's no fucking way you'd get away with acting like this. You need to understand your limits and stop being so damn stupid. You're an omega. You're too fragile to behave in such a careless manner."

"I'm not fragile!" she yelled, standing abruptly with her fists tightly clenched.

I jumped up and squared my shoulders, looming over her. My wolf growled at the rage etched on her face and the scent of anger rolling off of her. She had no right to challenge me.

"Yes. You are," I growled. The rumble pushed through my chest and into the air making her shiver. "You are not a warrior. You are an omega. You are meant for birthing and raising pups, not raising war. You need to stop being so fucking reckless and know your place." I moved toward her, closing the space between us. My breath quickened, and my temper blazed, rapidly spiraling out of control. "I refuse to let you continue to run around as if you're invincible. You're too impulsive, acting like you can't get hurt. I've let you get away with far too much, and when I tell you to do something, you fucking do it!"

"You do not get to tell me what to do! I'm not some weak, pathetic creature that needs your constant supervision!" She glared up at me, her mouth in a tight, unforgiving line.

My wolf snapped and snarled to put the disobedient omega in her place. To exert my dominance as the alpha.

I leaned down, looking hard into her eyes. I could smell her fear as she tensed, confusion twisting between her brows.

It only took Tzidal a few moments to feel my intention, and her eyes widened in surprise as I attempted to force her into submission. My scent became thicker and more intense.

Her eyes watered, and her breath hitched, inhaling the force rushing off me.

She broke eye contact and shoved me, but I stood firm. She needed to listen to me so I could keep her safe. Her willingness to put herself in harm's way, to possibly die, gutted me. I couldn't lose her like I lost Fennah. I wouldn't survive something like that again.

"Stop it!" she yelled, her lips trembling as my dominance finally started overtaking her. Sweat bloomed across her forehead as she struggled beneath my glare. A deafening silence lingered between us as she refused to back down, clinging to her pride. But my wolf demanded her obedience, and he would have it.

My heart beat wildly, and my head was pounding from the strain. I couldn't help but admire her even more as she fought so hard against me. She was so fucking strong.

"Please stop," she begged, fighting the urge to bow her head.

I grabbed her arms, holding her to me. She would listen. I would keep her safe if it was the last thing I did. She looked up at me with tears streaming down her cheeks. The pure desperation on her face caused my heart to falter, and I wanted to stop. I was hurting her. I needed to stop. But I couldn't. My wolf wouldn't let me. He pushed me to continue, forcing me to break her and keep her. Make her understand how much I needed her.

Tzidal leaned her head back and closed her eyes as a sob broke free from her lips. She whimpered long and loud, finally submitting to me, then her knees buckled. I caught her before she could hit the ground and pulled her to my chest.

I was disgusted with myself as she sobbed in my arms.

I broke her.

Fuck.

Through The Vaesen Forest

Tzidal

FOR THE NEXT FEW DAYS, we walked in nearly complete silence. I was still weak and a bit dizzy from Joon forcing his dominance over my wolf, and I would never forgive him for it.

He crushed and humiliated me, all to satisfy his pride. I hadn't spoken to the alpha since. He tried apologizing the following morning, but I slowly walked away from him without a word. No fight left in me. When he approached me again to talk, I continued my reign of silence, refusing to look at him. My wolf demanded I respond to the alpha, but it was easy to ignore her if I didn't look Joon in the eye.

Byriel seemed comfortable with the silence, traveling in peace and trying to be helpful when he could. He didn't even argue when I took his belt and dagger, hitching it to my hip and telling him I wasn't comfortable with him having it while we slept. He simply nodded in understanding.

The silence, however, was killing Lex.

He groaned and whined that he was bored, insisting we all stop being so huffy and entertain him. I just didn't have it in me. My heart hurt too much to fake happiness for my friend, which left him very moody.

We approached the edge of the forest just before sunrise. We had agreed it would be best to enter the city around dusk, allowing us to rest for the day. It would also mean the city's streets would be at their busiest, and the guards were more likely to be distracted.

The King frequently stayed in a castle just off the coast, but we wouldn't know if he was in residence until we entered the city. Byriel explained that it would be easier to sneak in if his father wasn't there since they only kept half the servants and guards on staff when he was gone. But he was confident Hida would be there.

"I guess I should eat before we enter the city," Lex said, looking around the brightly lit forest. The morning sun cast a vivid light over everything it touched. "Should be plenty to choose from out here. I just wish it was night."

"Do sirens not hunt during the day?" Byriel asked him.

"Not really. No one with good intentions sneaks around the woods at night. It lets me eat with a clear conscience."

"Lex," I gasped dramatically, mimicking his usual flirty tone. "You're such a softy."

"I am not," he snapped.

"Yes, you are," I teased. "You care who you kill."

"I do not, and I will not take this kind of abuse from you," he huffed, twirling his robes behind him as he stalked off into the trees.

"He seems to hunt a lot," Byriel said, watching Lex disappear. "Do sirens need to kill so frequently to live?"

"I think he just really enjoys it," I shrugged. "I try not to think about it too much."

"I bet it's hard to befriend a murderer while trying to

avenge your murdered mate," he said a little too casually for my liking.

I shot the alpha a fierce glare, and he immediately looked down, mumbling an apology. At least he had the grace to look shame-faced.

"Lex isn't a murderer," I said as calmly as I could. "He's a hunter. There's a difference." But even as the words left my mouth, I wasn't sure I believed them. I had spent too much time trying not to think about Lex's victims and their families.

"You're right," the alpha said. "I apologize. I didn't mean any disrespect. I've just never met a siren before, and I wasn't thinking about it properly."

"I've never seen an alpha bow down to an omega so quickly," Joon said, giving him a piercing glare.

Byriel squared his shoulders and tilted his head back. His eyes narrowed, but he didn't stand up to challenge Joon properly. "I offended the only creature here that's shown me any mercy or kindness. I'm not bowing down. I'm showing respect. I insulted her friend, and I'm sorry," he said in a loud, firm tone.

Joon pushed out a soft growl but didn't respond.

I couldn't help the smile that pulled at my lips, and I quickly turned my attention to the firewood in my hands to hide my face. I didn't want to encourage a fight between the two.

Sitting down next to Byriel, I arranged the sticks in the center of a circle of rocks. I could feel Joon's eyes on me, but I refused to look at him. Still too angry.

"Let me see your wound," I said a little more forcefully than intended.

Byriel immediately obeyed, tugging his shirt over his head and exposing his toned abs. I gently pulled at the bandages I made out of leaves and dried moss. Joon moved closer, the tension in his muscles almost audible, but his nervous energy was distracting and unnecessary. If Byriel wanted to kill us, he'd had plenty of opportunities over the last several days. While I didn't trust the alpha, I didn't fear him either.

"This is healing nicely," I said, gently applying pressure around the edges. "And there doesn't appear to be any more pus."

"Thank you," Byriel smiled. "You've been very kind to me even though you have no reason to."

"I'm making sure you're healthy enough to help me find Hida," I said flatly, dabbing at the still tender flesh with a rag. "I don't know if that makes me kind."

"It does," he said simply, leaning in to catch my eyes. "It makes you very kind."

Joon growled low in his throat, baring his teeth. Byriel glanced up at the seething alpha, then slowly sat up and leaned away from me.

I looked at Joon out of the corner of my eye. He looked ready to kill, his eyes glowing red. "You said the prophecy demanded you kill eight wolves?" I asked, turning my attention back to the wound.

"Yes," Byriel whispered, shifting his gaze to the ground.

"Did you get all eight?"

"No." He shook his head slightly. "We were still looking for one. We checked all the were-villages on the mainland. Next, we were traveling to the shared cities, elvish colonies, and the witches' settlements. Stone City is the only one we'd been to so far.

"Whoever bears that last mark has never shown it to anyone. Or at least no one is willing to admit to seeing it," he said, looking a little defeated.

"So you have no idea who it is?" I asked.

"No."

"Is the King's life still at risk even with just *one* wolf alive? Would one even matter?"

"Yes," Byriel said cautiously, glancing at me out of the corner of his eye. "Even just one matters."

"So if Hida and you both die before the last wolf is found, will the King send new guards to find whoever it is?"

"What are you getting at?" Joon asked.

I kept my eyes on Byriel, but my body pulled hard to answer the alpha. To obey his every word. "Will the eighth wolf be killed no matter what happens to you and Hida?" I asked again.

Byriel looked down at the fire pit and sighed heavily. "The last wolf will be found no matter what. The King will make sure of it," he frowned. "As long as that wolf lives, my father is doomed to die. There's no changing fate."

I nodded, finishing with his wound and moving to start the fire. I could feel Byriel's tense breathing behind me, but I kept my eyes down, working to spark the rocks in my hands.

"Tzidal," Joon said softly. He paused, waiting for me to respond.

My heart pounded in my chest as I tried hard not to answer him, my wolf and body begging me to respond. I hated him so much for forcing me into submission, my mind feeling as if it belonged to someone else. I shifted some dried grass and sparked a flame, making myself ignore him.

"Tzidal," he said more firmly.

My hands shook, and my jaw clenched, but I remained silent. I held my breath and stared hard at the tiny flame that flickered before me.

"Omega!" he yelled, and my head automatically snapped up to him, making me wince. He looked angry but also ashamed at my reaction. I didn't know why. This was what he wanted. My mindless obedience.

"Okaaay," Lex said, his voice laced with apprehension as he walked out of the trees. He was wearing the face and body of a lovely young boy with blue eyes and a tiny, pointed nose. He looked like a child. It was disturbing, and it made me happy he killed whoever craved the young boy in front of me.

"I've had enough with the weirdness between you two lately," Lex huffed, his hands on his narrow hips.

"You already ate?" I asked. "That was fast."

"So was he," Lex frowned as he shook off his appearance and melted back into his familiar form. "Why is Joon yelling at you?"

"She won't talk to me," Joon huffed. I suppressed the urge to roll my eyes. *Such an alpha, whining like a petulant pup.*

"What are you up to, little wolf?" Lex asked.

"When we're done with Hida, I'm going to find that last marked wolf and keep whoever it is safe from the King's guards," I said loud and clear, my eyes finally meeting Joon's for the first time in days, challenging him to argue. "The King ordered the marked wolves to be killed. If I can find that last wolf, the King will die. I want to make sure he does. I want the King of Wolves dead for what he's done to his pack."

Joon laughed, loud and long. "I do love your passion, omega. But there's no way you could find that last wolf."

"You don't love my passion," I whispered, narrowing my eyes at the alpha. I could already feel a sob working its way up my throat, but I shoved it down, not wanting to show weakness in front of him ever again.

Joon's smile fell, and he had the gall to look upset, almost apologetic. It made me angrier. Lex shifted nervously, moving his gaze between us.

"You think you're the only one here with a purpose," I said, my voice hushed and laced with the threat of tears. I stood up, trying to sound stronger than I felt. "You think you're the only one that's suffered and lost and has something left to lose, but you're not. I cannot let one more innocent wolf suffer like we have." I balled up my fists, feeling my rage flow through me. "I will kill Hida to avenge Korban. I will find that last wolf and keep them safe. And that will kill the King. He deserves to die for what he's done to us."

A few silent tears rolled down my cheeks as Joon looked at me quietly, not daring to speak. "I will spend the rest of my days hunting him down if I have to. Even if it brings about the end of the earth, and the stars fade and the Moon ends. I will not stop." My lips trembled, and I fought hard to keep my voice from shaking. I had to say my piece, though. I had to make Joon understand that I wasn't built just to obey and submit and raise pups. I might have wanted some small fragment of that life at one point, but that part of me died with my mate.

"I am not weak, and I am not stupid. I am angry, and this is my purpose."

"This is your purpose," Joon whispered, lowering his head slightly to better look me in the eyes. "And my purpose is to be by your side if you will have me. I will help you now and forever. Until the Moon ends."

Camp Before The City

Byriel

I HELD my tongue as I listened to the omega declare that she wanted my father dead. She talked so effortlessly about it as if it would be easy to find the last marked wolf and even easier to condemn our King to death. My wolf snarled and yearned to attack. To defend my father, my King, from their threat.

I moved uncomfortably on the forest floor and tried to force my attention to the weak fire. I nudged a few sticks and twigs, my mind racing as the alpha and siren spoke in hushed tones. I should have been listening to what they were saying, but all my attention was on the omega. She shuffled off into the woods, a little ways away from us, crouching down near a thicket.

She wiped at her face, tears still dripping down her nose and chin, and busied herself picking berries. She held them gently in the tail of her shirt, not turning to look at her friends as they spoke.

The omega was so small, typical for a wolf of her status, but I couldn't help but think she might be a real threat. She held a determination the other two just didn't possess. She acted as if she had no fear, and she also seemed to have no issue defying her alpha.

I had found peace in agreeing to help them find Hida. He was savage and violent, enjoying the fear and pain he inflicted on those we hunted. His death would surely calm the lands and appease the Moon. But killing my father was an entirely different matter. He was our sovereign, blessed by the Moon and stars, and meant to lead his people until his natural death.

As a member of the guard, I had pledged my whole life and being to protect my King. And as his son, I just couldn't imagine life without him, even if he was sometimes cruel.

"You look deep in thought," Tzidal said. She looked at me from over her shoulder, her big, brown eyes a little more tortured than usual. She stood up but stayed near the bushes, holding out a handful of berries.

I glanced at her alpha, making sure Joon was still distracted before walking over to her. "Thank you," I whispered, taking the fruit but finding it hard to meet her eye. I didn't want her to see my struggle with her new plan.

"What is it you're trying so hard not to say?" she asked.

"I will need my dagger back before we enter the city. It's a part of my uniform." I rolled a berry between my fingers before popping it in my mouth. The burst of tart juice on my tongue was muted over the bitter taste I held just thinking about what I might have to do if she actually found that last wolf.

"No," she said, her voice firm but somehow still sweet. "I'm not giving it back to you."

I nodded and sighed, "I figured as much."

"Are you still committed to this?" she asked. "Have you changed your mind now that you feel better?"

I moved my gaze over her face, taking in her soft features

and kind eyes. They were too kind, not capable of the revenge she craved.

"Hida doesn't deserve to live," I said, not feeling bad in the least for condemning an evil wolf to death. "He'll be in Vaesen. He left to return a few days before me, so I'm confident of that. You'll get your revenge. I promise."

I watched her carefully as she picked a few more berries, setting them carefully with the others.

"I'm sorry for what he tried to do to you and for how he acted toward your mate. It shouldn't have happened like that."

"But you aren't sorry you killed him. Are you?" Her voice carried an unsettling peacefulness that made my skin prickle. Her gentle composure set off a rush of panic within me that I just didn't understand. I rolled another berry between my fingers, not sure how honest I should be.

"I love my father," I finally said. "And I love my King. I serve him without question. As a member of his kingdom, do you not?"

"I could never love a King that would so easily sacrifice his pack based on a few words from a witch."

"You shouldn't make light of what the witches read."

"You shouldn't take something so seriously that demands the death of your people," she snapped, emotion finally lacing her tone. I found a little more comfort in it. I could understand rage, revenge, and hatred. But her serene composure, while comforting at first, was making my wolf pace and eyes twitch. It wasn't natural for a wolf to be so calm with so much intensity hanging in the air.

The soft movement of feet caught my attention. Joon's eyes were fixed on me as he edged a little closer to Tzidal, trying so damn hard to conceal a snarl. I was sure if the alpha let it slip, the omega would be livid.

"You're right," I said looking back at Tzidal. "Our pack

comes before everything else. I will help you kill Hida. I allowed him to torture too many for too long. I owe it to the dead to make it right. And I will help you find that last wolf."

Tzidal's expression went dark, and she looked at me with thick tension between her eyes as her fingers brushed gently over a leather strap tied to her wrist. It made my wolf bristle, feeling the challenge behind her glare.

"I need your help to find Hida. I don't need you to find the last wolf," she said firmly.

I nodded, figuring as much. I was so damn conflicted. The Moon wanted me to help them end Hida, but what was I supposed to do about her promise to kill my father? It was too bold and went against everything I believed. I couldn't just let her walk away after this to find that last wolf. Because if anyone could do it, this omega was capable.

"Will you kill me once it's done? Once you have your revenge?" I asked, thinking of how I had begged her to end my suffering when they first found me. The pain in my mind and body was too consuming at the time, but now, death didn't seem as seductive as she once did.

"Do you still want that?" Her voice was soft again, almost sympathetic. It was unsettling.

"Let's get some rest while we can," Joon said loudly, making Tzidal flinch. "This may end up being a very long night for us, and we'll need our energy."

"Come here, puppy," the siren cooed with open arms on the other side of the fire. Tzidal smiled and moved quickly into his embrace.

I couldn't help but wonder how anyone could lay so peacefully with such a dangerous creature. How did the omega not feel as if she was sleeping on the edge of a blade? One bad dream and the siren could flay her in his sleep with incredible ease.

I lingered on the edge of our camp, looking over the

familiar forest. The city was just within my sight—the blue and red rooftops peeking out between the tree's leaves.

I had been gone from home for so long, and it felt good to feel the friendly breeze on my skin again.

"I'm warning you now," Joon stepped up next to me, "don't try anything fucking stupid tonight. Do you understand me?" The alpha's fists were clenched tightly, his knuckles white.

"I gave you my word," I said. "I'll help you find Hida."

Joon rounded on me, his jaw clenched. I fought the urge to lunge at him, knowing I had no right to meet his rage.

"You murdered my mate," Joon seethed. "You are a gutless mutt with no right to walk this land, but Tzidal seems to think you have worth at the moment, and that is the only reason I haven't ripped you to pieces."

I listened, trying to keep from baring my teeth. His fuming scent hung heavy in the air, taunting my wolf.

"If you do anything, and I mean fucking anything to put her in danger," he gritted out, motioning to the omega, "I will end your pathetic life in the most painful way I can imagine." His face was red, and his shoulders shook slightly as he spoke, his wolf inching forward. "I've had over a year of tracking your ass down to imagine all the different ways I could torture you. Do not test me."

I held his eyes, trying like hell to push down my wolf's demand that I meet his challenge. I reminded myself the alpha's anger was justified, then I forced my eyes down to the forest floor, submitting to his rage. My wolf blazed with a violent fury inside me.

Tzidal's hushed whispers drifted toward us, and I looked over, seeing the omega and siren speaking quietly to one another while huddled at the base of a tree. Joon's eyes immediately softened as he looked at her.

I couldn't quite place their relationship. I assumed they

were together. She had a mating bite and reeked of the alpha, but she was so defiant. I had never seen an omega act in such a way to their mate, and I wondered what kind of wolf Joon was for allowing her to behave like that. No self-respecting alpha would dare to let such a weak creature have so much control over them.

Tzidal looked over the flames toward us, and her eyes caught Joon's. She stiffened, then rolled away, her movements sharp and deliberate. Joon deflated a bit at the action.

"Is Omega Tzidal your mate?" I asked. I knew the question would piss him off, but I couldn't help it. While I had no right to challenge him, I could still provoke him a bit. Tzidal was clearly tied to his heart, and right now, it was bleeding for the omega.

"Don't talk about her. Don't look at her. Don't fucking think about her," Joon snarled softly, the air crackling with his restrained fury.

"She doesn't seem very happy with you," I said, fighting the urge to smile.

"Shut the fuck up," Joon gritted out before stalking back toward the fire.

The Castle Tunnels

⟡

Tzidal

THE SENSE of unease within me grew the closer we got to the castle. Joon might be right about Byriel, but I needed to trust my gut, and it was too late to turn back now. Byriel would help us find Hida quickly, otherwise, it could take us days to figure out where he was, assuming he hadn't left the city already. But if he was in the castle, there was no way we'd be able to sneak in undetected. There were just too many things that could go wrong. We simply needed Byriel.

This was easier and safer. I hoped.

Byriel motioned for us to follow him into a tunnel off the coast, leading us into the castle's belly. The black entryway in the rock was difficult to see at night and I wondered why it wasn't guarded.

"Pay attention," Byriel said. "This is the way you'll go to get back out."

I glanced at Joon. His eyes moved over every passageway as

we moved deeper into the dark tunnels beneath the city. The paved ground became more narrow as a waterway came into view, flowing quickly next to us. A distant crack and loud splash made Lex startle, and he flung his arms around me, making me jump as well.

"You're the most terrifying thing down here," I said, feeling his arms shake slightly. "Why are you scared?"

"I hate the water," he squeaked, startling again when the rustling of something in the dark echoed through the tunnel. "What was that?"

"Calm down," Joon hissed.

"There may be a few guards down here," Byriel warned. "It would be best to keep it down."

The scratching of nails on wet stone drifted toward us as we wandered further into the darkness. Two glassy, glowing eyes appeared in the black void in the distance.

"What the fuck is that?!" Lex screamed, his fear hitting a crescendo. He squeezed my neck hard, pressing our bodies together, as his eyes darted all around. I tried pulling at his arms to free myself, but his grip was too tight.

"Calm the fuck down!" Joon gritted out in a harsh whisper.

"This might not be a good mission for you, Siren," Byriel said, his brows raised.

"No shit," Joon spat, a look of complete fury on his face. He turned quickly, scanning the tunnel.

Just as Lex's arms loosened from around my neck, a creature rushed toward us. Lex screamed, his voice reverberating off the walls and water. A large hound bounded forward, its tongue hanging out of its mouth as it rushed down the passageway toward the tunnel exit.

"Oh my goodness!" Lex gasped, letting out a nervous laugh. He released me and rubbed his sweaty palms on his knees. "It's just a dog. It's just a fucking dog." He placed his hand over his heart, nervous energy radiating off him. "You need to tell your cousin back there to not scare the shit out of me like that!"

"Cousin?" I snorted, trying to keep my voice down. I could see both alphas tense as they kept creeping forward.

"Yes. The dog," Lex said plainly. "You're a wolf. He's a descendant of wolves. You're practically related, aren't you?"

"We're all connected by the stars and the Moon," Byriel spoke softly. "We are all one another's brothers and sisters."

"Okay," Joon said, coming to a halt. He pointed at Byriel. "You are a bit much right now, and I don't have the energy for it." He pointed at me. "You need to stop encouraging him. And you." He pointed at Lex. "Need to calm the fuck down and stop talking about such stupid shit!"

"I'm sorry," Lex huffed. "I get chatty when I'm nervous."

"Really? Are you *always* nervous?" Joon asked, his eyes comically wide. "Because you talk non-fucking-stop, and I need you to shut the fuck up right now."

He stared at Lex, daring him to speak. The siren looked bored. Slowly, Joon turned and walked.

"Asshole," Lex mumbled.

Joon spun, his nostrils flaring. "I swear, if you don't stop talking right this fucking second, I'm going to —"

"What?" Lex snapped. "You're gonna what?"

"Who is there?" A voice called out, echoing off the walls.

Lex jumped and flung his body into the nearest passageway. Footsteps in the distance quickened, and a guard appeared just around the corner, searching for the source of the sound. I shoved Joon as hard as I could into the passageway with Lex. Thankfully, I caught him off guard, and he stumbled out of sight.

I grabbed Byriel's face firmly in my hands and crashed my lips to his.

Everything went silent but became so loud at the same

time. I could hear the heavy steps of the guard walking toward us, Lex's frantically soft breaths, and Joon's deep rumbling growl that seemed to never end.

"Byriel? Sir!" a female guard said, stopping and bowing.

I pulled my lips off of the alpha's and pretended to blush, pushing my face into his chest. He stuttered for a moment before pulling himself together.

"Vera," he said, clearing his throat.

"I'm so sorry, Sir." She stood at attention, her black ponytail swaying behind her. "I didn't realize it was you."

"Byriel," I said in a soft, flirty voice. "I'm cold, and you promised me a warm bed." Joon's feet shifted against the stone, and I closed my eyes, hoping he wouldn't do anything stupid.

"That I did...my omega," Byriel smiled stiffly before turning back to the guard. "Please don't tell the stewards you caught me down here. I'm trying very hard to avoid my responsibilities tonight."

"Of course, Sir," the guard said in a very formal manner before turning on her heel and disappearing back down the way she came.

We waited for the sound of her footsteps to completely disappear before Joon and Lex came out of the shadows. Joon glared down the tunnel where the guard just vanished, not meeting my eyes.

Byriel ushered us further into the darkness and toward the last passageway. He and Lex disappeared around the corner, but Joon grabbed me by the arm and held me back before I could follow. He pushed me gently against the cold wall and placed both hands on either side of my head, trapping me.

"Don't ever kiss anyone other than me ever again." His voice was calm, but his eyes were on fire.

"You don't get to tell me what to do," I whispered in a

stern tone. My wolf whimpered, but I felt a little stronger and more defiant. "I'm not yours."

"Yes, you fucking are," he gritted out. "Just like I am yours, Tzidal. All of me. You own me. You control me. You thrill me and fill me and excite me. You own *everything* about me." His voice was tight with emotion and desire as he leaned in, whispering with soft eyes. "You're mine, omega."

He gently ran his nose over the edge of my jaw, inhaling me deeply before pulling back, hovering just over my lips.

I wanted to kiss him.

And scent him.

And make love to him.

I hated him so much.

"I fucked up," he said, removing his hands from the wall. "I should have never made you submit, and I'm sorry. I'll never do it again. I promise on the Moon herself. I will *never* do that to you again."

He looked at me with so much tender love, waiting for me to respond. I gave a quick nod, wanting to give him everything and nothing at the same time. I shoved myself off the wall and away from the alpha, moving down the corridor.

Through The Castle

Byriel

"WHERE THE FUCK ARE WE GOING?" Joon snapped.

I shook it off. Again. I understood the asshole's anger and was trying to be patient. After all, I had a hand in killing his mate. He had every right to hate me, but I was trying to help, and it was getting hard to ignore his unyielding attitude. Especially now that I was on the mend, I had to constantly fight my wolf not to challenge Joon's aggressive behavior.

"The throne room," I said, opening a heavy, wooden door.

We stepped out of the musky passageway and into the fresh air of the castle. The hallway was empty, as I expected. This portion of the court rarely saw much traffic. There wasn't much over here that required staff or stewards.

"Is that where Hida is?" Tzidal asked, excitement and fear flashing in her eyes.

"No." I picked up my pace. "If Hida is here, he'll be at the guards' station house."

I rushed down a hallway and up a long, winding staircase. We needed to get to the throne room and leave as quickly as possible.

I would help kill Hida and right some of my wrongs, but then I needed to leave and get to the palace to warn my father. I couldn't risk his life. I wasn't the kind of guard or son that could allow his death so easily.

"What's in the throne room?" the siren asked.

"We can't shift here," I said, motioning to a small table as we passed. Wolfsbane sat in a delicate vase in the center. The dark purple petals looked wilted, in need of water. "It's everywhere. On every table hung above doorways, bundled under beds and chairs. My father likes being the strongest wolf in the room at all times, and doesn't allow anyone to shift around him."

I slowed, hearing voices, and glanced carefully around the corner. Two of my father's stewards spoke, strolling toward us. Turning quickly, I grabbed Tzidal and Lex's wrists, pulling them down another hallway.

"My father keeps two charms that contain bindweed and were enchanted by the Westland witches. They will allow the wearer to shift even if they were bathing in wolfsbane. He wears one at all times and keeps the other in the throne room. We'll need it."

The truth was, I might need it to defend my father, but that was for another fight. One I'd hopefully not be forced to have.

I rushed past a series of doors stopping at a large tapestry hanging at the end of the hall. I grabbed one side to reveal an entryway, motioning for everyone to enter.

Once we were all settled in the dark passageway, I leaned in to whisper, "the throne room is just through here. No one other than the King and his kin are allowed to enter without permission. It should be empty, but stay here just in case."

"How do we know you aren't just going to grab it and leave or shift and kill us?" Joon asked, his shoulders tense and his jaw jutting out slightly.

I hesitated, then sighed.

"The Moon hasn't let me sleep a single night since I murdered that pup. Until I met her." I pointed at Tzidal. "That night by the river when I agreed to help you, I slept more soundly than I ever have in my life. This is clearly the path I'm meant to take. And I don't blame you for not trusting me, but I give you my word. I'm done hurting innocents. I can't do this anymore."

Joon glared, the muscles in his jaw straining. He wasn't going to give me an inch, but I understood why. I didn't expect anyone to gift me forgiveness.

I remembered Joon's mate clearly, just like all the wolves I had killed this last year. She seemed to be an impressive beta, with a clear sense of pride. She fought hard, knocking Byna out briefly before we were able to overpower her. I had never felt anything when asked by my King to take the lives of other alphas or even betas, but everything about the prophecy was different.

Joon's mate was the second marked wolf we had killed, the pup being the first, and she seemed honorable. She fought hard and looked Byna in the eye when the alpha shifted and tore out her throat. She never once cried, begged, or broke. She didn't deserve to die.

But I hoped this would give me a chance to right a few wrongs—or at least one.

"I will be back," I assured, wanting to say so much more, but it was too late for that. Joon groaned in disbelief and turned his gaze to the omega.

I slowly pushed on the wooden door and stepped into the throne room. My footsteps echoed as I rushed across the smooth stone floor to the dais on the other side. I kneeled next to the throne and pulled out an intricately carved wooden box. Nestled within the velvety fabric inside was a circular medallion at the end of a long silver chain. It had the King's seal on one side and a paw print on the other.

"I'm surprised to see you here." Hida's rough voice startled me. He walked confidently across the room, his signature sneer firmly in place. "After what you allowed to happen to Byna, I'd have thought you smart enough never to return."

"What are you doing here?" I demanded, standing to full height and pushing my shoulders back. "You aren't permitted in these halls without the King's permission."

"I have more of a right to be here than you do," Hida seethed, displaying his pointed teeth. I edged closer to him, his stance rigid and alert.

"What the fuck does that mean?" He met my movements, stepping sideways, circling me.

"It means that you have deeply disappointed our King, my friend. Your unwillingness to do what is needed to save his life has not gone unnoticed. And it pains his majesty to know how little his son loves him."

I bared my teeth at his mocking tone, ready for the attack I knew was coming. Movement in the corner of the room caught my eye, and I glanced over. Vera, the guard from the tunnels, stood at attention, looking me hard in the eye. I let out a defeated sigh.

"You have no loyalty or backbone, and your father knows it," Hida growled, giving Vera a jerk of his head to dismiss her. She stepped out through the large wooden doors, but I could see her shadow beneath them. I wondered how many other guards waited out there for me.

"You know nothing of my father," I hissed. Hida loved to manipulate my father's affections for him, letting it fuel him to behave however he wanted. He played with his victims and taunted me when I ordered the alpha to act in a more humane manner, but that was all over now. It was his time to greet death.

"I have been ordered by Her Highness, alpha Strayton, to kill you should you return," Hida smirked. "She's tired of your failures tainting her father's legacy."

"My sister ordered this?" I snorted, not surprised in the least. While I had no claim to my father's throne as the second-born, Strayton had always been wary that I might challenge her for it. It was something I always made clear that I didn't want. "Is this a recent order, or has my death been planned since before I even started?" I asked.

"She knew you'd fail," he smiled. "You're too fucking soft. It's pathetic. You would have been less of an embarrassment to your family if you had been born an omega. You're obviously built to submit."

I roared and launched myself toward Hida, striking him in the chest and landing on top of him. The clatter of metal sliding across the stone floor pulled my attention, and I turned to see the locket skating toward the main doors. I moved for it, but Hida kneed me hard in the gut and spun us, pinning me beneath him.

He grabbed me by the hair and jerked my head up. I clawed at his arms and neck, but the alpha didn't budge. I wasn't at full strength yet and knew almost immediately I didn't have it in me to win this fight.

"How fucking pathetic," Hida laughed. "You'll be easier to kill than the pups we've tracked down."

He bared his teeth, prepared to strike, and I closed my eyes, ready to accept my fate.

The Throne Room

Joon

I PUSHED OPEN the wooden door, stopping the second it let out a deep, sharp creak. Byriel and Hida stood in the center of the massive room, speaking. I strained to hear what they were saying, but they were too far off and their voices too low. Whatever their conversation, it was clear from their posture that both were ready for a fight.

Tzidal pushed herself under my arm to see out the door and her body tensed. "He's here," she whispered in disbelief.

I slowly pulled the door shut and gently moved her back into the passageway.

"Please, I am begging you," I said as quietly as I could. "Let me go out first and subdue him. Then you can come out and do what needs to be done. Please, Tzidal. I know you need this, but I need you. Let me make this as safe as possible."

Tzidal sucked in a deep breath, her eyes glazing over with

tears and fury. She stared at the closed door, her heart fluttering wildly in the vein in her neck.

"I promise you." I squeezed her shoulders, trying to convey as much sincerity as I could. "You will have your revenge. I will make sure of it."

She swallowed as if a sour taste stuck to her tongue before slowly nodding. She stepped back away from me and closer to Lex. The siren wrapped an arm around her shoulders and nodded at me.

"It's okay, puppy," Lex whispered in Tzidal's ear. "We have him."

I opened the door again, seeing the two alphas circle each other. Byriel looked weak, his gestures slow, and his muscles reacting half a second after each of Hida's movements. He was an easy target and would probably go down without much effort.

Suddenly, Byriel roared and launched himself at Hida. There was a brief moment where he had the upper hand, but Hida quickly spun them and poised himself to rip Byriel's throat out. I reacted without thinking, launching myself out the door and sprinting across the room. I slammed into Hida with all my might, forcing him to the ground with a grunt.

I drew my fist back and punched the stunned alpha repeatedly in the face. Hida stuttered, swinging his arms wildly, completely caught off guard.

"Guh..guh..guards!" Hida finally managed to get out between fierce blows.

A rush of uniformed alphas ran into the room. I glanced up quickly and tried to shift. My bones were desperate to glide and move, but they held firmly in place. My wolf snarled within me, enraged at being denied the taste of blood.

Two guards slammed into me, ripping me from Hida and forcing me to my knees. I struggled and jerked but they shoved me down, keeping me in place.

"Byriel!" Hida roared, pointing at the weak alpha. "He's a traitor! Hold him down!" The guards hesitated, glancing at one another. "It's an order from the King himself! Hold him down!"

An unsure guard stepped forward and grabbed Byriel's shoulder, gently holding him in place. Byriel moved easily for him, his breath labored and heavy. He was going to be no help in this fight. I'd have to do this on my own. I just hoped I didn't lose Hida in the process. It would break Tzidal's heart, and I had every intention of keeping my promise.

Hida got to his feet and smoothed down the front of his shirt. "Who the fuck are you?" he demanded, rounding on me.

I ignored him scanning the room. There were seven guards in total, no clear weapons in sight, and only two exits that I knew of, the main doors and the passageway. I wondered if more guards were waiting in the halls. *Were these the only ones that had heard Hida call out, or was the whole castle aware of our presence, making escape impossible?*

"Wolf!" Hida yelled, trying to get my attention.

My eyes snapped to him, and he glared. Hida was just as I had remembered, dark, ugly eyes and the faint outline of a sneer constantly on his lips.

One of the guards shook my shoulder and growled low in his throat. "Answer Commander Hida when he speaks to you!" The guard sounded young as if he wanted to convey more strength than he actually possessed.

I looked over the alphas around me, realizing how young they all were. They appeared to have presented in the last year, maybe two. It was odd the King would allow pups to watch over him and his people.

"Who are you?" Hida demanded.

"I'm the last face you'll ever see," I smirked as one of the guards shoved on my back to force me lower.

Hida laughed long and hard. "I doubt that. But I do enjoy a challenge."

"Byna said the same thing before I ripped her throat out," I mocked, smiling at the fucker.

Hida's eyes went wide with shock and rage. He snarled loudly, the sound echoing off the walls.

I braced myself to attack when Lex's screams caught my attention. The side door burst open, and a guard walked out, holding Tzidal and Lex by their hair. Hida glanced at the pair briefly before doing a double-take and fully turning his attention to them.

"The omega from the Madra Village?" he asked with a pleased scoff-of-a-sound. A wide grin split his face, and he turned to me. "What is this?" Hida walked closer to Tzidal, keeping his eyes on me, mocking me with his leer.

It was clear he was hoping to elicit a reaction to see if the omega held any value to me. I tried so damn hard to keep my face blank, but the closer he got to her, the more unhinged I became. My wolf slammed and pushed against my boundaries, trying with everything he had to slip forward, but he was held firmly in place within me. It was agony for both of us.

"Is she yours now?" Hida asked, brushing his fingertips over the side of Tzidal's face. She glared at him, her eyes filled with a blazing rage and glassy with tears.

"Are you trying to avenge her mate's death for her?" he mocked, watching every twitch and spasm in my face. "Did she tell you to find me and kill me?" He laughed, scrunching up his nose as if this were the most wonderful gift anyone had ever given him.

My muscles jerked briefly, urging me to lash out. But before I could move, Hida gripped Tzidal's face hard, making her whimper. He turned, catching my eye, and laughed.

I froze, trying to think through my options. I struggled slightly against the guard's hold on my shoulders, testing their grip. My heart was pounding fiercely, and I could feel my control slipping. My body yearned to bathe in the blood of every wolf that dared to touch my Tzidal.

My eyes met hers, her soft features conveying so much patience and control, and she mouthed two words. Only two.

It's okay.

I nodded in return. The moment would present itself. I just needed to be patient. I needed to trust my omega.

An End And A Beginning

Tzidal

"WHAT EXACTLY WAS YOUR PLAN, little omega?" Hida mocked as he squeezed my face hard in his hand. "To break into the King's castle, track me down, and kill me?" he laughed.

I jerked out of his hold, rubbing my cheek. "I am in the King's castle, and I have tracked you down. I expect killing you won't be that hard either."

His smile dimmed a bit, but he kept it in place. "You actually think a little thing like you could kill someone like me?"

"I could," Joon growled, holding his head high despite the guards pushing at his back.

"I think I could easily kill you," I said confidently.

Despite my calm demeanor, my heart squeezed in my chest as Korban's bloody, pained face flashed through my mind; the fear in his eyes, the blood bubbling out of his throat, his shuddering last breath. My body burned at the memories. It was as if the threads that were holding my heart together were fraying and snapping apart, ripping my chest open.

My body thrummed with rage for Hida.

For the lives he took.

For the children he had killed.

For the moments he had stolen.

"Little things like you amuse me so much," he smiled. "Death is hard, pup. Harder than you could ever understand. Taking someone's life is difficult. It's messy and painful, and it fills you with a burning excitement that can easily consume you." His eyes flashed with violent lust. "You have to love it to want that kind of fire coursing through your veins. It would simply be too much for something like you."

"That was a lovely speech," I smiled sweetly. "Now, be prepared. Because I will flay your skin from your body and drape it over my shoulders as I watch you die. It will be messy and painful, and I cannot wait for it to consume me."

Hida's eyes narrowed as I spoke, then he burst out into a loud, cackling laugh. His voice echoing off the stone walls.

"You know." He tilted my chin up. My skin itched where his fingers grazed, but I held firm, not wanting to give him the satisfaction of knowing how much it bothered me. "I was denied my right to take this omega by this fucking coward." He motioned to Byriel, abandoning me for new prey. Byriel glanced up from where he was held on the floor, as Hida loomed over him. The rich color that had returned to his skin was all but gone, leaving him pale and sweaty.

"The weak are the spoils of war, my friend, and you had no right to take that away from me. But now, I'm going to kill you and this one," he said, pointing at Joon. "And then I'm going to fuck her before I rip her throat out."

Joon's whole body was tense and shaking, his wolf trying to rip out of him. Men love to talk, but beasts thirst for blood.

And my alpha was on the verge of losing all control. Every wolf in this room was about to be dead.

I softly nodded at Joon again. Then I reached into my robes and pulled out Byriel's dagger. Joon's eyes went wide, and he planted his feet. Once I was sure he was ready, I jerked.

I twisted to face the guard holding Lex and shoved the blade right into his gut. The wolf grunted and curled into himself, screaming.

Joon roared, and the rush of feet echoed as the guards sprang into action. I didn't turn to look but instead sprinted toward the throne, wanting to put as much distance as I could between me and the fight.

I crouched behind the massive chair, scanning the room. Joon was already covered in blood, dropping the body of a guard at his feet. Two others lay dead on the ground near him. Lex was circling and taunting another guard. The wolf was horrified and hesitated to touch the siren. Lex's teeth were long and sharp, and he swung his hands out in a teasing manner, his claws inches from the terrified alpha's face.

My eyes moved quickly to Hida, who was straddling Byriel, beating him mercilessly with savage blows. I moved to help him but stopped almost immediately. A guard caught my movements and sprinted toward me. I hunkered back behind the throne and eyed him hard as he stepped up on the dais.

"Come here, omega," he ordered, circling the chair slowly.

"No!" I yelled, my wolf snarling and snapping within me.

The guard jerked and lunged for me, but I dodged him quickly, moving around the throne.

"Come here!" he yelled.

He ran around the side of the throne, chasing me in circles. I moved swiftly as his bulky form lumbered beneath his heavy uniform. He suddenly stopped and stepped up onto the throne, bracing himself to jump over it.

"I said come here!" he ordered, his face contorted with rage.

I gasped and backed up, bumping into a golden pole with a small flag holding the King's seal at the top. I spun it in front of me just as the alpha jumped over the back of the throne. The pointed rod shoved hard into his gut and slid easily inside him, the fabric of the flag bunching up against his stomach. The alpha grunted as thick streams of blood dripped down the shiny golden spear. He gripped at it, his hands finding no purchase on the wet metal. He tried speaking, but nothing came out, just blood dripping over his lips. I shoved at the spear once more, causing the guard to fall sideways and smack onto the dais with a wet thwack.

I raced toward Lex. He was kneeling over a body that was ripped wide open. His face was dripping with blood, the alpha's guts tangled in his fingers. He glared, with bloody teeth, at a trembling alpha that was trying to gather the courage to attack him. Lex stood up and casually walked to the frantic wolf. The guard angled his posture to attack, but his fear locked him in place. Lex lazily swiped his fingernails across the wolf's neck, and blood poured out like a fountain. The siren's eyes glimmered, and he moaned at the sight.

I hesitated to move, not wanting Lex to attack me accidentally. He was lost to his inner beast...assuming sirens even had one. It seemed more likely that they were pure beasts all the time. Nothing restrained within them. But before I could move, a sharp grunt and a splatter of something wet pulled my attention.

Joon's hand was buried deep into the last guard's chest. Blood gushed out around Joon's forearm as he moved around inside the wolf. The guard coughed, and blood sprayed out of his mouth, covering Joon's face and chest, then he slowly fell to the floor, dead before his head hit the ground.

"You okay?" Lex said, grabbing my shoulder. Blood

streaked down his face and robes, and his arms were coated in the thick, sticky substance. The look in his eyes truly terrified me, but I nodded and took his wet hand anyway, relieved to have him standing next to me.

Joon sprinted across the room toward Byriel and Hida.

Hida's fists looked bloody and raw as he pummeled at Byriel's face and chest. Joon launched himself at Hida's body, knocking both of them onto the stone floor. Joon immediately struck Hida in the ribs, pinning him in place.

Byriel stood and swayed, his feet unsteady. I was worried he might keel over, but he wasn't my main focus at the moment. Joon was. And right now, my alpha was tearing at every piece of Hida's flesh that he could reach. Hida continued to fight back, ripping at his arms and face with his claws, not willing to go down easy.

Then it all happened as if in slow motion.

Hida reached down to his belt and pulled out his dagger, similar to the one I still held tightly in my hand. He reared the blade back and plunged it into Joon's chest before any of us realized what was happening.

Joon leaned back and examined the blade sticking out of him. The shock on his face had to mirror my own. He gripped the handle and slowly pulled it out, blood flowing freely down his already blood-splattered chest.

Hida shoved Joon off of him and dug his knee hard into his stomach, straddling his body.

"I am the wrath of the King!" he roared, his eyes wild and feral as he bared his teeth. "You cannot kill me!"

I tightened my grip on the dagger and flew toward them.

Hida grabbed Joon by the hair.

Pulled his limp body off the ground.

Opened his mouth wide.

And prepared to sink his teeth into my alpha.

I slammed into Hida's back, brought my dagger around,

and sliced clean through his throat. I moved the blade back into him quickly, sawing and tearing, desperate to feel his last breath. The dagger dragged and tugged as it tore through flesh and muscle. It slipped a bit from my hand as his slick blood poured over and down his body. Hida let out a strangled cough, spitting out a fine mist of red into the air, then he went limp, falling right onto Joon's chest.

I kicked and heaved at the dead body, shoving him off my alpha.

Joon's unconscious form stole my breath, and I froze. My head pulsed with a familiar all-consuming pain, the kind felt when you lose a mate.

"Nooo!" I cried, my voice shaky and broken. "You can't die! You're mine. Death doesn't get to take you. You belong to me." Hot tears poured down my face as I brought shaky hands up to his cheeks. A soft cough left his lips, and I gasped, turning to find Lex.

"He's alive," I whispered. "What do I do?"

The whole situation was too familiar. The pain, the blood, the panic.

"We leave before they find us," Byriel said, walking as quickly as his battered body would allow. He grabbed the medallion off the floor and flung it around his neck, tucking it securely in the front of his shirt. "Follow me," he said, struggling to heave Joon onto his shoulder.

Byriel shifted into his wolf. His heavy paws thumped across the blood-soaked stone toward the passageway.

The last time I saw that large, black wolf, he was disappearing into the woods after murdering my mate. Now, here he was, disappearing down a passageway, trying to save my alpha.

THE SWIFT WAVES rocked our small boat, making it feel as if we could be flung overboard at any moment. Byriel rowed at a steady pace, moving us through the rough, dark water.

I cradled Joon's head in my lap. The alpha was still out cold, and I was too terrified to think what might happen if he didn't wake soon.

"Will he be okay?" Lex whispered to me, an arm wrapped loosely around my middle. He held me the best he could in the small vessel.

Too scared to answer, I simply looked down and brushed my fingers through Joon's black, shaggy hair and down the sides of his face. He looked so frail. It broke my heart.

"Byriel?" I said.

The alpha looked slightly over his shoulder, still concentrating on rowing through the choppy water.

"How did you find the marked wolves?" I needed something to take my mind off Joon's labored breathing.

He paused, thinking, before pulling the oars up to rest for a moment.

"It hasn't been that hard," he said softly. "We ask around the villages and neighboring towns about the mark. There's always someone that points us in the right direction, whether it be because they just want to be helpful or they hold a grudge. Enemies are always willing to share too much information." He rubbed at one of his shoulders, stretching his arms out. "We werewolves like to show off our scars too much. Others tend to remember marks that stand out on someone's skin like that. But it's as if this last wolf doesn't exist. Maybe the prophecy was wrong, and there were only seven."

I unsheathed my dagger, trying to think everything through. Hida's blood still covered the blade. I dipped it into the water, watching the dark waves wash it clean before bringing it up to my face to examine the shiny metal in the moonlight.

"So the wolf you're looking for carries a mark in a place no one has ever seen, has no grudges, and no enemies?"

"Yes. What kind of wolf lives a life like that?"

"Omegas," I said simply.

"So our fate rests in the hands of an omega?" Byriel snorted.

I sheathed my dagger. "Doesn't it already?"

———

WANT to find out what happens to Tzidal and Joon next? Read the next book in the Blushing Moon Trilogy, The Blue Path.

THANK YOU FOR READING!

It means so much to me that you read my little book. I hope you enjoyed this story as much as I enjoyed writing it. If you did, it would be so lovely if you could write a short review on your favorite book website. Reviews are so important for authors and even just a single line can make a big difference.

Thank you so much!

Also by Kitt Lynn

The Hund Valley Series

The Casin Series

The Broken Omega Series

About the Author

Kitt lives in Oklahoma with her husband and stacks
on stacks on stacks of fantasy books. She writes not-so-exciting
technical things in her "real" job but lives for the evenings
when she can visit her paper friends in their magical worlds.

She is obsessed with fantasy, folklore, love stories, and horror
in general. If you dig these things then you might enjoy her
books. You can find pictures of her sweet puppies, her coffee
obsession, and the ridiculous things she says to keep herself
motivated on her Instagram @kittlynnauthor.

For information on books, signings, and content, please visit
www.kittlynn.com

goodreads.com/kittlynnauthor

tiktok.com/@kittlynnauthor

instagram.com/kittlynnauthor

bookbub.com/profile/kitt-lynn